Orphan
Book One
Surfacing

Orphan
Book One
Surfacing

Nathan Day

SEVENTH STAR PRESS

Cover art and design: Martina Stipan
Cover art in this book copyright © 2017 Martina Stipan & Seventh Star Press, LLC.

Editor: Scott M. Sandridge

Published by Seventh Star Press, LLC.

ISBN Number: 978-1-948042-04-8

Seventh Star Press
www.seventhstarpress.com
info@seventhstarpress.com

Publisher's Note:
Orphan: Surfacing is a work of fiction. All names, characters, and places are the product of the author's imagination, used in fictitious manner. Any resemblances to actual persons, places, locales, events, etc. are purely coincidental.

Printed in the United States of America

First Edition

To my Belle, my beloved and eternal muse.
It's true.

"For the mind governed by the flesh is hostile to God."
– Romans 8:7 (NIV)

PROLOGUE

The Earth stood defiant against the depths, visually as alien to the sun that warmed it as air to a newborn child. The planet's surface looked no different; vast blue oceans enveloped masses of green and brown under a shifting veil of grey and white clouds, but from afar, with Heaven's eyes, taking in the globe as a whole, sight would gloss over, as if looking through jade colored glass. That jade glass that was not glass but still a barrier, nonetheless; a cocoon of energy separating the globe from the universe comprised of flat geometric shards whose tips originate and end at golden winged spheres; simple, man-made satellites, but in numbers so vast that counting them could only be compared to standing on the ground and looking up to the Heavens to count the stars. Those who had engineered this technical marvel refer to it as The Shell and daily breathe gracious sighs that it served its purpose so precisely well.

Reflected colors crept across one such satellite: the form of a small child, floating freely along its belly up and away from the Earth, its determined eyes fixed on a point past the Shell into the space beyond. If one had Heaven's eyes, they would know that an end is near.

The child, at first glance, would appear unremarkable: fair-skinned and blonde-haired, seemingly shorter than average height for the age many would guess him to be, but the eyes, however, would be the giveaway. They shared the same eerie shade as the barrier, not just the cornea, but throughout, each a solid pool of haunting jade. The child wore no expression as it swam through the upper atmosphere without any visible means of propulsion. It did not expand its chest to draw air, nor did it blink. Its only movement was a constant twist of the lips, as if trying to voice a dozen words at once, and the sound that was born was not of a single muttering voice, but a chorus of tones and languages and accents each droning persistently against the others in a chaotic battle for supremacy.

Silently the child, if that is truly what it was, glided on a path that would send it past the satellite that wore its reflection and crashing into the Shell itself, but when it reached the jade glow, the child passed through it as if it were just light or cloud. There was no resistance to the child's momentum, and that too, was by design.

The child entered the open expanse of space, its pale skin completely unaffected by the extreme temperatures that should have destroyed it. The vacuum, likewise, was powerless against it, unable to even swallow the voices or rob its lungs of oxygen. The child served a purpose and such trivial things as laws of physics and science could not be allowed to hinder its progress. So, the child continued its path, an arrow shot towards the heart of Paradise. Alone in a sea of mute black. Until–

The light at first was faint enough that it could just as easily have only been the Sun reflecting off the Moon, as it should. It was too weak to illuminate the child's features, but became a hint in the abyss of the child's eyes. To the child it was without origin, a disembodied glow, but soon it took root in the dark. It began as a dot, a fraction of a pinpoint. It began to pulsate, a visible heartbeat in the void, and with each throb its shape doubled, as did its brightness. Its slow crescendo stretched for minutes as the child continued towards it. The intensity of the incandescence was soon at a degree that a human would be painfully blinded; yet still it could not reveal the child's shadowed features. The eyes of the child, however, drank in the light and reflected its brilliance.

The light grew to such a size that it eclipsed the Moon and outshone the Sun, but, in all the universe, nothing else could see it or be cast in a shadow it might cause. The light was here to meet the child, and the child alone was aware of its existence. The lightnreached the zenith it chose and in a matter of seconds shrank back to the size and form ofna tall man, broad and imposing in build, though its radiance never wavered. It regarded the child silently and patiently, arms hanging at its side neither threatening nor welcoming.

The stars themselves began to pulsate, and other stars appeared about them untilnthe whole of space was densely populated by their number. Each star, new and old alike,ngrew to a brilliance that, even though each was a pale comparison to the first, was awe-inspiring. The illuminations also began to take shape into the forms of men. Some bore the heads of animals or multiple animals and most had at least one set of majestically expansive wings. All wielded savage weapons made of the light they had first been. The vast host pressed in towards the child, weapons at the ready, but made nonattempt to hinder its progress.

At last the child slowed to a stop – as before, by no discernable means – and as itsnspeed dwindled, so did the voices that spewed from its lips. It swung its feet underneath itself so that it may "stand" to face the light. The child observed the light, regarding it almost as if it were its parent. Empty moments passed as neither did more than watch. Both knew the other and understood its motives. Neither saw the other as an enemy, but the child had come to slay the greatest of all the lights.

Finally, the child spoke.

"Are you the one some call God?" it asked in a single, monotone voice so young and innocent as to truly sound like a child.

"No." There was a deafening crack of thunder that echoed even throughout the vacuum of space, and a long blade of impossible resplendence formed in its right hand. The entity puffed out its chest, its wings spread so wide as to obscure all sight. It drew back high to strike–

"Be still, Michael," came a voice, calm and lovely as the very winds.

Something stepped into view from behind the archangel. It had the general form of a man, but its features were strangely indistinguishable and at the same time unremarkable – because that is what He chose – just an understated figure thinly rimmed with a light infinitely beyond any other. Michael's aura dimmed as he moved aside with a deep bow. Underneath the tempered radiance were hints of facial features; the squared jaw and unremarkable mouth of a man, but eyes like a stalking lion. Likewise, the multitude of angels came to an awed hush and bowed their heads respectfully.

The figure approached the child, its hands outstretched, palms open welcomingly. "My children, I miss you all," it said.

The child's eyes slammed shut and it spasmed. Pleading screams erupted from its throat, filling the silence with an agonized dissonance. Every angel covered its ears and wept at the sound.

The figure placed a finger to its lips, said, "Peace," and the screaming ended abruptly.

The child's eyes opened, and it studied Him evenly for a time as if nothing had happened. Finally it asked, "Are you God?"

"I Am."

"And you are here," it stated matter-of-factly in that singular voice, but suddenly a rush like an inferno shot forth from its throat as a thousand accusatory voices roared, "You are HERE! FAR and AWAY! Hands washed and clean of our filth!"

The storm echoed across the galaxy then calmed in an instant, and only silence lingered.

The child bowed its head, not in reverence, but in preparation. No more time would be wasted in this exchange. It had a purpose to fulfill.

The choir of voices began again, barely a whisper at first, born in its belly, moving up through its chest and into its throat, gaining volume as it traveled. Tones accompanied them, a grating moan too deep and piercing scream too high to ever be made by a human and when the voices hit the child's mouth they erupted in a maelstrom as violent and physical as a nova star. Dissipating threads of luminescence bled like sand from a windblown dune from Him in its fury. The populace of angels cried out in torment and folded in upon themselves as if struck.

Then, above the chaos, the singular innocent voice of the child spoke again.

"We have but one question to ask."

CHAPTER 1

The Pacific Ocean is keeper of many secrets. Its deeper waters, often serene and crystalline on the surface, belie the countless tales and treasures resting silently in its dark embrace. As much historian and scholar as jury and villain. It has been both the granter and destroyer of dreams. One such dream was the Fair-Haired Belle.

In the late 1940s fishermen were regaining their confidence, journeying in small, increasingly brave steps further west, closing the gap to Japan again. The horrors and scars of the attack on Pearl Harbor were still fresh, if not bleeding, wounds. Resilient captains, many of whom were retired naval officers themselves, sought to reclaim their trade in those fertile depths, some as fishermen, others transporting and shipping. They were often headstrong, but few were foolish enough – in their own not-so-humble opinions – not to bulk up what firepower they could afford to have on board. You never know what a recently defeated and bitter people might do, especially those driven to a raging insanity after the United States' counter-scars on Hiroshima and Nagasaki. Some chances you just could not afford to take.

Not all intrepid journeymen could boast a military background, many could claim the waves as their roots, having families whose livelihoods stretched back for generations by conquering Poseidon's domain. Fathers took sons and nephews for apprentices, teaching them to read the clouds, navigate the stars, where best to drop net and how best to handle the economics of it back on dry land. These too were a proud and driven people. To many it was not about becoming prosperous, but moreover surviving. You sailed and you fished because you had wives and daughters back home. You toiled because you did not have a choice.

Dexter Workman fit into neither of these archetypes. He could claim no time as a military man, and he had come from a family of lay-abouts and a few mechanics — though yes, mostly lay-abouts. His uncle Norman and Norman's eldest boy, Tommy, ran a modest garage in the no-horse town of Versailles in southern Indiana. Dexter's father, Clyde had taken to the bottle as if it were his job, leaving Viola, his mother, to make what little means she could by taking in the linen wash for the only roadside inn the Versailles economy could meagerly support. Versailles had virtually nothing to offer in matters of tourism – save for a seasonal festival boasting the typical livestock competition and barn dance – and was en route to nowhere significant. Little cash coming into town, meant little cash spreading through town, which meant the town folk had to scrap by in slow, perpetual cycles of survivalism from one generation to the next – and that was a reality Dexter could not accept.

He threw himself fully into his studies. He doubted he was getting the same level of education, as even someone a few grades behind him in a city like Indianapolis, but was steadfast in his belief that an open mind would lead to open doors. During the summers he would split his focus between whatever books he could convince Ada Hollifeld, the school's librarian, to lend him, and an apprenticeship under his uncle, Norman, and cousin, Tommy. For Dexter, it was not enough to just read about how a thing worked, he needed to take it apart and study it. The act of piecing a thing, such as a car engine, back together told his mind how each smaller part served its purpose in the greater scheme – the small brush strokes that, to him, painted the bigger picture.

It was during one such summer that Dexter discovered his love of the ocean. Granted, Indiana seemed to him about as far away as possible from any body of salt water, but Dexter's mind knew no geographical hindrances. He sat underneath a rotting oak, grateful for the cool late afternoon breeze that rolled across the cornfields of Ripley County and tried his best to focus his mind on *The Old Man and the Sea*. Normally Dexter read nonfiction – encyclopedias were a particular favorite because you could learn so much so quickly – but Ms. Hollifeld had felt the compulsion to force the book on him this go-round.

"Not everything there is to know can be learned from flat facts, Mr. Workman," she had said.

It was a captivating truth that he had never considered. He had hoped that that philosophy would lead him to new directions, learning about life through art. What could a painting teach about the inner struggles of its painter? What lessons did a symphony hold? The idea itself was mesmerizing and Hemingway's alleged masterpiece would be the key that would open that glorious new door. The problem was, however, that despite his willingness to glean the book's soul, Dexter found it to be agonizingly dull. He tried not to let its written voice throw his enthusiasm, but he found his eyes did not want to focus on the text. His mind could not retain what he had just read, and the further he read the less he wanted to continue. But the sea itself beckoned his imagination like some rolling, untamed creature of myth. And so, *Some men,* he decided, *just can't be told about a thing poetically. They need to see it as it is and let it show its own artistry.* And that was how it began.

Dexter had a new driving force. He had to see the ocean – any ocean – for himself. Having spent an entire teenage lifetime landlocked suddenly became an unbearably aggravating ordeal. He put the books aside and begged his uncle Norman for more work and pay. Norman accommodated as best he could, always believing that if anyone in this family had been intended for something better, it was Dex, but the killjoy beast that was Versailles ensured that Norman had very little extra to offer. Dexter was nonetheless undeterred. He took what little Norman could offer and sought out other employment wherever possible. A few local farmers were able to give him odd, single-day jobs here and there and a few nights Mr. James at the Dew Drop Inn had given him the gracious opportunity to sweep and dust for next to nothing. But each penny was saved, and each bead of sweat that fell down his forehead was one fewer he had to endure before he could set off.

Small towns have a way of killing big dreams and, at this, Versailles had a way of
excelling. Dexter quickly found that there just simply was not enough he was able to dirty his hands with that would help his progress in any realistic timeframe. Maybe if he saved every penny for a few years, maybe five, or maybe it was time he just quit school all together and work year-round. Maybe then he could be out by next summer. He realized that he had become obsessed – though others had known this for quite a while, and in a small town it was easy to become jealous of another's obsessions, especially if they lead to bigger and better things.

Clyde Workman was the very definition of an angry, bitter drunk – sweeping up shattered glass from flung beer bottles was a regular chore for Viola. Some fathers revel in seeing their children succeed, but Clyde took it as a slap in the face; an insult to what little he himself had achieved and a firm reminder of his many failures. He had worked hard once. He and Norman had opened the Workman Garage together, split-even partners. But Norman could not handle the fact that Clyde enjoyed his drink. Norman was a man of the gospel, a self-righteous-holier-than-thou as Clyde saw it. A straight arrow who couldn't deal with a loose curve, and so after six years in business, that pompous ingrate forced Clyde out. Nevermind how he spent many mornings sleeping off the dog that bit him or how his workmanship was dangerously sloppy. In fact, it was a faulty brake job that had nearly caused old Mortimer Kramer to run off the road into Milo Jones's house that had been the absolute last straw for Norman Workman. Norman loved his brother despite his flaws, as a Christian should, but a man had to be held accountable on Earth as he would be in Heaven. Norman's sole regret was what the long-term effect would be on Viola and Dex.

The time had come for that long-term effect to come into play.

Dexter had returned home late one night from the Dew Drop to find his father passed out on his rocking chair on the porch as if waiting for him. He was tired and sore from helping Mr. James add a new overhang to the door of the manager's office and just wanted to crash onto his bed and bid the world ado. He stepped over the empty beer bottles in front of the door, noting curiously the few coins that lay about them, and made his way inside. When he got to his room he stopped cold, eyes wide with disbelief.

Broken glass lay scattered across his floor, but not from another beer bottle. Clyde had shattered the mason jar Dexter kept his savings in and taken every cent inside.

Years of abuse taught Dex the lessons of quiet acceptance and burying emotions, but this single act was more hurtful and vile than anything the man had ever done. The time to fight back had come at last.

Dexter stormed out onto the porch, half-blinded by equal parts tears and rage. He slammed the front door hoping to wake his father, but when that did not work he stepped up and kicked the rocking chair back, toppling it and spilling its occupant backwards with a loud, terrible *thud.*

Clyde woke with a start. He immediately attempted to get to his feet before even looking around to puzzle out what had happened, but he was still considerably drunk and balance was his enemy. He fell hard on his chin, causing it to bleed and cracking a lower central tooth. Then it was as if the shock of the pain sobered him. He placed his hands flat on the porch and drew his knees under him. He paused to scrape his teeth together, feeling out what damage had been done, then pushed himself upright. Clyde was a ghost of a man, a skeleton wrapped loosely in worn skin that had the semblance of aged leather, but his appearance belied his strength and ferocity – a fact that Dexter knew well. Clyde's eyes were pits of acid and hate and they turned on his son with full force. Dexter staggered for a moment under the brutality of that gaze, until his eyes dropped and saw again the coins lying at his feet on the porch. His eyes rose, he could be his father's son.

Through the burn of tears he screamed, "What the hell have you done?"

Clyde balled his hands into fists and his arms began to shake. "You think you're a man now? You think you're better than me, boy?" he replied.

Dexter was a little confused by the response, but did not let it show. He would have his answers. "What did you do with my money? I've worked hard for that! What did you do?!"

Now Viola was at the door, half-in half-out, holding onto it like a shield. Her eyes were wide with worry. Deep down she always knew a boiling point would be reached, though she had prayed so diligently that it would never lead to this.

"Dexter, what are you doing, son?" she pleaded.

Dexter never took his glare from his father as he pointed an accusing finger. "He stole from me! Everything I've earned, he's taken it from me!"

At this Clyde snapped. "I ain't no thief, boy! You little piss-ant! You want your money it's out there," he pointed into the lawn, blackened by the clouded night. "You get out there and dig it back up! But I guarantee you that when you do I'm gon snatch it up and toss it out there again."

Dexter's shoulders dropped and his face went long.

"Why would you do that? I've worked all summer for that."

"Cause you think you better than me. Well you ain't nobody. You think 'cause you got your nose all up in them books that you're smarter than me? You think you gon git out of here into that great big world out yonder? And leave me here to rot? That it, boy?" Clyde took a threatening step forward.

"Clyde no," was Viola's weak plea. Her fear of her husband eclipsed her love for her son.

Clyde regarded her for a moment; his anger grasped a new angle. "Your mother works as hard as anybody, and you just gon leave her to sweat away, you ungrateful mutt. You got all that money, and you just gon blow out of town. Boy you need to give that money on over to your mother. We got things we need here. You need to be takin' care of me."

More words came from each man. The argument went around in circles, as such things do, until at last tempers reach their peak and the energy turns physical. From then on Dexter claimed that that was the night he became a man. He matched his father nearly blow for blow as they rolled around the porch, locked around each other, flailing madly with bleeding fists. Viola wailed and begged, but was altogether ignored. In the end, however, Clyde won as he always had. He left Dexter on the ground that night, eyes and mouth swollen, mouth and nose bloody, ribs bruised but not broken. Dexter would always wonder if his father's drunkenness had given him the advantage of strength and muted his sense of pain. As Clyde made his way into the house to sleep soundly in his bed, he only gave his son enough acknowledgment to stop and spit on him. Dexter managed to crawl through the high grass and up the front steps, but passed out there on the porch.

Dexter woke to a red, though sunless sky. He guessed it to be about 5AM. His body was a mound of agony. Every move he attempted brought its own special pain. His eyes were wet and sticky and burned when he wiped them, but he needed to see. He rolled slowly onto his stomach, ignoring as best he could the resounding complaints from his ribs. He crawled backwards to the porch steps and, by sliding his legs down them, was able to use them to get himself upright. Once he was standing he was not stopping, he turned east across the barren field and began the slow, agonizing trek to his uncle Norman's house.

It was around 7AM when Dexter finally knocked on his uncle's door. Norman and Tommy were both up and dressed, ready to start their workday. The moment he opened the door and took sight of Dexter, Norman knew exactly what had happened. After a few questions Norman handed Dex's care off to Tommy and took off down the road to confront Clyde. During the hour he was absent Tommy did the best he could, tending to Dexter's cuts and feeding him what scraps of eggs and bacon he had not finished that morning. When Norman returned his eyes were red from tears and his knuckles scraped.

"You live here now," was all he said.

Dexter Workman lived with his uncle Norman and cousin Tommy for less than a year. Norman accepted his decision to drop out of school and took him on fulltime at the garage despite the financial strain it caused. For Dexter's birthday, his uncle presented him with an old broken down Ford pickup that he had allowed Milo Jones to trade in for some work to his tractor. The three men made that truck their mission. Even after long workdays they would commit no less than three extra hours to its restoration. Their progress would hit the occasional snag when money was not available to order the parts they needed, but when it did, they attacked it like a pack of predators.

It was a cool spring morning when Norman finally gave Dexter the keys. He wished his nephew all the blessings God could provide and put him in the driver's seat. Norman's farewell handshake was firm and housed a small wad of twenty-dollar bills.

"This'll get ya a decent ways, God'll get you the rest." He said.

Dexter left Indiana that day and never returned.

He worked his way across the states, God had provided small and timely opportunities and graces just as Norman had said, and on the 3rd of May 1936, nearly a month later, Dexter crossed the Nevada border into California. He made his way southwest, finally stopping and settling in the metropolis of Lanza del Los Santos. At first the culture shock nearly overwhelmed him, but he found a bit of his old philosophy returning to strengthen his resolve. *If you want to know a thing, you must study a thing.* And so he came to embrace his new environment. He found work on the docks, a double-edged blessing as the labor that provided his livelihood demanded nearly too much of his body, but also put him beside the ocean daily. In time he came to know many of the fishermen that came to port there, and it was not long before one such captain took him on altogether.

Dexter spent his next five years learning by doing on a vessel christened, *No Shore.* He proved to be incredibly adaptive and fashioned himself into a jack-of-all-trades both on board and on land. The Captain, an old navy man known by most only as the Captain and not by his given name, was a mountain of a man. As salty and fierce as the sea he trod.

One night the Captain had called Dexter below deck to speak one on one. Steiger, as he revealed himself to be named – not his entire name, mind you, but it was undoubtedly more information than any of the other three crewmen had – told Dexter that he knew Dexter's calling was to have a boat of his own. They discussed a partnership based around the purchase of a second vessel and the potential of new buyers for their hauls.

A month later the vessel was bought. A modest beauty, but it would float in any storm and was the most that Steiger could afford at the time. Laslo, a wiry old seaman that physically reminded Dexter of the father he'd left behind so many years ago, was reassigned by Steiger to be Dexter's first mate and only needed crewman. As Laslo had no desire for authority, he was happy to oblige despite the forty years of experience on the sea he had over Dex. The new vessel was christened, *The Fair-Haired Belle*. Steiger fancied himself a poet and in one such poem, a decent though long-winded psalm to the waters, this was the name he had given the Pacific. The new venture was off to a promising start.

The *Belle* was the embodiment of all Dexter's hopes, and the reward for the sacrifices of yesterday. Upon its deck at high seas he felt transformed and emboldened. Free in a very tangible sense. He traveled at his pace, under his stars, without restriction other than those his responsibilities imposed. It was if the *Belle* were a living extension of his soul; the waters her blood and the wind her breath. With the infinite Pacific stretched across his horizon, the world – and life itself – fully opened before him.

And then December came, and Pearl Harbor was razed.

The chaos brought on by the attacks on American waters slowed the momentum of Steiger's plans before they really had a fighting chance. But a second factor crept into play that ended it entirely. Steiger had spent years ignoring the pains in his abdomen.

Dismissing them altogether to himself and anyone who happened to see how they caused him to tighten and wince as "indigestion" or "bad whiskey". In truth, the pains were the result of cancer, and in February of 1942, it claimed his life. Just before his passing Steiger had silently come to terms with his own mortality, knowing that something inside him was too broken to fix and too evil to give him much more time. In his foresight he deeded the *Fair-Haired Belle* over to Dexter solely and made efforts to reassure their buyers that despite the global turmoil the fish would keep swimming in.

Steiger's death crushed Dexter like ocean depths. Aside from his uncle Norman, Steiger was the only positive father figure he had known. Laslo took back command of the *No Shore* without protest. Dexter's own ambition faltered. He slowly took to the drink, laughing as he saw the irony his father would be quick to point out. He spent fewer days plundering the deep. He began to forget why he had come west at all.

Then the letter came.

Sometimes in life bad news begets bad news without any

regard to the strength of a man's spirit. Tommy Workman had written the letter, but they were Norman Workman's words, as Norman himself was illiterate. The letter was full of regret and sorrow, but also of encouragement in the face of tragedy. It seemed that finally Clyde Workman's deteriorating mentality had altogether collapsed and given in to the will of the demons within. On a rainy Sunday morning he had taken a hunting rifle and shot his wife, Viola, in her sleep and then proceeded to hang himself. *By the time this letter reaches you,* Tommy had scribed in Norman's words, *they both will have been buried inthe family plot on Mockingbird Hill. Beneath the willow there, just as your mother had wanted.*

Come home when you can.

-Norman

A lesser man would have crumpled under the weight of such tragedy. A stronger man would have found a sanctuary and allowed himself to cry. A man of faith would have prayed to God, and a man without would have cursed Him. Dexter just sat in the silence of the moment, letting it wrap around him like a protective cocoon. *The greater truths in life are the ones that never seem real,* he thought. Perhaps that was why he did not cry; he just simply could not connect to the reality of it. Maybe if he had been back in Versailles, in the midst of friends and family, caught up in their symphony of weeping and wailing, but here, a continent away, there was nothing more than words on a page.

And sometimes words hold little power.

Come home...

Dexter dwelt in this mindset for the next few days, though despite this he was only half-invested in any of his day-to-day functions. He floated through the motions of his livelihood with all the grace and enthusiasm of an automaton. His muscles knew their function and could continue their routine while his head remained checked-out. It even occurred to him at one point that he felt as if he were having an out-of-body experience, looking in on himself from the clouds. That thought, at least, did manage to sadden him in a very real way that the news of his parents somehow was incapable of.

The waters themselves seemed empathetic to Dexter's state, a constant humdrum beat of lazy waves rocked the *Fair-*

Haired Belle like a drowsy mother rocking her child's cradle. The motion further numbed the personae of the day, counting through the minutes like a lazy, slowing metronome, working its lackluster magic to dull the senses and awareness of the world around him And he continued this way day in and out for nearly another year...until...

The second letter came, again in Tommy's penmanship, but the words were his own...regarding Norman. He read, but at so fast a pace he was doing little more than skimming its contents:

...severe headaches...

...pain...nausea...

...dark spot...

...tumor...

...not much time left...

...please come home...

These words were different. They were tiny fangs summoned of ink. And they were sharp, and they bit, and the part of Dexter that had spent the better part of the past year hibernating behind his emotional walls woke like a roaring lion.

He worked quick as he could...

...not much time left...please come home...

...packing, sending word to Laslo of the situation and his intent to leave for an uncertain time so that the *Belle* might remain in safe harbor undisturbed, planning his route via bus line–

And that's where the snag caught him.

The year had been rough in more ways than emotional. Even though America's economy was in prancing stride, Dexter's zombie-esque state had gained him meager haul and therefore little revenue. Many of his usual buyers had given up on their reliance upon his catches months ago, and the few that stayed loyal did so at reduced rates for low quality stock. His rent and utility payments had fallen dangerously behind until finally Dexter abandoned the apartment and took up permanent residence on the Belle and spent what little he made on ensuring she had gas enough to journey out each day and paying into the insurance policy Steiger had insisted he get so that should she sink, Dexter would stay afloat.

In short, Dexter was broke.

He tried to meet with Laslo to barter for a loan, but the man was uncharacteristically cold to him. Dexter suspected Laslo knew of his financial state and either doubted Dexter's intentions and/or ability to repay the loan or Laslo himself was running on fumes. Either way Laslo was a dry well. So Dexter turned to his buyers, pleading for payment advances on future catches, but given his recent decline and the fact that he was using the money to travel back across the hemisphere, he was universally sent away empty-handed.

Days were ticking away and a third letter came.

...symptoms have gotten worse...

...so much pain...

...maybe only weeks...

...misses you and wants to see you one last time...

Dexter became increasingly desperate. Seeing no other option he offered the *Belle* for sale. First again to Laslo who again declined any financial arrangement and then by word of mouth through the docks and fish markets. Surely in all of Lanza del Los Santos there was some crew in need of a worthy vessel, but it was if the devil himself was against Dexter for no interest was expressed, no offers came and while Norman lay on his deathbed, Dexter sat night after night in the cabin of the *Belle* regretting the home and family he had left behind. Norman, who had been more of a father to him than his own. A man who had taught him how to work hard and earn a man's respect. Men like Steiger who–

Steiger...

When the thought hit Dexter shot up like a bolt in a clear sky. The insurance Steiger had so adamantly insisted he maintain - *forsaking all else but fuel to set you to sea* – that would...but wait...of course he had tried to sell the *Belle* previously. That would take her from him, but at least she would live on the waters, carrying his dream on the winds and waves until such a time that he could buy her back, but this...to destroy her entirely...

...what option was there?

On that very night he set his decision into motion. The winds were strong and the waves violent. This would cover for him as long as no eyes bore witness. He stood on her bow with an old gas lantern at his feet and with a claw hammer loosened the nail from which the lantern normally hung providing some visibility in thick fogs as well as alerting other vessels in the same foggy waters as to his presence. When he was satisfied that the nail would not long hold he bent low and lit the lantern then proceeded to carefully hang it from the nail. This done he saw fit to debark, hoping that his pace was more normal than it felt. Once ashore his legs fought his will for the right to break into at least a jog, but his will remained dominant and he steadily walked along the docks towards the slumbering juggernaut of Lanza del Los Santos. A living wind raged through his hair, over his shoulders and back towards the *Belle* with enough force to stutter his step and when he heard the crash and breaking of glass his knees nearly gave, his neck nearly snapped around to see, his heart nearly quit.

"I'm so sorry," he whispered to her. To himself.

He walked on as best he could manage, letting his dreams burn to ash at his back.

Two passing weeks found Dexter's boots back on Ripley County soil, but days too late. Norman was gone. The cancer that had ravaged his body had caused him immeasurable pain but Norman had held on through it as long as he could, hoping each day that that would be the day Dexter would come home. The funeral had been the midday before. The wind had been mild, but steady, sweeping through the cornfield that surrounded Mockingbird Hill stirring a rustled song like a distant choir. Nearly the whole town of Versailles had come. Norman had been well liked and highly respected by all and all shed tears as he deserved. The pastor had quoted several beautiful verses of hope and comfort, reminding all that this life is fleeting but the victory is reward eternal.

Dexter never again left Versailles, Indiana, for more than an hour or two in any direction and only as business required. He took up work at the garage with Tommy, and the two ran it steady for twenty more years until one unexpected day Dexter's heart gave out as he lay beneath a Cadillac DeVille doing nothing more than changing its oil. He never knew the love of a woman, nor married nor had children. He never let his mind wonder outside the County lines. Ripley was a bubble. A prison. It was familiarity and punishment. A warden that had at last brought a fugitive home to waste away the remainder of his days in regret.

But on some blessed nights, as the wind rolled atop the stalks, it carried with it the salt of the Pacific and the siren song of his *Fair-Haired Belle,* and on those nights as he slept he sailed lunging crystal waves towards unfathomable shores.

*****

The tale of Dexter Workman was but one of hundreds that plagued the mind of the angel once called Athiel by his brethren as he sat in the splintered, wooden corpse of the *Fair-Haired Belle* where it came to rest on the floor of the Pacific Ocean. His head hung to his chest, and his wrists lay across his knees, his whole body limp and drawn in. He had not met Dexter Workman nor watched over him directly, but Athiel knew him as all angels know all the hearts and lives of man. A gift of near-endless Knowledge blessed to them by the Lord of Angels and Man through His grace. In his younger days Dexter had been a devout Baptist, attending church every Sunday with either his mother (when she could) or Norman (when Clyde would not allow his wife leave their house, most often to help nurse him through the morning's hangover), but that routine devotion began to waver as the dreams of the ocean overtook him. The sea had become his new god and riding its frothing back, only thrice in those many years had Dexter accredited the magnificence of the waters to their heavenly Creator. The possibility that the tragic life that befell him, a life hard-fought earned and so cruelly taken, might have been his due for putting his new god before the True God was one of numerous constant questions running through the angel's mind.

In this physical form he had the appearance of a man, notably tall (just over eight feet), lean and athletic and classically handsome despite the fact that not even a single hair could be found on him. He was nude in human terms in that he was without garment, but more so in terms of the angels he bore no wings, only scars on his back where once they had been. He had placed those aside long ago, laid them at the feet of the archangel Rafael and then plummeted down to the earth.

He had roamed for a century, masquerading as just a man and bore witness to countless acts of both cruelty and kindness across the face of the mortal world. If asked, he would say the cruelty was far more abundant and that saddened him greatly. Being there in the wrappings of flesh, his perspective was quite different than before when he had both wing and Heavenly Knowledge. And thus, he had settled here at last, hidden away from the deeds of man and Heaven and Hell. Spending his eternity in the calm of the depths haunted by everyday ghosts of the world that God both created and let fall by the wayside.

A prisoner to his own rationalizations, he had not felt the absence of the one he had once referred to as both Father and Creator in some time. For most of his time since he fell, Athiel could sense the lingering presence of his Lord like heat from a distant star on the back of his neck, but somewhere along the way that sensation had left him entirely. The truth of it was that he was not sure when. He simply had not noticed its passing. And in his watery home, he no longer cared.

His thoughts meandered to a soldier he had glimpsed only briefly, a man he had been told would be his next charge and lead a life so profoundly cursed that it would cripple his mind, body and soul. Of all the tragic lives he had witnessed, this life to come had proven to be the final straw, the catalyst that would turn the once majestic being against his Most Majestic sovereign. Fraught with a troubled childhood only to later be far from his homeland, flung into a foreign war as men of power and greed set their pawns against each other only for the sake of…

Suddenly Athiel opened his eyes. His senses became fully alert. The heat from that distant star, long since cold and dead was there upon his skin, faint but demanding to be noticed. His eyes felt increasingly hot. He blinked and held them closed in hopes of soothing them. *Such a human gesture,* he thought off-handedly.

Then, just as abruptly as the sensation began, it intensified in a violent swell, the force of it raising him to his feet and bending his spine backwards. His head was thrown back and his arms thrown out; fingers bent into trembling claws. His eyes, oh how his eyes burned. His jaw gave way uncontrollably to the deafening roar that erupted from his throat, bringing with it a light so terrible as to blind any man or beast who would have seen it. His body began to hover above the deck of the boat, and the water about him hissed angrily as it continuously transformed into steam. Chaotic tremors ran through him as tears of golden-red blood began to flow from the outer corners of his eyes and down his cheeks, clinging to his flesh despite being submerged. As the tears fell down his face they seared painfully into him, etching sharp lines that burned like the fires of hell. His body convulsed as if struck simultaneously from many random angles. The light and scream from his mouth continued their up-surgence, the very force they sustained felt as if it were to rip him apart from inside.

And then it ended, all of it, the pain, the heat, the sound and the brilliance, even more suddenly than it had begun, as if a switch had been flipped and a light put out. Athiel's feet gently touched down upon the *Belle's* deck. He was weaker than he had ever felt in all his existence. His frame slumped forward as minor convulsions ran through his limbs caused more by the immediate memory of the experience than any real sensation. He touched a fingertip to the newly formed scar running down his right cheek, baffled by its cause and its meaning. Down-turned eyes vacantly roamed his surroundings as he tried to draw upon his Heavenly Knowledge.

That was when he realized the overwhelming absence about him. Before he had pushed thoughts of his King, the Creator, I Am, into the back of his awareness and had assumed that in the time since that the Lord had simply accepted Athiel's descent and had severed all Heavenly connection, but there had always remained a weakened state of the Knowledge that all angels held over the mortal realm. Now, however, it was gone entirely and with it an even deeper and severe void, like the life had been ripped from his spirit – from the entire universe – leaving only a longing so fierce that it made everything he sensed about him feel utterly hollow. It was as if the Father Himself had been...

Athiel straightened. He had always been told that he was gifted with far too active an imagination balanced against such weak insight. It was a trait that had set him apart from many of his brethren, and he felt it had been a gift he had received at his creation. But now that "gift" was turning against him, and in this mortal form he was more vulnerable to doubt and fear than he had been before his fall. He would not worry;

worry was a trick of the Enemy. He would go, and he would discover.

He stepped out onto the slanted deck of the *Fair-Haired Belle* for the last time and turned his eyes high towards the water's surface. His stretched his arms down out and forearms out with his palms facing up. Without a sound he began to rise smoothly through the Pacific, leaving the ocean once more to its secrets.

CHAPTER 2

Father Joseph Behanan took in slow, labored breaths. His hands hurt from how hard they had been clasped together and only as he released them did the blood start to return. His mouth felt dry to the point that the back of his throat was sore. His heart ran a marathon inside his chest. At the ripe young age (as he liked to think of it) of 33, Father Joseph had never received a holy vision before.

He was far from what one might expect a parochial vicar to look like in this part of the Lanza del Los Santos dioceses. True, the Cathedral of Saint Michael was in a rapidly deteriorating part of downtown, but it was still patroned by some of the city's social and political figureheads, including Mayor Consuela and famed nightly news anchor Kenneth Phelps.

As a black male in the prime of his life – "Don't call me Afro-American," he would say, "I was born and raised in North America, and I'm proud to *be* black!" – he had often received jeers from relatives and childhood friends about not keeping to his responsibility to his own community. The harshest among the complaints always came from his father, a fire and brimstone Baptist pastor still saving souls down in Arlington, Texas. Father Joseph had always expected that more than a little racism had flavored Reverend Jameson Behanan of the First Revival Church of Christ's view of how a black man should best serve in the name of the Church. Joseph understood the reasons, or at least some of them. The brutality and humiliation his father had suffered at the hands of bigoted white children all throughout his school years would certainly be enough to scar any man, but he would continue to pray for the good Reverend day in and day out until God chose a time and means to correct that view and heal those lifelong wounds.

In all truth Father Joseph was not sure what had led him to the seaside metropolis of Lanza del Los Santos in the first place. He had no doubt that it was ultimately God's will that brought him here, but the circumstances were considerably less than remarkable. He had come to visit his cousin at a local art school and had fallen in love with the vibrancy of the city and had thus stayed. He had already begun looking into centenary schools throughout Texas – as he had always planned on following in his father's footsteps into ministry – but had converted to Catholicism after falling for his cousin's friend, Harmony. The two dated briefly, but soon enough she found the "uncultured cowboy" from Arlington, Texas far less than interesting and went about finding someone else. To his surprise Father Joseph was barely heartbroken, and so he re-devoted his attention to the calling of the Lord.

The conversion to Catholicism had, of course, not gone over very well with the Good Reverend back home who quickly denounced all the flashy "hosh-posh" rituals of the Catholic Church as unnecessary and un-biblical. "They taint the very message of the Good Lord himself!" the Reverend had claimed, "the Lord, my God, concerns Himself with love and prosperity of the soul, not of pomp and theatrics!"

Joseph never saw it that way. He understood his father's views, but to him there was peace and beauty in the rituals and the incantations. They helped to bring the mind closer to Heaven. They were acts of respect and worship, but most importantly they rang true to his heart and *that* was what he believed mattered the most. He had conceived a simple slogan that had begun to catch on around the congregation – including Mayor Consuela's most recent press conference. It was that "The heart is the instrument through which God speaks to us."

His "fine flock" as he lovingly referred to them, was comprised mostly of upper- middle class white Johns and

Janes. Many were married couples in their late forties and upward. A strong awakening had started taking place among the teenage attendees a few years ago following a scandalous act of embezzlement from the church accountant that had brought the cathedral to the brink of closing — this had been the very reason Joseph was brought to serve at Saint Michael's. A few of the teens, spearheaded by a high school senior named Antonio Rodriguez had seen the scandal as a test laid upon the faith of the congregation and had taken up spiritual arms to combat the downslide of trust and confidence that had resulted. It was a valiant effort, but one that had seen a sudden and unexpected downturn for no discernable reason. This spiritual "quieting" may have been infectious because the overall attendance had begun to wane around the same time, and a church that had recently and publicly let cry a lion's roar to "claim this city!" had shied away to lambs virtually overnight. That had been some time ago. Around two years ago Saint Michael's had seen a satisfactorily consistent rise in attendance, but that had plateaued and now, once again, began to fall away. It was that very concern that had brought Father Joseph to his knees in prayer, under the compassionate gaze of the Virgin Mary.

Brian Keyland, Saint Michael's Choral Director, had finished the final pre-service rehearsal, releasing his singers back out into the world and their own lives, and had just himself said "Goodnight," and left. Joseph was alone in both truth and his thoughts and so brought himself to the feet of the Holy Mother and bowed to pray. His prayer had begun with thanks and praise for a God he truly loved wholeheartedly. He thanked the Lord for a heart that both listened and learned and for the offerings the Cathedral continued to receive, even if they were not what they used to be. He knew God would provide and thanked Him for that as well.

He moved on to the prayer list from this week's services, and that was when the vision struck. At first there was an odd ringing in his ear made up of several harmonic tones at once. It shook his concentration, and he almost started to pray for focus, but the sharpness and volume of the sound increased. It leapt from his ears into the very air around him, filling the sanctuary. The echo of it crashed upon itself like waves, but each crash only

25

complemented the next and the harmony grew richer. The dim light at the back of Father Joseph's closed eyelids at first dulled to a complete black and then pulsated a distant white. Then, all at once, his self-awareness left him, and he was as an eye in the Heavens.

He saw all the Earth from a distant place in the sky. Saw it surrounded by an unnatural green aura. He saw a Child that was not a child glide into the stars. He saw the Heavenly Host, too numerous to count. He saw the Light that met the Child, saw it take the shape of a man with a sword of flame, only to be gently upstaged by I Am. He saw the Child's eyes shine with the same hue as the Earth and its mouth move to speak, but could not hear the words. He saw I Am become encompassed in the green flame that spewed from the mouth of the Child. When the flame died he saw I Am no more.

He saw a man that was not a man sitting in the wreck of a ship on the ocean's bed. He saw the man writhing in pain as molten tears burned down his cheeks. He saw the man stand and rise up until he was head above the waves.

He saw a mother and her son in the contrasting light and shadows of the city streets. Saw the horror in the mother's visage, and the confusion in that of her son. He saw how they ran as if the devil himself were at their heels, then he saw the eyes of the devil that followed them, hidden beneath the face of a man. He smelled the putrid breath it exhaled as it chased them. Saw the delight it took in the chase. He saw the mother on her knees, pleading as she died.

That was when the vision broke and Father Joseph became aware again of himself and his surroundings. His mind was at odds; so fascinated yet so afraid. He had studied extensively about the visions of biblical prophets, but they were often very allegorical, at least in the "visual" sense. What he had experienced felt more akin to a flashback, as if he had actually been there to see those things firsthand and maybe that – especially given the devil in pursuit – was the most unsettling aspect of it.

With no conscious intent he turned his gaze upwards at the statue of the Blessed Virgin that watched over him on the right side of the sanctuary. His breath caught in his lungs, and his heart forgot to beat. Crimson tears ran down the Holy Mother's face, connecting at a point under her chin then running down the front of her neck as if she had been crying for more than a moment.

He had no way to sense the presence all about him as the angels fell to their knees and wept.

*****

The angel Dycliasses stood over the troubled priest, one hand placed firmly on the man's left shoulder. He had always felt great love and favor for this particular child of God and had followed him for many years in Texas before joining him in this Californian metropolis. Like Father Joseph, the angel stared at the face of Mary, the earthly mother of Christ. He understood the cause of the tears though he, himself, had not encouraged them to flow. He wanted to join his brethren as they howled before him and tore at their garments but he could somehow not accept the truth of what had happened. It was realms beyond impossible. The King of Kings knew no beginning and would know no end. The God that made the Heavens and the Earth could not be unmade. The very fact that the universe still even existed was proof against it. Man could not have succeeded where even Lucifer had failed.

There were truths hidden from him. His angelic Knowledge had lessened considerably some uncertain time ago. It was conceivable, nah, *likely*, that the two events were related. And he would discover the reasons and the means behind it all. Until then he would not weep. His Father was beyond the touch of oblivion.

All at once silence filled the sanctuary as a desperate pounding rattled the front doors of the Cathedral...the mother and son had arrived.

CHAPTER 3

A good life, it seems, can go one of two ways: it can spiral unexpectedly down into disaster and ruin or, as is usually the case, it can just keep getting better and better. A bad life, however, always seems to go from bad to worse. Traci Nicholas was unarguably a case for the latter.

At 35 Traci had already lived a life filled with enough drama, abuse and close calls to send the heart of any Hollywood executive racing. It was clichéd in a sense: the drug-addicted mother and her parade of scandalous male suitors, more than one of whom had spent "quality time" with Traci against her will. When she was 14 Traci ran off, leaving her mother and Chester, her mother's boyfriend, passed out in a drug-addled haze. She lived off the streets however she could manage; thievery, prostitution, grand theft auto, whatever it took to make it one more day. At 17 she even began a short-lived career in the adult film industry, but one physically aggressive, cocaine-fueled director later and she was "out of the biz" —his similarities to her mother's usual male "friends" were too much to tolerate, even for her — and back on the streets. Three months into her 18th year she became a drug mule for Salvadorian cartel players looking to increase their presence in various California cities and by her 19th year she had been caught, arrested, tried, judged, and sentenced to a five-year stint in a women's prison. That lasted for six months as federal agents saw the opportunity to use her as bait to catch something bigger for their fish fry. Their job done, they released her to a women's halfway house and placed her under the strictest of probation. The cartel were not idiots, and the feds were not concerned enough about hiding her assistance and soon a hit had been placed on her life.

After a brief chase through the slums of Lanza del Los Santos and a bullet to the back of the head, the assassin vanished into the night, but his task was not complete and Traci was able to drag herself through dank alleyways and eventually, miraculously onto the steps of the Cathedral of Saint Michael. The priest at the time, Father Leary, found her and called 911. She made a miraculous recovery, changed her identity and cleaned up her act. She attended church at the Cathedral regularly for a few months after, but soon her attendance fell off. Shifts waitressing at a small diner paid much better on weekends and she hoped God would understand that she could not live on bread alone. In time, she forgot she needed Him in her life to any degree, and the miracle of that fateful night and of Father Leary faded away to the back of her mind...until now.

Now she was running back down those very same alleys, gunning for the very same destination and desperate for the very same miracle. The irony of it was in no way lost to her, and the keen sense of déjà vu as she made each turn felt like justice from God Himself. But she had always believed (well, beginning from the moment she started to believe in Him) that God was, above all, a forgiving God and that He would spare her and the tiny hand that clung tightly to hers: that of her son Solomon.

Even under close scrutiny Solomon was a spitting image of his mother. The same auburn hair and high Cherokee ancestral cheekbones. The same full lips that always seemed to be puffed out like a pout. The car door ears and the ski-slope nose. There was no arguing whose child he was, and that was the devil of it, for all the features that Solomon had inherited from his mother, it was what he had of his father that was even more undeniable and infinitely unsettling. It was the eyes, dead blue orbs like a stagnant pool in late autumn, dead like fallen leaves on an old grave, dead like the weight of sin.

Traci looked down sorrowfully at those lifeless eyes as she pulled at his arm, urging him faster and faster down the cluttered alley. Just two more blocks. Two more blocks to Saint Michael and hopefully another hand-of-God miracle. She heard the loud crash of a garbage can being kicked aside and in her fear could not help but look back.

How was he already so close? It was impossible! At that speed he would reach them before they reached sanctuary. Solomon was just a boy, an innocent, but at that moment he was also dead weight, and that would be their undoing.

Drawing on the adrenaline coursing through her body she hefted Solomon off the ground and against her breast single-armed in one strong swoop mid-step. She bit down on her lip and demanded her legs move faster. She could hear the footsteps behind her like a drumbeat counting down their doom. Even worse she could hear his wretched breathing, the sound of stone on stone in the hollow of his...*its*...chest, and that made her recall the foulness of his breath. It brought to mind rotting meat and carrion. That goaded her faster.

Street lamps lit familiar stairs some five hundred feet ahead, displaying them like a prize for her troubles. At first the sight of them was such a tremendous relief that she nearly slowed her pace, but she heard Solomon's breath catch in fear, and her efforts redoubled. He began to slip loose from the cradle of her left arm and instinctively she grabbed him with her right to raise him back higher into his perch, but that too slowed her down, and she nearly tripped on a discarded cardboard box as she once more re-dedicated her efforts. In fear she looked back once more, certain any second now long fingers would wrap around her neck, but what she saw stopped her in her tracks. Her pursuer stood still approximately a hundred feet behind her, hands balled into fists, head tilted down so that it was conquered by the shadows. Only icy blue eyes shined through. Eyes as cold and dead as her son's – for this was his father.

Long moments passed with only the labored rhythms of their breathing playing against the odd silence of the night. Traci turned fully towards her pursuer, her right hand against the back of Solomon's head in a subconscious attempt to shield him from both harm and the sight of his father as well as a physical proclamation that she voiced aloud, "You cannot have him! He's mine!" This close to the Cathedral she felt a small surge of defiance and bravado.

The father did not reply, only watched. His unflinching gaze pierced the hard exterior Traci had erected. Fearing he – or it…whatever *it or he was* – was on the verge of assault, she spun on her heels and made one last mad dash for the Cathedral steps. The father took a deliberately slow step forward, followed by another. He/*it* was in no particular hurry. He/*it* knew where she would hole up like a scared rodent and he/*it* had all the time in the world. He/*it* was enjoying the chase too much to let it end so quickly.

Her heart thundered in her chest, the brief respite from running had done little in the way of allowing her to catch her breath, but she was nearly there. Twenty more steps across the empty street, then fifteen, then eight and then two and then at last she was there. As her left foot first landed on the bottom-most stair of the Cathedral she actually did slow to a walk. She would not have been able to explain it if she tried, but she knew with all her being that the Cathedral itself would shelter her from the unholy beast at her back. She never felt the need to look behind her as she ascended to the main doors, this was her home in dark times, her cleft of the rock. At last she was at the top and finally then did she turn to look behind her.

There he/*it* stood, smiling victoriously at the base of the steps. His/*its* gaunt frame barely seemed more than a skeleton despite the flesh he/*it* wore. His/*its* face was a patchwork of scratch marks and dirt, probably a meth-head now, making it seem like an entirely different face it – yes definitely an "it" – had worn when it had seduced her.

Impossibly, her heart sped up, as if sensing this it took a step forward up the stairs toward her. She dropped Solomon to the ground and made a try for the latch to open the door – locked. She looked back, he continued to close the gap between them. Closer and closer, higher and higher at a slow, deliberate pace. She hammered her fists against the grain of the doors and screamed for someone to open up and let them in. Please dear God let them in! It opened its mouth and gnashed its broken yellow teeth hungrily. It reached its hands out like a father welcoming a long-lost child home, smilingly invitingly and amused. She threw Solomon behind her, placing herself between the beast and the innocent, unsure of what she could do but unwilling to do nothing.

Suddenly the door behind her flew open, a middle-aged black man in priest garments stepped out towards her and asked, "What's going on? Are you ok?" His eyes darting from the woman to the child to the "man" and back to the woman again.

She spun instantly, scooping up the boy as she took her first step and bullied past the priest and into the safety of the Cathedral.

Left alone, the priest turned his gaze back to the "man" on the steps. No words were exchanged but the priest's body trembled with the knowledge that the devil stood at his door. It is the kind of moment holy men always prepare themselves for and question themselves about. If you stood face to face with the devil himself how would you fair? Would you proclaim the name of the Lord and send the Enemy on his way, like a champion of the faith? Or would you cower under the weight of his stare? Perhaps out of a degree of cowardice and perhaps simply out of the confusion of disbelief, Father Joseph did not stand tall like a lion on a hill, instead he stepped backwards through the doorway and closed it after him, keeping the devil in the night.

CHAPTER 4

Treygen Andros reached for the payphone receiver then hesitated. It was not the filth and gunk that had accumulated over the years, coating its scarred black surface, that gave him reason for pause, though at one point he had been a tried and true germaphobe (no, there were much more disgusting and dangerous things in the world now…well, they had *always* been around…but now he had confirmation that they were far more than just folklore and simple-minded mythos). It was the future that plagued him. Each action had an equal and opposite reaction…if you let it. He had been careful so far; watching over his shoulder for a "tail", driving an hour away from his current lodgings with enough change in his pocket to ensure this call could last days if needed (despite the ungodly rates carriers were charging these days), but it was always what you did not notice or never accounted for that always came up to bite you in the end.

Which future would he live out? If he got away with this undiscovered maybe he could weasel into a safely negotiated amnesty once the hammer fell. Maybe he would follow his initial instincts and simply disappear as soon as he hung up. No, they would find him, he had to remind himself of that. They could *always* find you, even if you somehow managed to disable the implant in your skull without them finding out – they had the Pillar, and *nothing* was beyond the Pillar's sight…he should know, he designed it. *Maybe* suicide was really the only option that made sense any more. There was no way he would not be found out, and what they could do to him with this technology was far, far worse than death. But no…if all this was real, wait… it *was* real, that was why this was happening to begin with, and that could mean that if he took his own life then his only reward would be eternal damnation. Was there any way around that now? To fool the system and cause yourself to die in a manner that would ensure you weren't cast into the lake of fire? If the Paradox Initiative had succeeded — and it certainly seemed that it had — then who would be left to judge your actions? Or, more to the point, was there even a Heaven out there anymore?

His mind raced. Too many outcomes in this life *and* the next. Too many possibilities unbalanced by too many uncertainties. And where was his evidence? He could explain the science behind the spiritual – or was it, in reality, the spirituality behind the science as it was clear now that they were one and the same – but would his words prove convincing enough, even to an old trusted friend, to spark the proper investigations and bring their ramparts crashing down. If only he had material evidence, but obtaining anything concrete would be far too risky, and he would be murdered by those he had slaved for.

What was Valdez's endgame with all this anyway? Immortality? Maybe that explained the hard push towards ramping up the cloning programs. Didn't matter. Only one thing seemed to matter anymore in this chaos Treygen felt cast into, and that was the truth, and the world deserved to know and judge for themselves how to deal with it.

There would be wars. The various religious factions of the world would collide as never before. Some – *many* – would claim that this was some ultra-elaborate hoax to win an unprecedented wave of new believers or the work of the devil, but potentially and most likely they would take arms against him and those he worked for. Surely Valdez knew that, just as surely as he had defenses against these eventualities already in place.

Maybe Treygen would be spared if *he* were the one who came forward. Or maybe he would be literally burned at a stake for his troubles. True old–world punishment. That seemed somehow fitting.

Nevermind, he had waited long enough. He pushed all thoughts of consequence from his mind and took the deepest breath of his life. It was time to decide where he stood and to plant his feet firm on that ground. He closed his eyes, felt his heart pounding in its cage, opened them again and picked up the phone.

CHAPTER 5

They called him the Blowfish for good reason although he was born Jasper Worthington. He was known throughout the streets of Lanza del Los Santos as a bit of a storyteller after a fashion. Always the juiciest gossip: "You know that the Mayor been courting some ladies of the night up at Broadleaf Pointe? You hear that them winos down at the old train depot disappeared 'cuz some government folk needed some cattle for their scientists to poke and prod on? You know that at night the ghost of the James Brown dances in the warehouses down at the docks for spare change and gives out sandwiches? It's all true, I've done seen't'it all with my own peepers, yes sir, yes ma'am." As much as he was known, he was known as a blowhard and what he witnessed tonight would be as highly regarded as the rest of the claptrap he was known to sling about in saliva-drenched tell-alls.

Blowfish sat in a long, moldy trench coat at the edge of an abandoned dock that jutted into the calm Pacific waters with complete disregard for the fact that, structurally speaking, it should have collapsed into those waters years ago. He kicked his feet jovially while taking deep breaths and puffing out his cheeks to their absolute maximum capacity while rubbing the green beanie cap that was as much his trademark as his stories. He was positive that this talent was why fellow transients called him Blowfish although he couldn't recall ever displaying it to anyone. He looked past his left shoulder at the shipyards about half a mile away. He supposed he should get ready to head that way, the Godfather of Soul would be out anytime now handing out them sandwiches. Oh, how he hoped tonight was tuna fish on wheat.

Blowfish turned back to give the Pacific one last fond look-see before rising to his feet, and that's when he caught sight of... well, something.

At first he thought it was a fish. It floated along the surface of the water at an even keel and shined almost magically in the moonlight, but a fish could not (or *would* not, you never know with the attitude fish have these days) swim in such a straight path at such an even depth. He cocked his head and rubbed his chin trying to puzzle out if the manatees would be migrating towards Indochina this early in the year or not and if this one had perhaps gotten turned around somehow. Maybe it was James Brown himself about to rise out of the water, sandwiches in tow. That had to be it, which meant that since he was coming out of the sea, yup, it was tuna fish on wheat night alright!

Blowfish licked his lips and leaned forward excitedly. His eyes tried to focus despite the bit of whiskey that kept them blurred. As the domed object neared it occurred to him how light-skinned the Godfather looked tonight. He shrugged it off to the moonlight. When the anomaly was within a hundred feet of the dock it began to rise, revealing itself to indeed be a man, although to Blowfish's extreme disappointment not the Godfather of Soul and Sandwiches. The man's skin was pale and hairless. Deep scars cut down his cheeks from his eyes. As the man came almost full out of the water Blowfish glared unabashedly as the being had no discernable pelvic anatomy. Soon the figure was completely above the surface, feet stepping along the water as if on dry land. It cocked its head curiously towards him, as if in some vague sense of recognition. Blowfish stepped back, almost toppling when his foot found a gap in the wood. He dropped to all fours and out of sight of this watery phantom.

Once more the night was quiet and serene. From his angle Blowfish could see nothing but the gentle heave and ho of distant Pacific waves and the star-filled sky they reflected. Sure, there were some antsy looking clouds hanging in the distance, but who knows where the winds might take them.

Before his mind could wander back to a much-desired tuna fish on wheat the phantom returned, rising impossibly above the dock and levitating there only a few feet away. Blowfish's heart did its best to leap out of his throat, and his elbows tried to give way entirely. Through lips rigidly twisted into a fearful snarl he heard himself utter the words, "What are you?"

At this the being lowered smoothly down onto the dock. It took two steps towards him with movements equally graceful and powerful. It still appeared to be very much male for all the rounded and cut detail in its muscle-build but so unnaturally tall. The look it gave held neither malice nor pity, only inquisition.

"I am no longer sure," it replied. So strange that its voice should be so deep yet so soft and somehow comforting. "But I ask that you rise and be not afraid."

In the warmth of the stranger's voice Blowfish found adequate strength to stand again. He continued to study the features of the entity before him and in his attempt to speak could only muster enough mental power to say, "You're naked."

The apparition looked down at itself as if realizing this for the first time, and then smiled. "Yes, I am. I had forgotten that."

Blowfish wiped a line of spit that was threatening to spill over his lip with his forearm and then looked down at his coat. He proceeded to remove it, and the beanie cap he wore and presented them wordlessly to the stranger. It regarded them with an exceptionally genuine smile and then took them. As it put its arms through the sleeves of the jacket it looked at him and said, "Thank you, Jasper, you have always been so generous." Impossibly, despite the phantom's proportions, the jacket and cap fit as if tailor-made.

Blowfish straightened his spine and tilted his head in disbelief. "You know me?"

"Not as well as I once did, but I remember your kindness very well."

The man born as Jasper Worthington felt his shoulders shed all the tension they had been holding. His clearing vision blurred again around the edges as tears fought for supremacy over his lids. The stranger reached a hand forward to cup his jaw; its touch held all the comfort of the world. It met his eyes levelly and smiled.

"You will be blessed again."

At that the stranger stepped past Blowfish and made its way off the dock, continuing its course for the heart of the city. Jasper fell to his knees, overcome with joy, and wept.

CHAPTER 6

Kenneth Phelps stumbled in his efforts to hang up the phone. It bounced harshly against the polished mahogany top of his desk, leaving an imperfection in its unnaturally dark finish. The line went dead on the other end, and now the piercing, inharmonic tone it produced was an audible dagger that cut to the heart of him. At 53 he had experienced enough of the insanity this world had to offer to accept almost any reality presented to him; that trait played an incalculable role in his success as a television newscaster (a profession upon which he now teetered on the brink of its pinnacle). He had seen the rise and fall of modern day empires. Witnessed firsthand the blood man could spill and the ignorant cruelty that was its byproduct – many nights he still woke in a cold sweat remembering the corpses of children buried in the rubble of exploded buildings, many holding hands, or the body of a young girl who had been raped then shot repeatedly by her own brother in a warlord's heinous forced initiation, all while juggling the burdens and hardships that came at the time with being an Afro-American professional in an often ignorant and prejudiced business. But what he had just heard…the veil that had been pulled back would have at one time shown him insurmountable joy and confirmation. Now, however, there was only the darkest void.

He prided himself on his mastery of the English language (and he was by no means a slouch when it came to French,

Japanese, or German either, he would have you know), but had never felt more at a loss of words nor could he imagine a situation that would induce that feeling half as much. Somehow he had to find a way to speak this truth out loud. The world would have to know. He felt no compulsion to be the bearer of this, the direst news conceivable, but someone had to be, and he had long ago been granted the pulpit with which to reach the masses. His throat was suddenly almost too dry to speak, but right now, despite his grief and his perplexity, there was one person that absolutely must be told.

"Sharon!" he called out to his wife, hoping she would hear him from across their penthouse suite. He had meant to add the words "I need you" but he physically could not manage another syllable.

"It's finally happened..." he whispered into folded hands, "...they actually..." He had not strength to finish the thought out loud. For months Andros had fed him information in coded, sporadic messages about something the scientist called "The Paradox Initiative" and now the full measure of that enigmatic scheme had come to fruition.

He could hear his wife in the kitchen, fumbling in the fridge. Over his distinguished career in journalism (first as a field reporter working his way up to larger markets, then to the anchor chair, and now to greater heights) she had always been his personal sounding board. He gave her the privilege of being the first to find out anything and everything he had uncovered. He would spare her no details, regardless of how gruesome they may be. She repaid that respect with complete honesty in her advice on how best to present each and every potential story to his producers and, eventually, to the world. Her opinion was always open-minded but forthright, often unapologetically blunt, and almost always right.

He had never needed her more.

"Coming!" she called back faintly. Her voice was soon accompanied by the staccato crescendo of high heels on the newly laid wooden flooring.

As he waited for her, his attention drifted slightly. First to the computer monitor that gave his spacious office most of its current illumination (even if it did cast the room in a fittingly haunting, pale glow) and secondly to the only other light source, a modest goldfish tank that held its sole occupant, Boris, in a stagnant world of plastic and glassy deception.

On the monitor was an opened e-mail from a legal assistant at CNN asking him to have his lawyer review the attached amendments to his pending contract with them. Every look he gave it should have made him feel like a kid again, moronically jumping for joy like it was Christmas morning and he got *exactly* what he had asked for twice. Instead it seemed so overwhelmingly insignificant.

Hovering stoically in his humble abode, Boris met Kenneth's gaze with practiced indifference. Kenneth admired many things about this fish (truthfully more than he admired in most people). One: he admired how Boris, like all his kin, grew to fit the size of his environment. He felt it was a trait the two had always shared, and it was how he chose to view his professional life. Two: he admired how content Boris was floating in his tiny world of fake plants with his lifeless neighbor Harry the Who-Needs-Modern-Diving-Technology-When-This-Old-Suit-Works-Just-Fine Diver who appeared to give up on his quest for the endlessly opening and closing treasure chest just inches away and satisfy himself with a life of merely watching it from up close. Now Kenneth was absolutely a man who believed any man could move a mountain and undoubtedly should when the world showed him a thing that no man, especially a Christian, should abide by, but sometimes it was calming to be reminded that God would grant the serenity to accept those things that you cannot change.

He felt the intensity of watching eyes and shifted his attention to his office door. Sharon stood there wearing a look of deep concern. Even now his mind thought about how intensely beautiful she was, even at 50. Her slender figure belied the fact that she had given him two equally lovely children (Dylan and Julia respectively), but the greatest aspect of her beauty lie in the brightness of her eyes. Though that brightness was now dimmed, it was not entirely gone from her.

"Ken, what is it?" she asked in so quiet a tone, as if afraid to shatter the edged silence altogether.

The pressure of building tears buckled his eyes, and as they began to spill forth so did the words from his now gaping mouth. He told her absolutely everything, as he always had, sparing her no detail, no matter how gruesome. He explained to her every uncovered truth and lie, from the catalytic knowledge to the chain reaction it had set off. He unveiled the single greatest discovery in the history of not just mankind, but of the entire universe, and the single greatest act of aggression ever committed against it. And it was more than she could bear.

By the time he finished she was curled into a trembling ball leaning weakly against the doorframe. He felt more than a tinge of guilt at having done that to her. Wrapped in the echo of her weeping he felt his own tears, for the moment, dry up. He wanted to cross the room to her and attempt to comfort her with the strength of his arms, but he felt too weak and doubted it would make her feel any less alone and orphaned than he did. He was strong enough to admit that he needed guidance, and so he reached for his phone and began dialing the only person who came to mind. He just prayed that Father Behanan could prove it was a lie, that his trusted source, a man who had never steered him wrong – purposely or negligently — had been misinformed or had misunderstood what he had taken part in.

He would cling to anything that sounded even half rational. Anything that could make him believe the sky was not falling.

CHAPTER 7

The night air was stagnant and vacuous. The distant cacophony of metropolitan noises pushed in against the shadows but could not compete with the sheer volume the silence that surrounded the Cathedral of Saint Michael spoke. Ocean breezes should have stirred the various litter that lined the streets. The anarchic chirps, buzzes and flitters of insect life should have played its nocturnal symphony. No passers-by passed by. No stray cat strutted. The air itself felt frozen in the grip of time. It was as if all the world turned away or altogether retreated from the intangible touch of malevolence that emitted from the figure standing statuesque under the Cathedral's threatening gaze. The gargoyles perched upon its stony brow snarled down in warning, but the superstition that had borne them long ago was powerless to remove the interloper from their province and knowing this, he smiled.

It was not a joyless smile – even the vile took delight in the vile – but still a thing made of mongrel teeth and bloodshot eyes, and the skin upon which it shone was now cracked leather and strained as if it was being pulled in upon itself, and soon the seams of the puppet would rip.

Reflexively he shook the body's gaunt arms, ready to be rid of it, but it was not yet time. He sniffed the air like a hound and tasted the night with the flick of a serpentine tongue. There were foes about, huddled together in their sorrow. Weakened, so very weakened. They were just as aware of his presence as he was of theirs, but their doubt was palpable. This turning of tides pleased him greatly, and so he lingered, letting their worry build. Worry was of the devil and a sin; it showed a lack of faith, and for the dogs of Heaven to lack faith…there was power in that knowledge.

That was how he had bested the first guardian; stood against it and beaten it down, then skinned it slowly as it cried out for its Father's mercy, and desecrated its holy flesh. He would do the same to these and any other that sought to keep the child from his grasp and its true destiny.

He felt icy drool cascade from the blistered lips he wore. This hunt permeated his being; the strongest of hungers. He would kill those within and then claim the boy, drag him into the night, screaming onward towards his birthright.

Eagerly, Uzahl stepped forward.

CHAPTER 8

It seemed to, on some level, further unnerve those around him how calm Solomon remained. What was it the priest had said it was? Shock? Although he was only 8 years old he understood the concept of shock and therefore knew enough to know that that was nowhere near the money. If they had bothered to ask him directly, he would probably just call it awe.

The night had begun as mundane as any other: Leslie, his babysitter, had fallen asleep on the couch as always, leaving him to his own devices – which meant staying up eating dry chocolaty cereal washed down with off-brand cola and watching cable television until mom came home from the diner. Leslie had been on thin ice with her job security on the line, and the *"...of the Dead"* marathon Solomon was tuned into when mom walked in turned out to be the nail in her coffin. Solomon left the room, letting Leslie take the brunt of mom's wrath and sat on the double bed the two of them shared to stare out the bedroom window. Their apartment felt every bit the "sardine can" mom kept calling it. One bedroom, a few ancient and barely working appliances that qualified the kitchen as being "furnished" and a bathroom comprised of a broken toilet – the super's coming tomorrow to fix it this time for sure! – and grimy tub that did little but collect shed hair and empty toiletry bottles. The view, however, was unbeatable, at least in Solomon's eyes. The bedroom window looked out across Ludlow Street at the eastern face of a sister complex owned by the same slouch of a landlord, presenting Solomon with a fantastic view of windows, each like his own private television, looking in on the lives of his neighbors...even the inhuman ones.

Each of the apartments was its own network show. The third from the left on the second floor was a sitcom about two temperamental sisters determined to make it on their own. Diagonally above and to the right of them a drama about a single man trying to get back on his feet and win back his wife and children. From there if you counted two right and three up was the musical about a college drop-out giving it all his might to make it on the big stage – complete with impromptu singing and dancing. Directly to the left of "Broadway" (as he called it) was a constant drawn curtain that he assumed to be a horror and mystery show too terrifying for young audiences. Each window held a stage for him, each occupant merely a player.

Maybe someone sat in a window across Ludlow, he often wondered, obscured in the shadows and enjoyed the opposing multi-channel view from that side. Maybe he and his mom and Leslie were all an after-school special to them that was about to reach an episodic climax and recast through the living room window. Maybe he was not as alone as he felt. Maybe someone could rewrite his story, and he could have a father.

If someone across Ludlow was watching his building, however, he held serious doubts that they could see behind the scenes as he did to other players that went relentlessly about their work, moving in tight invisible orbits around each tenant. Angels and demons. He knew them for what they were, not because he had seen enough television or read enough books, he simply *knew* deep down in the pit of his heart. The angels floated about with such a silky sense of purpose; they touched the people and imbued them with confidence and love and comfort, they stayed an angry tongue, they drank disease from an embattled body, they lifted the souls about them and fed prayers through them towards the sky. The demons, however, clawed into their victims, latching onto them like grotesque leeches and brought forth the worst in each soul. They opened emotional scars. They blinded minds from truths while whispering bold lies. They whipped hearts into jealous and violent frenzies. They stole away hope and charity.

Sometimes the demons and angels occupied the same rooms. Sometimes the angels brandished fiery blades and warded them away. Sometimes the angels stood aside, allowing the demons their play – this confused Solomon greatly. When was an angel a guardian and when was it a bystander? Was it a choice or an order direct from the top? If an order who, then, was worth saving and who should be left to suffer? Was it an order for him to be saved then? Is that why the angel fought and died at his doorstep?

It had been the first angel in a few years to come so close to his home. Solomon had gained his spiritual sight in an instant when he was only 3. He woke from a nightmare he no longer could remember and beheld an angel keeping watch above his bed. The angel looked down absently as if listening to a voice only audible by its ears and then met Solomon's eyes for only a brief moment before bleeding away into the night. The last thing he saw of it was the surprise in its eyes. It took a few years and some maturity for him to realize that surprise had likely been from the realization that Solomon had seen it. Since then no others had come near him, though many across Ludlow Street had seen him watching them. Demons kept their distance as well; never becoming more than prying eyes occupying distant shadows. . .Until tonight.

Solomon had seen the angel first. As he watched the neighboring building movement drew his attention to the street below. The angel stepped into the middle of the street as if it had been waiting at the entrance of his building, but was obscured from his line of sight. It stood silently for a long while, chin raised but eyes closed, just taking in the life of the night. Surely it could hear the last angry words coming from his mom's mouth as she paid Leslie tonight's fee and then escorted her to the hallway. It was waiting, Solomon was sure of that at the time, but he did not yet realize that more to the point, it was guarding.

In response to no stimuli that Solomon could detect the angel conjured a sword of flame from nothing in a flash so intense that Solomon had to shield his eyes. When he put his hands back down he saw another figure, stepping out of the darkness further up Ludlow, keeping a steady stride towards the angel. The demon was man-like in general shape, but seemed to be made of rotted grey scales with whisps of shadow infinitely deeper than any the mortal world knew oozing from the cracks in between. The angel took up a readied stance and called out its warning, but the demon strode forward as if it had not heard. In a final show of stark intimidation the angel stretched mighty wings that gleamed of golden and silvery tones. The wings spanned across the width of Ludlow and made the angel appear nearly three times its size. Nevertheless, the demon still would not relent; it kept the same uniform pace.

Without warning the wings gave one colossal beat and flung the angel upward and forward at its adversary. The demon instantly leapt and the battle was joined. The struggle was a savage dance composed of movements too swift for a mortal to follow and in the space of a second, was finished. The angel fell to its knees before the demon; the flame of its weapon sputtered out as it hit the ground, and its wings looked tattered and bloody. The demon grasped a wing in each hand and with a thunderous roar ripped them from the angel's back. The angel's scream of agony struck Solomon full in the chest, stealing his breath. It sounded so...so human. The demon put its hands upon the angel's scalp and sank its claws in. What took place after was an act so unholy that words cannot touch the depth of its sacrilege, and in those moments the angel called out a desperate plea to God in Heaven for intervention. When it was finished, the demon stood above what remained of its victim, a revolting mass of meat, blood and ash, like a skinned animal. To Solomon it seemed the angel had been made mortal before the dark ritual was finished. The demon raised a hand high, holding the limp flesh it had tore from the angel triumphantly.

Despite himself, Solomon let out a gasp, though he doubted entirely that that was what drew the demon's attention to his window. He could not make out its features, but Solomon was certain that it wore a satisfied smile at the sight of him and was surprised to find that that brought him no fear, only a roiling sense of curiosity.

The demon came towards his building and then was obscured from his sight, leaving the night eerily still.

Across Ludlow the various sitcoms and dramas and

musicals played out in their usual fashion, completely unaffected by the war that was waged moments ago outside their windows; not even the other angels stirred, which blew his mind. Solomon rose from the bed and walked back to the living room, knowing company was coming and wanting to receive it there. His mom stood in the kitchen staring at the dirty mass of dishes occupying the sink – yet another job function that Leslie neglected – and crying over the day's stresses. She caught sight of him in her peripheral and turned her head away long enough to wipe her tears, but he had seen. As she turned back to him she parted her faux smile to speak but was interrupted by a gentle wrapping at the apartment door.

"If she thinks I'm going to change my mind that girl is just..." Traci said as she crossed the living room to answer the door, never finishing her train of thought (audibly at least). She threw open the door in a show of anger but was stopped cold by recognition of the figure standing outside.

She shook her head as if it would clear away her disbelief and asked, "What the..? No, no, no. Where have you been? What are you doing here?"

Solomon leaned to see past her into the hallway. The man that came into view was sickly thin and road-worn. His greasy brown hair hung in nappy strands down to his skeletal cheeks. Thin, dry lips wore a weasel-like smile. Ignoring the question that hung heavily in the air the man leaned to his left to regard Solomon.

"Wow, he's a good-looking kid now, huh?" he said with great pride.

Traci stepped sideways to block his view. "What do you want?"

He straightened back up to answer her, breaking his contact with Solomon. The man reminded him of several vampires he had seen in movies while Leslie slept. Bloodsucking drifters who starved nearly to death in between meals, not the high class or emotionally sensitive type that seemed to be fan favorites this day and age. At the surface he seemed like your average American lowlife, but there was a strong hint that under the skin lay something dark and sinister. Solomon suddenly realized that he had forgotten about the demon that was surely creeping its ways up the building to find him.

The man responded to Solomon's mother, "I came to see my boy. Isn't that fair?"

It felt as if a cold hand had just struck Solomon's cheek. His mother spun to gauge his reaction with her mouth agape. He blinked through his confusion. He had never met his father, nor had he ever asked about the man. He just assumed that when the time was right, his mother would tell him all he needed to know. He was not the only tough- luck kid he knew. Not everyone had a mom *and* a dad in the traditional sense. The nuclear family was fast becoming an endangered species.

The look on his face must have ignited something fierce in her, for Traci turned back to the man at the door and began to forcibly usher him to the hallway outside.

"Out here, now!" she said, starting to close the door behind her. "Now!"

That's when things became much worse.

The man stiff-armed Traci; the motion itself looked rather feeble but the strength of it knocked her off her feet and against the door. The door flung back so hard the knobbput a hole in the wall and stuck. Traci flew through the air and tumbled backwards whenbher legs struck the coffee table behind her but fortunately the bulk of her upper body landed on the couch, cushioning her fall. In the next instant the man – his father – stormed into the apartment with long, purposeful strides, aiming straight for Solomon with an outstretched hand.

"Come to me, child!" he demanded.

It was then that Solomon got a clear view of his eyes and the truth within them. This man was a vessel, a beast of burden being ridden by the demon that had slaughtered the angel below. Still Solomon felt no fear, what he felt was, in a word, entranced.

The man's fingertips were inches away when, with a banshee scream, his mother rammed the man broadside with all her might, sending him crashing into the kitchen, yet leaving her sure footed at Solomon's side. She took full advantage and scooped Solomon up off his feet and ran out of the apartment as fast as she could.

What followed was a pursuit through backstreets and alleyways in a winding marathon that led all the way to the sanctuary of the Cathedral of Saint Michael where Solomon now sat quietly in a front pew, hearing only half of what his mother was able to force out through manic lips. He was much more interested in the other occupants of the

sanctuary: the trio of angels gathered at the base of a statue of the Virgin Mary sobbing into their hands and even more interestingly the fourth angel who sat away from them in a pew five rows back from Solomon, his mom, and the young priest. This angel was different, physically – in non-corporeal terms – larger than his brethren both in height and muscle-build, with wavy black hair that hung to just above his shoulders. His eyes were a pale sea of blue that held not a single tear, but instead held Solomon in a fixed and harsh gaze.

Bits and pieces of the conversation happening inches from him floated into Solomon's ear. He heard:

"I never thought he would come back for him! He's the devil! He really IS the devil and he wants to take my son away from me!" – his mom.

Then the priest asked a question.

"Straight to hell!" – his mom again in a voice that cracked with equal parts fear and trauma.

The priest mentioned something about calling the police then tried to stand, but Solomon's mother caught him in the grip of both hands and pulled him back down, nearly causing him to fall completely.

"They can't help us!" his mom cried, and the priest seemed to know this.

No words passed between them for long seconds. Just heavy breaths as if they were in the midst of combat.

And suddenly they were…

The solitary angel rose and spun around in a fraction of a heartbeat. In the next fraction the double doors in the back of the sanctuary exploded inward off their hinges, raining splinters half the distance to them. Solomon's mother screamed, and the priest immediately rose to his feet. The weeping angels stood and simultaneously brandished tall swords of fire.

The man – the *It*, his father – lurked in the doorway, emitting an unearthly cackle that sounded of grating stones. The large angel sprouted wings so massive as to completely obstruct the three mortals from the assailant's vision. The other three angels charged forward, and after a moment two of the three launched into the air, swords high and ready to strike the demon down.

CHAPTER 9

D ycliasses placed himself between the mortals and the fray, knowing any of his three brethren alone could best the creature that now defiled the house of the Lord, but smart enough to act as a safeguard should the demon somehow slip through. As the others leapt forward to swat it down, Dycliasses studied the demon, curious as to its identity. Not so long ago, in a moment that his thoughts blurred to recall, he and his brethren had felt their link to the Father cut. He could remember the sudden hollowness within and without and the accompanying fear and confusion, but he nor any he knew, could recall the day or the details. The event was a haze in the back of their minds, but with the loss of that connection came the loss of Knowledge and Prophecy. Studying the interloper as best he could he gained a sense of familiarity, but not recognition. Undaunted, he would determine who this fiend was and maybe better understand not only the reason behind its assault, but also the measure of its audacity.

Strangely the demon was somehow protected from true Sight. The poor soul in which it rode should have been as distinctly discernible as the creature itself, but all Dycliasses could make out were the frayed edges of it, the rest was a blur as if Sight just slid off the surface of its form. Of late and with rising frequency the whole of demonkind had become emboldened, but also disjointed in purpose. Their schemes bordered on truly chaotic, bringing him to wonder if their link with the Deceiver had been cut same as their own to Heaven. It would account for much, and if they knew the angels were disconnected from the Father then they would likely assume them weakened as well. To his great sorrow, he feared that they may be right, and the events that followed drove that belief home.

Trael and Periel had chosen to strike from above while Hersis, the smallest of the trio, came in low. The demon cast the body of its host high into the air at the larger two. To the humans in the sanctuary who only saw the possessed man leaping crazily, but with superhuman ability, at nothing, it must have been both a frightening and confusing sight.

"Wait!" Dycliasses cried out, sure of the strategy the enemy would use, hoping to warn his brothers. Before he could utter another word his fear became reality. The demon abandoned its host in mid-air – a sight of ripping soul and flame and blackest smoke – causing the now unconscious body to continue with the momentum of its flight through the incorporeal forms of Trael and Periel until it crashed into the sanctuary wall behind them, but by the time the body hit the wall two of the angels had been slain.

The demon dove out of its host at Hersis's feet. The angel swung horizontally, hoping to cut the enemy in half, but the demon was too quick. As it hit the ground it rolled past Hersis, smoothly coming to its feet and willing its own weapon, a chain comprised of blade-edged brimstone links that trailed smoke and smelled of sulfur, into creation. Before Hersis could react to defend himself, the demon spun, curling the chain around the angel's neck. With a ferocious cry it yanked back, unfurling the chain and severing Hersis's head. His body burst into light and dissipated upward before it could hit the floor.

Periel was the first of the remaining two to correct his course towards the enemy, adapting his flight path instantly with a tucked roll, like a swimmer kicking off the wall of a pool. He picked up speed as he darted at a trajectory slightly above the demon's head. Trael performed a similar feat immediately after but came at the demon lower and from its flank. Just as Periel was to reach his mark he extended his blade forward and down, in a strong vertical attack in concert with Trael who slashed diagonally, minimizing the demon's evasive options. The demon, however, anticipated the assault and contested it perfectly, twisting its body back and sideways evading first Periel's blade, then flipping and rolling just past the arc of Trael's weapon. It grappled Trael as he flew past, wrapping itself and its chain around the length of the angel's form. Dycliasses could clearly see the utter horror on Trael's face as his brother realized his doom. The demon released its grip and spun the opposite way, pulling its chain with it and cutting the angel into shreds of light.

Then the unconscious man collided into the wall with a massive crack.

Periel and Dycliasses both stood in stunned silence. The demon landed squarely and bent low, allowing itself to be seen more clearly. The visage before them was not its true form but something far worse. Dycliasses's emotional guard was shattered, allowing pure rage and grief to flood his heart. The fiend had clothed itself in the skin of an angel. The holy flesh hung off it loosely as any garment would when it was much too big for its wearer. The skin around the eye sockets had been tucked inward to hold them in place, but it was the demon's true eyes that shown through; hot yellow orbs, splintered with red, that mocked and smiled.

"Fiedr..." Periel's shoulders fell, recognizing the sagging face of his slain brother upon their attacker.

"Blasphemer!" Dycliasses roared, and the very cathedral shook, knocking dust from the windows and balcony, *"I will know your name!"*

The demon cackled madly as it had upon its entrance before answering in a low and oily voice that polluted the air of the sanctuary. "I am Uzahl."

It was a name Dycliasses knew. A trickster and schemer who moved in ways that would normally keep it far away from the presence of holy guardians; a servant of the Strong Man.

In his peripheral he saw the mortals retreating through a door behind the pulpit and into the senior priest's study. The child was being carried again by its mother, but watched their struggle with calm interest. That disturbed Dycliasses immeasurably. He heard the door lock behind them and the phone being dialed.

He knew the demon would hear this as well and likely turn his attention on them before any authorities arrived to further complicate matters. He had to end this now.

"You are no warrior. You are a serpent that crawls on its belly." As he said this, Dycliasses took a threatening step forward and conjured his own weapon: a battle axe with a hilt of silver and blades of light. His wings curved forward, their tips pointing towards his adversary.

Uzahl laughed again and swept his arms wide in presentation. "Look about you, coddled one," it said, "this feeble serpent slaughtered your ranks with ease."

Periel was overcome with righteous fury and charged Uzahl's right flank. Without turning to look Uzahl thrust his arm out straight to his side and caught Periel mid-charge under the jaw. He hefted the angel off the floor and as Periel swung his blade down at the demon's head, Uzahl merely swatted the attack away like a minor annoyance with his free hand.

The demon's sneer widened as its long fingers wrapped around the sides of Periel's head. It said to Dycliasses, "You are abandoned, and we serpents have risen." The demon tightened its grip, and the immense pressure produced a series of cracking sounds until Periel's head imploded with a blinding flash. Uzahl lowered its arm and batted its hands as if to shake off filth.

Its serpentine tongue licked out over decaying angelic lips. A taunt. A reminder. A declaration of war.

CHAPTER 10

Father Joseph brought Traci and Solomon down the short
hallway behind the choir loft and through the door to
Father Donovan's study. With adrenaline coursing so
mercilessly through his body he had very little trouble pushing a
nearby bookshelf against the door. He regretted the lack of tact
in his voice as he yelled for Traci to dial 911 but niceties would
have to, for now, fall victim to necessity. Perhaps that was for the
best because if it had not been for the sudden booming authority
in his voice Traci might not have snapped out of her hysterics
and done as she was told. As she ran over to Donovan's desk
to pick up the phone, he threw his back against the bookshelf,
hoping against the impossible logic of recent events that he was
somehow strong enough to ensure no one or *no thing* could
penetrate his improvised barrier. His breathing was a series of
tidal waves threatening to burst through his chest. Heavy beads
of sweat hung in his eyebrows. His eyes darted around the room
looking for anything that could be used to their advantage either
offensively or defensively. And then his eyes fell on the boy.

Solomon was like the eye of a hurricane, a totem of
unflinching calm in the midst of chaos. As Traci tried futilely to
steady her voice enough to answer the 911 operator's questions
and Joseph stood tensed, waiting for some forceful impact to
rattle against his impromptu barricade, Solomon just stood still,
breath light and regular, arms straight at his side, not trembling

in the slightest. His eyes, however, were terrifying in their own way. The child gazed off in the distance as if daydreaming, no...not daydreaming, his eyes danced about madly. It was as if he could see through the wall straight into the sanctuary and were watching some erratic scene play out. It was disturbing in fathoms so deep that a vicious shudder shot up the length of Joseph's spine.

Father Joseph was a man that held great belief in the unknown and the unseen. He spent his nights pondering not just the celestial majesties the Bible spoke of, but also the infernal depths and all the realms in between, and in this one night, in the span of less than an hour, it was as if a massive veil had been pulled back and all his beliefs had shown themselves to be so valid and tangible that all his imaginings before felt outlandishly fantastical, and with that tangibility came a very real danger of both spiritual and physical consequence.

He had known from the moment he first saw the man on the steps of the Cathedral that evil had come calling, not childhood Hollywood evil, but *real* malevolence. He was convinced the man was possessed, but it was so much more menacing than anything he had experienced in the two exorcisms in which he had, up to this point, partook. The way the man had looked about the sanctuary played on his mind. Had he perhaps been challenged by a host of angels? And did he actually snarl or was that a trick of Father Joseph's memory? And why did he fling himself so violently into the air so inhumanly high, only to crash aimlessly against the wall like that? Worst thought yet was if indeed the beast had arrived at his threshold, was his faith strong enough to turn it away?

Traci fumbled the phone back into its cradle. "The police are on their way." Her voice at least had found some small sense of stability now, but his mind could only ask if they would survive the wait.

CHAPTER 11

The angel had been right, of course, Uzahl had never been a warrior. He was, like all his kind, created with a very particular set of attributes for a very particular purpose. His trade skills were subterfuge and confusion; the subtle poisoning of a man's soul. But so much had changed of late, an unforeseen power had struck from behind a curtain and left their angelic vanguard somehow maimed while he and his kind discovered new might, unrestricted by the Lord of Heaven. It granted him even greater appreciation of why Lucifer had first cast his lot against his Creator and, even though he would not name it so, Uzahl's pride was about to reward him a similar fall.

After having bested the first trio of angels, Uzahl had so very little respect in reserve for the one called Dycliasses that had avoided the battle. Whether it had been angelic ego believing that he and his brethren were flatly superior or a strategic back-line defense of the mortals or even, and Uzahl had placed his bets on this latter option, that the angel simply sensed the presence of something that had ascended in grandeur far beyond him. Uzahl did not give weight to the reason, only to the fact that there was no longer an advantage of simple numbers. It came down to one on one, and in swift manner he would go and claim the child.

Uzahl attacked first, launching himself at an angle that at first appeared to be carrying him over the angel's head, and then suddenly swooping down and to the angel's left flank in a tight arc. Dycliasses stood his ground, glaring at the visage of his fallen brother now worn proudly as a grim mockery. The once-grand wings that carried Uzahl aloft now shown of blackened decay and burnt tips. Though their size never dwindled, they trailed streams of ash as the demon flew. When the demon's weapon lashed out at Dycliasses's flank the angel side-stepped and brought his axe up to block the attack, causing Uzahl's whip to wrap several times around the axe's handle. As Uzahl's arc began to carry him behind the angel his whip went taught and at that moment, Dycliasses pulled back sharply over his head with both hands against it. Uzahl was yanked back into the air, so caught by surprise that he lacked the wherewithal to release his grip on the whip. In the next instant Dycliasses tugged the axe back low past his right hip, causing Uzahl to rocket straight toward him. As Uzahl flew uncontrollably, Dycliasses brought the blade of the axe up in a tight circle meaning to cleave the demon in half. At the last possible moment Uzahl regained enough composure to roll his body towards his right shoulder, bringing his right hand to slap against the side of the axe-blade and alter his flight path safely towards the ground out of threat of his opponent's reach. He released the whip, leaving it bound around the angel's weapon. He allowed himself to roll across the floor, through several rows of pews, and back onto his feet. Though he need not confine himself to the laws of the physical world, Uzahl was amused, almost impressed at times, by his own theatrics, shifting between the physical and spiritual realms both for tactical advantage and flair.

The angel gripped its massive axe on the hilt and high on the neck, just under the blade. The hands began to glow golden-white, then the glow spilled down the length of the axe, and when it reached the whip, the whip disintegrated like crumbling embers. Immediately Dycliasses took after the demon, axe swinging back and forth as he ran. Uzahl hissed in both frustration and warning and spread his arms wide. Long blood-red claws sprang from underneath the angelic fingertips he wore, ripping them asunder as he ran forward to meet Dycliasses head on.

The combatants met, and for a moment it seemed the two were equally matched. Uzahl began taking the offensive in a storm of savage, swift strikes from seemingly impossibly random angles, but Dycliasses coolly parried or dodged each with a flowing grace. Uzahl lacked true experience and knowledge of battle, and as his attacks grew increasingly sloppy and desperate Dycliasses began to press his advantage. Uzahl swung wildly for the angel's throat and Dycliasses spun around his left shoulder simultaneously extending his right arm to catch the demon by the wrist. Having caught Uzahl off-guard, Dycliasses immediately released the wrist and continued with his spin, bringing the axe in his left hand around to the back of Uzahl's leg. When the axe struck, the angelic skin worn by the demon took the brunt of the blow with a thick, solid thud. The axe lodged temporarily as if the skin clung to it, and it took Dycliasses considerable effort to pull it free again.

Uzahl remained kneeling, unable to make use of wounded leg and so shook by the blow itself that he was unable to balance fully on his good leg. Looking up, he saw the axe angled high over Dycliasses's shoulder; the angel meant to behead him now. The severity of this rationalization snapped his mind back into control and his wings stretched wide behind him. As Dycliasses brought down the killing stroke, Uzahl's wings heaved forward with all their might, launching him up and backward in an attempt to avoid being struck. Dycliasses's swing narrowly missed as his enemy whisked to the far side of the sanctuary.

Dycliasses showed no hesitation and sprinted toward Uzahl even before he landed. After a few strides the angel launched himself full into the air just as Uzahl set feet to ground. The angel caught him square in the chest using his head like a battering ram and again sent him flailing back. For a moment the physical laws seized Uzahl, causing him to slam hard into the back pew, toppling it backwards as its backing snapped into chunks. He hit the wall of the sanctuary then fell forward flat on his belly. He managed to lift his eyes just in time to see Dycliasses hurtling towards him like a comet, axe raised high. Uzahl scampered sideways like a mad cat, but was not fast enough and the axe came down with all the force of Heaven upon his right wrist. Uzahl let loose a howl of pain and rolled onto his back, grasping crazily at the stump, now alight with smoke and flame. He kicked his legs wildly, constantly pushing himself backwards along the floor, scrapping deep ravines into the wood, gaining him safe distance from his foe. Dycliasses turned and began to stride once more towards him, the look in his eyes making it clear that he meant to end his wounded prey. In a frenzy Uzahl spun onto his belly and propped himself up haphazardly with his remaining hand. With a final, infuriated cry he sprung up, instantly entering an incorporeal state and escaping through the ceiling into the safety of the outside world.

Dycliasses fought off the temptation to give chase, but there were those here who needed his protection. He knelt down to pick up the hand he had severed and felt a great, bitter taste on his tongue. It was the guilt of knowing that he did not slay the fiend that had claimed the lives of four of his brethren, but he had aligned himself to the priest long ago and now, more than ever before, felt an overwhelming need to honor that.

He looked down at the hand, evil underneath the wrappings of his brother, and the tips of his fingers began to glow. It spread across the angelic flesh, absorbing it, releasing it from the hellish curse until at last it was part of Dycliasses. Now only the beast's hand remained; a gnarled thing of dark grey with long reddish black talons and open, oozing sores. He summoned forth a length of rope and affixed the claw to his waist so that it may remind him to be vigil. In his gut he hungered for vengeance. It felt like a rot under his skin, and he knew, given time, it would consume him little by little until either he give in to the savage urge or found a way to purge it entirely. But he was not ready to let it go, not yet. He would keep it burning down in the core of his being, fueling him, keeping him alert, because in his sinking heart he knew this would be the first of many battles to come.

CHAPTER 12

In flat understatement: the world had changed. In the more than sixty years he spent in the depths of the Pacific the fibers of morality had withered down to fine hairs. He could only imagine that the shifts had been so minute and subtle that they were hardly noted from one generation to the next, but to him they were glaring. Nothing stood out as such a stark example to him as modern advertising. Once the focus had seemed to be on taking pride in things like honest, hard work and family and living with a certain, though often exaggerated, sense of style and class. Men were depicted as hard working breadwinners and women were masters of house and home. Today, however, everything was sex and sarcasm and strong goading towards one-up-man-ship. Fragrances, alcohol, automobiles, even things as menial as foodstuffs were often marketed with scantily clad women or men who were suddenly transformed into something bolder, more sexual by the advertised token. Scripts filled with belittlement and slander replaced the seeming pleasantries of normal conversation. It was spread across storefront windows, billboards mounted precariously on building tops, multistory digital screens, and radio waves floating on the night wind from open car windows. The hand of the Enemy had moved further than Athiel had imagined it would, and now, caught up in the sensory maelstrom of it, it made him both nauseated and mournful.

All at once he heard very nearly his exact thoughts being spoken aloud and looked about for their source. Three men well dressed in suits of green and grey surrounded another in black who stood on a crate with a megaphone and shouted to passers-by about the moral compromises that the humankind continued to make.

"There is no God in your greed," he proclaimed. "You worship the trappings of this life and willfully blind yourself to the glories of the next."

The river of people flowing in both directions down the sidewalk crashed against Athiel only for a second when he stopped to listen. He ignored the disdainful remarks the busy pedestrians made and soon enough the river ebbed around him as if he were merely a stone.

The man continued his sermon.

"You set your goals so very low; a car, a fancy new cell phone, jewelry, clothes, a big house. These things are material, and all things material will one day turn to dust and blow away. Set your goals high," he exclaimed, "set your sights to the highest of heights. To the Lord above and to the mansion in Heaven He offers to each and every one of us who will but simply love Him."

An occasional passer-by would slow to listen to the man preach, but none would stop entirely. Most gave despising glances or swatted away the pamphlets that his associates tried earnestly to distribute. From out of a sea of passing faces a teenage voice shouted back, "Your God is dead!" but the speaker never stepped forward to be identified. The preacher took hold of this challenge and retorted.

"The Lord of Lords and King of Kings is never-ending, my friend. He lives in every heart, even those who refuse His love." As he continued he pointed into the crowd randomly as if any one there could have been proposing an argument. "It is the world that is dying! It is our hearts that are dead! Dead in shame and the sickness of sin."

Men in the passing crowd waved him off with visible disgust, but Athiel felt pride for the preacher swell in the pit of his chest. The man swam against the tide and never flinched at the slings and arrows that flew at him. The prophets of old would applaud.

Athiel turned his attention back to the pulse of the city about him, though aesthetically different, Lanza del Los Santos was fundamentally the same. The bustle and energy had multiplied in scale as the population grew and crowded both inward in high rises and outward into suburbs, but the heart of a city rarely changes. In such metropolises he always felt more connected with the heart of mankind, though their outer facades were thicker armoring here than in more rural communities. Here he felt more in-tune with the war every man wages against sin both knowingly and ignorantly. The boundaries were painted in tones of blurred grey, and it was within that shade that many true revelations were made. Here there was struggle that held a greater sense of immediacy. Here there were more souls to be saved. Here there was a greater unacknowledged need for God's love. Here he could serve.

He laughed at himself. The human-like heart in his chest pounded in ways both familiar and unsettling. It was like a surge of adrenaline, and as it tapered off, it was replaced by the hollow remembrance of why he had chosen this existence over his first; the desire to help embattled by the nature to serve orders with which he could not agree. An ancient ache arose and chipped away at what remained of his enthusiasm. He sighed deeply, one of many mortal habits he had picked up, and fell back into the flow of the people. Another cell in the blood that coursed through the veins of the city, being carried unaware to its heart and to answers he had yet to think of questions for.

CHAPTER 13

From his perch atop a billboard displaying a smiling woman claiming her love for a cheeseburger the Prisoner watched the once-angel wade through the mortal streets as if he were one of them. He felt a greater kinship now than he had when the two had served the Throne. He did not know the particulars of why his once-brother, Athiel, had cast aside his wings, but that question loomed over him with equal parts empathy and caution. He would watch Athiel for a while longer and see if he too was being pulled along by the same great thread that he felt. Maybe together they could both find answers to their individual questions. Maybe they could shake off the absence of their Father. And maybe the Prisoner could at last be set free.

He heard the approaching roll of thunder and looked out over the skyline. Skyscrapers bit into the night sky like rabid fangs, piercing into the fat gray clouds that threatened hard rain. He saw deeper, beyond the clouds and into the pulse of the world itself, and there glimpsed the edges of the true storm that was raging. No life, mortal or otherwise, would be untouched by its malice. And in the balance hung…perhaps everything.

He stood and turned in the direction his once-brother had trod and leapt into the possibilities of the night.

CHAPTER 14

The Cathedral of Saint Michael was now officially a crime scene. The first responders had arrived within five minutes of the 911 call with three news teams just minutes on their heels. The first to arrive, a thirty-something Sergeant named Paul Kennedy, was actually a parishioner which, to Father Joseph, was a tremendously calming blessing. Father Joseph handled the majority of the initial questions they were asked as a group and, watching closely in his peripheral, he saw Traci was surprisingly still not very forthcoming when they were questioned individually. She volunteered the name of the man who had invaded the Cathedral, but it took persistence to pry the more intimate details of their relationship from her, especially that he was her son's father. Solomon was rigidly silent and soon, by direct order of the Major on-scene, he was left alone entirely – for the time being.

Light examination of the body by a few officers came to the collective agreement that the body in question had been dead for a considerable time longer than the stories that were being told alleged, but that would be estimated more accurately once the coroner arrived. To further complicate matters no one in their group could give any explanation as to the damage done to pews in the back of the sanctuary other than they "heard a ruckus." Untrusting glances danced back and forth between various officers but none spoke freely.

After a time the Major asked Traci and her son if they

would like to be driven home, but she only shook her head "no." Finally, Father Joseph had volunteered accommodations built as an addition to the Cathedral itself, a half-way house that had never been finished due to an embezzlement scandal that to this day remained a black mark on the church's name. But there were beds, working plumbing, and a roof; and if Traci felt safer here, she was certainly welcome to stay. She gave verbal agreement, and for a moment the Major seemed to hang in indecision. He finally relented but informed them all that further questioning was likely, and for a time officers would be stationed outside the Cathedral.

A pair of detectives arrived along with the coroner and offered a second battery of questions, most were just revised versions of queries they had already answered, but Father Joseph and Traci answered truthfully. They escorted Solomon alone back to Father Donovan's office, thinking it a better way to draw answers from the boy, but he was still entirely unresponsive which they concluded was due to a state of shock.

Soon Father Gregory Donovan himself arrived, having spent a hectic five minutes outside the police tape trying to explain to the media that he currently had nothing to tell but would gladly speak with them after he had time to go inside and find out more himself. As soon as he was within the scene's perimeter he went about trying in vain to offer what assistance and comfort he could. Father Joseph told him of his offer of accommodations for Traci and Solomon, and Donovan agreed instantly, even offering to stay with them himself so that Joseph could go home, but Joseph refused, and in time fatigue earned by his own hard day wore Donovan down. Donovan took time to confer with the Major and Sgt. Kennedy so as to be as well-informed as possible. As the patrolmen and detectives left, carting the corpse of Solomon's human father with them, so did Donovan. As promised he gave as concise a sound bite as possible to the hungry media outside before making his way back to the sanctity of his home to call the dioceses' bishop and bring him up to speed.

After a long while they at last found themselves alone in a void comprised of harsh silence, huddled together on the front row of pews. An unspoken need took hold of Traci, and she clung to Joseph like a child to her father. She went limp into his arms, face buried in his chest and wept. Her fingers bit into his triceps, but he never let the pain show. He would endure what he had to for her sake. He could not read her thoughts, but she must have come to realize that her son had just lost his father, for she released Joseph and swept up Solomon into her sorrowful embrace. She petted her tears from his hair and kissed his forehead as she rocked him back and forth. Yet still the boy was quiet.

Father Joseph took his eyes off of the mother and child and looked about him in wonderment, bewildered that the officers had left them alone. Surely that was not normal procedure, leaving a crime scene not unattended, but worse: attended only by potential suspects that could use the opportunity to tamper with evidence. Blue and red flashes reminded him that officers were just outside while alternately tinting the stained glass that lined sanctuary walls and painting the soft features of the Virgin Mary. He could no longer see her red tears and wondered first if that was significant and secondly if he had truly seen them at all. He looked curiously at the smashed pew in the back, his eyesight was not strong enough to pick out details with any genuine clarity at this distance, but he knew the man had never impacted there. Of a sudden he realized that what he was searching for was not something he could actually see, but that an unseen presence lingered in the air about them. He felt like a blind soldier in the smoldering aftermath of a recent engagement. Considering that he and Traci and Solomon were still standing, he assumed, or rather he hoped diligently, that the victory, at least for now, had been claimed by angels.

He became very aware of the tension in his shoulders, and the rest of his body took that as a signal and began to tire. He turned to Traci and suggested that he show them to their room, but paused then asked if she would like for him to say a prayer. Through gritted teeth she nodded, and they bowed their heads, as did Solomon to his great surprise. Moments lingered heavily before he could find the proper words to begin. He firmly believed that all prayer should begin with an expression of gratitude, but he struggled to find gratuity in the night's events. At last the words came and with them an unexplainable but welcomed sense of lucidity and peace.

CHAPTER 15

As Father Joseph offered up the first words of thanks for the safety of their group, Dycliasses placed a loving hand on his shoulder and willed the priest to be strong. He ached to think that these prayers would float to Heaven and not be heard. Was the Throne truly now vacant? Not so long ago he would never have believed that such was even possible, but now, in his heart, there lay doubt and with it dread. He placed his other hand across the priest's scalp, closed his eyes, and offered up his own prayer in hopes that, somehow, it too would be heard.

CHAPTER 16

They all laughed at him when he told them about the man rising out of the water like an angel. Well, not *all* of them: Herschel never stopped his random pacing, all the while muttering to no one about the "ears that never stopped hearing," and Motor-Mouth Gillespie enthusiastically added himself into the story, but none of that dissuaded Blowfish from his vigorous retelling of the night's events at the dock. The further into his retelling he got the more it seemed as if he could see it play out from different angles which gave him a growing sense of clarity. This man was not a man; could not be *just* a man. And he knew Blowfish's name, his *real* name. His mind divided in two, one part the prolific spinner of tales and the other the studious bystander, listening only in part to his own tale-weaving all the while diving deeper into his own psyche. He knew many truths that others never seemed to have the wherewithal to accept, but this particular yarn held a more substantial place in his personal history. It was so tangible that it made other nights seem dream-like by comparison. The memories of each rendezvous with the Godfather of Soul and Sandwiches at the docks began to haze over, as did all those nights he saw the Mayor gallivanting about with a new tootsie or two, and that time he was knighted by the Pope during the second Great War. The smaller aspects of those times began to just kind of fall by the wayside. But the pier and the man…that was vivid in a way he could not fully comprehend.

He stopped mid-sentence near the end of his telling and

looked into the baffled faces about him. In each face he saw a colorful and tragic history. Bouts with alcoholism.The crushing of dreams. The fear of success. The abandonment by and of family. Abuse. Chemical imbalance so great as to cause genuine clinical insanity. So many lives that all spiraled to this same dark place in this same unforgiving world. And if he could look around him now and see this many lost souls just here, living in a makeshift camp constructed of torn tarps, soggy cardboard, and filth under the Lincoln Bridge, then how many more vagrant souls were out there on this Earth?

His vision began to blur from tears before he even realized it was happening. He no longer felt like such a victim of his own sorted history as much as he felt like a man nearly powerless to lift up those about him.

Embarrassment crept in and before it could overtake him fully he yielded the floor, as it were, to Motor-Mouth Gillespie. It occurred to Blowfish that in those same faces he could see a total lack of belief in anything he had to say, although a few did display a degree of amusement. He stammered back to his own personal piece of real estate, a pile of newspaper currently held in place by a few well-placed bricks, and was about to lay down when he froze in place. Home was not home any more. He had occupied many houses in his former life, had shared them with a wife and three kids, but they had always felt like rented space; someone else's property. This mangy heap was the one thing he had ever built with his own two hands. It was not much, but it was *his*. Or had felt like it was, until now. Until tonight.

There was an odd tickle running up the back of his neck that assured there was more to be had out there. It was not a presumption of material or monetary gain, but of something worth so much more. Something of *true* value.

With a huff, Blowfish compromised his newfound sense of purpose just enough to lay down on his crude bed. He pulled a few pages over top of him to guard against the night breeze but felt no real security in it. Not anymore. As sleep began to him (which was nothing short of a miracle considering that Motor-Mouth Gillespie had no concept of volume control) he could only smile and remember the words the man-that-was-not-a-man had gifted him with, "You will be blessed again."

CHAPTER 17

Kenneth Phelps was still awake when Sergeant Kennedy's name appeared on his cell phone. Sharon had only finally fallen asleep a half-hour before but still lay across his lap. He had not moved before for fear of waking her, but took that chance now. If Kennedy was calling this late, it had to be important.

As he gingerly slipped his arm out from under her and replaced it with a throw pillow he clicked to accept the call and whispered, "Hello?"

Mr. Phelps, this is Sergeant Paul Kennedy with the LSPD, I'm sorry to be bothering you this late. Hope I didn't wake you." Kenneth and Paul had spoken numerous times after Sunday morning service at Saint Michael and had long before come to a first name relationship, so the fact that Paul was committed to such an official tone immediately put Kenneth on edge.

"No Paul," for his own sake he attempted to bring the conversation down to a personal level, "I've been awake. How are you?"

"To be honest, Mister…Ken," a small, fragile relief settled on Kenneth, "not very well, there was an incident tonight at Saint Michael," and was instantly shattered.

Kenneth looked down at his wife to make sure she still slept soundly then left the room and retreated back to the confines of his office. As he shut the door behind him he bade Paul continue.

81

"A man chased his ex-girlfriend and their son into the church, and well, to be honest, we're not too sure what happened next." Paul hesitated.

Kenneth sat down in his office chair and leaned forward onto his elbows, his brow furled. These were not the apocalyptic tidings his gut had been expecting given his previous conversation with Treygen, but whatever news was coming was definitely not good. "Tell me what you know."

"Well, the girlfriend called 911. Father Donovan wasn't there, just Father Joseph. He had the three of them barricaded inside Father Donovan's office. Said he locked them up in there after the man, the ex-boyfriend...well...after he threw himself into a wall and broke his own neck or something. Allegedly he had chased the girl and her son from her apartment after a confrontation. Said he was pure crazy, but at least no one else seems to have been hurt."

Paul finally stopped to take a breath, leaving Kenneth with an opening to interject, but found he could not. He had no idea what to say.

After a tense silence Paul continued, "There were news crews from a few stations there, including yours, but I didn't know if you had heard yet, and I know that you and Behanan are kind of close. So, it just seemed like you should be in the loop."

Kenneth ran a hand through his thinning hair. That explained why Joseph had not answered his call earlier that evening. He felt selfish at wanting to contact him now, not knowing how traumatized his friend might be. True, the news Kenneth had to unburden himself was of infinitely greater consequence, but in his current possible state would Joseph be able to process it?

He became aware that Paul was patiently waiting on the line for any reply at all.

"I appreciate you calling me, Paul. I'll try to head over to Joseph's apartment first thing in the morning and check on him."

"Go to the church. All three of them are staying there for now. The girl didn't want to take her kid back home for some reason. I mean, the guy's dead, but she seems spooked beyond anything I think I've ever seen. In fact, didn't seem like she wanted to leave the church at all. The whole thing was just bizarre. Maybe Father Joe will tell you something more than he told us."

Kenneth frowned, Paul was trying to bait him into fishing for more information.

"Thank you, Paul. I'll talk to him tomorrow. Have a goodnight."

Paul grunted a hard syllable, clearly he did not intend for the conversation to endnthere, but he conceded.

"You too, Ken. Tell Sharon hello for me."

"I will. Good-bye."

Kenneth hung up and reclined in his seat, folding his arms tight against his chest. He could not filter his various thoughts into organized groups. Could not rationalize the bombardment he felt.

He exhaled heavily and asked aloud to no one, "What next?"

CHAPTER 18

The ominous clouds that had teased the dry streets below for hours now finally began their brazen offensive. Many of the pedestrians – either having lacked the foresight to carry an umbrella or did not own one – took refuge from the torrential ambush inside small storefronts or under crowded awnings. They had places to be but maybe if they waited just a few minutes the rain would let up just a little, just enough. Vacant taxis suddenly found plentiful fare; their drivers edging one another out, jockeying for prime curbside real estate. Others plodded along not seeming to mind the soaking. Those intuitive enough to bring umbrellas strutted about like peacocks whose feathers bumped precariously as they passed one another. To Athiel, all of this was beautiful.

Humanity had such a vitality about it. Trouble reared its ugly head and mankind adapted. Some chose paths of lesser resistance, which often led to other dark choices and further down the road to sin and ruination. Others stiffened their spines and craned their chins higher in defiance of the odds. But even in the face of great adversity, the human race carried on, almost simply because it could. It was a gift that the Father had granted at the dawn of mortal creation…a time, he told himself, when the Throne still loved unconditionally.

He wrenched his thoughts away from the Throne and the Heavens; they always led him to low places, close to those dark paths of ruination he now felt a greater vulnerability to. He would chose instead to embrace the majesty of the world around him and so laid his head back and let plump droplets bead down his face. They made shallow pools around his eyes and tasted metallic on his tongue. Water was life here, and as it danced upon his flesh he truly felt alive.

To his right a crowd began to form around the window display of a modest electronics store. A low murmuring began to crescendo until at last a woman let forth a wail of both grief and terror. Her knees gave up their strength, and she fainted backwards, clumsily caught by two gentlemen who had stepped closer out of sheer curiosity.

Athiel turned to offer some assistance but was immediately caught up by the images on the television screens that populated the window. The Vatican had been attacked. The Basilica of Saint Peter was burning. Flames like massive tentacles lashed out from shattered windows, whipping angrily against the early morning sky. Large sections of the building's face had crumbled inward and appeared ready to collapse completely. Rescue workers ran in and out, escorting survivors suffering from various degrees of injury. More than a few of those pulled from the maelstrom tried desperately to race back inside. As cameramen recorded live from half a world away another massive section of the building gave way in a downward crash of heavy rubble, flame, and smoke.

The image cut to a close shot of a Vatican worker who was far too emotional to remain still or by any shred rational. Though she snapped out short Italian syllables a network voice-over offered translation.

"The Holy Father," she said, referring to the Pontiff, "He may still be inside."

She began to shake visibly as if that very thought had just hit home to her. Offscreen a reporter began to ask questions which she answered with varying degrees of success. The two networked translations clashed with the original voices, dulling the emotional impact of the answers.

He asked, "What can you tell us about the explosion itself?"

"I was just arriving to begin my shift. I was approaching security when…it was so loud. My ears still hurt. My chest still hurts." She spun back to face the crumbling structure and screamed hysterically, "Holy Father pleeeease!!!"

Athiel stepped away from the growing crowd and let the gravity of the attack drive home. The Pope, spiritual leader of millions, possibly dead. And of even greater and graver consequence, that it was murder. This volatile planet was growing moreso in grand strides.

He bowed his head and searched within the tomes of his Knowledge. There was a plan, had always been a plan, carefully orchestrated, vigilantly monitored, and though it was wrought with hardship and pain, in the end, it was right. Or so he had once believed. His faith in the divine wisdom of the plan had faltered before his fall. In truth it was one of the many divisive elements that led him to it. Fortunately he still maintained vivid Knowledge of it…or he had. Now reaching back into his memory felt like oiled hands sliding across his scalp. He could not grip the precise aspects he wanted. Some drifted to the surface like bubbles only to burst, leaving him very little in the way of clarity or enlightenment.

He gave the televisions one more hard stare, hoping it would trigger something in the scrambled puzzle of his mind, but nothing. Deep down, in his gut more than his mind, he knew that somehow what he was seeing was wrong. It was not a link in the grand chain. Somehow the world was turning in ways against the Lord's design. And *that* knowledge gave him true fear.

CHAPTER 19

It was with a heavy heart that Treygen Andros watched the futile efforts of the Vatican rescue workers. A heavy heart and more than a shade of guilt. No, he did not set the charges—he was a man of science, not violence, but he was in league with those that did. He had no proof of their agenda, but there was no mistaking the link this horror played in the larger chain of events all orchestrated by Valdez. If he had not been so sickened by his own role in matters he might have marveled at how beautifully placed each piece was and how, now that things had been set in full motion, each domino fell without the slightest obstruction.

He wanted to run full-speed away from the throng of mourners that had already gathered outside the police quarantine. His eyes flashed quickly about the crowd as if somehow more than one of them *knew* he was involved. Maybe he was not as overcome with emotion as the rest and that marked him as a suspect. And if any of these simpletons could make that deductive leap then surely so could local law enforcement.

He bit his lower lip hard, almost hard enough to make it bleed. The paranoia was digging in again. It wanted him to believe that every random glance his way was a visual study of his character or every whisper he could not make out was all talk of his conspiracy. If he did not know better (for certain) he would think a demon was tormenting his mind. But no, not a demon. He knew how they operated and, more importantly, was now protected wholly against their powers. No, this was scientific. It was chemical, and it was treatable, and he reminded himself that in recognizing such, he knew how and when to act upon it.

He shook his right hand down into the inner breast pocket of his overcoat and fished out the bottle of pills that lay within. He had designed them himself. Tested them on himself. He called them his "fairy dust". A secret side project he conducted in *their* labs, under *their* noses. He reminded himself that if *they* still had not hounded out his secrets then this crowd was surely not detrimental.

He twisted off the cap and swallowed two pills dry before hesitating and choking down two more. They would take effect soon enough but even the fact that he had taken them worked a bit of placebo magic to calm his nerves.

He held out his right hand to test his control. Still shaky, but with focused effort he could tame it to a degree.

He watched the anarchy a few minutes longer, trying to predict the global consequences that could result. Despite himself he became mesmerized by the savage ballet. The pulse of the flame provided the bass tone, the emergency sirens the treble, as the dancers pranced and pirouetted to and fro the debris before a woeful choir of onlookers. And just for a moment, he wanted to join in their somber melody.

His phone vibrated in his pant pocket, startling him. Though no one looked his way or even cared, his cheeks felt hot with embarrassment. He clumsily fumbled his hand into his pants and procured the cell after its third ring. His screen read "Valdez," and he could not help but pause. Fourth ring. The call transferred to his voicemail. He cursed himself for being so mentally disjointed and scrambled to call Valdez back before the voice greeting ended. Whether he succeeded or not did not matter, the voice that answered his return call was impatient from the onset.

"Andros." Spoken in a rolling Spanish accent.

"Yes, Mr. Valdez?" He hoped his tone sounded infinitely calmer than it felt.

"We need to speak. It is of the utmost urgency."

His throat dropped into his stomach. "Yes, sir. I'll come right away."

"I expect that you do."

The line disconnected.

Andros's hands were sweating, and he felt feverish. He reopened his bottle of fairy dust and extracted two more pills. *With any luck,* he thought, *I can have a heart attack.*

He resealed the bottle and fought his way out of the crowd, hoping no one else could see his world falling apart.

CHAPTER 20

T he far side of the world is often, in effect, a different world altogether. Sometimes even a different room is a realm unto itself. The air can be sweet and nourishing, while outside it is vapid and choking. In the small makeshift bedroom in the unfinished wing of the Saint Michael Cathedral, the air was cool with the flavor of rain and, even with the night's dreadfulness, somehow the sweetness of relief and security.

Traci Nicholas lay in the fetal position atop a naked mattress (mattresses had been purchased at a discounted rate from a parishioner though funds had run short before sheets, blankets and the like could be procured) with her arms wrapped instinctively around her son. Even in the deepest of sleep a mother will protect that which she loves. Her dreams were of joyous things: a lake of calm water set against an amber sky, a sailboat that drifted without the need for wind, Solomon blithely drawing stick figures on the mud of the shore with a stick. It was the rest of the righteous untouched by the troubles of the waking world.

Nearby Father Joseph reclined in a heavily padded brown leather office chair he had wheeled in from Father Donovan's office, a gift from Matthew Hughes (proprietor of Hughes Fine Furnishings whom had generously discounted the mattresses) as a "thank you" gift for helping lead his eldest daughter, Angela, to Christ and then overseeing her nuptials a year later. Matthew had gifted this particular chair because it was the absolute finest he had in stock; ergonomically designed and artfully stylized with thick brass buttons running along the seams. The leather was deceptively firm, but when you sat and let the chair perform its brand of magic, you sank in as if on a cloud. Father Joseph had become well acquainted with this feature already during his tenure at Saint Michael. His last waking thoughts were how it seemed to melt away any burden you carried. He had smiled devilishly, uttered "Mana from Heaven," and then slumber had claimed him.

Dycliasses stood exactly halfway between the two dreamers, exhaling waves of peace that swam through the air in golden curls that found their way gently onto their lips. It was a small matter to grant them this serenity, there was surely more tribulation to come and they would need what rest they could afford. But he was discomforted in his own way. With every blessing he gifted to the mortals he could feel a bit of his own strength slip away in small shavings. This had never happened before to any angel, and its implications were dire. God was the source of their power, ever-renewing, absolute, and unending. And now his power was fading.

He felt the eyes of the boy upon him and turned to face the child. Solomon was cocooned tightly in his mother's embrace, and though he lay perfectly still, he was fully awake and aware.

It was the first true opportunity the angel had to study the child, and Solomon was likewise committed to studies of his own. Solomon was not the first human to have such sight, though it was rare to such a degree that humans would consider it myth. But there were reasons for that talent, and that was where the danger lie.

"You look at me as though you have seen many of my brothers," Dycliasses broke the silence.

Solomon nodded meekly.

"And when the demon came, you were as familiar of he and his kin."

Another nod.

"How long have you had this gift?"

At last Solomon looked away. He stared blankly and seemed to consider his reply before settling on a shrug.

Dycliasses stepped toward him and bent low to his level, and for one fleeting moment the boy seemed to almost shy away...or was it fear? Was the underlying repulsion the angel felt shared by the boy?

"My name, dear one," he forced the endearment, "is Dycliasses."

Solomon opened his mouth to speak, but his mother stirred—the angel's blessing was losing its potency—and he closed it instead.

Dycliasses brought a hand to his lips and kissed it tenderly, dousing it with another blessing and then touching Traci's forehead so that the blessing would pass on to her. She sighed and smiled, never waking. Her arms tightened around her son in a manner more filled with love than protection. Solomon closed his eyes, and with a sigh of his own, drank her love in. It comforted the angel to see that the boy was indeed very much just that...a boy.

"You were about to speak," Dycliasses's found his voice laced with a softness he had not intended, but was glad for it nonetheless. "What was it you wanted to say?"

Solomon bit his lower lip and found the strength to answer.

"I know your name. I've heard others say it. Both kinds. The ones like you say it with love. The other kind, the demons, they used to be afraid of you." The words were spoken with the voice of a child, but the surety of a man.

Used to be, the words stunk of fearful apprehension.

"You seem to know more than I, Solomon. Why are the demons no longer afraid?"

A flash of surprise crossed Solomon's face. "They say God is dead."

And there it was, spoken aloud, each syllable a nail in his breast. And right then, all doubt was swept aside. Now only emptiness remained; a void that dread would soon fill.

The boy continued, "They say the angels are weaker now. And people will be easier to control."

Anguish. Rage. Despair. All swelled up to assault the angel. He slumped to his knees. He wanted to cry out like his brethren had in the sanctuary, to tear at his garments like the prophets of old, but a rational thought occurred to him and, for the time being, managed to stabilize him, if only to a small degree.

He regarded the child.

"When did you hear this? Just tonight?"

"No," was Solomon's immediate reply. "For months. They say the sky closed up, and they won, but they didn't know how."

Dycliasses's jaw tightened. *The sky closed up...months ago.*

He remembered a day, vaguely, when a change came swiftly and unexpectedly. The Knowledge all angels possessed was near-omnipotence that flowed from the Lord Himself. There was a thread that tied all creation to the Throne, an ever-present love and power that connected all children to Father. But on that day the umbilical was severed. Thinking back on it now it seemed so clear, and he could not understand how he could have forgotten. All at once the Knowledge, the love, the wholeness of his being left him. And not he alone, but *all* of the angels suffered the disconnect. Somehow, as time went on, the memory of that day faded into obscurity. He turned his mind over trying to uncover new bits of what he may have lost, and he began to realize just how utterly he felt. Human. Uncertain. Grounded. As if...

"...We have forgotten how to fly." The concept took sound without Dycliasses being aware he had spoken, but he continued out loud, "The sky was closed. But we forgot how to climb to the Heavens, so we never knew."

Oddly Solomon seemed to understand all of this in a way deeper than a mortal should, especially a child.

"Are you becoming like me? Human?" the child asked with an air of innocence only a child can carry.

Until that second Dycliasses had not considered that possibility.

"No...it should not happen like that, but..." The doubt that infected his tone was cumbersome. "If the Lord were dead, then everything, everywhere, should have ended. Nothing can exist without His nurture. And we would not become mortal. We would die with Him," he smiled as best he could at the boy, "but He cannot die. Cannot be hurt or overthrown. Lucifer tried, but even he failed for our Father is almighty."

Dycliasses stopped. He had been rambling. His thoughts

were jumbled. His words sounded desperate to even himself, as if clinging to anything that would provide him any measure of hope. Kneeling and disjointed in this way, he felt like a child before Solomon. It was unsettling. Again the priest and the mother stirred, a direct reaction of their spirits to the angel's mood.

From the depths of Traci's embrace a small hand reached out and Solomon pulled her arms tighter around him. "They sound like you. They were all scared and sad at first, but now most don't remember."

"Nothing is clear for me, child. I did not even know how lost I was until now. Maybe you can help me to better understand." Dycliasses accented this with another smile, but it was not returned. Perhaps in time the child would...

A warmth ran up Dycliasses's neck, and the look on the child's face confirmed what he felt. Solomon stared beyond him, into the depths of the Cathedral.

"An angel is coming," Solomon confirmed, but with an air of unpleasantness.

It was an unpleasantness Dycliasses shared.

CHAPTER 21

Belethor was unnerved by Solomon's awareness and had asked Dycliasses to accompany him outside for privacy. Dycliasses refused.

"I will not leave their side. Uzahl has not finished with them."

Belethor stood in silence, puzzling out a compromise while Solomon scrutinized him unabashedly. The angel did not wear the seemingly standard white and gold robes of his kind, but instead donned a very modern black three-buttoned, double-breasted, pin-striped suit complete with a white dress shirt and solid black tie skillfully tied half winsor knot. It gave him the appearance of an undertaker or government agent, not a being of pure spirit, and in fact, the angel stood before them in physical form. Should either Joseph or Traci wake they would likely be startled by the presence of the stranger standing before them appearing to converse with the shadows.

"Others are calling for a gathering," Belethor said, finally, "At dawn."

"Who specifically?" Dycliasses asked, and when it seemed Belethor would not answer he pressed. "You may speak in front of the boy. He knows much," as he spoke he moved beside Solomon as if to demonstrate that the child was not a threat. "Maybe more than we ourselves."

The last part earned Solomon an inquisitive stare. While

Belethor was clearly unhappy with such openness in front of a mortal it seemed that he thought perhaps there was a thing or two that could be learned here. His gaze shifted from Dycliasses to Solomon, to the demonic trophy at Dycliasses's waist and back to the Captain before he finally continued. There was much to be curious about indeed.

"Juriel initiated. Already he has drawn Palius and Tristes to him. Messengers have been sent to gather any brethren left in this city. Juriel is insistent that all abandon their extraneous duties and attend."

Dycliasses rose defiantly, his wings exploding outward, taking up nearly half the room and causing Belethor to step backwards.

"As I have said, I will *not* leave these mortals to fend for themselves against a foe from which they have no recourse. Juriel can find me after should he still desire to speak with me." He proclaimed, leaving the challenge lingering in the air.

When Belethor regained his composure he took an expression both grim and saddened. Dycliasses's wings drew in slightly at the sight.

"Have we come to this?" Dycliasses asked. "United no more? We in-fight and lack direction."

"We are not ourselves," Belethor's eyes flickered again to the demon's hand dangling morbidly from Dycliasses's robe.

He sighed, turned away from Dycliasses and strode towards the open door.

"This is precisely why the gathering has been called. Juriel holds hope that we may reunify and make sense of all that has become of us." Belethor gave Solomon one last odd consideration. "I hope you change your mind, brother. There are greater matters upon us."

As he brought his attention back to Dycliasses, something haunted crossed his face.

"I love you, Dycliasses."

Dycliasses lowered his wings, likewise touched with sorrow and, deeper under the surface, the unfamiliar sting of shame. But he did not speak, only watched Belethor leave in silence.

As Belethor made his way down the hall he called back over his shoulder, "You know where the gathering will be held. I hope you will join us."

Dycliasses's neck went limp, and his chin fell to his chest, but the surrender he felt continued downward until his whole body threatened to topple. He allowed this. All he had been battling internally clawed just under his skin, and finally he was ready to let it have its way. He dropped low on all fours allowing all the pain and anguish and rage and fear to spill forth in near hysterical waves that rolled up from his belly and shot out from his lips in a blinding golden light.

Father Joseph and Traci writhed almost violently as their peaceful dreams suddenly turned dark and fretful. Once Traci clinched Solomon so fiercely that he cried out in pain. Still dead asleep Traci screamed Solomon's name and pushed out against the weight she felt touching her, knocking him to the floor. Solomon landed hard on his right shoulder but was too stunned to vocalize the hurt.

Even unconscious, mother's instinct kicked in and alerted Traci that she no longer held her child. She sat up, fully awake in an instant, and fought against her adjusting vision, trying to locate her son. She recognized the blurred shape on the floor before her eyes could fully focus and scrambled off the bed to him.

Across the room Father Joseph convulsed in his chair and roared, "Get behind me devil!" and kicked against the air, waking himself in the process. His startled eyes bulged with fear as he tried to familiarize himself with his surroundings. He caught sight of Traci cradling her child on the floor, Solomon holding his right shoulder. Joseph reached up and wiped away the trails of sweat escaping his hairline.

Among them, yet unseen by all but Solomon, Dycliasses brought himself up to his knees, still doubled over with his arms wrapped tight about his stomach.

In this small room, in each others' presence, everyone felt entirely alone.

CHAPTER 22

Gregory Donovan stood high on a hill covered with a mixture of soft grass and moss. A willow tree spotted with fluorescent purple petals loomed over his left shoulder and provided cool shade from a tyrannical sun. Below him a sea of eager faces waited eagerly in a colossal half-circle at the base of the hill. The on-lookers ran the complete gamut of human existence: elderly Afro-American couples cuddling tightly, Caucasian teenagers sporting tiny headphones trailing from cell phones, middle-aged Asian women holding hands with their children, Jewish leaders, Muslim students, young, old, male or female, all races and ages and religions were in attendance. Faces smiled up at him lovingly and many of those belonged to parishioners of his own congregation at Saint Michael. All came willingly, wearing their earnest anticipation upon their sleeves. They were the flock, seeking to be lead to greener pastures by he, their kind shepherd.

He smiled grandly to bid them welcome and opened his arms wide in a universal embrace. Every hand raised high to return the salutation. Their fingers stretched towards him as if to behold even the slightest sensation of his light. Some eyes closed and leaked sweet tears of joy. All loved him and all believed he would lead them righteously; they but awaited his word.

He let his left arm fall but kept his right aloft and asked, "Please, brothers and sisters, lower your arms and raise your hearts. I come to you with wondrous tidings!"

They obeyed like children rather than spiritual siblings. Many took hold of others around them and pulled them closer, so excited to share in the message they were about to receive, but all kept silent for fear that they would miss a single word of it.

Clasping both hands to his chest he continued, "I am but a humble servant of a love most high. An unconditional love that reigns down on each and every heart, regardless of if that heart should choose to accept it. That love is all encompassing and all knowing. It thrives in even the murky shadow of man's soul. And *even* there, can it find a foothold and metamorphose into a thing of life changing splendor."

Every face opened more to him, eyes and mouths widening, ears straining to draw in every droplet from his lips. With each line they believed more and more, that much was evident simply from their body language.

"The wages of sin are the wages we each have earned. We do so so very often and often so very meekly. We convince ourselves of the safety of our little white lies. That minor sin is of minor consequence. But all sin is a barrier we erect between ourselves and a loving God." His physical smile was momentarily eclipsed by an emotional one under the skin as the thought struck him, *this is why Joseph enjoys my sermons so much. I sound like a Baptist evangelist.* Remotely he realized he had not seen Joseph present in the crowd.

"Do you not feel *His* love cascading down upon you even now? Accepting you, every sin and every flaw?" He accentuated this point by once again reaching his hands towards the sky. He expected to see those below mimicking the gesture, but they did not. Instead many faces seemed confused. They gazed skyward as if any moment Heaven's light might shine down upon them, yet baffled that it did not. Low murmurs broke out in pockets throughout the multitude and many suspicious glances shot his way. His arms slowly began to fall back to his sides, and his face melted into a display of confusion.

"What troubles you?" he asked.

Many looked away or towards their feet like scolded children. Others returned stony stares. To his left a dense group spread out, and from their center Father Joseph stepped forward, the woman Traci and her son Solomon behind him as if he was their shield.

"The halls of Heaven have gone cold, Greg. The Throne is unoccupied, and the love you babble about is now just wishful thinking." Father Joseph's stance was both proud and defiant. Mixed with his words they stopped Father Donovan solid.

Behind him a weak breeze rustled the willow petals and the long, whip-like branches raked against the ground.

Gregory Donovan shook his head. He felt utterly betrayed. "Why would you say that?" He took a few steps down the hill at the exact same moment that Joseph began to step towards him.

As Joseph replied he turned as to include everyone in attendance. "An angel came to me. The flame of its sword had been extinguished and its wings stripped bare. It cursed the world of man and blamed our lack of faith for weakening the Lord."

Appalled gasps echoed through the crowd. A few braver voices called out "No!"and "How? Our faith is strong!" and "Forgive us!".

Joseph quickened his gait, matching the increasing brutal authority in his tone, "*WE* weakened God, people! But it was *they* who performed the death stroke!" An accusatory finger extended at Donovan. "We were led blindly down a path of greed and hypocrisy! We were pawns of men of influence, and it was *their* arrogance that stopped the heart of the Lord!"

All eyes turned towards Donovan and they all *believed*! In the span of five seconds every soul had turned against him and were now sure without the slightest hint of proof that it was all horribly and undeniably true. Fists clinched in indignant fury. Feet shuffled in the grass, readying to pounce. Teeth gnashed.

Donovan began to backpedal up the hill, sensing the worst, but every step he took only convinced the crowd more of his guilt. Joseph seized the advantage and trotted after him up the incline. His volume increased and his words came from a crazed smile accentuated with ravenous spittle, "*Your* pride has condemned us all! *Your* wickedness has plundered the meek to line your own pockets all while you claimed it was for the sake of righteousness! How *dare* you!"

The crowd fell in behind Joseph in a great collapsing triangle. The wind picked up, and the branches of the tree now slapped about madly. Donovan stumbled back and fell onto his bottom but continued to push back against the ground with his soles. Joseph was almost upon him, looming over Donovan like Goliath. Donovan spun onto his hands and kicked himself up and into a hard sprint. Joseph and the crowd instantly took up pursuit. He shielded his face against the lashing branches of the willow as he ran through them and down the back slope. At the foot of the hill was a wide river that he had not seen. Its waters were a raging torrent that dared him to attempt a crossing. It divided a lifeless valley of scorched, cracked earth that stretched far over the horizon. The flanking mountain ranges were jagged spines too steep to conquer, but with the mob at his back he ran to the river, knowing he must test his mettle.

When he neared the shoreline he saw the waters were a dark and cloudy gray. It was impossible to gauge the river's depth, and the current was much more vicious than he believed from afar. But he had no choice, and when his stride brought him close enough he flung himself in. His feet found purchase, but the water came to the base of his neck, and he lacked the strength to successfully fight against it. He kicked off the river bed and turned to swim with the current at an angle that would eventually bring him to the far shore. His first few strokes spoke of good omen, but suddenly the current spun him around and slammed him against an underlay of sharp rocks. They ripped into his side, and he cried out in pain. His control was lost. He grabbed at his side and kicked wildly to stay above the surface. The cut was deep enough that he could feel the very bone of his rib cage. He turned his head in time to see a taller rock that stuck inches out of the water like the curved fang of some great beast, but was too late to brace himself and once again he was victimized by the current's brutality. This time the point sliced into his cheek and again he cried out. With sheer luck he managed to wrap his right arm fully around the rock and pulled against the current until his left arm locked round it as well.

His body ached from fatigue and his fresh wounds began to burn from the saltiness of the water. He struggled to breathe as it splashed over the rock and into his mouth. Not only was its taste salty but also metallic and sour. He spit it out but more came to stifle his breathing. Panic took hold. He had no options left to him. The river fought to claim him. The rocks hungered to taste him. On the shoreline the crowd waited eagerly to either see him die or execute him themselves. Many began to look about their feet and picked up large stones and with maniacal sneers they hurled the stones at him. The first few splashed into the surface inches from him, but the third struck him true in the forehead. Its impact was blinding, and he nearly lost his hold on the rock. Blood began to run down his forehead and into his right eye. The crowd erupted in celebration then more looked about for stones and soon they were raining down upon him. They crashed into his shoulder and his ear. One bounced heavily off the top of his head and almost instantaneously he could feel a whelp forming. Voices cried out, "Heretic!" and

"Blasphemer!" and "Slave of the Enemy!". He saw another coming square at his face and instinctively lifted his left arm in a vain attempt at protection. It struck his elbow with such force that he felt a tremendous snap accompanied by a loud pop and right then all his strength was lost to him. His grip slipped, and he was pulled away from the rock and back into the mercy of the current.

The crowd adjusted their aim to continue their bombardment but after the first few tosses a loud voice demanded, "Stop!"

The jeers of the mob, the roar of the river, and the howl of the wind all came to an abrupt silence. The malevolence of the current gentled so much that Donovan was being carried along as if cradled. He strained to turn to see the owner of the voice but could only catch a tall figure in his peripheral on the opposite bank. His head pounded, and he could feel his pulse in every searing wound. He wanted to call out for help but lacked the strength. The figure, however, stepped down into the water as if reading his thoughts. It waded smoothly in waters that came only to its waist and when it reached Donovan it hooked muscular arms under the priest's shoulders and began to drag him back to the embankment. Once there it lay Donovan softly on the dry ground and turned once more to address the congregation and bellowed, "This man is a *true* and just follower of the Lord Most High! Shame be to you who so willingly succumbs to the treason of false prophets! Disperse so that you may go to a place of solitude and beg the Lord's forgiveness!"

The crowd's collective head slumped, and the people broke, going about their separate ways back over the hillside until they were gone from sight. Donovan struggled to open his eyes but could not until fingertips caressed his lids, and then they opened as if of their own volition. He drank in the beauty of the stranger who knelt above him and spoke the word as his mind formed it, "Angel."

The angel smiled. "You are safe now, Gregory. They cannot harm you while I am near."

The angel reached down and clasped Donovan's hands, and a great measure of strength was restored to him. It pulled him up so that he was sitting upright and then sat itself beside him so that the two might be on equal ground. The angel was the very definition of the word "celestial". Its hair was a shimmering waterfall of gold that fell to its shoulders. Its chin had the chisel of a man, but its lips the tenderness of a woman. Its translucent white robe hinted at the hefty musculature underneath. It was the embodiment of physical perfection with one stark exception. Its eyes. The angel's eyes at first were hypnotizing pools of blue sky, but closer observation betrayed dark borders of black, like poisoned waters at the edge of the pupils.

The angel caressed Donovan's forehead with the back its hand, and the wound there vanished and with it, the agony it brought. Its touch was overwhelming joy. It smiled once more at Donovan but spoke with a serious tone. "You are just as I claimed, a true and just servant, but like all who are righteous, you are beset on all sides by the wicked. There are wolves amidst your flock who carry themselves as sheep. One who would even assume to usurp you and spread his heresy as if it were the word of God. Do you know of whom I speak?"

Donovan nodded. His heart was heavy with the sting of betrayal. Joseph had become like a son to him. The young priest's love for the Lord and the church had seemed so pure. *Wolves as sheep.*

"Even now he brings demons into the house of God."

"The woman and child."

The angel appeared saddened. "I understand how difficult this revelation must be to you, Gregory, but know that your burden is also the salvation of those who seek your guidance.

108

You must be a hand of purity. You must strike down the devil that walks amongst you before he leads the righteous into damnation. Will you do this?"

Donovan hesitated, the weight of this calling bearing full upon him, but again he nodded.

The angel smiled.

"Go then and cleanse your house."

****

Donovan sat up in the darkness, out of breath and soaked in sweat. His bedroom was completely empty, but he clearly felt a presence watching over him. Waiting on him. Eager to be obeyed.

He threw his feet over the side of the bed, got up and walked to his home study. He sat down in his heavy leather chair – a twin of the chair in his office at the Cathedral, only this one purchased, not gifted – and pulled a bottled water out of the mini-fridge he kept beside it. He could not shake the feeling of eyes upon him, lingering just out of the light.

He picked up a notebook and pen from the table on the other side of his chair and wrote "Joseph" on the first blank page. He circled the name and drew question marks around it. His mind swam with questions, but the one bit of certainty he could cling to was that what he had just experienced had not simply been a dream, but a prophetic vision. He had never had one before but had listened to others, often priests like himself, share their own. It coupled too well with the resonating feeling he had had earlier that night when the Cathedral had become a crime scene; the Enemy was moving against his walls. The Enemy toiled in the shadows and birthed deceit, often in the guise of innocence.

He wrote the other names, "Traci" and "Solomon", and drew arrows pointing at them. This was spiritual warfare in a very real sense and Gregory Donovan was a warrior on the side of Heaven. He would defend his flock against any beast that come scratching at his door.

He closed his eyes to pray, but did not. Instead he began to evaluate and plot. The time for action was close at hand.

****

From the depths of the shadows just outside Donovan's study, the demon Uzahl watched with no small amount of pride as the seed he planted germinated. Mightier mongrels were falling so much easier as his power grew. Another small nudge might be required but the field had been sown, and soon he would reap its crop.

Satisfied, he slithered down the hall and back into the fading night.

CHAPTER 23

Destiny. Some believe it to be a calamitous chain of random events that pull random threads together to one point in time and space, as if life could be symbolized by a spiraling spider's web. Others believe that it is simply another name for the will of God, or whatever deity or deities they choose to follow. To an angel, it is the name of the path they were forged to tread, and although it is a path made of many parallel threads and unseen turns, they walk it on blind faith knowing that its destination is as assuredly decided as its origin. The Father chose these routes long ago and paved the way before there were travelers to populate them.

Now those who stepped in blind faith were simply blind and stepping. They no longer held a sense of purpose or direction. The destinations they rushed towards were dark voids on the horizon. It was a chaos only the unholy would revel in.

Athiel was somewhere in-between. Since he had chosen to step outside of Heaven's grace he felt each step he took was one of his own design and where it lead was a place no one knew. Angels were not meant to choose, they were crafted to obey, but his blind obedience had shown him dark vistas that the pits of Hell could narrowly rival. For many mortals Hell was a sentence from the moment they were forced kicking and screaming into existence. They were born addicted to the same chemical devils that enslaved their mothers. They were born to fathers who spoke in languages of temperament and cruelty. They were damned before they could rationalize any thought of an alternative. And some, when they could see with unblemished clarity the nature of their plight, chose to trade this living Hell for an eternal one. Their only salvation was often something they were never given the chance to hear of. Should a soul be destined to suffer? Where was the justice in that?

So on into the dwindling hours of the night he tread. Unknowingly plucking the strings of the spider web like an out-of-tune violin. The night cast a heavy shadow. The moral and the righteous and the self-righteous rarely invested themselves in the pre-dawn minutia. These were the hours of the sinners and the downcast. The ladies of the night pawing at the streets for one last scratch from the johns who were too drunk or feverish with lust to return home, many abandoning loyal wives. The homeless lay scattered about the corners and benches and whatever human-sized rodent-hole they could concoct, shivering from the night air or the addiction coursing through their embattled veins. The unlawful sought their dime through intimidation or invasion or bloodshed. These were the very people that the Son of God had long ago proclaimed to set yourself amongst. In each face he passed Athiel saw both hope and damnation, like their lives were spent living on the edge of a cliff, toes out over the drop and their balance faltering.

He wanted to initiate contact with each, but found himself at a loss for how to approach in such a way as to not trigger their guard. His heart was pulled in all directions at once yet would not move in any one. And so he walked. Deeper into the alleyways and obscure landscapes that most humans would avoid on instinct. Several times he saw figures tracking him from shadows. Heard their footfalls in step with his own from far behind, but no one ever approached. No one ever called out to him. They were never afraid, just somehow drawn but uncertain and so each in turn allowed him passage.

His progress took him in a closing spiral through downtown Lanza del los Santos towards a step-stone in his own destiny—whether it be preordained or haphazard—as if a magnet were reluctantly pulling at him from across a great expanse. He never felt its drag, and so he never fought against it, as he might have.

He first saw the park a few blocks east running parallel to the backstreet he followed, but thought little of it. He scanned every doorway, every window he passed for a hallmark of opportunity. They were as uninviting in their way as every forlorn face he had passed before, dark and vacant. There was so much here to be done, but he had to find his jump-off point, and the search in and of itself was unhinging.

He cut a slight left at a "Y" intersection where two policemen sat in their cruiser slowly finishing pastries and coffee across from a small group of prostitutes who grew increasingly angry that their business was being scared away. He passed on the sidewalk beside the driver of the car and both officers stopped their intake dead and eyed him curiously but soon their attention was stolen by the tallest of the working women who had come over to lodge a complaint.

Two blocks up a woman quickly exited the passenger side of a mid-80's sports car, parked and running on the opposite side of the street. The driver, presumably her boyfriend, jumped out of the car, slamming the door behind him and shouting obscenities into the night as he ran after her, trying to prevent her from making it indoors. The nearby apartment building windows were suddenly alive with lamp light or curious faces, but none would interfere as the man aggressively grabbed at the woman and accused her of things that no man should give name to. His drawn fist was stayed as a strange compulsion turned his head toward Athiel. The angel crossed the street at the crosswalk but did not break directly in their direction. The man, however, let go of the woman's arm and turned to face the figure in the long coat. She rubbed her arm where finger-shaped bruises would soon form and took the opportunity to turn and flee to the safety of the building. Her assailant did not attempt to stop her, he only glared like a rabid dog but never spoke a word. Finally the man got back in his car and drove away, not taking his eyes off Athiel until his driving forced him to.

Athiel continued down this street heading straight towards the greenery several blocks ahead that marked the edge of United Park. He had no intention of setting foot in the park. In truth he had no plan whatsoever. He was only following the compulsion of his own heart. No one dictated his journey, and no one would stay his feet. And blindly Athiel crept towards his destiny with the prisoner close behind.

CHAPTER 24

How did I get here?
The question rolled over Preston Titus like a thick fog. He was a world-traveler, thanks to Daddy's dime, but compared to all the things he had seen—bullet-riddled corpses in a burning pyre stacked taller than a man; children so starved that they lacked the strength to swat the flies from their swollen bellies; a young, tear-streaked woman cleaning her face minutes before catching a bus upon which she would detonate the bomb she was wearing, killing seventeen passengers in the name of freedom—none of it seemed quite as surreal as where he sat now. He had never felt claustrophobic before—more than once while filming *Unfaith* he was forced to either hide or crawl through sewer drains and spider-infested crawlspaces to avoid capture or harm—but here, inside this custom made behemoth of a van, in the middle of a squad of grunts that looked chiseled from granite and dressed as if they had stepped out of a science fiction movie, he struggled for each breath.

"Where you at, Hitchcock?"

Titus snapped to attention. Although nearly all of the nine Hellsbane soldiers were looking his way, gauging his expression and awaiting his response, it was the man codenamed Mariachi that was leaning forward, identifying him as the antagonist. In a million other possible social scenarios Titus would have handled himself like he was nobility and the peasants were lucky to gaze upon him, he thrived on the attention, but here he felt infantile, like the new nerd on the block about to be initiated by school bullies.

He forced as sly a smile as he could manage, tossing up a wall of cool confidence that had no hope of succeeding and replied, "Sorry, man, just getting ready." He patted "Faye" the outdated Canon XL1 mini DV camera that had become nearly as iconic as himself and laughed lightly, a quiet bounce in his throat that betrayed his insecurity. As the awkward silence that followed pressed in he tried to recover, "What can I do for you?" and clumsily added, "Like the Hitchcock reference, by the way."

"I was saying I saw your film, that *Unfaith* thing. Got to admit, it was thought provoking." Mariachi's smirk oozed of sarcasm, and the other members of the team chuckled openly as if they were all sharing in an inside joke at Titus's expense. Titus returned his attention to Faye and tried to ignore them all for just a few moments more.

"Ah cool, cool. Thank you, man." Titus tried to project an indifferent disposition, but no doubt they could see his hands shaking.

Unfaith was what brought him here in the first place. A few years back Preston had conned—he called it what it was, to himself anyway—his paraplegic father into giving him four hundred dollars to buy the used Canon and shoulder mount from a pawn dealer. After traipsing all over Lanza del los Santos filming nearly everything he could train his iris on he found a derelict colony of homeless under the Lincoln Bridge. The people he met there, so full of character and so beaten down by life, would plant the seed from which *Unfaith* would grow. One man in particular, with a penchant for wild tales— many of which revolved around James Brown and sandwiches—had said something that would likely stick with him for the rest of his life.

"Buddy boy," the man had called him during fleeting spurts of lucidity, "we're all where we've gotten to because of what we believe. Some of us believe in a higher power, some believe in ourselves, and that gives us two choices: do we blame ourselves or do we blame our gods? Well buddy boy, if I got myself into this mess, then I blame God for not existing to save me from it."

At the time Titus had laughed and brushed it off. But when

the quote came back around as he reviewed the footage, it dug in. He had never believed in a Christian God, or in any deity for that matter. He often imagined that if such a being were to exist that it should have taken up a more parental role to its wayward children, letting them discover life for themselves and suffer consequences as needed then stepping in obtrusively at times when mankind really ought to have known better. Somehow what was worse than a god that turned its back on its creation, was one that never existed in the first place, leaving no one other than ourselves to blame.

Titus had not bothered to get the man's, or any of the other tramps under the Lincoln Bridge, name, but the dirty lunatic had given him his hook, and that hook grew into a vision. So after filming the camp for the better part of two weeks he pulled another, much larger con job on dear old dad and began plotting a film venture that would take him around the world in search of even more tortured souls. He would collect their suffering on mini DV as proof that God did not exist and no amount of belief or faith could undo the symptoms of a sick and twisted world.

The finished film had, of course, been stamped controversial, and he unabashedly loved the free publicity that afforded him. Religious zealots attacked him both on online forums and openly, sometimes physically, in public. He had lost count of the death threats that had arrived at his doorstep. And when the documentary won multiple awards at film festivals the world round, it was like sticking a hot poker in the eye of everyone who told this spoiled brat rich boy he was going to hell.

Then Valdez had called.

Fingers snapped, bringing him back to the present. Back to the dim blue light of the oversized van. The van with padded benches running the length of its cargo space. With walls converted to weapon and armor racks covered with enough hardware to invade a small country.

"Stay with us, Hitchcock," Mariachi chimed.

Titus threw up a finger—but not the one he truly wanted to—to buy a second's time. When the camera was on, it was as if there were a barrier thrown up between him and the world. Peering through the lens made life feel staged and manageable. Like he was the one in control. He fumbled nervously with the

Eject/Load slider in a mad rush to reach that security.

Mariachi sensed his advantage and pressed it. "So you really think that showing all those sick and dying and impoverished people proves that there is no God? No Heaven and Hell?" his grin was unbearable and Preston wanted nothing more than to knock a few teeth loose from it. But the banter continued, "Just because they're praying and nothing ever happens?"

He continued to fight off the urge to use, "In case you didn't know, I'm kind of a big deal," as a comeback. Thankfully as the cassette slid snugly into chamber and Titus pressed the deck closed he could already sense his confidence finding some purchase. He had been asked this same question a hundred times, maybe more. Mostly by ultra-religious types, and always with the flavor of added disdain. But he had been here before and he had answered this so frequently that his response now felt preprogrammed though no less effective. "Ever heard of the scientific method? You form a hypothesis, you pick a study group, and you test your theory over and over again, and if the results are resoundingly identical...well, there you go. Theory becomes law."

Flipping the mode dial on the side of the camera to manual, he finally found the strength to meet Mariachi eye to eye.

"Obviously you're a fan of fairytales, so how about you explain to me why I should believe in an invisible magic man in the sky? You tell me you have a book of laws, you can even call it history, but want me to believe that the people who wrote it didn't influence it with their own prejudices? That it was written with 'divine inspiration'? You tell me to believe out of blind faith but want to reach into my pockets when your God doesn't provide enough to pay for your new church or feed the hungry but your preachers drive Mercedes? Come on, man. It's a con game. Pure and simple."

Now he was cool, he was in charge, and as he raised the view-finder to his eye he felt his trademark crooked smile impregnate his lips. As he waved the camera back and forth, however, testing the lighting and focus, adjusting for the vans very blue atmosphere, the smiles on their faces made it clear that their little group secret had become a lot funnier. A few were even shaking their heads as if to say, *poor guy has no idea.* Again, that gnawing unease took hold.

But then he was saved. From the front passenger seat, "People. We've got less than five minutes until we reach target zone. I want gear double-checked, and I want Mr. Titus to get on with what he came for. Understood?" It was Doomsayer. The leader of this wolf pack, with a voice and manner that gave no room for questioning his authority. In the field it was absolute and as far as his troops were concerned, he was god here.

The members of Hellsbane replied with a unison affirmative and immediately went about the business of examining and readying their equipment. Titus had been given a few intentionally vague pages of information on the unit, briefly covering both their biographies (abbreviated to only their home city/country and applicable backgrounds which were, in truth, quite diverse and fascinating) and the very basics of how they were organized. They were categorized into four unit types: Priests, Crusaders, Redeemers and a Prophet. The Priests served as the basic infantry and carried what appeared to be a science fiction novelist's take on combat assault rifles. Each S.W.A.R.M. had two Crusaders, which served as forward reconnaissance although neither was present in the van. Hellsbane also had two Redeemers that filled in as heavy weapon operators. Their weapons were made of oblong cannons with multiple muzzles that attached to bulky, strapped packs by thick tubing. Each unit was lead by a Prophet. In contrast to the padded black armor that each soldier wore up to their necks, the Prophet wore what, at first glance, seemed a rather mundane gray bodysuit that was only slightly less than form-fitting, but a glossy black exo-skeleton ran up the spine and across the back like ribs. Up the middle of this exo-spine was a runaway of small blinking red lights that gave Doomsayer a hellish glow.

Titus saw that Doomsayer was watching him through the rearview and decided it was indeed time to begin. He first turned the camera onto Anne Sciantarelli of Columbus, Ohio, codenamed Jazz, a former Navy Seal now a S.W.A.R.M. Priest—*Priestess perhaps?* He was not sure—and in his opinion the looker of the bunch. She was aware that she was in frame and straightened, waiting to be addressed.

"So, Jazz," Titus pulled the camera away from his face long

enough to flash her a smooth, arrogant smile, "You wanna tell me what's going on?"

The smile had no affect. She replied evenly in a rather cliché military cadence. "We have received intel from Crusaders Strafe and Splinter that a group of approximately fourteen halos have gathered near the central fountain in United Park."

Titus fought the reflex to lower the camera while addressing his confusion. "Rewind. What is a *halo* exactly?"

It was Hammer, former light heavyweight boxing contender Toma Hollenbeck, likewise now a Priest and an all-around beast of a man, that answered. "Halo is the given designation for an angel. Horn for demon."

This time Titus could not fight the urge and the camera dropped beside his leg. "Angel?" His eyebrow furled incredulously. "We talking like a biker gang or...?"

Mariachi, real name Rafael Espinoza, former DEA Spec Ops, found that same cocky grin as if he kept it in a holster ready to use. "Nope. Angels. As in Heaven's little foot soldiers."

Titus spun the mode dial on the camera to OFF. "If you guys aren't going to be on the level with me just let me out now. I'm getting paid an insane amount of money, even for me, to be here so while I'll film whatever little training drill you guys want me to, at least cut the bull."

"If Valdez chose you when he could've hired any camera jockey in the world, Mr. Titus, it must've had more to do with your skepticism than your ability." Mozart—Lewis Chamberlain, former British Green Beret, Priest—spoke up. Compared to his colleagues he was a stick of a man, smaller even than the female Loki—Amanda Bierbauer, ex-police officer hailing from Toronto, Canada, Priest. "He doesn't go for 'yes men'."

When Titus showed no immediate signs of continuing it was Doomsayer who spoke next. "You're right, Mr. Titus, you *have* been paid a very large sum of money to be here and are likewise under contract." He paused for effect then added, "Continue." The word was both a demand and a threat and Titus knew he dare not test the conditions of that threat. He turned the camera back on and turned the lens back on Jazz.

"So, why are we after these *halos*?" The word was a mockery of phonics in Titus's mouth.

"To exterminate them." She replied flatly.

The absurdity nearly unbearable but he pressed forward. "If you would," he goaded meekly. "How does this go down... exterminating halos?"

Jazz obliged as if she had never been stopped, "Local law enforcement has been ordered to secure a perimeter around the park to ward off civilians. We enter and engage targets at point blank."

Despite knowing better, a chuckle leaked. "You make it sound so simple." And to her it was. It was no different than saying that water was wet. "So why don't they just scatter when they see you coming?" Then the obvious question hit him. "Actually, how do you even hurt an angel?"

Crucible, a.k.a. Derek Harper, former Philadelphia SWAT team now Redeemer, replied before Titus could identify who was speaking, and it took a moment to locate and frame him up. "With these." To accent his point he raised his large, cannon-like weapon and tipped it towards the roof of the van. Titus shifted the camera's focus and honed in on a single word painted on the side of the cannon, SMITER. Brickbat, former Triathlon Olympic Silver Medalist Kobe Yoshida from Tokyo, Japan, now Redeemer, raised his own, identical except for the word JUDGEMENT and clanged the two weapon tips together like wine glasses in a toast. Cheers resounded throughout the van.

From the front, Doomsayer's voice boomed over all else. "Approaching entry point. All eyes forward, all mouths shut. On your ready."

All instantly obeyed, taking their seats and donning insect-like helmets that, combined with the segmented thorax look of their armor, completely punctuated the designation S.W.A.R.M.. All bodies were rigged. All minds were focused. Someone, although Titus was unsure who, uttered, "For the judged, we bring redemption. For those that judge, we bring execution."

All responded in unison, "For the judged."

CHAPTER 25

Paul Kennedy looked down at his watch: quarter til 5 in the AM. To say he was unhappy was an understatement of massive proportions. With just over three hours left in his shift he could easily say this had been in the top three of the roughest nights of his life. It began with a domestic violence call that came in as soon as he his shift began, giving him no time for his usual stop at Art's All-Niter for a large black coffee. The perp was a large male in his late 40's, easily three hundred pounds and six feet five inches. Paul could not help but to think of him as an ogre: a snarling, slobbery beast straight out of a bad dream. He was hopped up on some substance or another, Paul guessed cocaine but that was for the toxicology reports to decide, and had battered his wife so bad that she left a trail of blood that led to her hiding place in the ramshackle apartment's only bathroom. Luckily the blood had slickened the wooden hallway enough so that when the Ogre tried to break the door down with his shoulder, he had instead slipped and fell and fractured his left wrist. By the time Paul and his trainee, Paulie Rodriguez—it was only a matter of time before the moniker "The Two Pauls" or some similar annoyance caught fire around the office—arrived on the scene the Ogre was back on his feet and banging at the door with both fists. The pain of his injury would come much later when the affect of whatever drugs the Ogre had taken wore off.

Paulie had wanted to go in and try to take the brute down by sheer force (the curse of youth at their physical peak, they believed they could move mountains with a finger), but, as his training officer, Paul ordered him back and laid a quick series of verbal commands down for the Ogre. The Ogre did not acknowledge them and continued his assault on the door, with Mrs. Ogre screaming bloody murder beyond. Right as the doorframe gave, Paul unsheathed his tazer and hit Ogre with 50,000 volts between the shoulder blades. The man's body tensed up and after a few seconds he dropped to one knee, but he did not go down completely. He turned for the first time, the officers definitely had his attention.

Paulie, The Rookie, cursed and asked why the big guy didn't go down, but the Paul, Old Pro, was busy muttering a prayer under his breath and did not hear. The Rookie drew the .40 Glock from his hip holster just as the Old Pro got off the second tazer shot, this one hitting the Ogre in a spread around the left shoulder and breast as he was attempting to stand. The Ogre again went stiff and at last tipped towards his bent knee and toppled over. The Rookie was already in action, racing down the hallway, pulling his handcuffs mid-stride. When he reached the Ogre he slapped them on tight as possible. With that done the rookie let out a deep breath he had not realized he had been holding.

"Ah man, I think he had an accident," the rookie waved a hand rapidly under his nose, hoping to exorcise the stench of Ogre's bowels.

Paul realized that all had gone so very, very quiet and called out past the Rookie, "Ma'am, this is LSPD are you okay?"

When there was no reply the Two Pauls exchanged worried looks. As the Paul made his way down the hallway and approached the seemingly unconscious Ogre at the Rookie's feet he drew his gun. Because…well, you *never* know. The Rookie had put his own weapon away to cuff Ogre, but was quick to follow suit. The Paul nodded towards the door handle, though the door had been freed of the frame, it had opened only a few inches and most of the bathroom remained obscured on the other side. Paul feared the worst, and the Rookie had no idea what to fear.

Paul called out again, "Ma'am, this is LSPD *ARE YOU*

OKAY?" When a second silence fell he added, "Ma'am we're coming in. If you have any weapons place them on the floor and slide them away from you." He locked eyes with Paulie. "We're coming in in three...two...one!" On his nod the Rookie kicked the door inward only hard enough to swing it wide, but lightly enough to not hurt anyone that could be in its path. The Old Pro crossed in front of him and entered the room gun-first, he pivoted on his right heel to check all corners. No one. At least, no one living.

The Rookie entered a step behind him, dropping low out of the Old Pro's line of fire and swept the room with his .45 Smith & Wesson. Its path froze when it reached what was now the corpse of Mrs. Ogre. The Old Pro holstered his weapon, and when the Rookie did not he placed a hand gently on the muzzle of the Rookie's .40 and nodded down at the younger man. "It's ok, Paulie. Nothing you can do for her now."

The Rookie's daze was broken and he nodded back at his superior and holstered his own weapon. He rose beside the Old Pro and for long moments they studied Mrs. Ogre. Her eyes downcast at the floor tile, but Paul suspected the life left them long ago, long before this final gasp. Paul Kennedy would later learn her real name was Leeanna Hanger and her husband, Jack, had made regular sport out of rearranging her features for some time. It seemed now that Leeanna had finally had enough and had found a way to make it stop. Somewhere in the short span between the Two Pauls knocking on the front door, identifying themselves as police, and subduing Mr. Hanger with tazer guns, Mrs. Hanger had shattered the bathroom mirror and used one of the larger mirror fragments to sever her jugular and end her suffering. Now she sat with her back against the corner of the bathtub and wall, legs sprawled out, arms limp, as if now, at last, she could rest. The left corner of her mouth might have been crocked in a smile as if to say, "I win this one. And I win for good."

Knowing full well that she had passed from this life to the next, Paul Kennedy still prayed for a miracle and checked for a pulse. He bowed his head and sighed heavily.

The Rookie began to cuss at the unconscious brute laying in the hallway and delivered a series of hateful kicks to the man's exposed ribs. The Old Pro got up as quick as he could and pushed the Rookie back. He held him firmly against the wall of the hallway, beside a wedding picture of the (possibly) then-happy couple. The Rookie did not put up a fight and when Paul reached for his CB to call it in, Paulie only let his weight fall back and slumped down onto his hind end.

Afterwards the Two Pauls had had a long talk about police brutality and physical evidence and just plain terms of what is right and decent. The Rookie mostly just listened but seemed to be genuinely soaking the moral in. He suggested the Old Pro would be right in filing a brutality complaint against him, but the Paul shrugged and said nothing. In truth he was not sure how to handle the situation and wondered to himself what would be the "Christian thing to do". Mostly, though, his mind circled around Mrs. Hanger and an endless spectrum of "coulda, shoulda, woulda's" that could have saved her life. But that was a moot point now, and the voice of his late grandmother echoed from nowhere, reminding him as she once did that, "the world is a pretty simple place. It's people that make it complicated." Wiser sentiments from a wiser time.

Later that cursed night the call had come in about the incident at the Cathedral of Saint Michael. He was relieved to find that neither Father Joseph nor his new charges had been hurt, but the news of the death in this one gleaming sanctuary in the storm of his life unsettled him greatly. It was as if someone had spit at the foot of God. He was rather glad to have left the scene, but too much about the occurrence did not add up and Father Behanan had offered up little of real assistance. He did not want to believe that the priest would lie to him, but someone was, and so he had parked the cruiser at Art's All-Niter and sent the Rookie inside for some coffee and made a phone call to Kenneth Phelps. Paul felt like a first tier rat trying to be as sly as he could hoping that Ken would, out of concern, call the priest and somehow get the "whole truth and nothing but" out of him and persuade Father Behanan to come clean with the authorities, but when the call was ended, Paul felt the con was a bust, and that he had lost some degree of trust in Ken's eyes.

The rest of the night had been not uneventful, but rather routine. He and the Rookie had cruised by a few well-known hotspots for prostitution and scared off a few prospective clients, one of which had run a stop sign and was ticketed accordingly. After that they had pulled a swerving BMW over and arrested its intoxicated driver and had gotten back out on the streets when this final call came in and, as Paul was fond of saying, "the hits just kept on coming." This new order was to participate in a park-wide quarantine, sealing off United Park. No word as to why or who was going in to resolve what or who to watch for coming out. The standing order was simply no one in or out without the right credentials at the single designated checkpoint.

Now they sat quietly, their cruiser parked askew across the middle two lanes of Regent Avenue. Paul did not like being kept in the dark, and that is exactly how he felt about this entire night, one big rolling blackout of information. He noticed the Rookie text messaging beside him.

"Who in the world is up this early?" he asked.

The Rookie smiled proudly, though shyly and replied, "My girlfriend. Well, maybe my fiancée soon...I hope. She woke up again worried, so I'm just trying to let her know I'm ok out here in the war zone." His boyish charm was not doubt a big part of what attracted the ladies.

Paul returned the smile, he liked the Rookie. He could easily see the Two Pauls as a solid, lasting relationship. He turned away to let the Rookie finish his text and dropped back into the cloud of his own thoughts. Time seemed unwilling even to crawl by and every glance he gave his watch only added to the slow misery of the morning. He pulled his own cell from his pocket and began to click through his stored pictures at the smiling faces of his wife and daughter. It was good to remind yourself of the things that made sense.

And so he wrapped himself in the pictures and the memories each one carried. And that was why he did not notice the lone figure crossing Regent in perfect silence and disappearing like a phantom into the park.

Chapter 26

Their gathering was a matter of necessity born out of fear, confusion, and the kind of comfort that only family can bring. Their father was lost to them, and many of their siblings had likewise fallen. Their enemies were beginning to recognize the increasing limits of a new, unbridled power and were rapidly becoming bolder. There was an order to the world that had, it seemed, in an instant, slipped into utter chaos, and now they had nowhere to turn but to each other. For angels, it was surely the precipice of doom.

Juriel drew little joy from the menagerie of faces around him. Far fewer had answered the call than he had hoped, and when only five of the eight messengers he had sent out returned he feared the worst. The sun waited impatiently just below the horizon, threatening to crest and drive bad tidings home into the heart, but Juriel would wait just a few minutes longer.

Tristes approached him cautiously and placed a hand on his shoulder.It was meant to strengthen and calm. It did neither. It only served to prove to Juriel that Tristes was battling with the same fears.

"More will come. And I am sure that those that do not, simply cannot," Tristes said. "It is not in our nature to abandon our duties."

Juriel clasp the hand on his shoulder lovingly and nodded. "After we finish here perhaps we can seek them out and speak with them of what is decided here."

Tristes nodded and left the hand there for a moment longer. Angels spoke no more sincerely than when they spoke in languages of love.

The angel Palius walked up to join them. He was taller than both Juriel and Tristes by a head and much broader in form and sported a lush, curly beard so black as to appear blue in tint. Like Dycliasses he had served as a Captain of the Host, but straddled the role of the warrior-chief more than healer or diplomat, and so here at this gathering he let the leadership fall to Juriel.

"We are fourteen in number, but Belethor is just now arriving with a few more. I am unsure of how many." Palius pivoted to open a line of sight for Juriel. As he said Belethor was breaking through the tree line towards the fountain. One by one other angels came into view, but after the fourth newcomer appeared the procession ceased. Juriel whispered a prayer of gratitude and then bowed his head, not knowing if his prayer would be heard. He turned his eyes to the fountain, a great lion carved from stone standing on its hind legs and clawing at the sky. Where was the Lion of Judah now?

Palius strode over to meet Belethor as he crossed the clearing with Tristes just behind. The angels who had already gathered for a moment seemed to light up at the sight of the newcomers, but their thankful expressions dimmed when they saw there were so few adding to their number.

"Ho, Belethor," Palius greeted with an outstretched arm. Belethor clasped it high on the forearm and echoed the sentiment.

Belethor turned to regard Tristes and then past him to Juriel. He swept a hand in presentation past the four he had brought with him. "These four came without hesitation. Three others would not turn from their duties, Dycliasses among them. Others I could not find."

The two groups had now joined to a larger whole and while the angels mixed together in loving tidings Belethor lured Juriel, Palius and Tristes away from the others. His tone came across low and dark, at perfect pitch with Juriel's own mood.

"At least six have fallen that I know of. Godran and Yzierius were overwhelmed by lesser demons in the subways. It seemed an ambush. And Trael, Periel and Hersis fell at the Cathedral of

Saint Michael at the hands of a single demon, Uzahl," Juriel and Tristes exchanged fearful glances, but Palius remained stone-faced, listening. "Dycliasses was able to drive him away, but did not destroy him."

Palius's face tightened into a grimace. "What of the sixth?"

Belethor looked away in a mix of shame and disgust. He couldn't bring himself to meet Palius's eyes. "I found the remains of Fiedr on a street."

Palius's dour visage broke. He gasped loudly as did Juriel and Tristes. The sound of it drew the attention of the closer fringe of angels; they turned and began to listen intently.

Juriel was the first to speak. "His *remains*? How? What did you find?"

Belethor visibly steadied himself before he continued. "He lay in the physical realm, a pile of meat and broken bone...like a mortal."

The larger group had come over and began to circle around the smaller. All faces were twisted masks of horror.

Knowing his role Palius was strengthened by a necessary sense of command in front of his brethren and at last found his own voice. "Why do you say meat and bone?" He knew none truly desired to hear the reply, but they must. These were the seeds of war.

Belethor's eyes wandered around each face. He longed to remain silent. To spare them the gruesome details believing it would only shatter their hope further. But they had a right to know the fate of their brother and the dangers they now faced.

At last he replied, "His skin had been removed. Traced about him on the street were inscriptions of wickedness. A ritual had been performed, and our brother's life had been devoured by his killer."

Every grim face flinched as if physically struck. For some, the vileness was so great that it was quickly replaced with white-hot rage. Palius was foremost among them and spoke for them all. "They dare the unspeakable! They act as if there will be no one to enact judgment upon them! But this will not go unanswered!" Those who had not given themselves to anger were swept up in the tide of Palius's battle cries, adding their voices to the savage chorus calling for retribution; all but Juriel and Tristes who kept themselves quietly reserved. Caught up in his own momentum Palius fanned the flames. "Every fiend that dares to aggress shall be hurtled into the Lake of Fire! Every putrid beast that does not know its place will be cast into Oblivion! Every silenced brother shall likewise be avenged! I swear this!" Palius thrust his hand towards the sky in proclamation, and a blade of golden light materialized, flooding the gathering in its righteous splendor. The angels followed suit, wielding fierce weapons in a decree of justice.

Juriel felt the sinking of his heart and was moved to speak. "My brothers, heed my words: this is not our way! There is a law and a purpose that governs our existence, and we are in peril of heresy!" The energy coursing through the gathering abated, and one by one the angels lowered their blades and gave cautious attention. Juriel continued, "*Something* had befallen us. What it is I cannot say. I too have heard the whisperings from demonic lips that our Father has fallen, and I too cry out that this cannot be. My very thoughts have numbed, and I cannot remember when last I basked in the blessed

light of the Throne. I long to return home but cannot remember the path." Nods of recognition scattered throughout the gathering; even Palius was plagued by these same troubles. And Juriel continued, "There are answers to be sought and found and we will not find them if we take offensive course against our kinslayers. Our Father may not have perished—I will refute even the possibility of such—but we all can feel that we have been stricken from His sight, and because of this we become untamed and digress while the underlings of the Betrayer ascend in might and bravado.

"We were not created to live an un-anchored existence, and in this we are fallible. But we cannot let our trepidation lead us down chaotic roads, blinded by our need for vengeance. We do not *avenge*. We were not *created* for such temptations. These are the ways of Lucifer; and like him, *this is how we shall fall!*"

Every angel remained still, Juriel's words weighing heavily upon them. Never before had they been torn between the ways of Heaven and the ways of Hell—or even the ways of the mortal world. They had never stood at a crossroads and hesitated before taking their next step. They were servants, and now they were without master without evidence of how or why.

It was in the afterbirth of this stillness that Juriel recognized their collective need for leadership. There stood a dire need to locate at least one of the archangels. Gabriel would likely be in Heaven still, if only they could find their way home, but it was likely that Michael, the warrior, was among the mortal world making the necessary preparations from the coming Tribulations. He would speak here and now with his brothers for a time longer and plot as best they could. He would scatter seekers to the far corners of the Earth and find whomever he could for surely the ranks of Hell were already devising their own battle plans. They needed to go beyond the city of Lanza del Los Sans and see if the rest of the world was also in such a state. If so, the world of man stood at grave risk, and the angelic vanguard would likely be marching on to total war.

The sun bore the first strands of its glory over the peaks of the metropolitan landscape and bled the sky of its dark tones, but the shadows it created were heartless shapes that devoured the alleyways and rooftops. On one such rooftop, some twenty-eight stories high, from almost half a mile away, two pairs of predatorial eyes studied the gathering from enhanced lenses. They coordinated to others below in a perfect dance of skill and training. The gathering of angels shifted into a tight circle, preparing for the hard road ahead of them, but they could not have known that a shadow was falling upon them.

And they never saw their own deaths approaching from the south.

CHAPTER 27

The vehicle came to a stop. Crucible, sitting nearest the cab, reached up and closed a thick dark curtain obscuring the Hellsbane members in the rear, leaving Doomsayer and their driver, a blank shell in drab, non-descript military dress to whom Titus had never been introduced, to deal with the two police officers that approached the windows on either side. Though they could see nothing, the curtain did not impede any of the sound, and Titus kept the camera running just for the benefit of capturing the audio.

There was an authoritative tapping on the driver side window; a sure-cocked bit of arrogance that police officers seemed to have instilled in them (as Titus had discovered through numerous run-ins with other members of their fraternity). Both the driver and Doomsayer's windows rolled down and the driver-side officer spoke, "You the *specialists* we've been holding our breath for?" From his tone it was obvious that this cop was nursing a bit of a bruised ego. He and his were probably itching to go in "Charles Bronson style" and clean up whatever trouble they thought waited, but they had been benched and doubtfully even told why. So now that the big boys had arrived it was only right and fair to take it out on them. Neither the driver nor Doomsayer offered a response. The cop conceded and asked to see some sort of identification or paperwork. Doomsayer obliged, and soon the cop stepped back and waved them through with one last sarcastic snap, "Break a leg, folks."

The van accelerated, and for a minute or so followed the main roadway through the park, then veered to the right and into more rugged terrain. Titus had not anticipated the bumpiness and knocked his eye-socket hard against Faye's viewfinder before almost dropping her altogether. He recovered less than gracefully and went back about the business of documenting the soldiers, all of whom were geared up and ready to roll. In the eerie silence of the moment he heard a faint whisper that sounded suspiciously like "Father forgive me…" which felt entirely at odds with what he had been led to believe was the group's hostile agenda. With their helmets securely fastened over the heads and faces it was impossible to know for sure who had uttered the words, but he was fairly certain the voice he heard was Hammer's.

Once again the vehicle came to a halt and in quick order Doomsayer pushed back the curtain and took position in the center of his troops. He wore no helmet, only a thin device that was a combination earpiece, eyepiece and mouthpiece. Titus zoomed in for a tighter shot of this device and then traced down Doomsayer's length, stopping to focus on the Desert Eagle strapped to his right leg. This stood out in sharp contrast to the "science-fiction prop" feel of the other Hellsbane weaponry, but somehow felt much more threatening.

Doomsayer addressed his soldiers, "This is a simple point and pull, people. Shadow-Eye reports that another five halos have joined the previous group, but this changes nothing, and they do not appear to be anticipating our arrival. So let's keep this short and sweet. Standard Umbrella formation then locked perimeter. Understood?"

In unison the members of S.W.A.R.M. Hellsbane emphatically replied, "Sir, yes sir!"

Doomsayer nodded and reached up to touch a shallow button on the underside of

his left wrist and a low, electrical humming began to sound, but Titus could not determine what purpose this device served. Doomsayer, however, seemed satisfied with the humming and pointed to the rear door of the van. "Move out!"

Mozart and Jazz threw open the rear doors and waited as one by one the Hellsbane soldiers filed out of the van and formed a tight grouping until Doomsayer stepped down with Mozart and Jazz following. Titus was unsure of what to do but stood to follow. Doomsayer spun his head and looked at him coldly for a moment. Titus froze.

"That camera won't see anything," he said. Anticipating some unspoken command, Jazz turned back to the van and produced a small protective metal case much like the one Titus stored Faye in from underneath her seat. She held out one hand to take Faye from him, and the other offered the case in exchange. Titus swapped out, opening the new case as Jazz set Faye loosely in the one he had brought along. In the new case Titus found a smaller, sleeker designed camera that seemed to be built from the body of a High Definition Panasonic he had been researching online, but the lens was noticeably stubbier and tinted a bizarre jade-green. Beyond that the various settings, buttons and focus and zoom adjusters appeared to be normal. Satisfied with his new toy and eager to give it a spin, he stepped down among the crowd.

"Do not break the tree line," Doomsayer ordered. "There is ample zoom to capture whatever footage you need without you making a liability of yourself. In short, stay out of our way." Doomsayer turned away and marched around the van, Hellsbane a compact circle around him.

The van had come to rest in the middle of a thick patch of trees in such a manner that Titus could not fathom how the driver had managed such a parking job and for the first time he came to notice how very quiet the engine ran. He laughed to himself thinking about what he would now call the "Stealth-Van" and what kind of Knight Rider rip-off television show these weirdos could concoct. He fell in stride twenty feet behind Hellsbane and followed them as far as the tree line as instructed. When Hellsbane broke out into the vast clearing that encapsulated the center of the park with its large fountain, their speed doubled towards a focal point that Titus could not make out. He would have guessed they were making their way to the lion fountain ahead, but their course seemed slightly askew of it. In a flash of "duh" Titus remembered the new camera in his hands and went about turning it on. Once it was powered he raised it and flipped open the side view screen and instantly his jaw dropped with the force of a hurtling comet. He lowered the camera for a moment to compare what he saw onscreen to what his own eyes could tell him and was dumbfounded by the difference. He raised the camera again and zoomed in on the multitude of green-hued figures that appeared on the screen a few hundred yards ahead of the Hellsbane squad. The lingering thought was that this had to be some kind of elaborate trick this shadowy company was playing on him, trying with incredible gusto to sell the fertilizer they were shoveling, but as he panned and zoomed in and out he could not imagine any means by which such a hoax could be pulled off. So instead, he chose to go along for the ride.

He panned across the group, studying them first as a whole before viewing them individually. They were unmistakably human in likeness, but taller and somehow indefinably more beautiful. They were clothed in what seemed to be loose white cloth of various archaic cut, though that was a guess judging from the green-hue the camera cast them in. They were as varied as any human group that Titus had ever seen yet there was a resounding similarity to them, like a reunion of siblings or cousins. Most remarkably and telling, however, were the wings. Each figure carried two grand, eagle-like wings around their backs that folded in, hugging their flanks with the tips crossing across their laps and more than a few had other, smaller sets of wings that tucked over the top and bottom of the larger set. Despite himself Titus felt the word slip from his taught lips into the night air, "Halos". Titus was hit by the irony that, search as he might, he couldn't see a single halo floating about their heads, and he shrugged it off as just being a false part of the mythos. He laughed at himself, realizing how suddenly easy it was for him to accept what he saw as…well, as gospel. Here he was, Preston Titus, Oscar-nominated filmmaker who had staked his claim with a film that very proudly declared to a weary world that we were all alone in our misery, that there was no high-power to aid us in our time of need and certainly no angels fluttering about to lend mortal man a loving hand, now becoming Preston Titus, true believer, all in the span of seconds. He was astonished at his own astonishment.

He blinked to clear the stardust from his eyes and tried to focus on why he was here: to document. He zoomed out to a wider shot to capture both groups, the halos and Hellsbane as the latter went in for the kill. He found it strange that the halos seemed entirely unaware of the approaching soldiers. Surely they would have seen them and sensed the aggression of their advance, but as he watched the halos only congregated in a wide circle, not wary of the world around them in the slightest. Hellsbane pressed forward and began to spread out to encircle the halo perimeter. Doomsayer strode confidently and unnoticed straight into the center of the halo group. His intuition suddenly screaming bloody murder inside his skull, Titus felt a bitter surge of bile rising up from his stomach at the thought of the fast-coming slaughter.

Chapter 28

"Shadow-Eye to Spear-Tip, all targets enclosed. You have zero strays. The green light is yours."

And with those words, the massacre began.

The creation of the S.W.AR.M. initiative had begun immediately following the adaptation of trans-spiritual technology into weaponry. Valdez had foreseen early on the necessity for such "defensive" measures and Doomsayer had been the very first recruited to this end. Playing a large role in both the development of the program and the military stratagem by which they would operate, he was given absolute recruitment authority, beginning with the selection of a dozen candidates for the rank of Prophet and then stacking the talent of his own strike team. He carefully combed the globe searching out the most malleable and capable bodies and minds, regardless of their histories or levels of previous training. He needed warriors, men and women possessing ferocious spirit, not just rank and file cannon fodder and in this, he had succeeded gloriously. Now, under the indifferent gaze of the stone lion at the heart of United Park, the fruit of Doomsayer's efforts moved in deadly synchronicity to wipe the servants of the Most High from the face of the Earth.

Juriel had gathered his brethren at this precise spot at dawn in hopes of first uncovering answers—or at least clues—to the plight that had befallen not only their kind, but the world

141

and possibly the totality of the Universe, and then laying forth a course of action. There had been a time when much of the future and schemes of this world had been made known to them, and they were rarely, if ever, caught unaware, but a dark stroke had torn them from the One who gave them such Knowledge, and now they were like children, lost, frightened and, for once, vulnerable. They could not see the assassins in their midst nor could they sense their murderous intent. Could they even understand that their existence had run its course or the irony in that they were to be executed by the very beings they had been sent to help and nurture? Perhaps it was a blessing that many of their number never knew that oblivion had come to claim them until the deed had been done.

The soldiers of Hellsbane crossed the clearing in quickstep and, without further order, spread to form a tight perimeter around the gathering of angels while high above and far away two of their number, the sniper team whose call sign had been designated Shadow-Eye (the Crusaders: Splinter, the shooter and Strafe, the spotter) maintained silent vigil. The Priests took up position tight against the angelic circle and brought their weapons point blank to the heads of the halos while the Redeemers with their heavy weapons stayed slightly back from the group. Doomsayer stood dead center of both groups evaluating whether all was at the ready and keying in on the discussion in which the halos were engaged. This group had been summoned together at the behest of one. They were to be messengers, spreading word to the millions of their brethren within this city alone that the archangels needed to be found and consulted. They seemed frightened and grasping at straws. It almost made him wish they could see the smile spreading across his face. Valdez would be pleased.

An audio implant embedded surgically in his ear canal relayed the words of their overwatch, "Shadow-Eye to Spear-Tip, all targets enclosed, you have zero strays. The green light is yours."

His grin widened. He could not help it. After months of training and test scenarios, some even involving live halo targets, his team was poised to draw their first blood in the field. The sensation was warm and electric; the sweet tang of pride.

He had looked forward to this moment and now, basking

in it, indulged himself to toy with his prey. He spoke, "On my mark in 3…"

The angels instantly silenced. They each looked about for the source of the voice and were utterly baffled by the nothing they saw.

"2…"

The muscles of his men steadied, but remained loose. A few made last second adjustments to their aim.

"1…"

His grin felt devilish. He would savor what came next without the slightest shame. He fingered the button on his wrist, letting the camouflaging umbrella of trans-spiritual energy drop and freeing his men to–

"Engage!"

Juriel's eyes went wide with shock as the strangely armored humans materialized out of thin air. Although he had never seen the tools they carried, he instantly recognized the dangers they represented. He cried out, hoping to warn his brethren but they were frozen in their shock and wholly unable to react in time.

To a human a fraction of a second flutters by so quickly that our hyperactive minds cannot register and measure such seemingly insignificant intervals, but to an angel, for whom a day in Heaven is millennia on Earth, that span of time and all the horrors within it can last a slow and torturous eternity. Such was Juriel's torment as helplessly he watched as eleven of his brethren, screaming incomprehensible vowels that marked the only pain they would ever know, were torn from existence in flashes of searing light. They had been more than just avatars of Heaven, they were servants of the race of man and soldiers for the cause of righteousness, now martyred by the most favored children of their collective Father. The purposes of their individual existences, and the plans that had been laid out to them, crafted even before the dawn of time, were now irrevocably moot.

The soldiers left no room for error in their attack. The first kills had been simultaneous, eight flashes of icy blue light at point blank range to the back of the heads of their Heavenly prey, followed by a blinding barrage from the Redeemers' canons that ripped through their targets like a deadly hailstorm. Their victims burst apart in snaps of blinding gold. From a rooftop nearly a quarter of a mile away Splinter loosed his shot, catching Tristes between the eyes with absolute precision. Flakes like embers blown from a fire danced out of the exit wound. Cracks formed from both sides of the wound and quickly spread down the length of his body. His eyes rolled back into his head, and his knees buckled. As he dropped his body broke apart and burst into a brief brilliance before vanishing completely.

Without granting any respite the attackers turned to line up new targets. They were trained to the very height of physical perfection and further enhanced through means of science and technology. This, coupled with the element of surprise, served them well and in the next small eternity, all but Juriel were likewise slaughtered.

While most of the angels had only exchanged final, terrified glances or stared slack-jawed at the demise of their kindred, Belethor, had enough wherewithal to react. He launched high in an arc to attack Talon on the far side of the circle. To his credit, the angel made it within inches of his mark but Brickbat was able to anticipate the path of the strike and unleashed a rain of blue fire that met Belethor in mid-air, tearing him asunder.

The light he bled crashed into Talon, splashing against him like a golden wave before vanishing almost instantly.

At that same moment Palius, his battle-hardened mind also sharp and reactive, threw himself at Juriel, wrapping massive wings about him as a shield. Both Loki and Hammer had selected Palius as their second target, judging him a threat for his brute size. Miraculously Loki's shot sizzled harmlessly through the edge of Palius' beard, leaving the damaged ends glowing and smoldering, but Hammer's caught him in the left shoulder. The blue sliver tore a hole all the way through and sailed on into the tree line beyond. It whizzed past Titus's ear, causing him to drop his camera to the ground.

Palius refused to submit to his wound. His eyes hardened, and he loosed a monstrous battle cry which threw the S.W.A.R.M. troopers off-guard. They had expected him to fall after just a single hit. But their stun quickly wore off, and they trained their sites on him once more.

Before they could fire a second time Palius took Juriel by the shoulders. Quickly he whispered, "I love you, brother," before flinging Juriel toward the edge of the clearing and away from the conflict. As momentum carried him backwards Juriel looked upon his brother's demise with horrific clarity. He saw the broad and mighty Palius, his beautiful wings outstretched to form protective wall blocking view of his own escape. Palius's eyes gleamed with a love so pure and selfless that it defined all the glory of Heaven. But then the soldiers pulled their triggers, and their blue fire shredded those magnificent wings and tore through angelic flesh. They were thorough, not settling to pull their triggers only once, but again and again, potting Palius with dozens of holes that bled Heavenly radiance. The network of fractures that broke out around them like spider webs soon connected and the light beneath broke free, exploding outward, crashing against the armor of his slayers. And just before Juriel found purchase, that light faded into memory, and his brother was no more.

With all other targets eradicated the soldiers turned the attention to the sole survivor. Without hesitation Juriel spread his wings and launched himself violently skyward. He needed to find sanctuary where he could mourn the deaths of his brethren briefly before seeking out others—

Hot pain sent him spiraling out of control back towards the clearing a few dozen feet below. His right shoulder slammed hard against the ground with real physical force. His left wing fell across his legs, shot clean off by Splinter's skill. The other soldiers began to rush him, closing the gap to finish him off. The tears Juriel had reserved for later made hopeless golden trails down his cheeks. When a human died, they went to meet their Maker, but to an angel death was a finality. Nothingness.

Juriel wept for those who had just fallen. For the Father who had vanished. For his own sake, and for the world that would be left unprotected in the clutches of chaos and wickedness.

He whispered, "They know not what they do," believing this thought would be his last but suddenly a voice rang out, clear and threatening, ravaging the silence. It made a singular, unwavering demand, "You will leave him be!"

CHAPTER 29

His nostrils flared, and the air burned like acid against the dry walls of his throat. His heart thundered in a violent panic. His fingers were cold and purple in tightly clinched fists. He stood, legs spread and on the balls of his feet, poised to spring with his wounded brethren, a fading tangle at his feet. All he could feel was white-hot anger and a dire urgency to protect. Had he time to analyze and appreciate his current state, Athiel would have been surprised at the newness of these mortal sensations, not in that these were foreign to him, but in how they permeated the very flesh he wore. How it gave off real heat and soaked the beanie he wore with sweat. Only once before abandoning Heaven had he stepped fully into the physical coil and never at a time such as this.

The soldiers were stopped dead by both the intensity of his cry and his sheer size. A few tapped curiously at the strange, insect-like helmets they wore as if experiencing an equipment malfunction. One lowered his weapon, but only briefly. All seemed entirely perplexed by the abnormally tall figure who had so threateningly announced his presence.

One soldier, clearly the commanding officer dressed in less armored regalia, took a series of bold steps forward. As he closed the gap to Athiel he fingered the device that hung from the right side of his head. From behind him the largest of their group—formidable for a human but at least a foot shorter than he—spoke for the rest.

"Sir?" he asked, leaving the larger question unspoken.

The leader looked down at the wounded angel by Athiel's feet then back at Athiel. "I neither know nor care what you are. You're in my way and that makes you an issue. And issues are to be dealt with."

Their feet shifted. Fingers danced impatiently on triggers. Breaths steadied.

The leader raised his hand to keep them in check.

"Strafe?" he asked into his headset. Athiel could not hear the reply but apparently it was not the answer the leader wanted.

Then adjust position," his eyes never left Athiel, but their intensity doubled, "ASAP!"

He lowered his hand, bringing it to rest on the butt of his holstered sidearm.

"Capture or kill."

Once more the night exploded with the strobe of blue light. Four of the soldiers provided suppressing fire while their squad mates spread right and left to flank him.

Pain erupted from multiple pinpoints where their shots connected. Athiel could not deny the scream that sprang from his lips. It was not a surface pain, any more than a headache harmed the flesh, but a blaze that coursed through his very being and threatened to burn him to ash from within. It was unlike anything he had ever felt. Even the blade that had struck him during Lucifer's great fall had not pierced so.

Their onslaught was relentless. It could not react beyond dropping to his knees and throwing his arms over his head in an ineffective attempt to guard himself. The soldiers circled him entirely, clearly not concerned with friendlies in their line of fire. Faintly over the screeching of their weapons and the throbbing growing in his head he heard someone question why he had not died like the others. No one seemed to know, and the fear that cluelessness wrought visibly hardened their resolve.

Suddenly a warm, soothing sensation enveloped his ankle, a wondrous contrast to the torture that tore through him. He looked down to see the wounded angel's hand grasping him, pulsating with a dim white glow. It allowed him a degree of relief and focus. The angel gazed up at him with great concern and love.

"If you are my brother," he exhaled weakly, "then flee."

It struck Athiel that the firing had stopped. The agony he felt lingered but was fading. All of the soldiers stood with guns aimed, but were wobbling as if exhausted. A few cast sidelong glances to their leader, awaiting his word, baffled that their target had not fallen.

Their hesitation cost them. Athiel lunged at the soldier nearest his left flank, a good 30 feet away, hands like seeking talons. He landed hard on the soldier. Trapped as he was in the physical world he took advantage of his momentum. His fingers caught the sides of the soldiers helmet, crushing it slightly, keeping it locked on the wearer's head without damaging his skull. His grasp firm, Athiel flipped overhead and flung the soldier at a low but speedy arc. The man crashed back first against the trunk of a tall tree with a horrific crack. The soldier fell to the ground and lay absolutely still.

The others were, at first, awestruck by their foes acrobatic and physical prowess but renewed their assault the moment he had snatched their squad mate.

"Brickbat, Crucible, Jazz: Rodeo!" their leader shouted. "Loki, Mariachi, shine a light!"

Three soldiers ran forward, two mounting their weapons on their backs in mid-stride. Clearly they meant to bring him down by physical means. As Athiel squared up to face them two others tagged him repeatedly in the eyes, blinding him. Bolts of bright blue filled his vision buying enough time for the first of the on-rushing trio to reach him. The soldier held his weapon high over his shoulder it like a club. As he neared Athiel he added a burst of speed and rushed by, bringing the butt of the gun crashing against Athiel's temple as he did. The second soldier, a female, bent low and rammed her shoulder into the base of Athiel's gut, using her momentum to continue pushing him back towards the soldier who had clubbed him previously. That soldier had reared his gun back, ready for his second "at bat". As he swung Athiel reached out, catching his attacker's elbow in his right hand and the attacker's shoulder with his left even as he was being pushed. He spun his torso and tossed the soldier out into the middle of the clearing. The soldier rolled a considerable distance before coming to a stop some twenty feet shy of the fountain.

149

The woman had her hands firmly on Athiel's hips, guiding him back towards a tall oak, the last of the trio right at her heels. He let his legs go limp and dropped back into the momentum towards the ground. The female soldier stumbled over him clumsily before tucking into a guided roll. The third man jumped over him to avoid collision but spun almost instantaneously to confront him. Athiel, now on the dirt, kicked up over his head and caught the soldier square in the chest, knocking him into his female counterpart causing them both to slam into the oak.

His enemies kept up their fire on all fronts, stinging him from all sides, keeping him slightly off-balance but unable to bring him down. As Athiel would rush one their formation would shift so that no edge of their circle stayed within reach. He attempted to dodge, moving erratically but his foes adjusted with near-omnipotent precision. But despite the pain, despite his frustration, he did not, *would* not, go down.

Finally their leader had had enough. He ordered soldiers to retrieve their injured allies and remove them from the battlefield. But he himself did not move. He stood, shoulders squared toward Athiel only ten feet away. His right hand clenched in a fist and his left still dancing on the butt of his sidearm. As the soldiers broke in various directions to med-evac their comrades the leader, and the angel regarded each other with unblinking hatred.

"What are you?" the leader asked at last.

"You would call me an angel," Athiel replied cryptically. His first impulse had been to identify himself as an *angel of the Lord*, but that was a title he had long since shed.

The leader pondered this then replied, "No. You're not. I don't know what you are."

His answer boiled away some of the rage Athiel felt. Despite witnessing these soldiers slaughtering his brethren he had still expected a slight bit of fascination from this mortal as to his true nature, perhaps even intimidation. But Athiel found instead that he was the one unnerved.

A soldier's voice played in the leader's headset, but Athiel could hear each word clear as day. "Sir, we have Crucible and Jazz secured. But Hammer," there was a definite, anguished pause, "Hammer's in pretty bad shape. His spine may be broken."

The leader never took his eyes off of Athiel. A battle waged within them as his hatred of his foe balanced against his care for his ward. "Get the backboard and load him."

"Yes sir," came the reply.

The leader gnashed his teeth. "I *will* kill you. Whatever it takes." Without warning the leader drew his sidearm like a gunslinger as he began to briskly stride forward. There was a brilliant flash and a deafening pop. The bullet slammed square in the middle of Athiel's forehead. The angel went limp and unconscious but the leader continued to fire as he walked, each expert shot a new wound in Athiel's head. But there was no blood. Doomsayer stood silently, disbelieving that it could really have been ended so simply.

The down rush of wind coupled with warning cries from his soldiers gave Doomsayer only a split second to dodge away from the mighty sword of blue flame that came down in a deadly arc between he and the body of his victim. There was a blur of what resembled gigantic bat wings made of the same blue flame. They spread across the ground, hiding the body of the self-proclaimed angel then in the next both the wings and the angel were gone, rocketing through the reddening morning sky.

A curse came through Doomsayer's earpiece; it was Strafe from high above. "Sorry sir. I took a shot but missed. It was gone before I could line up a second."

Doomsayer was surprised to feel his heart racing; the suddenness of the second attacker had stopped him cold. "Any idea what it was?"

"None, sir." Strafe replied. "Just a blur."

"Acknowledged. Shadow-Eye return to sender. We did what we came to do." Doomsayer turned back to regroup with his men and leave. He vaguely heard Strafe's confirmation just before thumbing off his earpiece. Too many questions danced inside his head. He found Titus waiting for him at the edge of the tree line.

"I got everything." The filmmaker's hands were trembling. "Everything."

Doomsayer's pace never wavered. He blew past Titus, who quickly began to follow, trying to match Doomsayer. "Back that tape up as soon as you're in the van. Then you and I are going to go through it frame by frame. I want explanations."

Titus nodded, but Doomsayer neither saw nor cared. He had issued an order and expected it to be followed, even by this bystander. He was not a man to be questioned. As he approached their transport Hammer was being cautiously lifted into the back. His mind returned to the promise he had made. He would kill that *thing*. Whatever it took.

Although their mission was a success, Hellsbane loaded to leave carrying a deep sense of defeat. Silently they secured their gear and took their places. Heads hung low. Eyes transfixed on the most injured of their number. In their stupor they failed to witness as the angel Juriel crawled away safely into the breaking dawn.

CHAPTER 30

Treygen Andros stood nervously just outside the entrance to the Café di Paolo. He had taken four more pills of *fairy dust* after leaving the chaos at the Vatican and yet still could not control his nerves. It struck him as likely that he had already built up a bit of an immunity to their effect. When he had the opportunity—or rather *if* he had the opportunity—he would dig in and find a non-lethal work around. Living without the *fairy dust* was simply not an option any more even if it caused him tunnel vision and headaches. He refused to classify them as migraines; a "headache" was tolerable, but a "migraine" would be admitting that the side effects of his beloved fix-all held long term consequences. His hand had subconsciously wrapped around the pill bottle in his pocket. He stood at what, for him, was probably the entrance to the gates of Hell itself, and the devil that waited for him inside was more dangerous than he could handle without assistance, so he pulled the bottle out to gird on the armor of his security. He rattled the bottle. From the weight and sound there were maybe two pills left. He twisted the cap and looked inside and cursed himself for being right. Head thrown back, he downed the last two and hoped that this would be the tipping point that would overcome his tolerance to the chemical (not a "drug", no never a "*drug*"...he was no weak-willed junkie addict) and bring him enough calm and focus to navigate through the web of lies he would have to spin to survive this encounter.

His eyes scanned the surrounding rooftops. He felt foolish at first but reminded himself of the type of people he had allied himself with. The fact that he saw no one only strengthened his paranoia. The men these men used were the kind you never saw until it was too late. Still, and despite the potential direness of his situation, he could not help but take a moment and admire the absolute beauty of the pastel hues that had become synonymous with the coastal village of Positano, Italy. He made a mental note that when, or rather—again—*if* he had another opportunity he would have to return here and truly explore its richness. It was easy to see why so many of the artistic set had found it so inspirational back in the 1950s, leading (as such things often did) to its ever-growing popularity as a vacation destination for anyone seeking a taste of luxury and romance.

It had not been a convenient locale to reach, however. First he had had to make the arduous drive down most of the length of Italy from Florence to Salerno before catching the long ferry ride the rest of the way in. The rather obese husband and wife he had been forced to sit beside brought such a nauseating stench to his nostrils that he could only assume they were Americans, a hypothesis which was soon verified by their butchering of their mother language and their utter lack of sophistication. Treygen Andros considered himself the very model of European refinement and thus fit to pass such judgments, without regard as to whether his increasingly dour mood was in any way relative to his increasing proximity to Manuel Valdez. No, such things could justifiably be considered to exist in entirely different realities altogether.

As the passengers began unloading upon arrival, and his undesirable neighbors slide their weigh across their seats and into the aisle, Treygen found the claustrophobia he had battled had loosened its grip on his diaphragm, and he could not only breathe with greater ease but actually endure the act itself, as the repulsive odors of his ferry-mates had given way to the familiar comfort of salt water winds dancing on the tip of his tongue.

The moment his foot struck ground he was immediately overwhelmed by the old world beauty of the Santa Maria Assunta's majolica dome looming over the beachfront like the watchful eye of the One he had so recently helped to slay. And inside that storied church, its famous Black Madonna which had played a great role in the naming of the town itself. He was grateful that he had brought none of his T.S. enhanced gear with him lest he fall prey to the temptation to look inside the church and see the Heavenly host within. In truth he feared what he would see on their faces. He feared the weight of their knowing eyes. He feared the guilt inside him would swell up beyond his ability to cap, and he would fling himself off the cliffs of the Amalfi coast and make the crystal blue waters below his tomb.

Stiff as the grave he had trod slowly along Via Cristoforo Colombo, already a dead man walking, to meet his fate. And that had brought him here, outside the café, awaiting his demise.

He twisted the cap back on his pill bottle and made a mental note to refill the bottle the second he returned to his apartment. He *would* return to his apartment. He would. He had to tell himself that over and over. This meet was in public. He had been cautious at every turn. Valdez simply wanted to talk, and the subject matter could be near anything. Their research covered such a wide gamut of scientific need and curiosity that it was most likely that a new project was in the birthing stages and Valdez wanted Andros involved. Possibly even as project lead. There...*that* was the thought to focus on. That was the bright shining light that would help the fairy dust take hold and work its beautiful, wondrous magic.

He breathed in the positive and, with a mighty exhale, expelled the negative. He was ready to face whatever lay beyond that door. They would talk, they would eat, and they would leave separately. And how amazingly delicious did the plethora of odors floating through that archway smell! Life was grand. Thank you fairy dust.

He entered on a cloud and spotted Valdez almost immediately, tucked away in a far corner with his back to the door. His short-trimmed silver hair and stiff shoulders were unmistakable. The suit looked new. Either a shiny black or navy blue, Treygen could not decipher in the café light, but it was undoubtedly worth a fortune. Valdez had a taste for the very finest things in life, which is why he had selected this café. Not for its price tag, but rather for the richness of its cuisine. Every table

Treygen passed held such elegant looking faire, be it a thick, steamy sandwich or a divine slice of pie that had the sheen of a queen's jewels. He would certainly have a hard time selecting his dish. His ears glossed over bits of conversation about the tragedy in Florence. Offhandedly he wondered if the fairy dust had kicked in yet despite being deep in its buzz.

He reached the far corner of the café and walked around the table to sit opposite Valdez. The older man looked up from the cheesecake he had half finished and took one sip from his coffee before setting it down and wiping his hands on a napkin in his lap. His eyes locked on Treygen like a hawk gauging its prey. Treygen stood, the silver lining of his cloud starting to dissolve under this predatory gauze.

"Sit." Valdez's voice was even. The kind of even that was dangerous.

Like a puppet Treygen took a seat, immediately fixing his attention to the café menu.

"You're not ordering. We will speak then you will leave." Valdez placed his napkin on the table and folded his hands in his lap. He let an eternity pass in silence, watching each second shave the edges off Treygen's guard.

Indeed Treygen soon found himself quite eager to leave; the sweet smells of the café had turned sour in his nose. The air felt thick. He felt claustrophobic again with his back against the corner, like a trapped rodent staring down a hungry cat. He had to get things in motion because the quicker it began the quicker it ended.

"You wanted to meet, sir?" His voice shook. He hated himself for feeling so weak.

Valdez did not answer. His tongue worked around inside his cheek as if freeing up a morsel that had lodged itself in his teeth.

"Are you satisfied with the work you have been allowed at our facility?" The question caught Treygen completely off-guard, but even in his semi-doped up state he did not miss the two key words it contained. "Allowed". "Our". Valdez wanted Treygen to know where the power was held.

"Very much so." He replied, hoping it sounded sincere.

"Your contributions have been outstanding, project to

project." Valdez's voice held none of the flattery his words should imply. "I'm sure you feel adequately compensated for your time and efforts."

Again the reminders. He was a child being shamed and put in his place. This was not good.

"I can honestly say I never had dreamed I would be paid so generously for my work." This was true, but Treygen's voice was still trembling. He hoped if he continued to play the part of the whipped dog that he would avoid his master's wrath, whatever had caused it.

"I'm sure, but any denomination is insignificant compared to what you have achieved," Valdez's praise was unexpected. It sounded genuine.

Treygen grinned faintly and nodded. Then the hammer fell.

"So I am sure there is no reason for me to remind you of certain stipulations that are leashed to these endeavors: contractual clauses insisting on secrecy and deniability. Things meant to protect both our organization and our cause. Yes?" Valdez was a handsome man. Younger than his hair color implied. Everything about him—his nails, his goatee, his eyebrows—was neatly planned and trimmed. His jaw was strong and chiseled square. Just how one might expect the devil to look. But Treygen always told himself that when you met the devil, he would be smiling. The devil that sat before him showed no emotion whatsoever and, to Treygen, that was truly frightening.

"Sir, I am not sure what you might..." Even as he spoke Treygen tried desperately to will himself to silence. His was the futile argument of ignorance from a guilty man. He was caught, but he could not stop the idiocy that spewed from his mouth out of panic.

Valdez stopped him dead with a raised palm.

"We are done here. You will leave."

Treygen's throat choked off the next syllable but his mouth stood wide and silent. He only hesitated a moment before standing up. He knew if he did not leave now more incriminating denial would come from his lips and besides, with each movement that brought him closer to leaving Valdez's presence the more relief seeped in.

He bowed to Valdez as he left. It was little more than a nod.

It felt foolish but it was all he could think to do to encompass "I understand", "Thank you for letting me go", and "good-bye" all in one motion. As he walked away he heard Valdez return to his cheesecake. His fork made a harsh scraping like the sound of nails on a chalkboard against his plate. Treygen forced himself to focus on the exit. He had gotten a pass. He had gotten very, *very* lucky.

But…why?

As he approached the door two large men in designer suits entered the café. They were the very epitome of Hollywood "muscle". His feet froze in place, outright refusing to take him closer towards them. It seemed he had not gotten a pass after all and that this, here and now in an Italian café, would be his end.

The men just stared at him indifferently. Treygen tried to flash his life before his eyes, but the fading magic of the fairy dust only allowed him foggy recollections. He wondered what would happen to him now that the order of life and afterlife had been obstructed. With the Paradox's work complete would he be harvested for something else? And would he even be aware? He would know these answers soon enough…

…and the men turned away and took seats at a table, turning their attention to the menus they found.

Treygen's body unlocked with a quiver. He felt embarrassment from the weight of the multitude of eyes that were on him. He tucked his head and exited the café. As his feet hit the sidewalk he could not help but question if forgiveness was still possible now that there was no one left in Heaven to grant it.

CHAPTER 31

The sky was a soft red and orange flame of rolling clouds painting the mighty towers of man with a demonic red hue. At first glance it could have been the capitol of Hell itself, and with the vast sea of wandering lost souls that littered its bowels one would be hard pressed to argue the point.

It was early, way *way* too early to be awake and decently mobile. Blowfish mocked himself a zombie, strolling mindlessly down Eckhart Boulevard in search of sweet, sweet sustenance. On a normal day (which day of the week it was was of little consequence when one lived a life without a job, or home, or family…save for knowing who might be doing their "this makes me feel better about myself" volunteer stint at theSaint Michael's soup kitchen—that Phil sure knew how to pepper up a good tomato soup, bless him) he would have lazed about for at least another two or three hours before getting to his feet and going about whatever venture struck him as important that day. But last night had not afforded him much sleep. Three times he had laid his head down and tried to rest—since he was a child he had always found that if he imagined he was Superman, soaring above Metropolis or circling the sun or fighting off alien hordes that his mind would loosen its grip on consciousness and release him into slumber—but each time he had slept uneasily for only a few minutes and then lay awake and tossed restlessly, growing increasingly irritated until he had gotten up and walked about,

159

gazing up at the sky. It seemed so wrong in a way that he just could not put his finger on.

During his second walkabout a chill suddenly raced the length of his spine moments before the shuffling of feet informed him that he was not alone. He hesitated to turn and see who it might be; maybe the Godfather of Soul and Sandwiches had totaled out Blowfish's tab and it was finally time for dues to be paid. His visitor, however, was neither male nor imagined; instead she was miserably hunched and thin as a paperclip.

"What keeps you up at the witching hour?" Sylvia Crindle, or Sylvie as she liked

to be called, asked with a bitter edge. Before he had time to reply she scratched frantically at the ridge of her hawk-like nose and snorted loudly and repeatedly.

Blowfish just shrugged. He was not a fan of Sylvie and opening his mouth would only invite conversation.

But Sylvie never needed an invitation. "A good man has no business being about this late. That's gospel truth."

He wanted to walk away but knew Sylvie would just follow him and converse endlessly with his back. Besides, he had thoughts that needed vocalization.

"Do you believe everything you see?" Blowfish asked. Internally he braced himself; only rarely did Sylvie say anything that was not entirely negative in nature.

But she surprised him for a second time that night.

"I believe in what my gut tells me. That's how the soul tallies the truth." She stated and took a seat on a plastic crate beside him. Her answer was somehow comforting. She fixed him with a sour and inquisitive glare and right away he knew she was on the verge of ripping that comfort away. "You're too screwy in the head. Like you got nothing but oatmeal sloshing around up there."

He sighed heavily, which brought a hardy smile to Sylvie's face. "Name me one soul here who ain't a porridge-head? Well, one soul aside from sweet, docile Sylvie." She began to cackle like a witch from a child's Halloween story which Blowfish found incredibly unnerving.

Having decided that he was done, he turned his shoulder to her and waved dismissively. The cackling fell away, replaced by the same beak scratching and snorting as before. Through the disgusting cacophony she managed to speak in staggered syllables. "Ah come on…*snort*…dear. *Snort*. Don't get…*snort*… so sour. *Snnnnortttt*."

He kept walking. For a few brief moments he had felt on the precipice of genuine revelation and, as usual, she managed to strip it away. He was only glad to hear that shewas not following him. Maybe now would be a good time to try to lie back down and rest. Sleep at least brokered a small measure of peace.

But Sylvie Crindle was not done with him. She called after him, "You wanna know what's real, porridge-head? The shadows. That's what's real. They watch, and they listen, and when they've made up their minds, they come callin'. That's gospel truth."

That thought clung to him like a parasite and ate at his security as he lay down. It bored its way into the dreams he flittered through in a half-asleep, catatonic state. It birthed shadows hiding eyes. Eyes that calculated and quantified. Eyes that hungered. Ears that heard the frightened skip of a heart and the truth behind the lies a man tells himself in places of his soul so deep that he forgets they are not true. He awoke gasping, the sharp pain in his chest alerting him that he had been holding his breath. The chill of the night air bit into bone, and he shook. He felt eyes on him; a feeling so definite that he had to force himself to open his own to ensure that there was really no one or no *thing* staring him down. But the dark of night held no consolation. The world was awash in black and shades of impenetrable gray that seemed to undulate like a heartbeat. Everything seemed eerily aware and focused on him. He felt vulnerable, huddled as he was under a blanket of newspaper, tucked like a swaddling child. At least if he was on his feet he might be capable of mounting some meager defense.

And so again he crawled off his mound and stood up, stretching his arms to wake complaining muscles, but he did not stretch too far—the grander the gesture the morelikely he was to attract unwanted attention—and once he was upright it came to him that the best defense was a good offense and sometimes the best offense could actually be a full on retreat. And so he walked.

That walk continued for the next few hours. It was a constant struggle between sustaining the courage to maintain a normal pace and staving off the cowardice that demanded he quicken his pace lest demons nip at his heels. His journey took him across several blocks towards the heart of the city. He would stop from time to time only to pick up whatever change he found lying about, and as the hidden sun began to reclaim the sky his mood slowly brightened in conjunction. His pace became even and calm, and soon he found himself at non-descript, yet welcoming, convenient store. His hand went to his pocket and fished out the change he had collected. He counted it. $1.34. *Not bad*, he thought. He rattled the coins once in his palm and pointed his feet towards the entrance, his step now brisk and giddy.

A few feet away from the door he noticed a woman in his peripheral. Mid-to-late- forties, dressed in a decently expensive gray dress-suit. Her pace was slowing the closer she drew to him, but he would reach the door first regardless. He lowered his head, figuring to look at her directly would intimidate her, and reached for the door. He stepped back and pulled it open, presenting the doorway to her with a wave of his hand. The woman's step stuttered, but then she too lowered her head and picked up her pace. As she passed by him she gave a cursory smile, but said not a word. Blowfish was unaffected. He had long since grown accustomed to such behavior and besides, the smell of freshly brewed coffee that now floated into his nostrils was far too rich to allow anyone a bad mood.

He closed his eyes and stepped forward to follow that inviting aroma all the way to its source when a sneaker crashed into his foot and a hand instinctively landed on his shoulder in an attempt to prevent its owner from going down. He looked up and saw that he had tripped a bearded, dark haired, tanned young man, probably late teens or early twenties, wearing a solid green hoodie bearing the logo of what was most likely some obscure band. The young man laughed and said, "I'm so sorry. I got a bit presumptuous I guess."

Blowfish fumbled with the door then stepped back to let the young man through. "Not at all," he said.

Once inside Blowfish felt like a kid in a candy store. The $1.34 in his hand might as well have been a million dollars. He felt like he owned the joint. Whatever he wanted was just an arm's reach away. Life this fine day was simply good.

He made his way to the coffee pots and waited patiently and quietly for the nicely dressed woman to pour her cup, using that time to decide what size and flavor to get. His stomach and taste buds begged for a large but at the price tag of $1.29 that would eat up the majority of his newfound fortune and no matter how enticing that sultry brown liquid may be, he also had a hankering for something to gnash between his teeth.

The woman was stiff, trying to ignore his presence and when she finished pouring her cup and adding in a few packs of creamer and sugar, she turned to her left and made a huge arc away from and around Blowfish, overtly avoiding looking directly at him as she did. Still he was unphased. He grabbed the smaller eighty-nine cent cup and began to fill it with steamy, caffeinated Colombian brew. He stepped to the side to allow a newcomer access to the various pots and cups and went about the business of selecting three packages of French vanilla creamer and four packages of real, no foolin' sugar.

The cup warmed his hand as he perused the shelves in search of the perfect mateto his beverage. He sipped it lightly, not wanting to drink too much before he had breakfast in hand; such things were best enjoyed together. At last he found a display of cheap, sugary snack cakes and at the bottom by his toes were boxes of single-sale granola bars beautifully priced at a quarter each. He grinned and snatched up a honey oat flavored bar and headed towards the register.

At the register line he again found himself facing the back of the forty-something woman. She was digging through her purse, mumbling curses beneath her breath as she searched for her credit card. She soon found it and handed it over to the cashier who tried three times to swipe it before resorting to punching in the card numbers manually.

"Must be the magnetic strip," he said with a patient grin.

She countered with her own less-than-heartfelt smile and began tapping her nails on the counter top impatiently. She glanced once over her shoulder at the man she clearly regarded as trash, and her nose twitched disgustedly. She turned back to the cashier and said aloud for all to hear, "Some people have no business being out in public if they don't even bother to bathe."

The cashier paused in disbelief, and his eyes darted briefly up at Blowfish before proceeding to enter the last few digits. The woman huffed loudly and asked, "Can you please hurry? Someone in here flat out reeks."

She had finally managed to penetrate his defenses, but with the hot coffee and granola bar in hand he was determined to keep his focus on the good. He forced a laugh and told the back of her head, "Long is the way, and hard, that out of Hell leads up to the light, ma'am."

The woman's head spun in response, and she gave a revolted snarl. "Don't talk to me," she said coldly.

Fortunately the cashier had at that moment finished her transaction, and the woman hurried to leave. Blowfish shook his head and stepped forward to pay. He set his haul on the counter and smiled at the clerk who just shrugged indifferently.

Blowfish began to rifle through his change, calculating his meal's cost, when a soft voice spoke up from behind him.

"Can I pay for that?" it asked.

Blowfish turned around. It was the young man he had collided with at the door. He had gentle eyes that complimented his genuine smile.

Blowfish lifted a hand in refusal and said, "It's okay. I've got it covered. But thank you though."

"Sir," the young man persisted, "hope this doesn't sound weird, but I really feel like God's placed it on my heart to help you out." The young man tucked the bottled water he was carrying under one armpit and pulled out his wallet. In quick succession he opened it and removed the few bills therein. He held them out to Blowfish. "It's not much, but it's all I've got, and I want you to take it."

Blowfish had no words. He stared at the young man and felt his eyes go wet. He attempted to again raise his hand in refusal, but the young man stepped around him and hand two singles to the cashier, the rest he tucked into the pocket of Blowfish's shirt.

"Please, just take it," he pleaded, "You'll be blessing me more than I can bless you."

Blowfish's mouth was agape. He slowly reached into the pocket and pulled out the cash. Three five-dollar bills and a one. He reached out and pulled the bottled water from under the young man's arm and placed it on the cashier's counter with a five beside it. The cashier added the water to the previous total, changed out the five and handed the change back to Blowfish.

Blowfish turned back to the young man and extended his hand in thanks. The young man took it. His hand was small but his grip was strong, much stronger than Blowfish expected. It was a good handshake.

"Will you tell me your name?" Blowfish asked rather shyly.

"Antonio, sir. And yours? I'd like to keep you in my prayers if that's ok." Blowfish drew a blank. He searched through the fog in his head; it had been so long since anyone had asked. It came to him in an image, a story in his head that he could not remember whether or not it held any truth. A man, tall and beautiful, rising from the ocean depths. The man had called him something...what was it?

And then he remembered.

"I'm Jasper Worthington. Pleased to make your acquaintance."

CHAPTER 32

Blowfish had not been the only one who had suffered from a troubled, restless night. Father Gregory Donovan spent the remainder of the long night following his dream in his study. The red light on the base of his land line flashed hurriedly, indicating several calls had been missed (although only a few actual voice messages had been left). He refused to give it any great consideration. His time at Saint Michael's speaking with police had drained his spirit considerably. He supposed the calls and messages could potentially be of importance, but he was a mortal man with mortal limits and he had had all he could take in for one night. Whatever it was would have to keep until the morning.

He sat quietly in the wee hours jotting down notes in chronological order detailing how Father Behanan had come first into his life and then ultimately into his circle of leadership. The young priest had an affinity for people. Race, creed, age, level of poverty or wealth, none of it mattered, he was a social chameleon that was never out of his element. During his rigorous studies at centenary Joseph Behanan had still made time to volunteer and get involved with the crumbling community that was Lanza del Los Santos's heart. This had won him great favor with the local Diocese, and in the end they, in what was now questionably either their wisdom or through other, darker influences, had assigned Behanan to Saint Michael's so that he could be, in their view, an effective and shining beacon of God's love for the most downtrodden of His people.

That was the story, on the surface at least. Like everyone else he had warmed up to Joseph right away. The young man had an innocent and sincere charm, like his heart was big enough to take in the woes of the entire world. But looking at the timeline on paper in front of him, frankly it just all seemed too perfect. Too planned to be happenstance. The book of Revelations told that in the end times wolves would come in sheep's clothing to lead the Lord's flock astray. These interlopers would hold lofty positions and through their word, claiming the name of God Himself, would poison a great multitude.

Joseph could be such a wolf. That was certainly what the dream—no, the *vision*, it was definitely more than just a dream—seemed to suggest. And these current events, what parts did they play in the grander scheme? The boy and his mother had already brought death into the house of God. And Joseph had been so willing to stay with them. Did the Enemy get a foothold and now deliberated within the heart of the house as to hown to tear it down from inside?

His heart ached at these thoughts. He had truly loved Joseph as a friend and almost as a son, oddly. He did not want to believe that such things were even possible, but the Enemy came at you by means of your weaknesses and from unseen angles. It was almost undeniable what was occurring, no matter how it hurt him to admit it, but the vision had been clear.

His time to truly serve was fast approaching. He whispered, "If only, Father who art in Heaven, you would take this cup from me."

Several times throughout the overly long night he could have sworn he had caught sight of a large figure in the shadows out of the corner of his eye. Each time he would stare, keeping his gaze fixed until his eyes could fully adjust to the darkness beyond the power of his desk lamp. Each time nothing, but time and again that feeling was there; that he was not alone, and that he was not entirely safe. But each time he would sum it up to residual energy from the impact of his vision and recommit himself to his work.

When the morning light had finally pierced through

his window and begun to overpower the lamp light he sighed remorsefully and stood up to stretch. Every warrior needed rest and refueling. Chosen or not he was still very mortal. He waddled flatfooted to the kitchen and went about the chore of cooking a decent warrior's breakfast: eggs, bacon, sausage links (never patties) with low acid orange juice (his ulcer was an angry beast of late) and grape jelly to scramble into the eggs. The act of cooking soothed him. The weight on his shoulders melted away with the sizzle of bacon grease. Life was full of many such trivial respites.

He ate in his living room and listened intently to the roaring quiet of his home. He never regretted the solitary life he chose (it was all part of the trade-off to give his utmost to the Highest) but at times the space felt cavernous. He often mused it was like residing in the belly of a whale. The silence soon became overwhelming, however, and he reached for the television remote.

Gregory harbored such deep hatred for watching television news, but always believed through it one could watch the movements of the Enemy on a global scale. The wars, the downward moral spiral, the unfolding of prophecy, all at the click of a button and plain as day to any who would truly watch and listen. That was where he had ended his viewing the night before after returning home from the scene at Saint Michael's, and that was where he picked up again this morning over the best eggs he had ever made.

The image faded in. Fire. Mourning. Death. Fear. The Vatican razed and the Pope believed dead inside. It was as if the Enemy had struck the earth with a fiery fist and claimed an unprecedented victory. Authorities were tight-lipped about nearly every detail, but it was clear that no one could believe that or understand how such an abhorrence could have been accomplished.

The phone rang. Father Gregory had been so focused on his television that it startled him to a full stand. His knee flipped the plate that had hung precariously off of the coffee table, spilling its delicious contents all over the rug. Gregory bit his tongue, barely stopping the cuss that threatened to fall out. He picked up the cordless phone off the end table to his left (he was still old fashioned in that he refused to be tethered to a cell phone) and answered. The voice that greeted him was heavy with fear and sadness. It was Bishop Terrence Graham at the Diocese, calling to inform Gregory of the horror in Florence.

"I have tried repeatedly through the night to contact you!" He began with a huff.

At first the Bishop's voice held a slight edge of condescension, but even in mid-sentence it wavered and finally trickled down to a tone that belied a worried sense of duty.

"Have you heard about the attack?"

"Just now."

"I need you to be out in front of this, ahead of your parish. It's what they'll need

from you."

"I know, forgive me but my night was filled with… tribulations." Gregory said,n"I'm watching the news as we speak."

"We have no real way of approximating how greatly this will affect so many aspects of the Church, but trust that I will keep in close contact with you and everyone within our Diocese. From time to time I may need to rely on you as my liaison in certain matters. Is that ok?" Bishop Graham was fumbling to find an early sense of order in this chaos and, truthfully, was doing a respectable job of it. For the most part he was able to keep the emotion out of his voice and letting his reason do the talking.

"Of course! I'll do whatever I can."

"Thank you, Gregory. Begin, as always, with prayer. These are times of tribulation, just as you said, and we will all be tested in our ways."

Of that, Father Gregory was certain. His eyes turned down to scan the meal that lay scattered about his feet. "I will begin to fast and pray the moment we hang up, Father."

"I know you will. I wish I could talk with you more, but I have so much to do and many more calls to make. I will try my best to call you later tonight."

"I've got to head over to the cathedral to follow up on last night."

"Sure. Sure."

"So try me there first; otherwise I'll be home as quickly as I possibly can." Images from the vision flashed in Gregory's mind, they all included the child and mother. It was not time to move yet, not without a clearer sense of what was asked, but there were still legal and liability issues to be addressed. The mortal coil, for the time being, trumped the spiritual war.

"Keep me apprised of that as well, but later, when there's time." Bishop Graham's voice gave for a moment; a slight quiver and woeful sigh. "So many battlefronts. So few of us to fight."

Gregory pitied the man the weight of his station.

"Good-bye, Gregory. Be vigil and be forthright."

"I will. God bless you."

"God bless you as well, Gregory. I pray He truly does."

Gregory Donovan hung up the phone and set it back down on the end table. He muted the television and just let the images sink into his brain. He let the need for retribution they brought settle in. Bishop Graham had been right, there *were* so very many battlefronts and so few soldiers to fight in the name of the Lord, but his own was obvious, and he was eager and willing to wage his war. He was behind the Enemy's lines. And right now, that was *exactly* where he wanted to be.

He got dressed and left the house, ready to begin.

CHAPTER 33

Manuel Dominic Valdez had watched Treygen Andros make his way back towards the café entrance via the reflection off a glass painting hung across from his table. Their brief interaction had confirmed all of his suspicions even without having them confirmed by Andros' watcher. The gloss over the man's eyes and warble of his neck denoted that he had taken at least a few of his personal medication. Pity. Andros was possessed of a mind that rivaled Einstein but of character as brittle as glass.

Manuel had taken some measure of amusement watching Andros squirm when his bodyguards had entered the café. The two men were veritable hulks, but were more or less decoys. The true men he trusted his life to were blended perfectly amongst the café patrons. To date four attempts on his life had been foiled simply because the overt brutes had drawn attention away from the vigilant eyes of the counter-assassins that trailed him. There were not the best in the world, but the best in the world had been their mentor.

Manuel had withdrawn his phone from his pocket, prepared to call that very man, but then paused to check his watch. It was not time yet. Approximately twenty minutes left to wait, but there were a gamut of pressing matters that demanded his attention. In truth that twenty minutes would be too small a window to accomplish what he needed to. He would have to prioritize.

His first call had been to his direct subordinate, Herzog Krieger. and it had been productively short and to the point. The Paradox had re-entered the Shell and recovery teams were en route. ETA was forty-three minutes. Valdez was unpleased with this, but Krieger assured him that the pace would be accelerated. End call.

His second call had been considerably longer. About half way through it a waitress had attempted to include Valdez in her rounds, but one of his hidden guardians ran interference, keeping the lovely young woman occupied with touristy questions regarding Positano culture and the local, though world-renowned, boutiques. She had hoped to make enough between her tips and wages in the next two weeks to afford an elegant though admittedly demure dress to wear to her sister's wedding. Valdez's associate, claiming to be an American banking executive, assured her that he would fatten her tip and used that promise as leverage to keep her from wandering too far away from his table.

The call itself was a jumble of positive momentum and setbacks. It seemed the first strike team to go live in the field had found victory at a high cost. The gathering of "halos" had been eradicated down to one, but a seemingly complete unknown had entered the fray and brought casualties—though not fatalities—to their number as well. That was unfortunate, but expected. The Pillar had foreseen this entity without being able to describe it with any clarity. For the time being it was enough to know that this figure was in play. Next was to determine to what ends and then to locate and deal with accordingly.

At the conclusion of the second call Valdez returned his phone to his pocket, finished the last morsel of his surprisingly delicious lemon cheesecake, and decided that it was time he take in a few more minutes of Positano culture. As he set his credit card on the table in front of him his secret bodyguard brought his conversation with the pretty waitress to a close, kept true to his promise with an astronomical tip, and then exited the café.

Moments later another man quietly, casually, left his money on his table and made his way to the café entrance as well.

Finally as Valdez exited, the two well-dressed brutes followed suit.

As he made his way down Via Cristoforo Colombo his eyes

wandered up to the tip of the dome of Santa Maria Assunta. He found it hard not to sneer at the many eyes that certainly followed him from upon it. He had been marked long ago as a threat, but never once had *they* struck at him directly. They did not know what he had done, or even what he was capable of, only that he was involved in their downfall. That knowledge empowered him. Man was now lord of creation, master of his own destiny. Risen like Zeus to devour the titans.

He reached into his inner pocket and retrieved what appeared to be normal, designer sunglasses. Placing them on he could just barely confirm his suspicion. A small band of angels stood atop the dome; as to whether or not he was the object of their attention was not a subject of doubt in his mind. He gave them a cheerful grin then thumbed the trigger built in to his watch. He only wished he could more clearly see their faces as he suddenly vanished from their view.

On all sides of him angels and demons went about their natures. Whispering in ears, poisoning minds, mending broken spirits, unaware that their time as puppeteers was slipping away. An angel held the hand of a little tourist girl separated from her family until another angel led her mother back to her. Valdez noted how frail they were already beginning to look. A demon comprised of smoke and gnashing teeth and boney hooks constricted around the heart of a man who bullied his way through other pedestrians to some unknown, likely unimportant errand. It was a sick masquerade. It was the *true* definition of blasphemy. And soon…it would cease.

He spied a squat old man at the entrance to a shop, beckoning passersby to have sandals custom-made "while you wait!". A demon of equal stature stood between him and the crowd, weakening the volume of the man's calls and working to turn away the interest of any who might notice him. Likely the demon sought to ruin him financially; the outside of the shop itself was in dire need of paint and repair, and the man's clothes were ragged and dirty. Upon short observation it was clear that the shop owner's enthusiasm was a forced effort, and slowly but surely his spirits were sinking. So Valdez would intervene. The great lummoxes that accompanied him blocked the oncoming flow of foot traffic allowing Valdez to cross over to the shop unhindered. He stepped up and offered the man his hand. The demon at the door could not see him and therefore did not react until the shop owner gave a cheerful greeting. The demon spun around in confusion, snarling at the owner, but remained unaware of Valdez.

The sandal maker ushered Valdez graciously inside, Valdez thanking him in Italian performed with a perfect Sicilian accent. A few lines into their dialogue— discussing Valdez's preferences in footwear—his phone rang. The twenty minutes were up. Valdez answered, but after greeting put the caller on hold. He returned to his conversation with the sandal maker, apologizing that the call was necessary but that he would pay triple the standard fee for sandals that were a true representation of this master's craft. The sandal maker clapped his hands and laughed joyfully, his spirits reinvigorated. He sat Valdez down in modest leather chair, bade Valdez to continue with his phone call then set about his work.

Smiling down as the man removed his left shoe, Valdez began to speak in fluent Cantonese.

"Have you arrived?" He asked.

"Nearly. There was a slightly longer delay at the airport than I had anticipated." A man's voice in equally versed Cantonese replied.

"Then I can assume you have not been compromised."

"Correct."

"Your work never fails to impress."

The voice on the other end was not used to flattery from Valdez, no one was, but it hid that fact well. "Thank you."

Out of the corner of his eye Valdez spied the demon. It had followed the sandal maker inside and was baffled as the man went about making sandals for no one it could see.

"Stay in the villa for the next three days. A new directive will be delivered then." Valdez knew these orders would not be well received, but the Pillar was always to be considered.

Surprisingly there was no argument.

"Will we be meeting again in the foreseeable future?" the voice asked. With his mind on the Pillar Valdez almost laughed at the irony of the question.

"No," Valdez replied, "but I will need to meet with the Rose. I would like you to arrange this."

The voice was silent for a moment.

"I will call her tomorrow. She checked in with me an hour ago and was lying down to bed. Apparently she hurt herself finishing her last task."

"Nothing life-threatening I trust."

"No."

"Then that will suffice." Valdez looked down to admire the skill of the man toiling about his feet. He held genuine respect for men who spent a lifetime mastering their craft: both the lowly sandal maker and the man with which he spoke.

"I'm pulling up to the villa now. You obviously spared no expense. I'm flattered."

The voice held no trace of sarcasm.

"You earn such things." Valdez replied.

He could hear the car beeping as the assassin known only as Whisper opened the door.

"Three days," Whisper said. The car door slammed shut.

Valdez took that to be an end to the conversation.

"Three days," he echoed.

Valdez once again returned his phone to his pocket and gave his full attention to the sandal maker, studying the bulging veins shifting on the back of the man's well-worn hands as he worked. He considered how the callused skin on the man's fingers had become as coarse and rough as the suede he shaped. Finally his mind settled on one thought and in it found a moment's bliss: man would, at last, truly reap the harvest of his toils.

CHAPTER 34

Paul Kennedy, the Old Pro, stood in his two-car garage stripping off his uniform. It was a habit he had picked up from his wife, Samantha, his high school sweetheart, the prom queen that this nerd-turned-jock/cop had somehow managed to woo. Time and again whenever one of his brothers-in-blue would make the clichéd joke, *how did you get* her?, he would laugh aloud and shrug the question off. To him, though, it felt like the plot of some knock-off John Hughes teen drama from the 1980s. He had certainly "come into his own" during his early twenties, but the fact was that Samantha had always been, and was *still,* exactly what society would expect a magazine covergirl to look like: tall, toned and unexplainably radiant. She was a "perfect 10" that this "7 at best" had managed to land simply on the merit of personality, charm and, over the course of years, trustworthiness and devotion.

They were the cliché that broke the cliché.

He grabbed his house robe from the peg next to the kitchen door and tossed his uniform in the adjacent basket that held a few pair of her scrub uniforms. Samantha Kennedy was a ten-year surgical technologist for the labor and delivery ward at the Patrick Morraine Hospital in downtown LS. This routine of stripping off their work clothes in the garage was the result of her work. She was deeply in love with the act of helping to bring new life into this world and the limitless possibilities and hope

179

that each brought. Her long, skinny fingers made her popular among the surgeons that practiced at Pat Morr (although Paul himself suspected that more than one had more unprofessional reasons for enjoying her company in the OR).

The only downside to her profession, that is to say, what *others* but not Samantha might consider a downside, was that often her scrubs would be decorated with the remnants of cesareans and even normal delivery. Blood—sometimes that of hepatitis positive patients or worse—afterbirth, and other byproducts of nature's wonder that most had not the stomach for. Add to the equation that, although it would be stretching to label her a "neat freak", she was borderline obsessive about the cleanliness of their home. The sum of these factors had been the routine she implemented, claiming that as natural and beautiful as such things were, she did not want to get them all over their house.

She would pull into the garage after her shift, usually around 7:30pm after pulling a 7-to-7, strip down to her unmentionables, place them in the hamper basket she bought, grab her robe and then enter the house, saying a quick hello to Paul and their daughter, Kat on her way to their bedroom to wash up and redress.

It was after nearly a month after Sam's implementation of the process that Paul came home one morning and, as he entered into their kitchen from the garage, noticed dried blood on his pants that had belonged to a heroine junky that had gotten beastly violent during the course of his arrest. Sam's sentiments came billowing through the cavern of his weary head and before his foot hit the tile, he stepped back into the garage and called to her to bring his robe. The warm, gracious smile that she had given him upon handing it over relayed more gratitude than an "I told you so" would have.

Now her ritual had become his, and their robes waited side by side like quiet lovers. As an added benefit he found that somehow the simple act of shedding his clothing in this way seemed to unburden him of all the negativity and hardship from the shift he had just ended, as if all those things had stained into the very fibers. But this morning the stains had soaked through the fabric and were tattooed on his bare skin. He felt a very tangible weight pulling on his shoulders and with edges of frost.

Now, standing nearly naked in the garage, his robe in hand but not on, he felt too filthy to walk inside.

And then the kitchen door opened. Just a sliver.

She peaked through the crack and emitted a girlish giggle, and in that instant the hell he felt burned away. His shoulders eased, and his knees nearly gave. He barely heard the sigh that escaped his lips. She giggled again, on the verge of outright laughter, and flung open the door.

"What you doin' in here?" she boomed in her deepest, fe-fi-fo-fum voice, wearing a comical visage to match.

He smiled. Her control broke. She let out a laugh as sharp as it was wonderful, leapt past the steps and slammed hard into his chest, nearly taking them both to the cool concrete floor.

"Baby!" she said, accenting it with playful pecks around the whole of his face.

He began to blush and tuck his chin into his neck.

Her palms caught his chin and brought it up to meet her stare.

"I've been missing you," her playfulness gave way to a sweet sincerity.

Paul could not fight the red in his cheeks nor the heat that accompanied the color. He stiffened his lips as best he could to try to speak.

"You've been missing me?"

Samantha's smile broadened, and her eyes lit like stars. She nodded and gave an "uh huh".

At this Paul himself giggled, with slightly more masculinity.

"You've missed me for about what? An hour and a half that you've been awake?" he asked sarcastically.

Her smile cocked to the side, and her necked swooned flirtatiously.

"Try all cold night long alone in our marital bed," she retorted.

It struck Paul how, after all these years together, Samantha still made him feel like the awkward and shy teenager he had been. His vocal chords locked, and his brain began spinning wheels in a futile attempt to say something, anything at all to continue this sweet game he and his wife were playing. He came up empty.

Fortunately her lips knew the score. She pressed them softly against his and parted them over and under his bottom lip and then pressed a little harder. Paul dropped his robe to the floor and with both hands embraced his beloved, returning the tenderness of her kiss threefold.

After a full minute their lips parted and Paul laid his chin on his wife's shoulder and pulled her close against him. Another sigh escaped him unwittingly.

Samantha cupped the back of his head and wrapped herself tighter around him. They both closed their eyes. Her embrace was his earthbound heaven and he gave in to it as much as his consciousness would allow. His muscles for the most part surrendered and relaxed, but the tension in his neck was unyielding. It ached with the pangs of last night's trials. He lifted his chin slightly and turned his head to the right hoping to relieve it some by stretching.

Samantha knew him well and sensed beneath the surface. She pulled back to look him in the face. When he proved unable to meet her studious gaze she spoke.

"Honey, what's wrong?" she asked both quietly and motherly.

He tried to force his mouth to reply, but it was uncooperative. He sighed his frustration. This she always misread and took personal. When her eyebrows tightened he found the strength to speak.

"It's okay, baby. Just…just a hard night. But I'm fine."

Her expression remained quizzical so he added, "I promise."

She took a moment to consider, but respectfully decided to not press the matter. He found that this made him want to tell her everything. Always. The fact that she gave him the space to do so on his own terms, in his own time. It was a large part of what made their partnership so strong.

"I don't want to go into detail," he began, "at least not right now. I'll tell you more later I'm sure, but…it was just a lot to handle in one night. Back to back, stacked up like that."

Samantha nodded her understanding but said nothing. Her genuinely interested and concerned look prompted him to continue.

"It was the kind of night that really starts to make you

question how many good people are still out there in the world, you know?"

She nodded again and flashed a sympathetic smile.

"Makes you question how much hope people have any more...in *anything*."

She reached a hand out and rubbed it up and down his shoulder above his left arm.

"That's why I'm so thankful for our faith in God," she said. "It allows us to look ahead, beyond the troubles of this world. And to feel sheltered in the meantime." She gave him an elfish wink and added, "Don't cha think?"

His lips curled to one side in a half-cocked smile, and he agreed. He drew a deep breath and searched around the garage ceiling for the strength to tell her what he had spent the end of his shift considering.

Her eyes narrowed. "Paul, you ok?"

He looked at her square and let the breath out. His smile widened with purpose. Looking at her he knew what he was feeling was right; it had a way of making good ideas seem epic.

"I've always heard people say that they would feel evil bringing a child into this world the way it is and where it all seems to be headed," he said.

Her expression grew confused but curious. "Okaaaaaay...," she said, "but don't let Kat hear you say that." She laughed. His body shook from silent laughter.

He continued.

"But here's what I think. I think, yeah, sad but true, the world has a lot of misguided people out there. Some are faithless and have lost their way. Others just seem to enjoy their apathy. Whatever the reason, times are getting tough."

"Yeah, ok," she agreed.

"Don't you think the world could use more good people in it? People who try to help their fellow man? Do unto others and so forth?"

His smiled broadened in anticipation of her reaction. She recognized this but had no idea what he was expecting of her. Her eyes darted about but kept returning to his face. She shook her head and shrugged.

"Sure," she said comically and added a "Right on!" with a

raised fist for good measure.

He pulled back and sighed. She was not following him. He had a way of being vague, and she had a way of not getting him. They each knew it but the could not find a work-around for this particular quagmire in their marriage. But it was minor and often entertaining.

He gave her another few moments, hoping somehow she would grasp his meaning from mid-air.

She smacked her hands against her thighs and asked, "What?"

Paul straightened his spine, felt the fierceness cross his face and said bluntly,

"Let's have another baby."

Samantha's face instantly fell pale. Her smile vanished completely, and her shoulders dropped and for a moment Paul misread her entirely. Her lips swam but produced no sound. They did not need to for the tears that began to fall said it all. Her chest heaved backwards for a second, and her mouth parted longingly. Still no words came but "Yes!" she nodded. Again and again "Yes!".

Her hands went to the back of Paul's head and pulled him close. The kiss that they bore was equal parts passion and love, and he met it evenly.

There were no more words. The thoughts and feelings that were shared were spoken in a language far surpassing sound and syllable. A language gifted to man and wife. And there, on the cool surface of the garage floor, was the epitome of love spoken.

CHAPTER 35

Long morning shadows fell across the charred remains of what was once a proud and true house of the Lord God. Ashen pews stood silently, waiting for the touch of believers that would never return. The pulpit, where once a righteous man had spoke the true word and lead many a soul to salvation lay on its side and smashed even before the fire came to deface it. And behind that a large crucifix that had once hung high, drawing the eye to Heaven, lay on its back as if prepared for the body of the Messiah once more.

In the center of this blackened sanctuary, the angel Athiel stirred to consciousness. He blinked, coaxing his vision into focus. It was a sensation far beyond strange. Angels did not slumber. There were no periods of lapse. Yet in his mind's eye there lingered a present and haunting void. It was beyond his grasp to understand.

He lay still for a minute, setting his thoughts about this enigma, gazing up at a morning sky that was angry with red and stripped with burnt crossbeams that could no long suffer support for a roof that was no longer there. He rolled onto his right cheek to view his environment and beheld the desecrated pulpit with what might once have been a crucifix inset on its face. A house of worship, he surmised, but such places should hold a serenity and fire that were the touch of the Father. This forlorn place held only emptiness and regret and sorrow.

The flooring he lay upon became increasingly uncomfortable, and he drew back his elbows to prop himself up. A soreness in his head screamed out, and instantly he recalled the soldiers and their leader and the bullet that had hurtled him into that unconscious void. His hand immediately went to his forehead to feel for a wound, but he was much weaker than he had guessed, and when his balance shifted his lack of strength caused his left arm to give up its support, and he fell backwards hard. The back of his head slammed downed on a large, sharp splinter of ember that was just solid enough to stab him before crumbling to ash under his weight. Athiel cried out in pain.

"Careful! You will do yourself more harm!" a gravelly voice called out from somewhere in the sanctuary.

Athiel slipped his right hand under his head to wipe away the ash from his new wound. He cradled his head as he attempted to torque his body and search out the owner of the voice, but all his efforts wrought him was a stab of fiery pain that emanated from where the bullet had hit. Again he cried out.

"Still yourself! I will come." The words were accompanied by dragging feet and the rattle of chains. With every few steps a deep and rumbling growl came forth that stretched for seconds. The closer the sounds drew the colder the air about him became.

Goosebumps rose in Athiel's flesh. Outside his peripheral the being drew closer—*drag rattle grooowwwlll drag rattle grooowwwlll*—until when, only a few feet away and "above" him, all movement and sound ceased, leaving only a frigid bite to signify the stranger's presence.

After a lingering silence Athiel tried to speak, finding his voice shook in the chill. "Are y-y-you th-th-ere?"

The growl rolled out followed by the voice like flint on stone, "I am, brother. I will not abandon you." And then once again the quiet.

Athiel stretched his neck despite the pain in his head, trying to catch a view of the voice but could not tilt his head back far enough to see, but he endured the pain and tried to roll to his chest...

"STILL!" the voice roared, and a hand suddenly came down upon his head and pinned him to the floor.

The touch of the hand was stronger than any Athiel could

recall feeling, but far worse it was bitter cold like the void of space and jagged like ground rock. Sharp points on the palm threatened to break through the skin of his forehead.

"You are not what you were," the voice had calmed and was almost remorseful. "You have become fragile. Vulnerable. If you do not rest you will not heal."

Athiel found he could not struggle against this being—*was it a captor or host?*— neither was he possessed of a mind to try. He let his body go limp.

"This is not flesh. It does not heal," the once-angel protested.

The growl that answered had an irritated tone. "It is now," the voice contested, "of a sort."

The hand lifted, and the pressure in his head lessened considerably. Chains rattled as the stranger rose. Feet commenced their dragging in an arc around to Athiel's flank. The growl seemed to envelope the whole of the structure, shaking the brittle walls that wearily stood. At last the voice came into view.

It was an angel, or had been once. The face it wore seemed beautiful if studied intently, but the angelic flesh upon it was pulled and showed spots of brown rot and gray decay. Loose bits of flesh hung at the edges of tears over the surface of its body like paint peeling away. Like Athiel, the angel bore no hair, and its only covering was a tattered loincloth that had once been part of its robe. Thick iron shackles adorned its wrists, ankles, and neck. Tendrils of decomposition seemed to grow from underneath each shackle, threatening to crawl down his extremities. From each shackle a chain fell endingin sharp, broken links. As the angel circled to Athiel's side he caught sight of larger chains embedded in several places on its back and back of its head, each also ending in broken links. The chains themselves seemed familiar. Each link was etched with angelic script except the broken links, which were rusty and worn smooth. Its deep black eyes looked out from under thick vertical strands of iron that had once held them shut. Similar strands hung broken from its lips like rugged teeth.

"Tartarus," the angel read Athiel's eyes, he raised his wrists to display his bonds. "I was a prisoner. Until recently."

Athiel concentrated on the angel's face, battling through such a strong sense of familiarity in hopes of recognition, but a mist lingered in his mind, and he came up short.

"Yes, brother, you know me. You knew me very well." The angel sat down with a heavy clattering, bringing himself almost to Athiel's level. "I am surprised you do not recognize me. Time, I am aware, has been…unkind," he chuckled darkly. The angel's eyes scanned the length of Athiel's body like a predator taking measure of its prey, and suddenly Athiel did indeed feel vulnerable. As if he sensed this, the angel grinned. "To us both it seems."

"If you are my brother," Athiel asked, "what are you called?"

The growl that answered vibrated through the floor and inside Athiel's chest. It was not threatening, but rather sad somehow.

"Not yet," he replied, "but soon, I think."

The angel stood, its chains scrapping against the burnt floor, tearing tracks in it as it did.

"I tracked you through the city," he began as he strolled towards the pulpit almost casually, his feet no longer dragging. "From the moment you surfaced I heard you call to me. It was a sickly siren song: that of a mortal dying in loneliness and neglect. I had just returned to this plane from my internment, as lost and uncertain as you felt I am sure." The prisoner knelt by the fallen pulpit and traced the carved crucifix with a fingertip. "The difference is I remembered you. Knew you on the ramparts. Knew you when you knew yourself," he turned back to Athiel, "not this *waste* have become."

The prisoner rose and walked back to the larger crucifix on the floor. He continued, "And I wonder…where were you going? What was your purpose?"

Athiel stared at the sky; the fiery clouds were quickly giving way to cool blue.

"I…I do not know," he said.

The Prisoner bent down and took hold of the crucifix, stood it up and then leaned it back against the nearest wall. This done he clapped the ash from his hands and stepped back to admire the symbol of Christendom.

"You and I are much like this place: ruined of our former glory, hollow and ultimately abandoned. Perhaps even forgotten."

The Prisoner rubbed his chin thoughtfully. "Not so unlike the Son are we?"

From on his back, Athiel shouted, "That is blasphemy! Your words…you speak as would Lucifer."

The Prisoner turned to Athiel and then back to the cross. His head and his voice lowered. "You are right." The Prisoner turned and made his way back to Athiel's side. "That was not my intent. I remember clearly the folly of the Light-Bringer's pride. I have no wish to follow such a path. I just believe that in some way I can understand the anguish of the Son, the Christ, both in the garden of Gethsemane and tortured on Calvary. Such ponderance brings with it a certain understanding."

Athiel rolled his head to look at the Prisoner.

"Of what do you speak?" he asked.

For a brief instant sorrow painted the Prisoner's face, but a blink wiped it clean, and he faced Athiel with a cool countenance.

He replied, "That, too, in time."

"Then what of now?"

"The riddle you have become, I think, and of course the grander scheme at play." The Prisoner once more took a seat at Athiel's side. He reached a hand out and placed a finger on Athiel's forehead where the bullet had struck. Athiel tensed with pain.

"It is a physical wound; a *mortal* thing," the Prisoner spoke, working his finger in a small circle. A warmth began to emanate from the finger's tip, soothing Athiel somewhat, but not entirely.

He continued, puzzled...astonished, "You should not feel this; its mark should not linger, especially beyond my ability to heal."

Confusion flashed in Athiel's eyes, and he made as if to prop himself up again, but instead relaxed and lay still. He collected himself before speaking.

"What do you mean it lingers?"

The Prisoner looked up and about the room as if searching. After a moment he stood and stepped over Athiel and disappeared towards the back of the sanctuary. Athiel rolled his head to watch. The Prisoner bent near wide double doors that had once served as a portal for worshippers to enter the sanctuary of the Lord but now stood gnarled and neglected. The Prisoner rose, and a brief glare flashed from the object he now held in his hand. He returned to Athiel's side and presented it: a picture frame. The picture itself had been consumed by the flame long ago, and the frame was badly marred but remained intact. Along the bottom edge of the frame was a small metal plaque that still read, "Guatemala Missionary Outreach, Summer 2010." Athiel supposed the frame had once housed a picture of a Guatemalan village and in the foreground local peoples and the visiting missionaries.

All at once Athiel saw it in the reflection of the glass: a round, open wound in his forehead that curled inward at the edges and in its center a pool of glossy red that looked ready to overflow but did not. Athiel began to reach a finger towards the wound, but the Prisoner grabbed his wrist and offered a grim smile.

"What is it the mortals are fond of saying? Leave it alone, or it will only get worse?" He paraphrased and laughed.

Athiel let his arm relax in the Prisoner's grip until the other released it and then set the frame down.

"They seemed as stunned then as you do now," the Prisoner stated flatly.

"They?"

"The soldiers you fought. The men who slaughtered our ilk."

The blankness in Athiel's mind began to ripple around the edges, allowing faint images to come through. He remembered violence: the horrified screams of the holy, a gauntlet of blue light, the snapping of vertebrae and bark and finally the smell of gunpowder and smoke. The remembrance awakened a new round of fire from his wound bringing Athiel to cringe.

"How can man kill an angel? That could never occur," Athiel rebuked, but lacked surety in his protest.

"I would like to agree, and I do not know, but it seems they have found a way. I have been told that they can be quite enterprising," a crude enjoyment flashed in the Prisoner's eyes.

"You…" Athiel stumbled verbally, "You speak as if you do not know mankind." A concept he found entirely alien.

The Prisoner smiled down at him, but it betrayed an old and enduring torment. "I have been absent for a long time, brother."

Again the sense of familiarity about the Prisoner struck

home, but again it would not develop into recognition.

The Prisoner turned his attention towards some distant horizon. "*How* they can bring about our end is important, yes, but moreso I believe the question is: *why?*"

The throbbing of his wound intensified and Athiel groaned. He desired to engage more actively in their conversation, despite his indomitable ignorance, but the pain would not allow clarity of thought. Angels had never felt such things firsthand and were apparently ill prepared to deal with them. The Prisoner must have sensed as much. He leaned forward and placed his palm inches above Athiel's eyes. A low growl built from the back of his throat, and he bade Athiel, "Sleep. There is time for such queries when you are rested."

Athiel wanted to resist, but felt warmth wrap about him like a cocoon and gave in to its embrace. His mind slipped eagerly back to the newfound comfort of the welcoming void.

As he slept the Prisoner stood sentry, eyes raised considering the sky, ears alert eavesdropping on a maelstrom of fear and discontent that wafted in from the city beyond the decrepit walls. His tongue flicked at the bitter taste mortal thoughts and pandering left in his mouth. He had been told much about the Father's favored creations, but now that he was finally able to appraise them firsthand he already began to find them lacking and scoffed at what passed as acceptable of the Father's forgiveness.

As the sun rose to stake its claim, the Prisoner sighed, all but certain he was too late.

CHAPTER 36

T he alleyways were constructed of cold and damp stone. Steam hissed overhead as it made its escape from pipes dripping with condensation. Somewhere in the distance the enraged barking of a rabid dog provided the only ambience and echoed from every surface making the lone protester sound like a ferocious pack, but no surface the maddening sound more than the hollows of Traci's head.

Traci's lungs hurt like they had been frayed with a cheese grater, and her knees felt ready to snap. The arches of her feet seemed to land on pebbles with every stride, but she dare not slow her pace despite the pleading of her body, despite the doubt that clawed at her mind, despite the fear that threatened to overtake her, she must go on, around the next corner, if not there then around the next and the next and so on until Solomon was safe back in her arms, and she dare not pause to give her body mercy, because *it* was searching too. It no longer wore the face of a man. No, it had shed that visage at the cathedral. The mask it wore now was the very decay of elegance, the twisting of beauty into cruelty and malice. It was more comfortable this way, closer in form to the beast it had always truly been. She was not sure how she knew for certain, but it was close, like breath on the nape of her neck, it was there, somewhere just behind. Its ravenous hunger would not be satisfied by her, it only wanted Solomon, and when it had her child in its gnashing jaws it would make her watch and beg, but in the end, it would leave her alone in the dankness and darkness to wallow in her failure and that, in truth, was the unending death.

She came to a four-way junction that forced her to hesitate. She cursed under her breath; it was more time than she could afford but something inside her demanded that the path she chose now was critical. Her head whirled, but each was identical. Panic wrapped about her chest, and she put a hand against it instinctively. Tears fell from sockets puffed from long spells of weeping. She screamed Solomon's name in desperation, but the only reply was the return of her own echo like a madman's mockery.

To the right...footfalls in a puddle...light of weight and small of gait.

Her hesitation broke instantly, and she threw herself full speed, into the alleyway. A child's shadow raced along the walls in front of her, matching her pace. She cried out to him, begging him to stop. She was his mother. She would keep him safe.

Close behind her the beast cackled, and it frightened her so that she tripped on her own feet. She smacked the ground hard with her palms, but saved her face from hitting. Her right palm was cut open. The blood was warm.

As she lay she turned to look behind her, afraid the beast was upon her, but it stood at the junction, its physique masked in shadow but its fiery red eyes shone brightly through the blackness that clothed it. It roared, a sound of both threat and victory, then turned on its heels and took off down the opposite alleyway, cackling as it went.

A deeper panic set in and Traci forced herself to her feet, kicking off to run as she rose...and stopped dead a mere inch from a wall. The alleyway before her had closed off. It had been a trick of the beast. She spun around as she broke back into a run, nearly tripping herself again as she did, but miraculously maintaining her balance against the momentum. She blew through the junction and down the opposite alleyway after the demon. Unnatural shadows bled off the walls, darkening the further she went, daring her to continue, but she had no choice. The barking of the dog seemed to be closer and somewhere in front of her. Soon the shadows blinded her completely. She put her hands out in front of her, feeling for any sudden turn or barrier, and tried her best not to slow.

Solomon's scream pierced the night and ended as abruptly as it had begun and left only silence in its wake. Traci screeched his name, she had no control over it, and tucked her arms again by her side and recommitted her effort for speed. He did not respond. She cried out again and again and again. In the blackness ahead the beast roared triumphantly. Traci shouted her agony and defiance...and suddenly her right foot hit slick stone and shot backwards, throwing her back down, but this time she was unable to protect her face. The impact seemed to be inside her head, originating from the middle and expanding like an explosion. Her central teeth bit through her lips, and she tasted warm, wet iron. Her skull throbbed and stars filled her vision for a moment then began to clear. In fact, she could see the ground beneath her. Everything was gradually lightening. She placed her palms beneath her to push herself up and heard the rabid growl of a large dog above her. She felt hot breath on the back of her neck. She defied the fear that welled up inside her and looked up, expecting to see a crazed wolf or Doberman, but worse...*it* stood there, a mass of swirling black mist that drifted upward, dissipating before the sky but never disconnected or uncovered its true body. The eyes, like red-hot coals, stared unblinking. Unseen lips parted, reveling jagged daggers in a victorious grin, and that's when she saw Solomon standing quietly at its side. The beast looked down at her son and laid an arm across his shoulder in an almost loving fashion, but Solomon did not recoil, only stood silently. The beast's smile broadened as it turned back to her. Traci drew in breath, preparing another scream when the beast suddenly tightened its grip on the boy and in the blink of an eye pulled him into the darkness of its body where he was instantly consumed.

Traci shrieked as she shot up in her bed at Saint Michael's. Her heart pounded and her lungs burned. Her eyes slowly began to focus allowing her to recognize her surroundings, and she begun to ease until she realized that Solomon was not by her side. The panic rushed in anew. She found herself too horrified to call out for him, so she threw her feet over the side of the bed and literally hit the ground running. She blew through the room's open door and into the hallway beyond. The hall stretched to either side like the alleyways in her dream, but was lined with doors. Taking a cue from her nightmare she turned left instead of right and tried to first door she came to. Locked. She sprinted to the next, which was also locked. The thought that she was still in an ongoing nightmare flashed through her mind.

There was a corner that cut left ahead of her, and from it she heard the clanging and scrapping of metal. She ignored the last door in the hall and ran towards the sound. A few feet past the corner a door stood open on the right. She ran to the doorway and inside and stopped herself after two strides.

Father Joseph Behanan started when she entered, dropping the skillets in his hands on the stove top. His hand went to his chest as he tried to catch his breath. He was alone.

"Traci you startled—"

She found her voice at last and cut him off abruptly, "Solomon! Where's Solomon?!"

Father Behanan blinked in confusion, and his shoulders dropped.

"I thought he was laying with you. He was when I got up."

Traci's heart stopped. She stepped backwards preparing to turn and sprint back into the hall and search the entirety of the cathedral, but a soft voice spoke up.

"Mom?" Solomon said sleepily from behind her in the hallway.

Traci's stomach convulsed, and she nearly vomited. She turned to see her son wiping the sleep from his eyes while her own began spilling tears.

"Solomon!" the word was weak but joyous from her lips. She threw her arms around him as if needing the physical reassurance that he was there. The very feel of him sent a wave of relief washing over her.

Solomon stiffened, keeping his arms by his side instead of returning her hug.

"Why are you crying?" he asked.

Traci gripped his shoulders and pushed him back so as to look him in the eye.

"Where were you?!" she tried to keep her voice from shaking, but could not. Sheimmediately hated herself for the confused shame that she saw in Solomon's face.

"I…I just had to go to the bathroom." His shoulders jerked, and he sniffed as if about to cry. She touched his cheek and then pulled him close again.

"No, baby, no, you're not in trouble. I'm so sorry. I just had a nightmare, and when I woke up you weren't there, and I got scared, that's all. I promise." She stroked the back of his head lovingly. It did her as much good as it did him.

Father Behanan went back about his preparations at the stove, trying to leave the mother and child to their moment. He turned two burners on and then returned to the fridge nearby to retrieve the bacon and eggs therein.

"Do you want some help, Father?" Traci asked. She was already leading Solomon over to sit at the small dining table the kitchen contained.

Father Behanan smiled over his shoulder and replied, "Thank you, but I've got this. And I'm actually not half bad, either."

Traci took a seat next to Solomon but made sure to face Father Behanan at the stove.

"Anything would taste like fine dining this morning, Father," she said.

"Joseph. You don't have to keep calling me 'Father'. It's appreciated, but unnecessary." Joseph produced a large clay bowl from a cabinet over the stove and went about the task of cracking the shells and dumping the egg yokes into the larger of the two skillets. Joseph laughed to himself and said, "I hope you guys like your eggs scrambled because that's honestly all I know how to make."

Traci stood up and answered, "We do." She walked over to the counter beside him and picked up the opened package of bacon. "Hope this doesn't sound rude but let me help. Your eggs are going to be done long before the bacon like that."

Joseph looked down and blushed. "Guess I'm not very good at this after all."

Traci smiled warmly and winked at him. "It's the thought that counts, padre."

They both laughed. Traci needed it more than she realized. Joseph pulled the skillet with the single egg yoke off of the burner, but went back to unshelling the remaining eggs. They worked in a disjointed partnership, but it was good that way. Joseph was funny and mindful, which made Traci feel empowered on a small scale, but on this morning that small scale was not quite so small. The kitchen became a whole other world, one without the memories of the night before. She barely took note of how much more she smiled in it than she had out there in the real world. This was a place with function and structure. Simple tasks providing satisfactory results. It was life siphoned down to its purest and best.

"That poor kid," Traci said quietly, stealing a glance over her shoulder at Solomon. "He really needs a man's influence in his life, but…well, all he's got is me."

Joseph's brow furled, and he likewise stole a glance.

"He seems like a pretty good guy. I'm sure your influence is a lot more positive than you think."

"You're sweet," Traci giggled, but it held a sad, defeated quality. "But dead wrong. I'm overbearing, overprotective, I barely make enough money to keep us going. He's gotta deal with all my stress because I'm too weak to hide it when he's around. He's only eight, and he's gotta compensate for my being single." She shook her head dismissively. "Sorry, now I'm unloading on you. I don't even know why."

"I'm happy to listen, don't worry."

"You're…you're just really easy to talk to."

When the time was right she allowed Joseph to place the eggs back on the burner and gave him a fair, yet joking, amount of grief in the process. Their eyes locked, but no attraction or affection passed between them. True, he was a very handsome man in her opinion, but in her heart she felt only gratitude of the purest nature. The circumstances had been horrid, but she felt she had found a sudden, genuine friend. He had an ease about the way he carried himself and went about his every action that was infectious. He reminded her of the older brother she had lost.

With the cooking finished the three sat down at the table and joined hands then bowed their heads.

"Holy Father," Joseph began, "we come to You this morning in a spirit of thanks. Thank You for the delicious meal that is about to satisfy our bodies, certainly, but Father, thank You for the mysterious paths upon which You set our feet that lead us to people and places unforeseen. Thank You for the comfort in the knowledge that wherever we tread, You take our hand and guide us through. I thank You, dear Lord, for the trials we must endure for we know that they serve Your higher purpose, despite the limitations of our vision."

Traci's grip on his hand tightened at that.

Joseph continued, "Holy Father I ask that you watch over Traci and Solomon. That their hearts be healed of the difficulties they have already faced and that You carry them through what else they may lie ahead. Be their strength, their refuge, and their portion. In the name of the Father, the Son, and the Holy Ghost, amen."

Their hands released and Joseph traced the cross over himself. Traci tried her best to copy the gesture. Solomon only picked up his fork and set to stabbing his eggs. As Traci finished her impromptu crucifix she saw Joseph watching her and laughed in embarrassment. Joseph laughed along.

A throat cleared in the doorway and all turned. There stood Father Donovan, arms crossed and a forced smile on his lips.

"That was a beautiful blessing, Joseph." He turned his attention to the mother and child. "I'm sorry to intrude on breakfast, but if it's alright, Ms. Nicholas, I'd like to speak with you and your son in private."

CHAPTER 37

Patrick Morraine Hospital. Critical Care Unit. 7:36 am Pacific.

Anne Sciantarelli, call sign Jazz, had seen her share of war and bloodshed.

Running covert ops in over twenty countries as a Navy Seal she had experienced brutality and death in nearly every climate and against nearly every foe the world had to offer. On a night raid in the embattled country of Darfur she had lost her CO to bullet fire from a scared child who had been forced into warfare. In Somalia she had taken a bullet in the leg and was forced to hold an innocent family at gunpoint for four hours so that she could hide in their apartment until militia forces gave up the search for her. She believed that behind enemy lines any means of survival was justifiable and that all wars had casualties. That was hard fact, not romanticism.

But this war was like nothing no human had ever dreamed. Against a foe most believed were fairytales. Preparations had been in the making for years, but only now, at last, had the first shots been fired. The first blood had only just been drawn. And already she was sick of it.

The chair she occupied in CCU room 431 was stiffer than she would have believed physically possible. It was pushed back tight into a corner close to the head of the bed her brother-in-arms now lay in. Normally she would not have been allowed to stay, but her employers could pull the highest of strings. The world was full of puppets, all at their disposal, which meant nearly nothing was forbidden to she and hers.

A small stack of books sat on the floor next to her chair, the Koran, Kings James Bible, the NIT Bible, Dante's Inferno. Tucked into the front of each were their accompanying cliff notes. Currently she was occupying herself with a thorough study of the book of Enoch, which she was told dealt largely with angelic folklore but was never canonized as to be an official Biblical text. She understood little of what that meant, all she wanted to understand was her enemy. *Know thy enemy*. The creed was tantamount to victory and, on a more personal note, revenge.

Had she not read somewhere, in the Bible perhaps, "an eye for an eye"?

A deep moan came from the bed. She looked up but saw just what she expected, Toma lay completely still. It was sign of progress, albeit small, but progress nonetheless.

The world beyond his room was a place of beeping machines and whispering nurses. A constant humdrum that quickly faded into the background and then was forgotten entirely…to an average person. But Anne's ears were ever alert. She was here as a friend and comrade, surely, but also as a guard. As in any hospital she knew the building was a hornet's nest of halos and horns alike, and it sickened her to be rooted behind enemy lines with neither weapon nor even optic gear, but Doomsayer had been stern. He knew her, had she seen either she would act with extreme prejudice, and despite their "global green light" and the puppet masters high above, brandishing even her TS-sidearm would set the building into a state of anarchy.

Goose flesh rose on the back of her neck which only served to feed the anger she was so skillfully containing. She was being toyed with. She was untouchable spiritually, the TS-implant she and all under the same employ had saw to that, but something wanted her to know it was near. Halos did not play such games, but horns…horns saw mankind as one giant sandbox. This one was smart enough to know that even just adjusting the temperature of the air around her would rouse her, and if it was that attune to her awareness then it was smart enough to know that it was being stupid to a dangerous degree.

"Keep it up and you'll be next on my hit list," she said aloud to the room.

She sighed heavily and looked again at Toma. It was their first rodeo as a unit and he, of all people, was their first casualty. *There's* NOTHING *casual about casualty,* she thought. She thought of the unseen entity in the room with her...in the room with *him.* It brought the bile to her throat knowing that the demon was surely taking pleasure from this. Had not Toma suffered enough through the years?

"Last time I'm going to tell you, freak, leave now. That's not a warning, it's a threat," she promised. From what she read and what she had believed prior to knowing the "whole truth" as it were, she believed that the minds of demons and angels were of a higher level than that of man in many ways, so she pressed her threat and laced it with logic. "I know you know that there's something keeping you from touching me inside, so consider that it's what you *don't* know that you should fear from me. Leave now."

After a few seconds the room felt significantly warmer.

She heard the rubbery squeak of military boots approaching. From the gait and the strut she knew it to be Doomsayer. And he was not alone.

The door to room 431 opened. Doomsayer held it wide allowing Titus to enter, camera in use.

In a flash Anne's composure broke. She sprang up from the chair, spilling the book of Enoch and its cliff notes on the floor. Her right hand went to grab hold of the camera lens.

"Get out! You are NOT doing this to him!" she shouted.

Titus managed to step back in time to keep his beloved Faye out of her reach.

"Have a seat, soldier! Now!" Doomsayer barked from behind him. His voice. His tone. Anne stepped back instantly but did not sit. Her cheeks went bright red, and her heart thumped like a hammer.

"He deserves better than this, sir," she said as matter-of-fact as she could manage without being openly defiant.

Titus kept filming, pulling his focus out and panning the camera around just enough to capture Anne in the right side of his frame without her knowing. As a documentarian he was very skilled at such covert maneuvers.

"Agreed. Now sit." And this time, Anne did.

Doomsayer made his way past Titus to Toma's bedside. If she didn't know him better Anne might have thought that he was trying to work his way into the filmmaker's shot, but no, Doomsayer was a soldier above all, and the well being of those who served with him held great importance. He leaned over Toma, examining him, then turned to examine the medical monitors. He seemed sufficiently satisfied with what they told him.

"We are privileged are we not?" Doomsayer said to her over his shoulder.

"Sir?"

"We have seen the truth with our own eyes."

"Yes, sir." She straightened her spine, not realizing she had been slouching. Soldiers did not slouch.

He turned to speak to her directly.

"And why do we deserve that privilege, but not the billions out there who are as much a part of this conflict but remain blind to it?" His face was stone.

Anne considered this for a moment before she replied. "We are not, sir. The sides were decided long ago, and it's always been *all* of us against *all* of them."

He seemed pleased with her response and added to it, "But in this they, our adversaries, have always had the advantage of knowledge over us. And that," he paused to turn back to Toma, "is coming to a close. Knowledge is a weapon, and we cannot win this war with so many unarmed and unaware. That's why Mister Titus is with us." He turned his headed towards her slightly. "Am I understood?"

Her response came out much meeker of voice than she intended, "Sir, yes sir."

Doomsayer walked back to the door and opened it wide. "I will return shortly. As you were." He gestured to the open door. "Mister Titus if you will accompany me."

Titus reached forward to his lens and made a hastened tweak to his current shot then rounded to get a parting shot of Anne who sat there looking like she had been thoroughly reprimanded. She tried hard to keep her face stoic, but her eyes betrayed her, and she was quite certain Titus's camera would capture that vividly.

Titus lowered Faye and walked out, bowing awkward as he did. Doomsayer followed, shutting the door behind him.

She was alone again with Toma. But now somehow she also felt like a casualty, or, and more to the heart of it, helpless, and in Anne Sciantarelli's mind that was unforgivable.

She picked up the book of Enoch off the floor and resumed her studies.

CHAPTER 38

With a guiding hand, Father Donovan ushered them through his office door. The smile on his lips was only skin deep, but seemed enough to fool the mother. The boy remained virtually unreadable.

Without being offered, Traci took a seat at Donovan's desk, but Solomon remained standing, his head down-turned as if the carpet held some vast interest. Donovan circled the room, hating how he felt very much like a vulture waiting on a body to give up its ghost, then leaned against his desk close to Traci. Towering over her in fact. He hoped that would swell his advantage. He steepled his fingers upside against his thighs and let out a deep breath he could not remember having been holding.

Here we go. First step off this ledge, and you're free-falling. But you've got no choice, do you? For the life of him he could not decide what made these matters truly feel so urgent.

"Were you able to rest well? Despite….," was his opener. It was a kind jump off point if not the best, but it certainly sounded genuinely tender and heartfelt. He left the question open-ended. She knew what he was referencing. No need to drag the previous night's horrors into the forefront…yet.

Especially should he be wrong.

Traci let out a snort, it was not quite amused and did not seem entirely intentional.

"All things considered…no, not really."

Donovan hung his head and nodded solemnly.

"That's entirely understandable. But I have no doubt that Father Behanan did his very best to make you and your son as comfortable as possible," he glazed this last bit with a grin that felt uncharacteristically serpentine. He tried to wipe it away, fearing it would raise the woman's defenses, but she appeared not to notice, and he could not force his muscles to relax.

She nodded as well as shrugged, "I guess he did his best."

"Well, God be praised that you were able to find a haven in your time of need." He had meant that to be a question, possibly concluded with an *amen*, but the word fell silent in his throat, and when it escaped her lips instead, Donovan was visibly rattled.

"Yes...amen," he echoed hastily.

He stood up, feeling his advantage had been stripped from him.

The Enemy has many devious ways to shake the foundation of the righteous.

He walked around to behind his desk, the sudden need to distance himself from this woman, this *vessel*, was simply too strong, and the desk provided a protective wall of sorts, even if it was only a placebo effect.

"If you'll pardon my saying so, you don't look familiar to me. Have you ever attended mass here at Saint Michael's before?" He hoped his façade was more ironclad than his insides felt. Already he worried he was pressing her too hard, had not taken enough time to soften her up and lower her defenses. He felt so far off his game plan, and over what? Her "amen"? One simple word. One *HOLY* word. *The Enemy is a serpent winding its way through the garden of our tranquility, amen.*

Traci yawned through the first part of her answer and restarted.

"I'm sorry," she laughed at herself, and his spine crawled, "what I was *trying* to say was yes, but it was a very long time ago. Back when Father Leary..."

He caught her off, a feeble attempt to regain some sense of control, and it succeeded.

"Father Leary! Oh really?" he too laughed, it felt wholly unnatural. "He was a master of words, but get him on a golf course and he could barely speak. Too many slices wide right, and all he wanted to do was curse. Silence can be golden, right?"

She shared his laugh, but only out of courtesy and with little conviction.

"I'd never heard that about him." Her eyes shifted nervously. *Good.* That was very good.

He pressed.

"So, why here? Why all of a sudden?"

She gave him a confused look as if he had asked her to swallow hot coals.

"I'm sorry, Ms. Nicholas…"

"Traci, please."

The interruption almost threw him off stride again, but no, he had found a foothold and was now beginning his ascent. He was on top of the situation and had no intention of going any which way but up from here on out.

"What I meant, Traci, was that I feel considerably out of the loop about what all happened last night." The smile he offered was gentle and inviting, but it nearly faltered when he caught sight of Solomon in his peripheral. The boy had been so quiet he had almost forgotten entirely that he was even in the room. The child still gazed at his feet, but was that a smile tucked into his chest?

Traci cleared her throat and shifted uncomfortably in her chair. *Perfect.* Donovan choked back the ounce of guilt threatening to rise in the back of his skull, but thought, *why shouldn't I be enjoying this? Watching the puppet quiver as its master loses focus. A victory against the Enemy is a joyous thing.*

"He came to our apartment. I had to do something. We ran for so long, but…but it felt like I was being lead somewhere. Like I was never just running blindly. And all at once it hit me, that we were coming here. To the one place I always felt safe." She looked up at him, her eyes big and glassy as a frightened doe. "Is that not okay?"

Donovan leaned back and opened his palms to her.

"Of course it is. Of course."

"I never thought beyond what was going to happen when we got here. Like if I just got inside that it would all just go away. I didn't mean for any of this to happen, I swear!" The strength of her voice was giving way. She fidgeted nervously with her hands and looked as if she expected to be booted from the premises or even worse, physically struck for her offenses.

But the boy…yes, definitely a smile. The tips of his teeth showed over the edge of his lip.

It suddenly occurred to Donovan that there might be two enemies at work here, a hellish alliance conspiring against him, or even that the boy was the true fiend and the woman still just a puppet. Each scenario was frightening in its own way, but Donovan had to press on, he would not cower in the presence of his foe.

Onward Christian soldier.

"I know that, Traci," first to her. "And I'm glad you're both safe," then to the boy.

Solomon raised his head fully into view, but the smile was gone.

"Do you feel safe here, Solomon?" Donovan asked, feeling the edges of his conviction start to fray.

The child nodded.

"Do you like Father Joseph? Has he been good to you and your mother?"

Another nod.

"He really has. We'll never be able to repay his kindness." Traci intervened. Perhaps a mother's protective instinct, perhaps a string being pulled.

Donovan ignored her and focused on the child.

"Have you ever met Father Joseph before, Solomon?"

Traci straightened. "I don't understand. What are you getting at?"

Donovan waved her off casually. "Traci please, I know you haven't been around the church in a while, I'm not suggesting you're lying."

Anger took hold and Traci leaned forward, hands gripping the armrests of her chair so as to keep them steady.

"It certainly sounds like you are! I don't like the way you're talking to my son!"

Donovan took a deep breath, letting the air in the room settle for a moment. Traci remained silent but eagerly awaiting his reply. He let her stew for a moment. He hated this cat and mouse game. Felt horrible at it and for it. Hated how much he was enjoying it.

He spoke to her in a voice both calm and authoritative. "Ms. Nicholas, a man died in my sanctuary last night. And from what I've been told the circumstances were most extraordinary. You have a history with this parish, and it is my responsibility before too much word spreads to our congregation to find out any and every bit of information I can. The family of the Saint Michael Cathedral will doubtless be unnerved and possibly even terrified to know that such a tragedy has taken place here. I'm sure many will find it hard to worship in a murder scene."

Traci was taken aback. She put her hand to her heart and her mouth worked for several moments before she could summon her words.

"Murder scene? The police didn't call it that last night."

My point exactly, Donovan thought, but aloud he said, "Strangely convenient that you weren't taken into custody, Traci."

"Convenient?!"

Donovan ignored her and continued on his own tangent. His words flowed cohesively but inside he heard his monologue unraveling into a nonsensical swill. He became confused, surely a trick of the Enemy, but would not turn back from his course. Somewhere along the way he would find his clarity again as long as he pressed forward.

"The media could easily spin this however they see fit. The mayor is a parishioner here, and it could be suggested to the public that he is involved in covering this death up."

She looked at him as if he had gone insane.

"Add to that that the persons involved were sheltered in this building as well. It all seems overwhelmingly coincidental, doesn't it?"

"None of that makes any sense! I can't believe this! You're calling me a murder?!" In her rage Traci stood up and took a step towards her son, but Father Donovan still felt ten feet higher. She continued, "I came here to protect my son from a man who was violent and crazed! I came to the one and *ONLY* place I have ever felt the hand of God keeping me safe and now, *YOU*, a *supposed* man of God is accusing me of...of...", she could not get the words out through the downpour of tears that began to flow.

Part of Donovan felt very pleased with himself. Another

part felt remorse. Something about the way her chest heaved as she gasped made him question everything: his motive, his accusations, his gut. Something was very, very out of place.

He dug his fingers into his leg. *No, the Enemy wants you to doubt. To doubt is to doubt God. It is a sin.*

Solomon stepped from behind his mother and came to Donovan's desk, stopping opposite the priest. There was stillness. Even Traci quieted her crying. Donovan waited and watched, knowing the boy had something to say. Utterly unprepared for what that something was. The boy placed a trembling hand on the desk. No, not trembling, *convulsing*. His entire body gave to a series of violent spasms. A wet choking sound came from his throat. Traci screamed and started towards him but just as suddenly as it had begun the seizure stopped.

Solomon dug a fingernail in a tight circle into the desktop, marking the wood.

"You're poisoned, and your faith is misplaced. You're the victim of shadow and ego."

Donovan felt a disembodied cold wash over his body.

Solomon continued.

"*YOU* are the puppet. And you will die for your troubles."

Traci gasped behind him. "Solomon, no," she whispered hoarsely.

But the child concluded nodding at the phone on Donovan's desk, "And so will he."

In slow time Donovan cast his eyes down to the phone on his desk, one of the multitude of receivers networked throughout the building. A red light signified one line was in use…

…In the office of Father Joseph Behanan.

CHAPTER 39

Father Joseph Behanan was indeed on the phone.

When Father Donovan had interrupted their impromptu breakfast, Joseph had nearly protested that Tracy and Solomon speak to Donovan without him, though he had no real clue why. A hunch really. Just a pang in the pit of his belly that said something was amiss and that bad tidings were on the way.

He chalked it up to the dire events of the previous evening and set himself to the task of cleaning up the kitchen. He pulled plastic containers down from the cabinets and sealed up the leftovers in case the others got hungry later and placed them in the fridge. He turned on hot water, put the stopper in the basin and scrounged under the sink for the steel wool. He pushed bottles of various cleaners aside in a huff and finally found the small steel wool ball hiding in the back by the trash bags. He rose up, tossed it in the rising water and grabbed the bottle of lemon detergent. It slipped from his hands and splashed into the sink. He instinctively hand-dived in after it and searing pain shot up his fingers to his forearm. The water was scolding.

He jerked his hand out immediately and stifled the swears his mind conjured.

He stepped back and took a deep, cleansing breath.

Gather your chi there, Hoss, he laughed to himself, trying to force his foul temper away. But that's when he heard the voices.

He could not make out any words, nothing beyond a random

syllable or two, but it only intensified that creeping feeling that shadows were closing.

Without thinking he took a step in the direction of the hallway then stopped himself.

What are you thinking, man? Why the sudden mistrust? That's not like you, Joe.

But he did step out after shutting off the steaming, running faucet. He paused once in the hallway like a nomad at a crossroads, and the temptation to eavesdrop was so heavy it was almost physical. His saving grace was a muted, sharp coo from the direction of the room in which they had slept.

His curiosity won out, and he returned to the room to find the noise was the vibration of his cell phone against the cushions of the chair he had slept in. He had not realized that it had fallen out of his pocket. The screen flashed an irritated blue bearing the name Kenneth Phelps.

He reached to answer but it ceased its mechanical dance as the call was forwarded to voicemail. After a moment the print on the screen changed and informed him that he had missed seven calls altogether. He opened his call history and saw that all calls but one had come from Kenneth.

I guess he heard about last night. Probably wants the story. It was a disappointing thought considering his esteem for the man he called a friend.

As he hit the send button to return the call he noticed that the power bar was blinking and sure enough the phone died in his hands. It was insult to the injury he had been feeling for the last few minutes.

He paused for another cleansing breath with a side-order of one-liner prayer, *Lord give me patience,* dropped the phone back into the chair and headed to the phone in his office.

Once there it took him a few tries before he could correctly remember and dial Kenneth's number, and he kicked himself for procrastinating on buying a rolodex like Father Donovan had suggested. But finally the connection was made...and finally shadows began to envelope.

The conversation began with Kenneth asking if Joseph was alright and apologizing for calling so frequently but with insistence that no matter could be more important. He sounded thoroughly worn and ragged, voice was weak and grating as if he had spent the entire night crying. Joseph briefly told him about the scene in the sanctuary, sparing the most unbelievable—yet true—details. He counted Kenneth high among his peers, but never forgot that the man was a journalist.

Kenneth apologized robotically for what had happened and then took over the rest of the conversation. He told Joseph everything Treygen Andros had revealed—minus his informant's name, of course, and that was out of professional habit, not personal choice.

He spoke with such intensity and urgency that Joseph did not even attempt to get in a word edgewise. He only listened silently until Kenneth finished.

"You've got to give me a minute to take all this in, Ken," Joseph breathed.

"I…I know. I'm still not grasping it entirely, myself."

"This is ridiculous, you know? Ridiculous to the point of blasphemous, actually." But he could not repress flashing images of his vision in the sanctuary just before the mother and child and *something else* had arrived. He remembered the blood flowing from the Virgin Mary. The voice of many voices. The child that was not a child. The Light.

His heart stopped cold for a beat.

"No…" his voice trailed into nothingness.

Kenneth was astute. He caught the demise of Joseph's argument and the falter in his tone.

"Talk to me, Joseph. Do you know something?" His voice was pleading and desperate.

"I…" did he dare tell him? Was he even strong enough to describe his vision out loud, especially now knowing that he may have witnessed the unholy truth, that the Eternal Lord of Heaven had somehow been murdered?

"Joseph, please. You must…"

And he did. His words spilled forth like a waterfall in an earthquake, his body shaking as the words poured out. And all throughout his recollection he could hear Kenneth faintly pleading, "No. No. No."

Together, in the search for answers and hope, all they accomplished was tearing each other apart.

CHAPTER 40

Moments after Kenneth Phelps and Father Joseph Behanan concluded their long and terrible conversation another call was made.

"Yes?" Manuel Valdez answered.

"We have confirmation, Andros told him everything," the voice on the other line informed.

Valdez hung up without saying another word. He flexed his toes to test out the fit of his new, custom-made sandals. When he was satisfied with their feel he paid the sandal maker triple his usual fee, as promised, and asked for a few minutes of solitude.

Once granted, he opened his phone and began shaping the fate of fools.

CHAPTER 41

Dycliasses was not there when Father Donovan began weaving his dark web. He did not hear Father Joseph and Kenneth Phelps compare their terrifying accounts of the slaying of the Lord Thy God nor did he dry their tears. When Traci needed strength and assurance in the face of spiritual assault, he was not there to grant her a measure of courage and resolve nor would he be there to stay her son's lips when they spoke foul prophecy.

As the mortal souls within the Cathedral of Saint Michael were waging their own pitched battles, the angel was not there to save or aid them in anyway, instead Dycliasses stood perfectly balanced on the very tip of the crucifix that stood atop the proud steeple on the face of the Cathedral of Saint Michael as a heavenly sentinel barring the entry of the very creature whose vile machinations had brought all these embattled souls together in the first place.

A presence darker than the shadows that embraced him, the demon Uzahl crouched on the low rooftop of the office building across the street, licking the nub on his arm where once a hand had been, like a cat and grinning like a rat with a secret. The folds of the wrinkled angel flesh he wore were already turning brown with decay; such unnatural things could never last. Uzahl laid a finger inside a crease on his right cheek and ran the finger through its length before pulling it free, placing it in his mouth and sucking loudly.

"The fruit is starting to rot," he mocked in barely more than a whisper, but Dycliasses heard it perfectly. "Maybe soon I'll have to lower my standards and wear something new. Something borrowed. Something…" it laughed, "you."

It cradled the stump forearm to its chest like an infant.

"Would be divine to have a hand as strong as yours."

Dycliasses did not respond. He would not be baited. The demon was quick, possibly even quicker than he, and should he be foolish enough to rush at his foe, it might give Uzahl an opening to access the cathedral and those within.

The city sang all around them; a song of car engines, televisions, street conversations and radios. It glistened like a thousand dull stars laid on the ground. The wind blew from the east at Dycliasses's back. Uzahl sniffed as if it actually carried some savory aroma then licked its lips hungrily.

"You cannot forbid me forever. You wane, and soon I will find one to invite me willingly and when that happens…" One by one Uzahl placed each finger in his mouth and sucked the tip like a glutton savoring his most recent feast. "It would be best if you killed me now."

Every voice in the cathedral below could be heard plainly, but Solomon's suddenly sounded with a booming presence that turned both their heads in the child's direction.

"You're poisoned, and your faith is misplaced," it said, "You're the victim of shadow and ego. *YOU* are the puppet. And you will die for your troubles."

Uzahl's chest swelled with pride, and he opened his arms victoriously.

"My boy! My beautiful progeny, sing to me your dark song. His voice is quite enchanting, don't you think?" He clasped hand over stub against his chest. "He gets that from me."

"And I got *this* from you," Dycliasses lifted the severed hand from his belt and waved it at its former owner.

"Adorable," the demon sneered joylessly and rubbed the stump as if plagued by a phantom pain.

"What do you expect will come of all this? Of all of them? With the gates of eternity sealed there is no reward or punishment waiting for them when their miserable lives are spent. So what, then, is the point of their continued, short-lived existence?"

Dycliasses remained silent. It was the only response suitable for the asinine question. In truth, however, it was something over which the Captain had pondered and worried. Death had become an unknown, at least until a solution to that—among the myriad of all their problems—could be found.

"Your silence speaks volumes," Uzahl taunted. "Seems even you can grasp the validity of my point."

The demon hunched forward like a cat ready to pounce, eyes wide and alert, tongue tasting the air as it spied the mortals under the angel's guard.

"The horrors I cannot wait to unleash upon them," it flashed Dycliasses a serpentine smile, "...through them."

A flash of light and Dycliasses's great axe was again in his hands. In the same instant his wings spread out like a golden wall. The compulsion to spring forward and end this wretch was sinfully powerful.

"Oh, pretty peacock," Uzahl chided as it began to walk backwards drawing the shadows around it like a cloak, but as the night enveloped it its voice lingered.

"You'll wish you had when you could have," it taunted. "You'll wish you had."

CHAPTER 42

A war on any scale, be it battle or campaign, is fraught with the fallen and the maimed. It is the totality of their numbers that tip the balance of the struggle until it points squarely to the victor. This is not happenstance or on the occasion, in the science of war, this is law.

And this cold, unfeeling truth was a reality that Toma Hollenbeck had come to know all too well.

Toma was always a child of war; lead into from the wound. His childhood was a series of battles; the little conflicts that are the cells of the body of war. He had always seen his adolescent years as typical Americana, though not the kind Norman Rockwell had illustrated or Andy Griffith had whistled about. His was the darker side: the streets. It was the Americana that had become the stereotype of the black child: you learned to run because speed was your salvation, you learned to fight when your speed was insufficient or moot, you learned to lie because the truth brought punishment, you learned to steal because nothing was given and the others were already poised to take. The one indisputable truth was that you did what had to be done to survive.

He had not always been a street tough character. In his early grade school years he showed incredible prowess academically. His father was not a washout or lowlife. He was a skilled mechanic and highly supportive and involved as best his schedule would allow. His mother was a housewife, though his father's income

223

barely allowed for such, but it was a choice they had made and agreed upon for the sake of raising their two sons, Toma and his younger brother Tavares, as they felt best. They lived in a low-income neighborhood referred to as Charlotte Court that was not impoverished, but stood adjacent to the projects. Their two brothers were taught early on what type of characters and areas were best avoided and told the honest reasons why. They were nurtured but not coddled, educated but not forced into pessimism. Life was a crawl through a trench, but it maintained its forward progress, full of potential.

As is often the way of life, circumstance intervened.

While working late on a transmission Johnson Hollenbeck, Toma's father, had promised to finish (and people throughout the minute metropolis of Lexington, Kentucky knew that Johnson Hollenbeck's word was worth twice its weight in gold) he had been assaulted and robbed. The two perpetrators had snuck up to him and without warning came upon him with aluminum baseball bats. They had done other things, filthy violations and humiliations that Johnson would never in the remainder of his lifetime speak of to his wife and children, but Johnson had been allowed to live. They could have killed him easily, if for no other reason than just to be sure that he could not identify them to the authorities, but leaving him lying broken and defiled to forever remember the brunt of their torment was so much worse.

After that night Johnson Hollenbeck was a shell of a man, drawn in upon himself so deeply as to appear hollow altogether. He spoke very little to anyone, especially his sons. Rarely would he even look them in the eye as if afraid to see the pools of shame his had become. He began to avoid the outside world and the multitudes that populated it altogether as if he were a stalked man. The few words he would offer were always tomes of distrust and hate. He would not work. Arnelle, his wife, had to secure and hold down two jobs (a hotel maid and a kitchen worker at a facility for criminally ill patrons) just to scrape by. The body lived, but the man had died, and his corpse was a cruel haunt cursed to them all.

In short order the boys became unruly and angry, lashing out openly and sometimes violently at authority. They needed to blame someone for the downward spiral they were cast into and any victim would suffice. This grew worse through the years. At age twelve Toma had gained a reputation as an outright bully and thug. He had been recruited by a gang called the K-Lo's and as part of their number, took on various illegal tasks, such as drug-running and distribution, but when he asked for a gun to carry, the leader of the K-Lo's, known as Reason, had denied Toma, saying he was too young and had yet to earn his gun.

Reason was a man in his early fifties. He had once had a carrier in the marines until receiving a dishonorable discharge for assaulting his commanding officer. When Reason returned to civilian life he was angry and poor. He had been trained as a killer He had a sharp mind that was keen on strategy and espionage. He put these talents to work and founded the K-Lo's just shy of his twenty-sixth birthday. He saw them as his own private army and molded them in his distorted image.

Reason took notice of Toma. Saw the eagerness in him, the desire to lash out and the unspoken (and unrealized) need for discipline. He kept Toma close, an act which garnered jealousy and resentment from others. They turned on him slowly, and in time would have possibly even killed him had Reason not seen the way the winds were blowing. He sheltered Toma, in ways babied him, until one night Reason tried to make sexual advances on him. Toma fled but told no one. After that night he disassociated himself from the K-Lo's as best as he could, but the past has a way of returning.

From there his contempt for father and authority figures escalated. Once he had even been arrested for assaulting his physical education teacher whom Toma accused of racism, despite their shared ethnicity.

"Go ahead, Uncle Tom," he had shouted as he struggled to free himself from the grip of two policemen, "baby them white kids!" He had followed this with expletives and racial slurs that had left every mouth in the gymnasium agape and more than a few eyes in tears until he was forcibly removed.

How Arnelle had wept that night. She broke down and on bended knees literally begged Johnson to speak with his oldest, but Johnson only stared past her emptily and said, "That's not my boy."

The polar opposite of Toma, Tavares had grown distant

and caulis like his father. He kept his nose pinned to notebook paper where he would draw near constantly. His art teachers had marveled at his talent and attention to detail, but always warned of the darker messages hidden in his work. Counseling sessions had come time and again between principal and teacher and parent and child, but none made any positive progress and after each, oh how Arnelle Hollenbeck had wept. Saints bless the woman, how often she had wept.

The final straw came when Toma and Tavares became separated by the bridge of middle school and high school. To Toma the transition had little initial affect, but for Tavares it was like losing a grip on a lifeline. He had lost the subconscious assurance of knowing his brother was roaming the same halls and worse, Toma had left behind a lot of enemies, enemies who now regarded Tavares as unprotected game and who had kept internal lists of all the wrongs visited on them by Toma's outlashings. School hours became more and more troublesome and over the course of that year many nights Tavares came home bruised and bloodied. Each time he would make directly for his room and lock himself away until the next morning. He would not open his door for poor pleading Arnelle (who would later weep) and neither of the other men in the house expressed a semblance of concern over the matters. Tavares would lie on his bed, starving, and draw his freedom, his peace…and most vividly, his revenge.

A back can only bend so far until it must either break or stiffen and on the final day of school in 1993 pain and torment came to its apex. A group of preteens who had done the most significant damage to Tavares over the year had decided to give him a grand summer send off. The five boys got off early at his bus stop and walked slowly behind him until the school bus turned out of sight. In that unsupervised, unguarded instant they fell upon him. Knuckles and knees and shoe tips and heels crashed down on him as he lay in the street curled fetally in a defensive ball. He kept his body tense as long as he could until at last, under the constant thunder of their justice, his strength surrendered and he unfurled only to befall more blows in his face, his chest and his groin.

They called him names as they pounded him, some vicious from the core and others utterly nonsensical, but, to a child, no less damaging and there, as he was beat into the pavement, although he would never realize it, Tavares Hollenbeck felt nearly exactly what his father had felt on that life-destroying night.

Only Heaven knows how long the punishment would have lasted had a neighbor (unbeknownst to all, guided by an angel) not seen the affair through her window and run out to the streets, screaming at the top of her lungs and waving a wooden baseball bat. As the other boys ran, the smallest among them, he who had suffered the most at Toma's hand, hefted a brick high and before the elderly neighbor could intervene, brought it down on Tavares's head.

The woman cried out as the child ran off, disappearing into a backyard and around the back of the house. When she bent low to examine Tavares her eyes went wide and immediately rushed inside to call 911. Tavares was taken to an emergency room but although the blow had not been fatal, he was to be kept at length so that tests could determine just how bad he was truly hurt.

That night and for the next five nights, Toma stayed at his brother's bedside.

Helped the nurses that came to take care of his baby brother in any way they would allow. It was determined that Tavares had suffered extensive brain damage and would be mentally disabled for the remainder of his life.

Around seven o'clock on the sixth night, Reason came to visit Toma in Tavares's room, having heard about his brother's tragedy. His hair, once a tight field of cornrolls, was now shaved clean and he wore a thick, oily beard. His presence in Tavares's room felt like sacrilege, but despite his anger, Toma found himself disquieted and cornered just as Reason had always made him feel.

Surprisingly Reason kept his distance, simply standing at Tavares's bedside and shaking his head.

"This is what happens when family falls apart," he forced into the awkwardness.

Toma sat silent, refusing to look up.

"What you gonna do now? You gonna soldier up or you gonna walk away?" Reason asked calmly, almost as if expecting no answer at all.

"That's my brother," Toma interjected, "it's my fault he's

here. I did this."

Reason shook his head and gave a *tsk, tsk, tsk.*

"You were strong. *Were* strong. And you let that slip. Dogs can smell weakness just like they smell fear. They smelt it on you, and they smelt it on him," he nodded towards Tavares.

Toma's fear broke and he stood up, fists balled in rage, ready to attack. Reason only cocked his head to the side.

"Oh, so *now* you're strong? Is that it? Now you're a bull ready to charge? Well where was that anger when it was needed? You want to use it now, but it's misdirected, youngblood. I'm not the one who did this. *YOU* did. *Just* like you said."

The blame hit Toma broadside. His body began to tremble. Reason saw this and pressed his advantage, closing the gap as he continued.

"You *still* wanna hate me? Fine. But you're not thinking clearly, you're not stopping to see that I'm here to empower you." He stepped over a few feet away from Toma. He formed his hand into a claw and tapped it on Toma's chest.

"You need to take all that hate, all that rage and hurt in your heart and use it where it's needed. You know who did this, and you know where they are, but you're sitting here, like a coward. Sitting here isn't helping him, there's nothing for you to do here except hide."

Reason stepped back and clasp his hands behind his back.

"One thing I know...the one thing I've *always* kept my sights on...is family, soldier. I love my family. I *protect* my family." He turned towards Tavares. "And when the need arrives, I avenge my family."

Toma stared at his own feet. The words snaked through his defenses and wisdom and gripped the base of his spine. He swallowed hard.

Reason turned to make sure the door was closed and that they were alone. His hands moved behind his back and the past flashed in Toma's mind and once more he stood ready to fight. Reason laughed.

"I'm not your enemy, soldier, I'm your family." Reason brought his hands around. In his right he held a black .22 pistol. "Family helps family."

Toma had caved, taking the pistol and setting out into the

night to enact revenge on Tavares's behalf. That night would set the course for the rest of his life; a course that would ultimately lead him here: in a hospital bed just like the one Tavares had laid in.

He stirred, troubled by dreams that played out as vivid memories, forcing him to relive the worst episodes of his youth. He woke slowly, wanting to remain unconscious regardless of his dreaming because even in this semi-conscious state his body was aware that to awake meant to face a reality it was not ready to accept. Slumber was comfort. The waking world held the real nightmares.

A soft hand moved across his, and a voice called out his name from across a vast expanse. Somewhere in that touch and in that voice he found the strength and desire to will himself fully awake. The first light his eyes met shone from the face of an angel.

"Anne," the words escaped his lips like the exhalation of a long held breath.

Anne Sciantarelli, the S.W.A.R.M. Hellsbane Priest (they saw themselves only as soldiers; gender had never factored in) codenamed Jazz, sat quietly at his bedside bearing an expression that foreshadowed bad tidings, although at the sound of his voice speaking her name there was an unmistakable, but momentary, wave of relief.

Hellsbane was a fraternity, a family whose water was thicker than blood, but somehow some deeper, unspoken bond had developed between these two. Although not outright romantic, there was a sense of attraction and romance about it, but something far more profound than camaraderie and laden with the highest of respect. And so, without hesitation, without an overflow of sympathy to elicit him emotionally, she gave it to him straight.

The facts were thus: Toma was currently a patient in the CCU of the Patrick Morraine Hospital in downtown Lanza del Los Sans. They had expected his near-comatose state to be brief, but even still he had regained consciousness ahead of their estimations. This is where Jazz hesitated. She could only be so strong for so long until the humanity overtook the soldier in her. Her eyes became glassy but never loosed a tear. She was still that strong at least.

"I may not get this exactly right, but I believe he said that you have what's called an ASIA A classification, where there is no preserved motor or sensory functions in your S4 and S5 sacral segments."

She stared long and sorrowfully into his eyes.

Finally she wrangled enough sense of responsibility to spit the last rotten morsel out, "They don't think you'll ever walk again."

Silence.

*****

Silence still.

Toma gasped so loudly and suddenly that it actually startled Anne. She had not realized that his breathing had stopped. It was violent like a corpse reclaiming life or a drowning man breaking the water's surface. He let it out slowly, and it shook terribly as he did. His eyebrows furled, and as he blinked rapidly she could see the gears spinning, but he spoke not a word. Like her, the pool forming in his eyes never broke the dam.

A rap at the door broke the mounting tension, for which Anne was grateful. At first. The door opened with all the slow caution of a thief mid-craft, so Anne called back,

"He's awake." All subtlety cast aside, Doomsayer swung the door wide and stepped inside, the vermin filmmaker on his heels, camera already in action. She turned back to Toma to bite her tongue and found it was harder to do so when Toma's face clearly telegraphed that *now was NOT the time*. But the soldier in her subdued the human, and she swallowed her disapproval whole. Orders were, after all, orders.

Either out of intimidation or some order Doomsayer had given outside (Anne had hoped for the latter) Titus gently kicked the door behind him shut and stepped forward only a step, satisfied to document from afar and occasionally shifting his weight in effort

to capture shots in various frames. He made almost no sound; a fly on their wall.

Doomsayer walked to the far side of Toma's bed and placed

a hand on his shoulder. He had a gift for reading situations instantaneously and knew that Anne had already given Toma the news.

"This facility is obviously not as capable as what we have at our disposal. Remember that." Surely, Anne thought, Doomsayer had meant the words to be sympathetic, but his tone was completely matter-of-fact.

Toma only clinched his jaw and nodded in response.

"A team is already en route to transfer you. They should arrive within the hour." His grip on Toma's shoulder tightened slightly, some small sign of emotional reassurance. "I have already spoken with Valdez and have his assurance that his very best will be attending to you." He pulled his hand away. "You'll be fight-ready in short order."

Doomsayer came around the bed and stopped briefly at Anne's side.

"Return to Hotel ASAP," *Hotel* being the designation of their makeshift barracks in Lanza del los Santos, "We're airborne in fifty."

Anne nodded. Doomsayer left, Titus at his heels like a parasite. Time stagnated. There was something, surely *something*, to be said, but whatever it was it would not come to her. Toma's hand pulled away from hers and he said, "Go."

She did.

CHAPTER 43

Preston Titus hated hospitals. Had ever since a group of inept surgeons had bungled a simple operation and taken his mother's life. The settlement money was considerable, but the Titus family was already *very* well off. Numbers printed on a check seemed a poor substitute for having his mom. She was worth more than any they could have offered, but he guessed the Board of Directors could only see people in terms of numeric value. Hospitals were not places where people came to be healed, they were asylums where people came to die.

As soon as he and Doomsayer had exited Toma's room, Doomsayer stopped to speak with the two gorillas in black Armani suits stationed outside his door. The acrid smells of urine and saline played at his stomach almost as much as the incessant beeping of machines and hacking of the sick hammered his ears. The chaotic mix was making him physically ill, and so he continued down the hall away from Doomsayer and towards the waiting area nearest their exit.

He busied himself with the buttons on his camera, pointlessly making adjustments and then immediately undoing them so as not to ruin any settings.

"Woah! Excuse me!" came the irritated complaint of a hurried nurse he had not seen but had nearly run over.

He stopped and huffed rather than apologizing, watching her disappear into a nearby room where a family huddled around the bed of an elderly woman. The family's sobs were accompanied by a high flat tone that spoke of the woman's passing. Her eyes remained open and stared up at the ceiling, through it, and upward to Heaven.

An idea came to Titus.

He raised the camera to his shoulder and activated its TS modification. He could see the family and the nurse as she examined the read outs on the various machines, but did nothing to resuscitate the patient. Just as he had hoped an angel stood in their midst, unseen to all but he. It was tall and slender, with flowing black hair and robes of purist white. Great wings wrapped over its shoulders and swung behind the mid of its back. As he recorded it bent low and kissed the patient's forehead and grasped her left hand. A soft golden glow spread from her hand and across her body, and he suddenly realized what he was seeing was the outline of her soul. The angel pulled back and her soul lift out of her physical body with unbelievable grace until it stood beside the members of her family. The soul shared her face, but was hard to mark out in its sheen. She smiled lovingly at her family and reached out as if to caress them one last-

"Hey! You can't do that in here." The voice was soft, but demanding without being angry.

Titus turned but left the camera high and running. A nurse in white scrubs with dirty blonde hair pulled tight in a bun and a name badge that read Constance stood a few feet to his left, arms crossed low over her stomach.

"There are laws about privacy and beyond that simple common decency."

Titus smiled awkwardly, but kept the camera rolling, determined to capture as much as he could before she shut him down.

"Now or I call security."

"Mr. Titus," Doomsayer called from further down the hall. "Would you be so kind?"

The jig was up.

Titus lowered the camera and turned it off, confident it contained more gold than he had himself seen.

"I know," he fumbled out, "and I'm sorry. I just got this thing and hospitals make me nervous so I just thought I'd test it

out to take my mind off things."

Constance was neither impressed or convinced. She stepped in uncomfortably close, even for a woman so beautiful, and eyed the camera before shifting her attention to him.

"I know who you are, Mr. Titus. I've seen your work."

"Really?" He loathed the idiotic grin that jumped to his lips.

"You know your way around a camera and narrative, but not around life."

And it was gone.

"With so much diversity in the world, why do you focus so heavily on the negative?"

"I focus on the reality," he countered, but the shaking in his voice undermined his resentment.

"Or your perception of it. And perceptions change when presented with new revelations, don't they?"

He took a step back and eyed her warily.

"The world is full of people who never want to see the bigger picture. That's a sad thing." Her toned softened, sweetened to the point she was smiling at him. "But what amazing things would happen if they stopped viewing it through the windows their pain create and opened themselves to real hope?"

He wanted to reply, but came up short. Behind her Doomsayer left his conversation and made to intercept theirs. As if on cue Constance walked off past him, patting his shoulder as she did and finished, "There's so much more out there to see, Preston. Keep your eyes open."

"Keep that off," Doomsayer snapped, "we don't need the attention."

Titus nodded, still thinking on the nurse. He looked the way she had left but she had already vanished elsewhere.

"We have places to be." Doomsayer marched off towards the exit, not bothering to see if Titus was following.

Titus quickly took after him, but as he did Constance's words echoed. They were recycled rhetoric the likes of which had been flung at him many, many times since *Unfaith* was first shown, but something about them….something rang true.

He bit his tongue to shift his focus and patted the camera at his side. He was ready to be away from the hospital smells and noises and ready to see what else he might have captured minutes back. Most of all, however, he was ready for the next revelation.

CHAPTER 44

His coffee gone, Blowfish plunged his tongue deep inside the cup, tilted his head back and lapped at the dwindling streams of cold, brown liquid running down. When he was satisfied he had gotten every possible ounce he reopened the granola wrapper and picked out the tiny chunks that lay in the crease at the bottom then went about licking the dots of melted chocolate from its walls, all while strutting down Joyce Avenue like the cock-of-the-walk and humming "Ain't No Sunshine".

"Sweet melody, but you know it ain't mine," came the all too familiar voice of the Godfather of Soul and Sandwiches with a playful jab.

Blowfish stopped dead, the tide of pedestrian traffic crashing against him briefly before cutting around him on both sides. No one gave him more than a disgusted glance before they veered away, too afraid that his smell might rub off on them to get too close, or that he might ask for some change, but he did not notice. Rarely did any more. Instead he raised his toes and spun one-eighty on his heels, his grin so wide it came around before the rest of him.

"James Jimmy James!"

"Heeeeey!" came the Godfather's gleeful reply, arms open as wide as his smile.

Blowfish threw out his hands, unaware he dropped both his cup and wrapper in the process, and offered up a colossal hug.

"Where you been?" he asked.

The Godfather pursed his lips and blew hard, showering him with spittle. "I been around, and I ain't been." He closed his left eye, causing the right to squint, and leaned into Blowfish's face. "You the one who didn't come to see me down at the pier last night."

Blowfish was taken aback. He cocked his head and retorted, "I was there, man! I waited for time and time and time, but you never showed."

"Well I was gonna, but you had to go fishin' people outta the water now, didn't ya? You ain't right in the head. You know that, right?"

Blowfish's face soured, a real prize-worthy pout. He swayed back and forth like a drunk, momentarily breaking the surface of the pedestrian river to his right, winning another angry curse from a passerby, but it did not even register in his private world. The people milling about him like ants no more existed to him than the Godfather did to them.

It was a mutual ignorance and, baby, was it blissful.

"So tell me, what that fish-man do for ya, anyhow? He grant you a wish?" The Godfather was pressing in on Blowfish's personal space again, but this time Blowfish did not back away.

"Nothing, he just talked to me. Told me something nice."

"Well ain't that a marvel? Good ta know, my friend, *good... ta...know*." The last three words were each punctuated with a stiff finger stab to the sternum. The Godfather pulled his hand back and smiled a giant, toothless grin (it had never occurred to Blowfish that this Godfather looked, acted, and sounded very little like the true Godfather of Soul). "I know he didn't bring ya no sandwich, now did'ee?"

Blowfish could not hold in his laugh.

"No, sir, he did not."

"Ah, heeeeeey!" the Godfather cheered in poor imitation of the real James Brown. He pulled his arms close to his side strutted like a rooster past Blowfish further down Joyce. He began caterwauling his own rendition of the true Godfather's "Get On the Good Foot" and curled a finger, beckoning Blowfish to follow.

Blowfish giggled childishly and scooted after him.

"Where we going?"

The Godfather added a slick skip into his step and replied, "My friend, you 'bout to win da great sandwich lotto. All ya gots to do is follow my stride and conjure up dem magical numbers. Easy peasy, ay Japanesy?"

Again Blowfish giggled, "Easy peasy."

He was giddy and intrigued, like he was being lead down the yellow brick road to a city of emerald delights. He wanted to skip, but barely had the energy. The long, sleepless night was starting to overtake him.

Their journey took them—*him*, actually—a few blocks down Joyce past the trendy clothing stores, past the never-ending stream of city dwellers—some blind to him by choice, some holier than thou with upturned noses or contemptuous glares—past the blocked off construction site, all the way to the bus station and a collection of payphones.

"What are these?" Blowfish asked, pointing to the nearest one.

"This? These? Man, they's magic boxes. Step on up and play them magic numbers an' you gon' gets sandwich after sandwich after sandwich."

Blowfish stepped forward to examine the nearest "magic box" closer. There was a grouping of buttons with numbers on them underneath what looked like a hard black banana with a metal umbilical chord. His fingers began rubbing anxiously against sweaty palms.

"What's the lotto number?"

"I ain't gonna tell, man. Ain't gotta. You already know."

Blowfish turned to tell the Godfather just how crazy that sounded, but lo and behold the Godfather was gone. He scanned the bus station, but his companion had vanished entirely.

He hobbled up to the magic box and picked up the black banana for easier access to the numbers. It felt hard and grimy, and from it came a tone so unpleasant he let it drop and hang by the umbilical. He chewed on his lower lip as he studied the numbers carefully. After much deliberation he pressed a few. What beautiful notes they played, so beautiful that the harsh tone coming from the banana stopped to listen. But beyond that... nothing...no sandwiches. He pouted.

From behind and nearby a voice called out, "Sir? Um… sir?"

He had no reason to think it was meant for him, so he ignored it, setting his mind to the mysteries of the magic box.

"Um…Jas…Jasper! Mister Worthington?"

Somehow that seemed familiar, in a very dream-like way, but still, the box demanded his attention.

A gentle tap on his shoulders broke Blowfish's concentration making him want to curse, but he bit it back and turned to investigate what else could be so important. The young face before him matched the strange sense of déjà vu the voice birthed. The dark beard and green hooded sweatshirt before him were surreal.

"Mister Worthington! Hi! How are you?"

Blowfish shook his head, trying to rattle his brains into recognition and came up short. The stranger realized this.

"Antonio," he patted his chest, "we met at a convenient store just like twenty minutes ago."

The jumble in his head began to spill out Blowfish's lips in a low mumble. His head continued to shake. The confusion became contagious, infecting Antonio. The young man felt an increasing awkwardness and made a play to divert it. He pointed to the payphone.

"Were you trying to make a call?" he asked.

Blowfish raised a tremulous hand and pointed to the magic box, still mumbling. A few words came out loud enough to understand. "Numbers…sandwich…" and again,

"Numbers…".

Antonio leaned down and picked up the receiver, unintentionally grimacing at its stickiness. He placed it back in its cradle then began to dig through the depths of his pockets. After a few seconds he produced a handful of change and presented it to

Blowfish.

"I'll just shove a bunch of these in, and you dial whatever number you need to call, ok?"

True to his word Antonio slid one coin after another into the change slot until over two dollars had settled in its belly. He handed the receiver back to Blowfish and stepped back.

The annoying tone from the black banana returned and Blowfish nearly dropped it again, but then, if the stranger had given the banana back to him there must be a solid reason for it. He focused again on the numbers. They were silver puzzle, a combination that barred access to his reward, but the Godfather had told him he knew the answer and such awareness brought with it a breadth of clarity.

He reached out, the tip of his finger settling on the two, but then he withdrew it. No, two wasn't right. It was close, but not quite right. One. He pressed one, and the banana fell silent. That was good. That was *progress*. He reached out again, both with his thoughts and his finger. He knew what was next. He *knew* that he knew. Give it a second and it will come...*three!* He giggled.

From there it became a flow, a natural progression from one number to the next until the eleven-digit combination had been unlocked. He shook with excitement. Any moment the sandwiches would come flying out...

A vibrating tone sounded in the banana. Odd. Then another. No sandwiches came. A third tone. A fourth.

And then a woman's voice.

"Hi, you've reached the Edwards' residence. We can't come to the phone right now so please leave your name, number, and a brief message after the beep, and we'll call you back as soon as possible. God bless."

And then a final sharp *beeeeep*.

Blowfish was stunned and underneath that anger was starting to build. It bubbled out like a geyser building intensity in another series of mumbled syllables until it was strong enough to gain coherency.

"Where are they?!" he spit out, "Where are my sandwiches. I got it right. I got the numbers, and now *I want my sandwiches! GIVE ME WHAT'S MINE!"*

Blowfish threw down the banana but the umbilical went taught and kept it from crashing onto ground and breaking apart like he wanted. He loosed a primal growl and stormed off back in the direction of Joyce Avenue, completely ignoring Antonio as he passed the young man by.

Antonio stood there for a minute, watching him disappear down Joyce and then closed his eyes and said a prayer.

CHAPTER 45

Treygen Andros sat on a moldy rug in a low rent motel bathroom watching the front door by way of the vanity mirror. He fought against the yawns and increasingly crushing weight of his eyes, knowing it was just a matter of time before they come for him. Every few minutes his right hand threatened to drop the Beretta in its grip. He never had to use it before, a fact that had him worried that when the time comes he will freeze up and not pull the trigger and that will be the end of him. The toilet mocked him. It would be such a better, more comfortable place to sit and might ease the cramping in his back and legs. But it would make it almost impossible for him to stay awake and leave him more exposed when they came charging through the front door. *When,* he reminded himself, insisting reality snuff out any residual hope of "if" and "if not". So he endured the cramping in trade for the small tactical advantage of huddling in the corner. Deep down he just wished they would arrive already and take care of their business, come what may. The suspense was killing him.

*****

Toma "Hammer" Hollenbeck was airlifted from Patrick Morraine hospital in an unremarkable chopper so as not to draw undo attention. They ferried him to the LS International Airport

243

and transferred him to a private plane where a medical team was waiting. During the long flight back to Haven they "took care of him" which consisted of partial sedation, heavy questioning, and all around annoying him. At least they kept him occupied. Sometimes the worst thing to do was lay and think. That was a lesson he had learned while serving in Afghanistan. He asked if there was anything they thought could be done for his spine and was told to "have faith", the irony of which made him chuckle. The numbness of his limbs only served to amplify the feeling of helplessness, and he began to wonder if this was to be his new "normal". The worst part was not knowing. Whatever the diagnosis, whatever the reality of his situation, the sooner they told him fully and truly, the sooner he could face it head on. He wished they would sedate him fully.

*****

Traci Nicholas stormed out of Saint Michael's Cathedral with Solomon under her arm and Father Joseph running after her pleading. He feared for their safety and asked that they stay at the Cathedral a little longer to try to figure something out. He had no plan to speak of, but if they were with him, maybe he could keep them safe. She would not listen. Father Donovan's accusations made her feel violated in a way she had not known in a very long time. And to have spoken to her son in such a way. Was this how men of God showed compassion? If so she wanted no part of it, or Saint Michael's for that matter. It was like she had forgotten Joseph's kindnesses altogether. Joseph returned to Father Donovan's trying to stifle the righteous indignation in his belly, but the Senior Priest had already left. With all that had happened during the previous night, Joseph needed the counseling of his mentor more than ever, but this instant put a rift between them that Joseph was not sure how to gap. His pride stung at how blazé Donovan had been about brushing him aside to speak to the mother and child, but mostly he was dumbfounded how the senior priest could so readily turn on those who needed the love and compassion of the church the most. He sat in his own office with noise reduction headphones on, using the Beatles *Abbey Road* on vinyl to both distract and relax him.

"…because the sky is blue it makes me cry." He would calm his heart and gather his strength for the fight he could feel coming, even though its true nature eluded him.

The church was still the "house of the Lord", a well-oiled and demanding machine. There are duties to attend to, but before he could see to oil those gears and bring others to a grinding halt, for just ten minutes he needed to be just a man. Logically prayer felt like a pointless effort, but he committed himself to it regardless. Maybe out of habit, maybe out of far-flung hope. Either way, he could not sit idly by.

*****

The Prisoner traced the scars that cut from Athiel's eyes down his cheeks and marveled at what lay before him: an angel that was mortal, yet far from human. Stuck in the physical world, yet free of its constraints. A creature of ceaseless toil and power, but now wounded and unconscious. The Prisoner smiled, wondering what wrath he will incur when Athiel learns his name and remembers their shared past. Like the oxymoron before him, the Prisoner too was once something more. Something beautiful. Something pure. He waited silently for Athiel to awake, eager to speak with him again.

*****

Manuel Valdez boarded a private jet in the midst of his seventh conversation since leaving Positano. Four have been with Herzog Krieger, his direct subordinate.

He sat in silence, running through a mental checklist of the haves and must-be dones: Eclipse, the Paradox had been secured and is en route back to Haven, as was he; the repercussions of Treygen Andros's betrayal had been set in motion, Hellsbane CO Doomsayer brought him up to speed on everything there was to know about Toma Hollenbeck—a.k.a. Hammer; an Arizona Senator and German diplomat were on the verge of breaking crucial promises, promises he knew would be broken before they were even made, and this was well and good as those agreements had been designed so that, once broken, those figureheads could be justifiably removed and dealt with as Valdez needed. He checked his watch, satisfied that his schedule was running almost perfectly in sync with events they had gleamed from the Pillar directly. The only current wildcard seemed to be the lead investigator of the Vatican bombing, a devout catholic who could not be bought or persuaded to see the bigger, truer picture. Such would be an easy thing to deal with, however, and contact with a proper fixer had already been made as well as a new investigator, one more in tune with mankind's best interests, was already waiting in the wings for appointment. He finished his call, silenced his phone, and opened his laptop. More updates from a multitude of sources flooded through, and a phrase echoed through his mind, *no rest for the wicked*. He chuckled. Wicked was a point of view. Maybe he *was* wicked in God's eyes, but God, Lucifer and all their spawn had been wicked in his. He was a guardian of man. Against all adversaries. So he concentrated on his screen, filtering emails by priority and forwarding on what he felt of urgency. His body was weary, but sleep would have to wait. There was much still to be done.

*****

Juriel wandered through the streets of Lanza del los Santos feeling weak and inconsequential. The slaughter at United Park replayed in his head a thousand times a second. Every fear relived, every brother lost once more. He did not believe such a feat was possible, and yet...Darker thoughts crept in. If man could kill angel...what could the absence of the Father mean?

His trek took him drunkenly through the city streets, past angels and demons alike, paying them no mind. His was transfixed with one purpose, to find his brother Dycliasses in hopes that he would know what to do. Perhaps Dycliasses would agree that

an archangel must be found and that perhaps even know where one may be. The very order of existence was collapsing around him. He could already sense the weakening spirits of the people as they went about their lives unaware that an end, *the* end, a *true* and *final* end could be nigh. It occurred to him that his true motivation bordered on revenge; to see those responsible brought to a swift and severe justice. Maybe it was wrong, but it was enough. It was *something*. And something had to be done.

*****

Paul Kennedy, officer of the law, devout husband, rejuvenated Catholic, lay awake in bed next to his wife, Samantha. He should have been asleep long since, having been awake for over 30 hours with another night shift on the horizon. It was early in the afternoon and their daughter, Kat, would be in school for a few hours more. He kissed Sam on her forehead gently so as not to wake her. He had never been more in love with her than he was at that moment and fought off sleep to soak in the sight of her resting peacefully, the sound of her shallow breathing, and the feel of her body, completely relaxed, in his arms. He thought, *If I died right now, that would be ok because this is the greatest moment of my life.* Their conversation in the garage came back to him along with the excitement of having another baby with his partner and best friend. He closed his eyes for a moment to say a prayer of deepest thanks and, in that brief and smiling moment, faded into slumber.

*****

Sharon Phelps was on the telephone with Kenneth's station manager. He asked (not so politely) that Kenneth not to come into work tonight, but he refused to provide any explanation other than the station's owner would contact her husband directly later in the day. She relayed the conversation to Kenneth, parroting his words verbatim and fighting back the desire to add a few choice words of her own. Kenneth could barely comprehend any of it. A storm raged in his belly, holding him captive in their master bath. It was the side effect of an ill-defined fear, causing him to expel all the fluids from his stomach. With every retch he felt a part of his spirit draining. *Retch!* His joy. *Retch!* His sense of security. *Retch!* His capacity to endure the cruelty of the world of man. *Retch!* His hope. When the worst of it subsided he was able to pull himself up to the sink to wash off his face and hands. He stared at the water as it circled down the drain and thought, *This is where we are now…but how much longer will the center hold?* before collapsing to the floor.

*****

Preston Titus loaded his film equipment and personal affects into a taxicab having been instructed by Valdez to travel separately from the S.W.A.R.M. unit he was being so handsomely compensated for shadowing. Valdez, ever a man of few words, had told him next to nothing. He knew he was catching a flight to Las Vegas and spending the night in a luxury suite at the famed Bellagio Casino and Hotel and given a thousand dollar expense allowance, and while that was certainly enticing, he would rather have been thoroughly briefed on the unit's upcoming assignment somewhere in the Nevada desert. Part of him felt like he was being ditched by his prom date, but the other part was glad for it. Since leaving Toma Hollenbeck's bedside and returning to his hotel suite in Lanza del los Santos he had watched the previous night's footage in its entirety no less than five times and *still* could not believe what he himself captured. It flew in the face of what he had ardently believed and shattered the relevance of his greatest achievement. There was no comfort to be had in the fact that his anti-God/religion documentary was increasing in popularity when soon the world would see just how wrong he had been. But the very proof it would take to convince a rational, thinking man like himself was right in his hands, and captured by them. He settled awkwardly against the stiff seat back of the cab and attempted to drift off in hopes that he could escape into sleep all the way to the airport and then fall back asleep on the plane. His mind was not prepared to tackle the ramifications of these discoveries. It would deal with them later, slowly, and on his own terms. Right then he just wanted the world to go away.

*****

Jasper "Blowfish" Worthington returned to his grimy patch

of earth and was ceremoniously greeted by members of his commune. Despite the fanfare he was quick to notice how Herschel sat far removed from everyone with his back turned as if in time-out or exile. Every once in a while someone would walk up and speak to him, but each attempt was waved off with a furious flurry. He strained his ears to listen and managed to catch his friend babble, "They won't stop listening. They look and they see, but they won't give me my head back!" Something drew his eye away, and he caught sight of Sylvie Crindle tucked in the midst of the midday throng of their "hobo city", her eyes wide, unblinking and fixed on Herschel. She sat on an old tire, her fingertips together and clicking her tongue against the back of her teeth. Every so often she let out a faint cackle. For a moment his mind connected marionette strings from her fingertips to the back of

Herschel's skull. When that moment passed she turned without provocation and stared Jasper down. A smile played at the sides of her cracked lips before she mouthed the word, "Shadows." His stomach rumbled as if in retort and reminded him of the black banana and how it had cheated him out of today's sandwiches. He took a seat on an overturned milk crate and spun away from her to allow his mind freedom to address more boggling issues. He would go back to the pier that night and wait for the Godfather to return. Maybe he would even see the floating man again. He tried to picture the floating man's face, but it came to him with all the clarity of a window smeared with Vaseline. The only thing he could grasp firm hold of in the slippery recesses of his mind were five words playing over and over like a skipping record. "You will be blessed again."

*****

Jack Edwards kicked open the front door, his wife, Roxanne, trailing fifteen feet behind. He was agitated (severe understatement) about being home so early and blamed it entirely on Roxie. He was home because he had had to close his dental practice, he was angry (getting warmer) because it was indefinite. The West Virginia Board of Dentistry had ordered it so which was Roxie's doing. She had had the power to prevent this, but stood aside on grounds of her ethics. He held to a belief that ethics had only a marginal role in the modern capitalist office, but it would seem she no longer appreciated the luxury *his* work "ethic" has provided *her*. He let the door shut before she, carrying a large, heavy box full of various paperwork and questionable patient records, reached it and did not go back to open for her. Why should he do her any favors? He set his keys on the kitchen counter while his thoughts circled the word "divorce" but weighed the consequences should the board call for a full-scale investigation. He saw the blinking light of their home answering machine and walked off. He had no compulsion to speak to anyone; no compulsion to do much of anything but pour three fingers of scotch and disappear into his home office, which he did without a word. Outside his sanctuary walls he heard Roxie drop the heavy box onto the counter. The flatness of the impact only worked to enflame his ire, and his mind began conjuring ways to punish her. She pressed play on the answering machine and despite himself he strained to hear each message. The first was Roxie leaving a reminder for herself. *Brainless,* he thought. The second was his brother, Eric, reminding them that his wife's birthday was the next day. *Carol can rot.* The third was odd: a man's voice, sounding at first confused before suddenly exploding into a tantrum about...what? Did he say "sandwiches"? Then a heavy thud followed by silence. He stormed out of his office thinking she had dropped the box— whether by accident or intentionally was of no consequence— it provided him with an excuse to unload his rage on her, but when he stepped into the kitchen he stopped cold. Roxie lay in a fainted heap in the kitchen floor.

*****

Events in life link together in an infinitesimal, overlapping chain. The stories that trace their roots back to one life will find that the importance of their bulk comes to fruition in the tales of another. Lives are often extinguished at seemingly unpoetic or inappropriate interval,s but this is part of the story's transition. And as each life, mortal or otherwise, rocks upon the altar of its own importance, they cannot see the next step, the step that could set their foot into paradise or inferno, the first step on their mountain-high climb or off the cliff into the unending void, but every step is progress towards an ultimate end.

CHAPTER 46

There was singing in the bathroom, too muted to make out the words, but the tune was strangely familiar. It was upbeat and playful which in terms of Samantha Kennedy meant very, very happy. Paul wanted to get up and join her in the bathroom, no matter what she was doing (with obvious exception), he just wanted to watch her. He marveled at the way she floated across every surface like a dream made flesh and when she sang…wow…even grown men got butterflies.

He was preparing to will his body into motion despite its tired complaints, but then two things happened in rapid succession…

Samantha popped out of the bathroom door, and as the words, "Well stud, looks like you're awake. Interested in another roun…" were escaping her lips they were cut short when…

With the lightest and quickest of raps on the bedroom door Kat barged in.

Mom and Dad cried out in unison, *"Don't come in!"*

Instinctively shielding her eyes as she backpedaled and said, "Sorry! Sorry!" Kat escaped back through the door but left it cracked open the tiniest bit so they might converse.

"Sorry guys!" Kat repeated, "I didn't see anything."

Although mostly covered Paul had flung the covers up, burying himself to the neck. Samantha, even though safely concealed in the pink robe Paul had recently surprised her with, had fled back into the master bath. She emerged, face bright red, trying her best to collect herself and simultaneously failing to hold back an embarrassed laughing fit.

"It's ok, hun, but don't come back in," Sam called out.

"I won't," Kat exclaimed in that exasperated tone that only teenagers can nail, "believe me."

Paul eased the covers down a bit and smiled at his wife, but only for a split second, any longer and they would both erupt in giggles. "What'd you want, child?" he asked. His eyes flickered back to his wife and laughter broke through her façade in a snort, but he maintained well enough to compress it into his smile.

"I just, um, can you hear me ok?"

Sam turned her back to Paul. She *had* to in order to compose herself. "Yes, hun. What do you need?"

"I just wanted to check in and let you guys know that Lila and I are going to run to the mall and see if we can exchange those earrings you got me before Get A Life."

Get A Life. The first time Sam heard that term in reference to Kat's church life group she nearly popped a vein in her forehead. To her it meant that the group was not taking its responsibilities seriously, just a bunch of teens making what they thought was a clever pun, but then Kat had explained it to her. The girls were, in fact, taking the purpose and responsibility of their group with the utmost sincerity. The name came from a conversation from their very first meeting when one girl, fifteen year-old Lindsay Wheeler, broke down and admitted to everyone in the group, most of whom had never met her prior, that she was unsaved and felt like she had never experienced *life*. Life to her was just a mundane series of habits that were daily dragging her deeper and deeper into apathy. She was lonely and depressed and more than once she had given suicide careful consideration. She had no life, she needed to get one so that her life, her soul, might be saved. After that, to Sam, it made absolute perfect sense and she respected the girls, and—with all due bias—especially Kat, a little more. It had been like watching her daughter mature ten years from the story's beginning to its end.

Sam faced Paul, her brow scrunched, "Um, I didn't hear a 'please' anywhere in that sentence, did you?"

Paul shook his head. "Nope, not even remotely close."

Although a huff leaked through the crack in the doorway, they knew their daughter was grinning along. Even though the door obstructed they could both picture with perfect clarity how she straightened her back, placed her hands together curling her fingers in a prim clasp, cocked her head to the right and fluttered her eyelids before speaking in her most proper and schooled British parody accent (her Keira Knightley impression was spot-on, if you closed your eyes you would be very fooled).

"Dearest muthaw and faaaawthaw, 'tis but rude of me to intrude, and I do so hate to be a bawthaw but would you *PLEASE* be oh so ever kind as to grant me permission to trollop through ye olde shoppe? It would be ever so wondiferous."

The parents lost it. Sam doubled over in laughter, and Paul buried his face in the covers while actual tears rolled down. Strange yet absolutely logical that they should be so proud of their daughter's talents in the epicenter of her sarcasm.

On the other side of the door Kat cracked up too, but even Kat fell into certain stereotypes and, as a teen, was rather impatient. Her laughter broke first, and she asked for clarity, "So is that a," her voice again altered, this time in a comical parody of her mother, "*'yes, my beautiful child, you may'?*"

Paul replied, "Yes," proud laughter, "Yes, our beautiful child, you may."

Kat was already rushing down the hall as she called back, "Thank you! I love you! I'll be back after group!"

They heard the front door open and hurriedly shut, but without the stereotypical parental degree of worry. Kat had proven time and again she was both responsible and trustworthy. She would be home about fifteen minutes after group ended, approximately 9:15pm.

She was gone and once again they were alone.

"I'm very blessed. I really, *really* am," Paul declared out of nowhere.

Sam joined him on the bed and he leaned in knowing she meant to kiss his forehead, and she did. "All three of us are, sweetheart."

"Of all the things I worked for and prayed for and begged for in my life, this: you, Kat, me, us...*this* is what means the most to me." He took her hands in his. "Thank you for this. And literally thank *God* for this."

Sam's eyes were wet. "Thank God," she echoed.

She leaned further and held him as tight as she could. He accepted this and let his shoulders melt, but his arms held her firm. He kissed her neck and began to rock her gently. She sighed lovingly and squeezed somehow even harder.

Then the moment came that all husbands and wives this deep in love know. They parted and drank the sight of each other in. Their thoughts became one; their desires entwined. Sam's grin grew mischievous and Paul's began to reflect the shift. Their eyes locked. The hands touched. The room, its walls, the world outside faded away.

CHAPTER 47

Paul Simon's "Slip Sliding Away" was finishing its last melancholy refrain when Dycliasses returned to Father Joseph's side. He had been perched atop the steeple watching Traci storm away with Solomon in tow. Once they had hesitated, and the boy turned to stare at him high above. His young eyes held the hollow sadness of a jack-o-lantern and, just as true, there was fire behind those eyes.

He continued his vigil until they were gone from his considerable sight. He expected them to be followed, but Uzahl did not appear. Dycliasses felt pulled towards them as if tethered—they were not safe, the demon would not abandon its goals—but his place was with the priest, and so he remained.

He peered into Joseph's heart and saw the burden there. The young priest's fear for the mother and child was great, and he clearly harbored the same yearning to accompany them home, attempting to do so would have been futile. Dycliasses put his hand to Joseph's chest and drew a portion of that weight from him. As he did the hand turned an ashy grey and became numb. Dycliasses bore this, but understood the truth of it. Without the wellspring of power from the Father he was weakening even more. So much troubled the young priest, but to drink it in entirely could bring the angel far too low and should Uzahl return here, Dycliasses would be no match against the fiend.

In a voice no man could hear Dycliasses whispered, "I wish

to do so much more for you, Joseph, but at this time I cannot, and for that I am deeply sorry."

When Paul Simon had finished, Joseph lifted the record from the player and replaced it with the Rolling Stones. Soon the jangling chords of Keith Richard's guitar ushered in "Gimme Shelter," and Joseph sat back down and laid his head on his desk.

"Lord give me stren…" he began, but stopped. Dycliasses knew the priest felt as if he were suddenly lifting his prayers to empty Heaven, and with that rationale the

priest's conviction to himself, to the world, and to the faith to which he had committed his life waned almost beyond repair. The angel drew more strength and brought his hands, warm and comforting, into the physical realm so that Joseph might feel their weight upon his shoulders and believe that Heaven might still be above. The touch was subtle, a slight relaxation of the muscles and a tingling sensation that nearly startled Joseph.

Joseph turned his head and asked into the emptiness, "Is someone there?"

For a moment Dycliasses debated whether to reveal his presence and address the priest face to face, but he opted instead to wrap his arms about and through Joseph until the two occupied the same space. Joseph's breath caught, and his head came up. His trembling hands crossed over his heart as if attempting to return the embrace.

His words were drawn out with awe and punctuated with a stream of tears, "I feel you. Blessed be the name of the Father and the Holy Ghost, I can *feel* you." Laughter that bordered hysterics sprang from his gaping mouth. "Please, may I see you and know you?"

Joseph waited, earnestly expecting his request to be granted, but Dycliasses withdrew. The breaking of their connection was instantly apparent on the man. Joseph stood and searched about him while his fingertips lightly clawed at his chest, his mouth still wide.

"I hope you can hear me. I hope that you're still here." Knowing that the angel would appear if it desired Joseph chose to stabilize himself by sitting back down at his desk. He put his weight on his elbows, clasped his hands together and leaned his head against them. He continued as if in prayer. "I don't know if you have been at my side for a while or if you have been sent to me just now…or maybe I'm just imagining you…but if you are here, please, I am in such need. The things I have *seen*. You *must* know what I've seen, and if you do then you understand why I need answers." He paused. "Why I need hope."

He looked back up expectantly but still Dycliasses did not reveal himself. Joseph sat up straight in his chair, and his tone took on a more business-like quality. "There is a family, a mother and son, named Traci and Solomon. They came to me in a time of crisis. They came seeking God's sanctuary from…" he searched for the right description, "from an agent of Satan. I know it. I saw a man flung threw the air in a way that is physically impossible. I felt the presence of evil in the House of the Lord. It was sickening. So please, I beg of you, help me."

Silence. Disappointment. Despair began to take root. Dycliasses took an indirect approach to killing it before it spread: he bade the phone to ring.

At first Joseph did not answer. Dycliasses touched his hand and beckoned it to pick up the receiver. It was not control, it was an urge, just the gentle suggestion that this was of importance and Joseph conceded.

With a voice rasped by emotion he answered, "This is Father Joseph Behanan. How may I help you?"

An elderly woman's voice responded. It was Sondra Burchett, the church's administrative assistant. Miles away in her apartment she too was feeling alone and afraid. Word of the death at Saint Michael's had spread, and she was unsure of how to feel about such news. Although she had hoped to speak to Father Donovan (who was not answering either his office line nor his home phone) she needed the reassurance of a man who she felt held a closer relationship with the Lord. Dycliasses knew this and reassured her that he could always be counted on as a source of strength or, at the very least, a patient ear.

The two spoke for nearly twenty minutes. In that time Joseph assumed the role for which he was hired and shed the sense of spiritual vertigo to which he had nearly succumbed. He was a man of focus and foundation. He did not lie to Sondra. He recounted exactly what he witnessed. He told her that although he was positive a devil had come to holy ground, that he was even more positive that it had been turned back by the ranks of angels and that the mother and child had been saved by putting their faith in the protection of a loving God. Sondra found this very comforting.

"I've seen a lot in my life," she said, "I've seen the evil that men do, and I've seen the evil that the Enemy creates. Father, I tell you wholeheartedly that on more than one occasion I've come under demonic attack myself—now I know that may sound a bit blunt, but that's who I am and how I communicate—but I trust in God, and I trust in His church."

Joseph told her how he appreciated her candor, and she actually giggled. Then she sighed happily and asked him if he had any business she could assist him with. He nearly declined her help until he glanced down and took note of his calendar. He asked that if she had time she help call the leaders of a handful of church clubs and life groups that were scheduled to meet on church grounds and ask that they temporarily relocate (at least for the next week). She was more than happy to oblige, and once Joseph gave her a short list of names she thanked him for his time, asked that the Lord bless him, and hung up.

After the call Joseph returned to leaning his head into his clasped hands. He concentrated on his breathing and reflected on the conversation he and Sondra had just had. He realized how it had consumed his thoughts and provided just the perfect distraction. It had allowed him to build up another and that, in turn, always built him up as well. He had always been complimented as one who, when business was there to be dealt with, he dealt with it from a level and steadfast perch. Problem A could be solved by Solution B and thus create Outcome C. And when he was in the midst of such an equation the business at hand was all that mattered.

A smile touched his lips. "Thank you," he said aloud to the presence he hoped was still nearby.

"Pardon my ignorance, but for what?"

Joseph jumped in his seat. Shortly before he had been hoping to hear such a voice, but now that one answered it sounded entirely too human. It lacked the mystical, otherworldly qualities that he had foolishly expected. There was good reason for that.

Standing in the doorway to Joseph's office, with his hand

raised as if about to knock, was Mayor Aurelio Consuela.

"How are you, Father Behanan? May I come in? We need to talk."

CHAPTER 48

Treygen Andros was asleep when they came for him. The Beretta clutched lazily in his hand, leaning its muzzle into the bathroom rug like a night watchman slumbering at his post. He had one knee raised to his chest and the other leg stretched out almost fully with his heel against the sink cabinet. When the commotion in the main room woke him he kicked hard with both legs, the bent left leg slamming harshly into the right which thudded against the cabinet door, cracking it loudly. In that instinct-driven instant the massive advantage he had had was completely lost.

A short burst of curses came from the bedroom area. Treygen was by no means a tactical genius and had zero military background or training, but the one flicker of brilliance he had had this night was to place a length of fishing wire across the width of the room like a tripwire, one end tied to the bedside lamp which he had placed precariously on the window sill and the other to the leg of the rickety wooden chair in the opposing corner. He doubted it would throw any intruders entirely off balance, but had hoped in the least it would create enough racket and confusion as to alert him and give him a few precious seconds to get the drop on his assailant. Now that the time had come, however, all was already going wrong.

He had not meant to fall asleep, had fought it as hard as he could (with the aid of fairy dust) but the fighting itself had worn him down. Now he was in an abrupt state of shock from being nervous-to-bed and startled-to-rise that caused his hands to operate in a realm entirely out of his conscious control. The gun dropped onto the rug, and he fumbled for it, but only managed to knock it onto the linoleum and send it sliding across to the side of the bathtub. He felt out of his body, watching in utter disbelief as the comedy of errors occurred.

And then from the other room the cursing voice evolved to a more friendly and searching tone. "Mr. Andros? Is that you, sir?"

In his waking dreamlike state the tone was as lost to him as his gun. All his mind registered was *intruder. Killer. Time running out. Dying time has come.*

He could hear the man in the other room wrestling to free himself from the fishing wire, though not violently hurrying. And although the stranger *did* seem annoyed, he sounded surprisingly calm and poised for the most part.

He called out again, "Mr. Andros? Sir? My name is Mr. Levi. I've been asked to return you to Haven. You haven't answered your phone, and your presence is greatly needed. Sir, can you hear me?"

Treygen had not answered his phone because he had flung it into a sewer drain two hours before. Fortunately, the remembrance of the moment was the start on his road to clarity and control. His hands refused to cease their chaotic shaking, but he willed enough dominance into them to at least pick up the Beretta and thumb off the safety. His jaw worked, and his vocal cords revved but would not produce a single sound.

Then the stranger was knocking on the bathroom door sending Treygen's heart into wild palpitations.

Again, "Mr. Andros?"

At last Treygen found his voice. "Stayoutgetoutleavemealo neI'mnotgoingany-where!" It all came as a long, frantic jumble rolling out faster than he could think it.

The voice outside the bathroom took on a weight of authority. "Mr. Andros I have been instructed by Mr. Valdez to retrieve you. You are leaving here with me and returning to Haven. This is non-negotiable."

"I have a gun! You come through that door, and I'll put a hole in your head!"

"Mr. Andros I am not here to hurt you. There is no need for a weapon. Please place it on the floor, I'm coming in."

"I'll kill you! I swear I will!" His control was evaporating. His hands were trembling so violently that he feared he would fire the gun accidentally, but he could not afford to take his finger off the trigger.

"Mr. Andros I'm going to count to three, and then I'm coming in. I'm unarmed. Ok?"

"Don't you do it!" The words came out in a hoarse rage that tore his throat as they were born.

But the stranger had a job to do and Valdez chose such men very discriminately. He would not be deterred by threats.

"One..."

"No!"

"Two..."

"Pleeease..." he was crying now, totally engulfed in his fear.

"Three."

The knob turned, there had been no mechanism to lock it, and the door swung wide. Treygen tried to watch the mirror through the salt water in his eyes. He saw a vague form enter. The gun in his hands turned to the opened door, whether through his conscious control or a result of the anarchy governing his nervous system, but the trigger was squeezed, gunpowder ignited and a bullet tore through the bathroom door and into Mr. Levi's right leg. He dropped to the floor and immediately began to backpedal to the relative safety of the other room. In the next instant the motel room door flew inward off its hinges and three more intruders, *armed* intruders, burst in.

Mr. Levi cried out through his pain, "The bathroom! He's got a gun!"

Treygen quickly attempted to wipe the tears from his eyes to clear his vision so that he could effectively use the mirror. He kicked the bathroom door shut and kick-scooted backwards until he felt the tub against his back. He heard movement from the other room and deciphered that Mr. Levi was being drug to safety outside the hotel room by probably just one of his associates.

Then silence fell. Relative silence. The hammering in Treygen's chest was so aggressive he was afraid it would betray his positioning. His jaw muscles ached from clinching. More water filled his orbs.

He tried to speak. Had to. Anything to eradicate the stillness.

"S…s…stay back," he said meekly.

"Mr. Andros," a new voice, but the authority was a spot-on match for Mr. Levi, "we've been instructed not to kill you, but unless you drop the gun now and walk out slowly with your hands high I can promise you that this is going to be the very definition of painful."

There he sat, Treygen Andros, arguably one of the greatest unknown and unrecognized (publicly at least) geniuses of the twentieth and twenty-first centuries, developer of technology simply undreamed of by both the common man and noted men of (supposed) academia, trapped in a dank motel bathroom with no possibility of escape. They wanted him alive—*Valdez* wanted him alive—but the jig was obviously up. If Valdez did not want him killed then that meant that he had something far worse in mind and, in truth, Treygen knew he deserved it. Not for betraying Valdez, no, that at least he had been right for doing, but for the part he had played, no...he was no mere pawn, for what he had *engineered*. No less than the destruction of everything. Complete annihilation. The clock was already counting down. Nothing could hold should the center falter or, more accurately, be removed.

It struck him suddenly that he had surpassed Judas Iscariot as the single greatest traitor in human history, possibly even outranking Lucifer himself. Because where Lucifer had failed, Treygen had ensured others succeeded. There was no punishment severe enough to lay upon him. Even the lake of fire would be too kind, but it would have to suffice. He would suffer, but not to the satisfaction of Valdez, or the one who held his leash.

Judas Iscariot…Iscariot Grey. Treygen wondered why he had never drawn that correlation before, but now, at the end it seemed overwhelmingly obvious. As the bathroom door crashed inwards and two new strangers raced in, guns drawn, that last connection, like the most basic of algebraic equations, *Iscariot = traitor²*, drew a crazed smile on Treygen's face. It was the last conscious thought he had before he pulled the trigger of the Beretta that lay pressed to his temple.

CHAPTER 49

Cairo, Egypt.

In a slum apartment near the outskirts of the city, empty except for a small wooden desk bearing a fat computer monitor and outdated tower with a singular flashing red light. Silent except for a low electric hum. Unvisited for some time. Suddenly the light turned green and others burst into life, dancing in seemingly random intervals accompanied by a series of clicks and beeps as multiple processors and fans clicked into action. Slowly the monitor woke to fill the room with a weak but increasing ambiance, displaying the words:

Osiris Protocol initiated...

Sending packages...

The automated system hijacked access to ten different wi-fi sources across the greater city and began to jettison fragmented bits of encrypted information across the internet, all weaving through various networks and servers until the pieces landed milliseconds apart on a single IP address over 5600 miles away.

The monitor updated:

Packages sent...

Hard drive purge initiated...

Purge complete...

Osiris Protocol complete...

Another red light flashed on a digital trigger hardwired between the computer and a block of C4. Spark of flame and thunder. Shrapnel and superheated air filled the night sky. The apartment and many around out were no more.

CHAPTER 50

Even at a relatively short height of 5' 5" Mayor Aurelio Consuela was an imposing figure. His mannerisms, poise, strong handshake, the way he always looked who he spoke with directly in the eyes, all these things colored him with the kind of gravitational pull one would expect of nobility. This man had found his calling in politics and given that he was already half way through his second elected term, it was clear the public agreed. He was a rare blend of conservative and liberal, the kind of leader who knew when money had to be spent or withheld for the true bigger picture even if it meant going against the popular flow, but then when such circumstances occurred, he had the charisma to make the populace understand why he chose his stance and often times, the majority of minds were changed at least to the point of acceptance if not full agreement. But what Joseph Behanan admired most was the ease in which he could shrug off the political regalia and just shoot the breeze like a commoner. By the casual droop of his shoulders, Joseph knew the man who now stood in the doorway was the man's man and not the sovereign.

"Hope I didn't catch you at a bad time, Joseph," Mayor Consuela leaned against the doorframe as if he was not wearing a thousand-dollar tailored suit.

Joseph eked out his best "all is well with the world" smile and stood to invite the man in. Consuela met him halfway across the room, hand outstretched. When their hands joined Consuela pulled Joseph in for a one-armed hug which Joseph secretly needed more than he could express.

Consuela released him and studied him for what felt like minutes. "You can't trick a trickster, Joseph, and you needn't try."

The Mayor ushered Joseph back to his office chair and sat him down. Joseph allowed himself to be lead; to let someone else take the reins even if just for a few seconds. As Joseph sat Consuela paused and leaned in, listening intently.

"Is that the Stones?" Consuela pointed to noise-dampening headphones that sat atop Joseph's desk.

Joseph smiled, almost genuinely, and nodded. He had forgotten that his record was still playing.

"Sorry, just would have expected it to be something more spiritual." The Mayor laughed.

"It's not 'Godly' necessarily, but it's spiritual in its own way, I suppose," Joseph let himself relax, just a little. "I'm human. I've got my secular vices."

Consuela took a seat across the desk opposite Joseph, crossed his legs tight in a manner both professional and casual, and set his clutched hands in his lap.

"As do we all. It's ok." He winked. "I could rattle of the name of a few television shows I should probably mention in my next confession. Nothing too racy or violent, mind you, but most of them could stand to lose a bit of the language and tone down the subject matter." His attention shifted as he traced the cord connecting the headphones to–

"Is that a record player?" Consuela pointed and asked.

A minute mixture of pride and embarrassment painted Joseph's smile. He nodded, "Yes it is. Belonged to my dad. I think I was seven when he gave it to me. Still works after all these years."

"Not a fan of digital, huh?"

Joseph shrugged, "It's not that, I honestly just think they sound better on vinyl. Remasters are too polished. It takes the life out of the music."

Consuela nodded, paused, then asked, "Who are some of your favorites? I may have a few records of my own I would donate to your collection."

Joseph's smile broadened, not at the offer, but at the kindness underlying it. "The Stones and of course the Beatles..."

"Of course," Consuela agreed.

"Some Zeppelin and Skynyrd..."

The Mayor's eyebrows went up, and his mouth curved back in a surprised but jovial grimace. "Skynyrd. Really?"

Joseph laughed. "Absolutely. Also Hendrix and Stevie Wonder."

"So classic rock, the *greats* of classic rock, I should say," Consuela interjected.

Joseph concurred, "Pretty much, and Stevie." Then quickly he added, "and some Marvin and Nat King Cole. Can't leave them out."

Consuela chuckled quietly. The tension had not fully left the air, but had faded into the background like a whisper for the time being.

"We like what we like, right? I myself listen to a lot of contemporary Christian. Casting Crowns, Newsboys, Third Day, but would have to say more than any others, Jars of Clay. 'Worlds Apart', love that song. Have you heard it?"

Joseph had.

"That kind of sounds like where we find ourselves now, doesn't it? In a world apart?" Consuela hoped the transition would be somewhat painless, but the slight drop of Joseph's head told him otherwise.

"It is. Absolutely." Joseph agreed.

Consuela regarded him with a warm smile, that of a friend with a soft shoulder and patient ear, but for now it was the Mayor who had to speak.

"I just returned this morning from a conference with our sister city in Italy, so I apologize for not being here sooner." Consuela began. Joseph raised his hands to protest the apology but the Mayor would not be swayed. "Out of my hands, I know, but still I regret I was not here to help in whatever way I could. My mother received a call from one of the first responders and had the foresight to ask him that the news teams be kept outside. From what I've seen there was minimal coverage that night. Soon as I found out about it I set what things I could in motion to make sure that the hounds had bigger stories to chase."

Only now did it dawn on Joseph that he had not seen a single news story regarding the sanctuary death. He was considerably impressed by how quiet it had been kept.

"There haven't been any officers by since then either, though I was told they likely would." Joseph added.

"Again, my doing. I asked that I be allowed to speak with you first, and Commissioner Harris owes me more than a few favors."

"That's not," Joseph chose his words carefully, fearful of treading on rocky grounds, "obstruction or anything is it?"

Consuela stopped and studied the younger man. The buddy personae giving way only slightly to the political. "They've already gathered all the evidence. They received all the eye witness testimony. In no way is the investigation being slowed or hindered, I promise you. I adamantly believe, however, that both the church and, more importantly, the surviving victims of, well, *whatever* occurred should be allowed a degree of normalcy. There's no denying it's what brought me here to see you. I've read the reports, spoken to investigators, but I'd really like to hear it from the horse's mouth. If you don't mind to indulge me."

Joseph straightened as if preparing for a full presentation and felt oddly defensive as if some measure of guilt lay at his feet.

"Well, I was in the sanctuary…" images of his vision came rushing back, and he had to stifle his tongue from spilling the details, "…praying. I heard someone pounding at the front doors and, of course, went to check. It was a woman and her son, and they were frightened beyond anything I think I've ever seen."

Consuela listened patiently, hands clasped, nodding as if to signify that the stories matched up. The nodding made Joseph nervous, like he was under investigation, but he continued as composedly as he could manage.

"As I let them in I saw a man cross street like he had been following them, maybe chasing them, but, and this was so strange, he stopped at the bottom of the cathedral steps."

Consuela leaned forward. "Why is that strange? He saw you were helping them, and if he had been chasing them, sounds like he wised up." Although that was true, Joseph knew in his gut that there was more to it than that.

"It reminded me of how kids in Texas used to creep up on an electric fence, just listening for the hum to see if it's on." Joseph said.

"You mean like testing a defensive barrier for weakness?" Consuela asked. He jumped a few steps closer to what Joseph was driving at faster than the priest was prepared for.

But Joseph conceded. "Yes, just like that. Your Honor–"

Consuela threw his hands up to protest the title. "Please Joseph, just Leo." In the third grade a friend of his had tired of saying his full name and shortened it to its end.

"Leo," calling him that only added to Joseph's discomfort. "I'll get into this more in a minute but this is a house of God" that knife came back, stabbing him deeply in the chest. A lump caught in his throat. "and as such is…protected, if you will."

Leo's face tightened slightly but he said nothing. After a moment he waved for Joseph to continue, but he continued with the facts as they were in mortal and verifiable terms ending with how the man flew through the air in a manner that seemed impossible and died.

"You're right, Joseph, strange things. I'm thankful no one else was hurt."

"So am I."

"What about the mother and son? Traci and Solomon, I believe."

Joseph nodded "They…" he flashed back to how Father Donovan had pulled them suddenly out of the kitchen and how, after the private meeting that followed, Tracy and Solomon had stormed out. "They went home this morning."

Consuela seemed satisfied. He sat quietly, considering, before looking at Joseph square.

"Father Behanan," he began, the politician now, "I am a man of faith which we know in this day in age comes with a certain social cost. Especially for a man in my position. But I believe the Bible from beginning to end. When people ask me how I could be crazy enough to believe such wild stories and ideas I say, straight-faced, that my heart knows the truth. When they say that the Bible was written by man and ask how I know that it wasn't tainted by man I say, straight-faced, that if God is all-powerful, don't you think He would see to it His words remained unblemished? I know these things to be true. My heart tells me so. Don't you agree?"

"I do."

"I know you do. I've even heard you say more than once that the heart is the vessel through which God speaks to us. I've stolen that line and used it numerous times myself. So I'm listening to my heart, and it tells me that you really believe that that lady and her poor son are still in trouble. Am I right?"

A sudden kick of relief hit Joseph, forcing the air out of his lungs. "Yes. Without question."

Consuela leaned in. "And how do you know?"

Joseph answered earnestly, "Because my heart tells me so."

Consuela leaned back. "I can see on your face that it does."

The Mayor rose from the chair while simultaneously pulling his cell phone from his inside jacket pocket. He held down the digit 4 for a moment, and the phone began to ring.

A man answered.

"Peter, it's Leo." Peter Harris, no doubt, the police Commissioner. "Regarding that situation at my church."

Commissioner Harris spoke, but Joseph could not hear what was said.

"Right, well, I'm a bit concerned about the wellbeing of Miss Nicholas and her son. Do you think we can spare a unit to sit on her house for the time being?" He asked politely, but in truth was more order than request.

Harris replied at length.

"That's precisely what I hoped to hear. Thank you, Pete. I'm with Father Behanan now, and I'm sure he'll also be happy to know our finest are looking after her."

Harris spoke.

"You too, Pete, tell Laura hello and have a good night. I'll ring you tomorrow from my office."

Consuela hung up and turned back to Joseph.

"We're dedicating a car to watch the house. Standard shift lengths, but we'll swap our boys out and make sure that someone's there for at least the next three days."

Joseph wanted to rise and shake his hand, but his legs refused.

"Thank you, so much. Can't tell you what that means."

Consuela walked around the desk and extended his hand. Joseph shook it gladly.

"We'll take care of them, Joseph. In the meantime I need you to take care of you. Understand?"

"Yes sir."

Consuela began to walk off, smiling. "Sir?" his mouth played like the word left a sour taste. "We're going to have to work on that." He winked and was out the door.

In the stillness of the room the needle began to skip at the end of the album. Joseph pulled it away and turned the player off. He was truly grateful for what had just occurred but as the minutes ticked by despair reclaimed a foothold. What did it matter now if any of them lived or died? The only true choice that remained was whether or not to throw his hands or tread onward in futility.

Chapter 51

A ngels do not sleep, but Athiel could and did. Angels do not dream, but as he slept, Athiel remembered.

Her name was Mary Cartwright, and she was cold and terrified.

July 7th, 1842, the general location was a sizeable acreage at the base of the Tennessee Smokey Mountains less than 20 miles from the flatlands of Cades Cove. Only a few years before the land's original native settlers had been removed and relocated to the Oklahoma territory allowing Europeans to flourish off the land unhindered. To Mary, however, her habitation and personal living hell was a twelve by twelve foot icehouse painted virginal white where she lay naked in a corner, drawn in fetally with a wool blanket wrapped around her both to amass all the feeble warmth she could and to keep her skin from freezing to the hundred pound blocks of ice stacked around her. The floor was covered with sand to allow for the melting ice to drain and sawdust was packed against the base of the stacked blocks. She had tried to keep her feet tucked completely under the blanket but it was not quite long enough, and after the first day they became painfully irritated despite the numbness the cold brought. She was gagged, but underneath her teeth chattered so hard she feared they might break. It was black as pitch inside, robbing Mary of any sense of time. She was not aware that she had *only* been his captive for three days. To Mary each minute was a frightful eternity that threatened the possibility of his return.

And on occasion he did. Her first warning was the snap release of the lock followed by the slow, threatening rattle of the chain, like a metallic serpent uncoiling. He would open the icehouse door slowly, drawing tension out of every second. Once the door was fully swung wide his considerable mass would fill its frame, and his eyes would linger on her, wrapped in the ineffectual armor of her blanket. He would smile. Oh that smile, like all the foulness of hell lay just behind his clinched teeth.

Finally he would enter, remove her blanket and leave her fully exposed. He had not touched her, not in any indecent way, but his gaze, the apparent joy at her anguish in his grin, birthed more fear than any touch could have. It was a look that prophesized of more wicked torments to come. She did not know how she continued to survive in the arctic environment that was her cell, but in the long, black hours of her suffrage she began inviting death. She considered removing the blanket and letting the bitter cold take her. But the suffrage would be drawn, and in the deepest recesses she still clung to the hope of rescue.

If Mary could see with angelic sight she would have likely been far more afraid. Here was a place of demons. A place where the wicked came to worship and make sacrifice. Hundreds of demons fluttered in the air; sentries guarding the small, unremarkable shack tucked quietly further back in the woods some three hundred yards from her frigid prison.

She would have felt damned.

But she was not alone.

Scores of demons stood outside the icehouse, hissing and taunting, daring Mary's unseen companion to challenge them. Mary knew none of this. She did not realize that the small ember of hope locked in her chest was a gift, and that Athiel, standing watch over her, was its giver.

The nefarious causality behind her fate had been conceived weeks before, but it was not until the night of July 4th that Athiel saw into the heart of her captor, Samuel O'Neary, the owner of the land and *all* structures upon it. Samuel was wealthy, but had gained much and much *more* when he committed himself to the worship of Lucifer. A powerful demon, whose name was unknown even to the angels but came to be known as The Strong

Man, ruled from a throne inside Samuel's soul and was mighty enough to obscure both his dominion and schemes from angelic discovery.

But The Strong Man was a demanding master, and it thirsted for pain and blood. Regular sacrifices were necessary to appease him, and nothing brought him greater joy than the suffering of the innocent at the hands of the damned.

Samuel was only the vessel, a priest of his order, taking delight in the malicious and perverse thoughts that engulfed his mind, believing them to be his own. Even he was unaware of the presence of The Strong Man. As were the twelve that followed him, including his lovely young wife, Esther.

On that cursed eve' over a hundred persons of means and influence, along with a few handpicked servants, had been invited and gathered at the O'Neary estate to celebrate the nation's independence in grand spectacle. Cups overflowed with ale and hearts overflowed with cheer. It was wondrously chaotic, joyfully deafening. Expertly planned and executed.

Esther had played the trickster, cozying up to Mary while her father, a foreman who oversaw the O'Nearys' many slaves, was distracted by drink at the hand of his employer. Meanwhile Mary was continuously tempted into several secretive sips of wine. Esther kept with Mary talking about her future, whom she might wed and what life she may then lead. Mary was indeed a pretty thing, if not of the most respectable lineage, but Esther went about convincing her that if she learned to wield her womanly wiles she would be a gamely catch for nearly any handsome bachelor in the region. Talk shifted to the estate itself and even though Mary had visited the household on the rare occasion, Esther baited her to a tour of parts she had yet to see.

From afar Samuel watched his wife's treachery with glowing pride, and when the women slipped inside the house he put a meaty arm over the shoulder of Mary's father and offered a toast to his family.

It was the toast that had alerted Athiel. The angel was in attendance watching over the local sheriff, a man whom God had tasked with a burdensome career, kept busy by the spider-web of deceit, lust, violence and greed that spread out from the little building hidden in the woods like a plague upon the land. The circle of thirteen that made sacrifice to Satan there went out into the world to corrupt and cause harm, but they were intelligent and influential; pawns masquerading as puppet masters controlling other pawns. So when Samuel O'Neary offered his toast, Athiel could sense the pride and lust swelling from him and took to investigate.

Athiel was hardly the only angel at the O'Neary estate that night. Seven in all had come with the various souls in their charge and they, in turn, were watched from all sides by a multitude of demons; many in the air, some in the bodies of patrons but most from afar in the woods by the little building.

When Mary was led into the house another angel, Losrael, attempted to follow her, sensing impending danger, but even without leaving the body of Samuel O'Neary, The Strong Man proved mighty enough to bar him entry. By flexing its might The Strong Man betrayed its ambiguity, but gave away only the vague certainty that it hid somewhere deep within the lord of the manor.

Athiel came to Losrael's side as did another, Nelerith. The remaining angels stood at the ready, their actions having antagonized the plethora of demons into an angered frenzy. Finally The Strong Man relented, but only to Athiel, and as he crossed the threshold, Athiel sensed the fiend was leaning forward upon his dark perch, smiling.

Losrael and Nelerith compelled persons about them to enter the house, hoping to prevent the two women from being alone, but The Strong Man moved Samuel to intercept them and form a conversational barricade at the doorway, allowing only his slaves and servants access.

It took mere seconds for Athiel to find Esther and Mary as they were making their way towards the home's sizeable kitchen. A demon rode Esther's back, its form a ball of smoke from which spider-like legs jutted and interlocked around Esther's torso and pierced her skull. At his approach the legs shook and made a hollow rattle in warning. Esther had been speaking to Mary, pointing out intricate details of various household décor, but suddenly stopped and looked back as if suspicious of being followed. When Mary inquired what was the matter Esther only smiled and said she thought she overheard her husband in a drunken stupor disclosing marital details too private for respectable company. The women laughed—Mary sheepishly and blushing–then continued into the kitchen.

The kitchen bustled with the chaotic to-and-fro of colored slaves and white servants; men bringing in dirty wares and taking out full mugs of ale or food for the ravenous guests just as quickly as the women could prepare it. Esther regaled the naïve girl with descriptions of exotic meals a capable woman like herself could prepare in such a kitchen, or, and she accented this with a wink, if she could afford to own a few slaves of her own. The slaves, Mary noticed, worked quietly and with down-turned eyes, purposely avoiding their mistress's gaze. The youngest among them, a girl of no more than nine years old, flashed Mary a sidelong glance, and in that quick flittering movement, Mary saw her dread.

Standing quietly in a corner, stopping a male servant to sample a pudding with a pudgy fingertip before it was taken to the guests, was a man Mary recognized. Thomas Finch was a portly banker with a snout like a pig that her father feared and often spoke ill of. Mary honored him with an abrupt curtsy, and he responded with a minimal show of interest before returning to the affair of the pudding.

Athiel could sense the presence of one of The Strong Man's lieutenants, a manipulative demon called Uzahl. When he reached Mary's side the fiend stepped into full view. Uzahl had not been one of the angels who fell after Lucifer's rebellion but was created shortly afterwards, a fact in which it took pride. Here and now it took on a tall, bipedal form with black, ashy bat-like wings, a purposeful mockery of the angels he forever held in disdain.

Uzahl smiled and prompted the demon saddling Esther to compel her to continue. Esther laced her arm around Mary's and lead her onward to a door on the far side of the room. Athiel made to follow but Uzahl extended a hand, blocking his advance.

"Only watch." The demon mocked and then stepped aside. It could not have stopped Athiel outright, but somehow knew that Athiel had not been instructed to intercede.

Ahead of them Esther opened the door with a flourish and bade Mary enter, asking if she had ever seen a wine cellar.

Excited, Mary stepped through and descended a flight of steps into the soft lantern light below.

Once the women disappeared through the doorway Uzahl leaned to whisper in the banker's ear, all the while peering at Athiel and smiling. Athiel could hear the coercion plainly. "Go play, pig."

Mr. Finch retrieved his finger from the pudding, gave it one last satisfied lick then wobbled down the stairs with Athiel at his back.

The plan coalescing around him remained clouded by the unexpected power of The Strong Man, but it was clear the girl was in dire straits. Athiel called out to Losrael and Nelerith, asking them to compel the girl's father to enter the home and search for his daughter, but The Strong man held sway and denied the inebriated father any such idea. Athiel turned his voice to Heaven and pleaded for permission to intervene, but, just as Uzahl had taunted, was instructed only to watch.

Once they reached the bottom of the stairs Finch picked up a leather-wrapped bludgeon that had been conveniently stashed on an upended bourbon barrel. He snuck up behind Mary with surprisingly stealth for a man of his girth brought the bludgeon down on the back of her skull. Mary crumbled to the floor alive but unconscious.

As the night drew out the number of guests dwindled until only a select few remained: a congregation of thirteen, including the O'Nearys and Finch as well as a few select slaves who stood silently, fearfully by while the paid servants cleaned the manor before finally dispersing just before the witching hours. Mary's father had long-since passed out drunk when two slaves threw him in the back of a wagon and bore him home. The thirteen gathered in the wine cellar as two of their number bound and gagged Mary as she stirred to the verge of consciousness. Knowing she was physically outmatched Athiel reached out and deepened her slumber to spare her the terror of waking to find the cadre circled over her drooling. Behind him Uzahl laughed and somewhere in the blackness of Samuel O'Neary's soul Athiel sensed amusement befitting a man watching an insect slamming headlong into glass.

The other angels had left the gala with their respective

charges, but Athiel had, for the night at least, abandoned the sheriff for Mary's sake. He would face the hellish forces alone, without fear. Mary, however, was terrified, and so he knelt down, kissed her eyes and touched her head. He blessed her with pleasant dreams of her childhood and family. He led her back to her baptism and let her once more feel the strength in her father's arms as he drew her from the river, dead to sin, reborn to glory.

Mary had awoken as she was being laid in the icehouse. She attempted to kick and scream but there were men, each far stronger than she, holding each of her extremities and a length of burlap had been wadded up, placed in her mouth and tied around the back of her head to serve as a gag. They dropped her hard onto the sand floor, the very top of her forehead went back and slammed into a block of ice, giving her a bruise and a headache that only recently subsided. As she lay there first nursing the hot, pulsing knob that was forming they tossed the wool blanket over her. Someone made a joke at her expense, but it was miles away from her ears, which could hear only her own frantic heartbeat.

In the first few hours she had beat against the thickly insulated walls of the icehouse, it made an anarchic percussion that was accompanied by a chorus of laughter from a portion of her captors who stayed outside for some time, discussing their plot in volumes too low for her to make out.

Athiel stayed with her, asking again for the permission to create the circumstances that would set her free, but again was told only to bear witness. Athiel put his hands upon her shoulder and bade her be calm. She did. Even still she struggled to regain her breath with the piercing air filling her lungs with coldfire. Athiel touched her eyes and bade her to see the wool blanket. She grabbed it and curled inside. Athiel wrapped himself about her, providing her with enough warmth to make her situation livable.

Once The Strong Man and the demon Uzahl came to examine the girl, riding their vessels and The Strong Man beyond sight. Samuel's presence was enough to cripple the girl's spirit and further extinguish the diminishing flame of her hope. In those encounters Athiel would stand tall and proud and spread his wings in warning. Uzahl would keep his distance, but The Strong Man, unimpressed, pressed his vessel upon the girl to steal her blanket, leaving her body open to the chill and her soul open to his poison for long, torturous moments before finally flinging it back and exiting in a fit of hysterics that bordered on mad.

And for the first three days, that was all that had been done. Until that third night, just before 3 o'clock in the morning…

Mary was asleep, but Athiel remained vigilant and saw Uzahl approaching alone and without his vessel. It strutted in like the lord of the manor, a sulfuric grin smeared across its charred visage. Its impossibly black eyes twinkled like captured moonlight.

"I pray this night finds you well, angel," it greeted in oily tone.

Athiel did not grace it with another display of intimidation; this creature was utterly unworthy of such presentation. He only replied evenly, "Speak your business then leave. You have no power against her."

It cocked its jagged head and knelt to examine the girl. "Not with you here, no. Pity that. I would like to saddle her soul and show her mindseye such…" it lifted its chin to Athiel, "*wonders*."

"I command you to leave," Athiel's words were low and firm and without threat. The demon must obey.

Uzahl rose into the air only a foot above the icehouse floor and tucked his body in tight. Its wings extended down to the floor as if propping it up. Its fingertips danced hungrily on its lips but it was not the girl who held its attention, but Athiel.

"I shall, momentarily, as you command. But, spawn of the tyrant, allow me that moment to stand before you in awe." Although overtly sarcastic, there was some underlying genuineness to the demon's tone.

Athiel stood. He tired of this game and meant to dispose of the fiend by words or by force. Few demons could loiter once commanded by an angel to leave, and this Uzahl was not their equal. The Strong Man must have been near.

"Flee in this moment or perish in the next," he said and a sword of brilliant golden flame like purest sunfire was born in his grip. At this the demon did recoil. It dropped low and cowered in the far corner of the icehouse, its wings out before it like a shield.

"I leave, master, but hear that I know you. My lord curses your name and will delight in your troubled presence when this child is sacrificed for his glory's sake." Uzahl's voice was a trembling hiss punctuated by rage.

"Never!" the cry erupted almost without Athiel even hearing it and was exclamated with a sidelong slash of his blade. Uzahl leapt to safety outside the icehouse, but the blade came so close as to singe the tip of its leathery wing. He could hear the demon scream as it retreated towards the structure in the woods.

Beside him Mary twitched, her dreams shifting to nightmares in the wake of the demon's presence, but Athiel reached down and caressed her head, and the dreams became more fond memories of her father.

For a while there was silence and calm.

And then the lock was unfastened and the chain unwound. The door flew open catching Athiel somehow unawares and likewise Mary was startled awake. The Strong Man had masked their approach. There were seven of them, including Samuel and his wife, stalking like royalty behind their foreguard lead by the piggish banker, Mr. Finch. The men fell upon her almost faster than the scream could form in her throat. Finch pulled her blanket away, and the others seized her limbs with such force that she cried out in pain. Again she tried to fight, but again they were too strong. They pulled her limbs wide leaving her torso unshielded.

Then Samuel entered, his right hand hidden behind his back and his step full of purpose. He muttered wicked words, vile syllables that no human tongue should have the knowledge or ability to form. As he neared he revealed the cattle brand he had been concealing. The unholy symbol it bore was red and smoldering like the fires of hell. He took a knee and touched the tips of his left fingers to the tenderness of her cold flesh as he recited his satanic incantation. He reared his head back then drove the cattle brand home–

"Awake!"

The voice that broke his slumber would brook no argument. Its stony resonance

reverberated throughout his body and rapt him fast awake.

It was the chained and decayed once–prisoner that had

saved him from the Soldiers. For a moment it seemed to Athiel that he could almost remember his savior's Name, but in the anxiousness saturating the air, the moment was quick to pass.

"What troubles you?" Athiel asked quickly, sitting up with no regard to the sharp pain it caused him.

The prisoner's low growl seemed to echo inside the pain. "The one you saved, Juriel. He travels alone. He is lost and increasingly hopeless." The prisoner shook his head in disgust. "How is it our kin tolerate such devolution?"

"How do you know this?" Athiel asked, wincing.

"The smell of it overwhelms. Can you not taste it? No, of course not, you chose a different way. He reeks of desperation. And *they* sense it too."

"Who?"

"Lucifer's spawn. Even now they circle him like carrion." The prisoner sniffed the air melodramatically. "It truly is intoxicating. Even..." he smiled devilishly, "*heavenly*."

Athiel struggled to his feet without too great a strain and instinctually flexed to stretch his wings, but his back was as bare as pieces of his memory lately seemed. The prisoner circled behind him, put a palm to Athiel's back and growled deeply.

"They are there, but denied of you."

Athiel pulled away.

"Perhaps later we will speak of your fall," the other suggested.

Athiel did not reply. The prisoner stepped forward and extended his arms.

"We should make haste. I can bare you." Athiel took the prisoner's hands in his own and instantaneously the two were a blue comet streaking unseen across the deepening night.

CHAPTER 52

To an ant a yard should be a maze, filled with obstacles and twists, but despite the dangers, an ant will find its way. To a man a metropolis should be a labyrinth, but in time he will grow familiar. To an angel, however, the world should hold no geographical mysteries; the lay of the land a map imprinted within them, shifting through near infinite variations over the course of history and future. To the angel Juriel, however, the universe had spun on its axis and all was a blind man's bluff.

Since his creation Juriel had served flawlessly, but remained unrecognized by the tomes of mankind and religion. He had performed a great multitude of lesser, "everyday" miracles at the behest of a loving God, but none had been written on parchment or etched on stone for prophets to heft. No man would ever speak his name or tell of his majesty, and that was as it should be. Juriel served a Father he loved and in turn loved His mortal children in the most selfless manner possible.

Never would he have believed that those children would turn at him to bring slaughter. But never would he, or anyone, have believed, or even conceived, that the God of Heaven, Yahweh, I Am, The Creator, could die. Now the never-ending had concluded.

Now all was aftermath and with the beating heart of the universe itself silenced, how long could life on any plane continue?

Juriel felt lost to a capacity that none had ever experienced; far beyond the minds and woes of mankind. He had been given knowledge of nearly the entirety of the plot of existence. He had known of the expulsion of Adam and Eve from Eden, the birth, life and death of Jesus Christ, the rise and reign of Adolph Hitler, the opening of the seven seals and the unfolding of the Great Tribulations, the Rapture, the Millennial Reign and Armageddon all before they were even set into motion. Time was not a splitting web of possibilities, it was an arrow flying straight towards a single destination but crafted with near infinite feathers on its shaft. Mankind held the great and underappreciated power of choice, but all choices were *known* to the omnipotent Creator, and the illustrious pattern that each, as a thread invisibly wrapped around every other, wove crafted one unchanging tapestry. The many decisions made daily by the populace of Earth were each locked into their own sliver of time, and for one who existed outside of time and space, nothing was unforeseen.

So how then had death found He who could see all choices and who held complete power over death? A frightening and confounding answer occurred to him: that it was what the Lord has *chosen*. He tried in vain to push the idea from his mind, but it was the only conclusion that made any sense. The concept of Deistical suicide was unfathomable even to one who could fathom every intricacy of the universe.

And thus, continued his spiral.

His mind spun on every axis knocking even simple geographical knowledge into limbo, and now he was an ant robbed of sight and sent, spinning in circles, on half its legs waiting for a scorching midday sun and a cruel child with a magnifying glass. The only concept that he could hold onto with any degree of consistency was the desperation for leadership; someone with the composure and wisdom to calm the winds and return to him purpose. Dycliasses could fill such a role, but although Juriel knew he resided within the Cathedral of Saint Michael, his innate compass was broken leaving him with only a general sense of direction as if Dycliasses was some faint, distant magnet. At least desperation held the endearing quality of necessity, which forbid one to give up.

So, he trudged through the alleyways of Lanza del los

Santos. He need not be confined by structural walls, but they gave him some tiny sense of course. Little things felt familiar: a red awning with a white printed dragon over the storefront of a Chinese take-out restaurant, a bench at a bus stop with the words "all that is, isn't" written in permanent marker, a jazz club with an actual velvet rope by the door that was seldom used for more than cursory show. Each was a vague waypoint bringing him closer to hope.

As he mused over these landmarks he caught first sight of them. Some kept to the air, circling hungrily like buzzards, others peeked out from behind walls and shadowed alleyways. Most seemed to be lesser demons, but a few above and on the ground were of a more vicious breed. Their number was hard to approximate as his stalkers hid and exposed themselves in quick, taunting intervals, but there were more than enough to delay him. Several let out venomous chuckles as they matched his pace and drew steadily closer. Somewhere in the recesses of his mind it came to him that only days ago they never would have been so bold, but this was one more thing that had changed...and did they seem somehow...darker and more fierce?

A shrill scream cut through every sense and gave Juriel his only warning as the first flyer came at him. As were all his kind, he should have been quicker than the hellspawn, but tonight he was not himself, and they were something different as well. He attempted a dodge to his left but the first and biggest of the flyers, shaped like a man with a face that looked grotesquely melted and a gaping maul housing rows of dagger-like fangs, easily corrected its flight path and tore into his shoulder with slender claws before taking back to the sky. Coming up behind it a flock of smaller bat-like demons swooped and broke against him like a wave. Each bit weakly into him before scattering back skyward. The attack came so swiftly that Juriel barely registered what was happening and flailed around clumsily.

A chorus of howls and laughter erupted from all around him as his ground pursuers came full into view. Those of human-like design strutted forward while the others slithered or crawled or oozed about. Those with eyes carried in them a proud gleam while those with teeth gnashed them hungrily. Juriel forced himself to settle both his inner and outer balance as the sphere of enemies collapsed towards him.

"I command you to disperse, foul creatures! *I command you in the name of the Throne and He who sits upon it!*" he yelled with all he could muster as he summoned his fiery golden blade into being and spread wide his wings.

And for a moment it worked…

…until the largest of their number tossed its skeletal head back, bayed mightily and spread long, bat-like wings. The lesser minions around him echoed his cry and shifted back and forth. In that moment, Juriel became acquainted with a new kind of fear, one he had not truly had time in the park to study. The human soldiers had attacked so suddenly and effectively that even an angel had little chance to think and react. The demons, however, had given him ample time to assess and fret at his situation. They were stronger and bolder than even a few days ago, truly, but he could feel them drinking in his dismay. He saw how it charged them. They wanted this drawn out as long as they could stand before stampeding in and tearing him into oblivion.

A smaller flyer, either too brave or too weak of will, darted for his head, but as it arced down Juriel successfully brought his sword into its path and slit it into two halves that caught aflame and burned out of existence before they could meet the ground. This gave the other demons a moment's pause, but it was not to last. The largest bent back and roared, accented by a hellish red glow that etched his frame like veins. The demons took that as a command and began their full press.

The flyers were the closest and quickest. The bat-likes split into three spiraling lines and came at him from two high angles and one low as the large flyer that had struck first blood charged straight, confident of its strength. Juriel grabbed the hilt of his sword with both hands and then split it apart, now brandishing an identical blade in each. He leapt into the air towards the closest flock of bat-likes and spun counterclockwise to their clockwise spiral with his swords out like propeller blades. The bats were agile, but not enough, and the entire column was ripped into fast-burning ash.

The next closest group scattered higher in fear, but the large demon redirected and slammed broadside into Juriel's back. It hooked a thin but surprisingly strong jagged arm around him and carried him higher all while slicing into his side repeatedly with its free arm. Juriel let out a pained cry then flapped his wings backwards hard against both sides of the fiend's head. Its flight faltered for a second, but it did not lose its grip. A second wing-slam made it howl angrily and claw more frantically into his side. Juriel brought his wings straight out in front of him parallel to each other, drew his chest in then threw his shoulders and wings back as hard as he could. The wings slammed back with enough force to crush through the demon's head and touch. The demon's headless body went limp then began to fall before it caught fire and disintegrated.

Juriel rolled his belly to face the ground just in time to see the third bat spiral only ten feet away and bearing up at him. He had little time to strategize and swung reflexively. His lips quivered for the smallest fraction of a second as a light sparked from his throat. The glow grew so radiant that his entire head glowed and beams like molten gold began stabbing from his eyes. He threw open his jaw and let the full brilliance of the heavenly light show forth. Instantly the bats and several of the lesser demons in the light's path on the ground below were reduced to nothing.

His reserves nearly spent, Juriel's wings relinquished their strength, and he fell hard to the ground.

He attempted to rise as the demons pressed cautiously inward, but could not even make it to his knees. The largest demon, wanting to claim the angel for itself, roared as it picked up speed, and the other demons fell back. Its steps became purposefully physical and heavy; it wanted Juriel to feel his demise approaching. It picked up speed and intensity. It was almost upon him, its claws raised high to cleave downward and sever his head-

-a streak of silvery blue fell from the sky and pierced fully through the demon like a spear. It struck the ground, pinning the demon mid-stride a full second before the fiend exploded in a blue flame that rolled across the battlefield and dissolved as suddenly as it was born. In the ground remained a resplendent sword of blue flame, long and wide and toothed savagely on one side. The lesser demons that remained searched the sky for the sword's source, but before they could flee a blue comet fell from the pitch night sky and slammed into the ground. A shockwave of blue flame blew out from its point of impact and consumed all the remaining demons before they could even scream. As the wave came at Juriel he could only watch, believing the end had truly come but it parted around him like water against a stone and washed over the demons at his back.

There was the stillness then that Juriel had longed for. He turned his head to see not one but two beings had come to his rescue. One, he was surprised to discover was his savior from the massacre at the park. The other, however, raised instant alarm that Juriel lacked the strength to vocalize. As the two approached the second gave a long guttural growl. His movements brought the broken chains embedded in his body to clatter and suddenly Juriel was not sure he had been saved at all. His blades had winked from existence when he loosed his inner light, so now he tried futilely to conjure another. What little hope Juriel had was likewise beyond return.

As the approaching figures closed the gap, Juriel summoned enough strength to ask, "Did you desire the honor of killing me yourself, Ter Greiel?"

CHAPTER 53

It was more than an hour past dark when Father Gregory Donovan finally and warily crossed his threshold. The taint that lay heavy upon him was bleeding so venomously out from his soul that it was affecting him physically. He had been fully prepared to confront Father Joseph outright, but after conversing with the woman Traci and her son he had felt off-kilter, or more to the point, afraid. The child Solomon's final words were terrifying in their own right, but the horrific deadpan gaze with which they were delivered was an incorporeal knife jutting its tip into his throat. At a time when he was in dire need of the strength of his faith, he found himself tested and had thoroughly failed. Facing Joseph would have been foolish. If he could not stand his ground with the lesser evil that this child embodied, then he was utterly outmatched for the greater devil that had taken up roost in his house. He would need to endure the defeat suffered in this minor battle and regroup to win the longer war ahead.

And so he walked to United Park.

As a child Gregory, or Greg as he was known then (or even Greggy by his mother who refused to let him grow into a man), had come to United Park as often as possible, most frequently as a young teenager once given enough free rein to venture out into the world with friends unsupervised. If time allowed they would take the train from the suburbs of Vineyard Hills and spend as much time as they could steal in the heart of the city. The bustle, the noise, the energy, all were intoxicating, but nothing engulfed the senses so perfectly as the wind carrying the mist off the fountain at the park's center to bid him welcome like a sorely missed friend. It broke through the heartache of the world like the kiss of an angel.

...but the park no longer held comfort. When he first caught sight of the fountain he was certain that his eyes were deceiving him, but when he closed the distance he saw for sure that the water had been shut off. It felt like an ill omen, but he rationalized it as coincidence and approached anyway. He sat on the fountain's walled-edge and peered into its depths. A shimmering sea of coins too numerous to count lay before him, most probably a wish long forgotten or only momentarily meant, but some had the weight of true burden and love.

Two dull pennies that she loves me.

A scratched nickel that I get that promotion; my family is in need, and this nickel is too large a portion of what I lack.

A shiny new quarter so that my dad goes into remission and his cancer is taken away.

Each was a prayer; deposits made for the long distance call to Heaven. Surely angels gathered in such places and, from there, carried the prayers, hopes and heartache straight to the Throne so that God may know that His people need Him whether they believe in Him or not.

Gregory reached into his pocket and fought around his wallet to find the few coins therein. He pulled them out, opened his hand and sifted through them: a quarter, three dimes and four pennies. He closed his hand and jangled them for a time and gazed at the fountain top, hoping without cause that it would water would spring forth suddenly like a sign that God was listening and ready to take his call.

Maybe all that was required was the toll be paid.

He stretched out his arm, turned his palm down then ceremoniously released the coins into the dry fountain. They crashed against their kin and danced with them only for a moment in a joyous display until relinquishing their gaiety to gravity's demands and from thenceforth remained silent.

Gregory Donovan dropped to his knees, leaning his forehead against the cool cement of the fountain's wall, and he opened his heart and his mouth, and in a heavy whisper he did pray.

"Holy Father who watches over us, Holy Ghost who haunts our souls, Holy Son who died so that we may live, I ask of you, heed me."

He searched for the words that rang truest. God would know his thoughts no matter what he spoke, but for his own reasons he had to find them.

"I am under attack. This is nothing new, but it *is*. Every day demons dance around us. They laugh at our folly and take joy in our sorrow, but this…this is so much more than what I've seen before. You have chosen to spare me from the necessity of the rites of exorcism, although it is part of my calling, but never once have you asked of me to engage the Enemy in such a way. I know you portion out the strength blessed to us so that it is always enough to persevere in the presence of calamity and that you will never give to us that which is insurmountable through our faith, but Father, I *fear*."

Tears threatened to spill from his eyes, and he had to sniff to keep mucus from escaping his nostrils. In the background, faint but audible footfalls slowly approached, barely registering.

"Maybe I never have been strong enough to stand in the same room as one possessed of a demon. Maybe you have spared me from this because you know that in such a trial I would fail, that I would fail *You,* but now this cup has been given me and despite its weight I *know* that I *can* be victorious. I know that in a place so deep inside that only you can touch. But Holy Father, I *need* Your strength to bolster my own. I *need* Your guidance to navigate this darkness. I *need* You!"

From behind his back came laughter. Boys not yet teenagers from the sound of it.

"Are you kidding me?" One asked. "Is he really praying out here?"

"That's the stupidest thing I've ever seen," the other answered.

Gregory's eyes opened, and his jaw locked, but he stayed his tongue. He felt demons at his back, mocking him openly, challenging his conviction, and defying his faith. He concentrated on his breathing, letting the sound of it work to drown out whatever else their tongues might spit at him. He doubled his resolve and once again closed his eyes and continued.

"I will do what is needed of me, Lord, despite the pain in my heart. I have loved Joseph to the best of my ability, but I see now that I have been deceived. You warned us that the wolves would come to lead Your flock astray and devour them on the dark sides of the hills, but even still I am appalled by the gall of the Enemy's aggression. I am thankful, *so* thankful, that you brought this into the light so swiftly so that the Enemy's plans might be beaten back."

Hot air hit his neck. One of the kids had leaned in. He could hear the smile behind the breath. The boy whispered darkly, "Who are you talking to, Priest? Angels don't live here anymore."

Gregory spun on the boy, being both angered and startled, but there was no boy. No one near him at all. In the distance patrons enjoyed the park in their various ways, but none had come within a hundred feet of him.

His heart tightened, and he put a hand to his chest. A man who lacked faith would believe his mind was slipping into insanity, but Gregory knew better. He drew out each breath to slow his heart rate. He had committed his burdens to the Lord, and the Enemy was already working to test for weaknesses in his resolve. He thought of Solomon and the prophetic threat he had given. He was under attack because he was just and his cause righteous. The Enemy and all those who followed him were afraid. Yes...*they* were truly afraid for when a man righteous with the power of the Lord stood against them, surely they would fall.

Gregory rose to his full height, chest swollen in defiance and left the park. He had left his car in public parking on the other side of downtown closer to Saint Michael's so that he could ride the subway. It was not entirely the same as riding in from Vineyard Hills but was familiar enough, both to and from, to placate some small unrealized longing for a simpler, more ignorant time. During the return ride he felt the power of his conviction eroding at the edges. Every rider he made eye contact with seemed to be nothing more than a mask with snakes slithering underneath. He was behind enemy lines and possibly the only warrior left to carry on the task. He felt isolated and vulnerable. He tried to steel himself, knowing fully that the Lord would send him what he needed to continue, but the courage that swelled within was self-induced and false. It was courage based on an impending empowerment that really never came.

He exited the subway and made the short walk to his car. Each step felt heavier as it echoed the ticking seconds that brought him closer to whatever lied just over the horizon. But he made each step just the same.

Because he had to.

The drive home was intolerably long, and although he was finally away from the myriad of masks, he felt no safer. He turned on the radio, welcoming what little distraction it provided, but when he finally pulled back into his driveway, he was unsure how much longer he could bare up his cross alone.

He wanted to voice his worry and disappointment out loud, but what was the benefit? In the end it came down to one question: *Are You abandoning me?*

Being back home offered no respite. As he walked in he neglected to flip on the entryway lights; a repeating red flash had caught his attention. It was his answering machine boasting to him that it held a hefty thirty-six messages. He sighed. His first instinct was to ignore the machine until later, but that many missed calls…there had to be importance.

Reluctantly he pushed play.

"Father Donovan, this is Charlie Mackey from Saint Michael's," a deacon in fact, and Gregory knew his voice, the clarification was unnecessary, but that was a part of how Charlie spoke under duress. "I can't stop watching the news, but no matter how many times I see it I *can't* believe it's real! How could this have happened? I don't want to sound like I've lost my faith, but Father, how could *God* have allowed such a thing? How?" In the background Olivia, Charlie's wife, said something inaudible. "Please, Father, I know you have to be overwhelmed with everything right now, but Liv and I really need to talk to you. Thank you."

Blinded by the maelstrom of his own problems it took until the middle of the next message (this coming from another church member, Mrs. Hillary Cameron) for Gregory to piece together the reference. He had nearly forgotten. The bombing of the

Vatican. The assassination of the Pope.

He skipped to the next message.

Lester Higgins, one of the oldest members of his congregation. His fears and his pleadings were the same.

Then the next...

Sondra Burchett, church administrative assistant. The same.

And the next...

Thomas Coy, the choir director. The message: the same.

The next...

Jesse Winchester. The same.

Diedra and Malcolm Ross. The same.

Micah Friedman, an active member of the church youth. The same.

After the twelfth nearly identical message Gregory pressed stop and then erase. He simply could not take it any longer. Hearing their tears and knowing the uncertainty that consumed them all. He wished desperately that he was capable of shouldering such things for them, but the truth was, he was beat down and, at least for the day, all but finished.

He walked over to the couch, ready to collapse on it...

And then the angel appeared.

Gregory had just started to realize just how dark, how *unnaturally* black, it was in his home beyond the little streams of light that flooded in through the windows from the street. Without warning a blinding flash of golden light tore apart the shadows, heralded by a trumpet's blast. It was the most beautiful sound he had ever heard. His hands rose to shield his eyes, but they provided little protection. Strangely, miraculously, however, the light did not hurt him.

And then, just as suddenly, the light faded and the shadows pushed in to reclaim the tall form at the light's center. As the darkness closed about it the figure hunched lower as if wounded.

Gregory froze in place, unable to move or speak or even think. A turbulent mixture of fascination and dread took hold, effectively anchoring him in place. His breath caught and held in his chest for several long, silent seconds until at last his lungs, burning in protest, violently wrestled control over his paralysis and sucked in a cooling gust of air.

As if it had been waiting from him to show a sign of life, the figure stepped into the light. The first step was proud and long in stride, the next a clumsy stumble, but the visitor maintained its balance. Gregory stood captivated as the streetlight climbed up the inhuman height of its frame. The *flesh*, if it could be called such, was a gold hue that shimmered like a hundred minute stars bursting, but inset on the limbs were jagged, pronounced veins of dark grey. In contrast it made the golden skin look sickly and in the process of ruination. Its third step was more of a slide and on the fourth, another slide, it came fully into view.

"I am Rewinel," its voice was not a single voice, but a conjoining of tones and octaves as lovely as it was unnerving. Its face was the face of a man, at first, but for a the slightest fraction of a moment seemed to morph into something resembling a lion, then immediately was human again. Deep crags like talons reached out from the corners of its eyes and mouth yet somehow it was achingly beautiful. It was a statue of flesh that had been ravaged by time and the elements.

"Are you..?" Gregory began but could not finish.

"I am what you see and little else."

With those words all of the worry, uncertainty and fear that Gregory had been carrying inside was swept away. He fell to his knees and grasped the angel's right hand. Its touch had the icy insensitivity of a corpse, but he could not keep himself from kissing it.

"You have come in answer to my prayers. Thank you! Praise you!" Gregory wept.

The angel Rewinel pulled its hand away from the priest and placed it on his head.

"There are things that must be done. Great and terrible things that are set before you to perform. You are made unwhole by them, are you not?"

To Gregory the cold palm touching his head felt as if it were holding him upright while his body wanted to crumble to the floor.

"Yes, I am," he said trembling.

"Would you do as I ask of you to see such things undone?" the choir of its voice fluctuated to mostly deeper octaves.

"I would. I will. Command of me, and I will do."

Rewinel removed its hand from his head.

"Then rise and hear what I would ask of you."

With great effort Gregory brought one knee to his chest to help force himself up. His body continued its refusal, but his power of will was too strong, and he finally brought himself to a stand.

"Please, tell me." He pleaded.

Rewinel attempted to rise again to his full height, and in the labor nearly toppled over. Instinctively Gregory moved forward to assist him, but stopped short, unsure if he had the right or even *could* touch the angel. The notion of him, a mere man, aiding a divine creature in such a way struck him as otherworldly.

In answer to his unvoiced concern Rewinel, now hunched over painfully, put a forbidding palm forward and said, "I am weakened nearly to the point of death." Rewinel must have seen the confusion flash across Gregory's face or, being an angel, read it in his soul. "Yes, Gregory Donovan, we too can perish, and many of us so recently have found our end. The world of man plunges so willingly into the bonds of sin, and as man turns his eye from grace, as the power of the church erodes, so do we."

"The church? You are dying because the church is dying?" Gregory was perplexed. He had never been taught that angels were strengthened by the faith of man, moreso the reverse was true, that they themselves strengthened the faith of man as God orchestrated, yet here stood an angel, the only he had seen in his meek life, and indeed it appeared at death's door. *And where does an angel go when it dies?* He pondered. *Oblivion? Do they just cease to exist, even beyond the resurrective power of God?*

"I am the patron of Saint Michael's, Priest. My service on this Earth is to it and its people, and as they turn from the Father, I fade."

Gregory began to ask how, but the answer came to him even before the angel spoke.

"The Priest you sire, he is a blight upon the sanctity of our church. He is an infection that is poisoning its blood, and if left unchecked, he will bring down its very walls. The souls within will be misdirected and lead into the lake of fire for that is the fate of the master he truly serves."

In the recesses of his mind, there had been pockets of thought that clung hopefully to the idea that Joseph Behanan was not truly a servant of evil and that Gregory was falling victim to stress and worry. So many horrifying things had occurred in the past two days, nearly at the same time actually, that the logic centers of his reasoning had tried to override the spiritual messages he had been receiving and tell him that Joseph was as much an innocent as he, but face to face with an angel—a *dying* angel—the wounds those thoughts had created were cauterized. Now it was known beyond doubt, Joseph was an enemy. A servant of *the* Enemy.

'My dreams, these thoughts in my head, have you been trying to speak to me, angel?"

Rewinel nodded.

"I thought I had heard you, but I was afraid to believe. Everything you've been trying to show me..." he was fumbling for the words in the wash of the dark relief he was beginning to feel. "...I...they...it was all happening...being shown to me... so fast that I..." his face went flush with embarrassment, "I was afraid I was going insane somehow. Forgive me, angel, and my lack of understanding."

Rewinel rose as best he could and put a hand on Gregory's shoulder. "Now you must fear no more, for what strength remains to me is yours to use. Do as I ask, and glory shall be restored."

At that moment Gregory Donovan felt more warrior than priest, and never before had he felt so convicted to his task.

"What about the child, Solomon, and his mother?" he asked.

"The false Priest holds power over them both, but the child is an innocent and can still be saved. His mother, however, she participates willingly and wishes to see the boy fully corrupted. She must be slain, and the child must be brought to me."

"And Joseph? Am I to kill him as well?" But Gregory knew the answer.

"Yes, but not yet. First the mother and child."

A shadow fell on Gregory's heart. He had no desire to kill, but would not defy the angel. Just as the prophets and heroes of the old testament had been called upon to slay the wicked, so would he. What troubled him most was allowing Joseph time to cause more damage to Saint Michael's and its congregation.

Even in the presence of an angel you doubt? How DARE

you! He ridiculed himself. *Do as you are commanded and trust in God's plan.*

He feared the angel heard his worry and tried to push it far away from him. He amassed the boldness he felt within and asked, "When should I do this?"

The angel Rewinel smiled. "Tonight."

Like a squire called to be knighted, Gregory took a knee before Rewinel's feet. He bowed and committed, "Thy will be done."

Rewinel gave instructions on how this task was to be undertaken and then sent Gregory to rest until the hour grew late enough. As the Priest retired to his bed Rewinel slid back into the shadows. He let go of the power he had delegated to alter the appearance of the "flesh" he wore, but the knowing smile remained. As he took to the air the demon Uzahl was indeed feeling jovial. Such a deception would not have been possible before with the Lord of Heaven reigning from His throne, but that had changed somehow, and Uzahl cared neither how nor why, only that it had been done. The ruse was also made so much easier because the seed of jealousy that had lain dormant in the priest, probably since the younger priest had first taken position in his church and stealing even a fraction of the heart of his congregation. When at last Uzahl gave water to that seed it began to germinate at a magnificent speed. Such unattended sins were so easy to exploit, especially now.

As he became one with the night, in transit to reap the harvest of his infernal labors, Uzahl looked down upon the multitude of vulnerable souls meandering about in blissful ignorance. He felt utterly sanguine. The city was a meal waiting to be devoured, but beyond its borders lay a bold new world ripe with opportunity.

CHAPTER 54

Immediately sensing the hostility in the air Athiel put himself in between both the wounded Juriel and the being whom he had just learned was named Ter Greiel. It was a name that struck a disharmonic chord somewhere in the cobwebs of his memory, but that enigma was currently of secondary importance.

Ter Greiel remained statuesque, his chains swaying as if moved by some otherworldly wind. Juriel's strength had failed him, and he lay flat on his chest trying his best to keep Ter Greiel within his line of sight. Juriel's face shifted erratically between the shape of a man and that of a lion then a ram, and his wings crept slowly back into his shoulders, giving the illusion that they were shrinking.

Secure in the belief that Ter Greiel would not follow, Athiel approached Juriel and knelt beside him. The dimming light that surrounded his weakened brother gave off little warmth, and that brought Athiel concern.

"If you will allow it, brother, I will heal you as best I can," he offered.

Juriel gave a faint nod. It was all he could manage. As Athiel approached, Juriel caught sight of the bullet wound in his forehead.

"How can this…?" Juriel trailed off, extending a finger towards in captivation.

"I do not know," Athiel replied.

Athiel reached his hands out, open palms facing Juriel. He drew away the taint of demon touch; it sizzled and cracked as it was burned away, trailing smoking. Once it was gone Athiel released his own radiance. At first it fell like glowing embers from his fingertips, but it became more concentrated like a solid beam. Juriel's back arched and a deep sigh escaped his lips. The process continued for a minute more until at last, exhausted, Athiel stepped back, letting his radiance fade.

From behind him Ter Greiel commented, "I did not believe you had the ability. Not yet."

Athiel looked down at his own hands, equally surprised. "Neither did I."

Juriel made an awkward dance of getting upright. When he was mostly vertical he studied Athiel blatantly.

"Athiel? Is it truly you?"

"Yes."

Juriel placed a trembling hand on Athiel's face. "How is it you are tethered to both worlds?" he asked.

Athiel was again surprised and turned both to gauge Ter Greiel's reaction and receive confirmation. The other gave only a slight, stiff nod.

"I did not know that I was." Athiel exclaimed, turning back to Juriel.

"I see you entirely. You cannot leave the physical state, can you?"

Athiel had not given thought to this before, and now that it had been broached he tried to fall away to the spiritual realm and was unsuccessful. He could not sever the ties that held him in the world of man.

Juriel's eyes went wide and without warning a flaming sword appeared in his hand. Chains rattled, and the familiar low growl rumbled through the silence as Ter Greiel came to stand beside Athiel. He gave Juriel only a cursory glance before speaking to Athiel.

"I would have preferred we had discussed such matters before, at the church. But," and he gave Juriel a stern, disapproving grimace as he said, "timing did not allow."

As if it had just occurred to him, Juriel asked, "You both came to save me?"

Both Athiel and Ter Greiel gave only a nod.

"Why? A traitor and a renouncer. What need have you of me?"

"Traitor?" Athiel asked, looking at Ter Greiel.

For a long, silent spell Ter Greiel watched Athiel and Juriel watched them both, waiting to see what Ter Greiel might say and ready to counter it.

Ter Greiel held out his arms to his side and invited Athiel to examine him.

"Do you still not know me?" he asked.

"No."

"The chains!" Juriel nearly screamed. "Do you not even recognize his bondage, now somehow broken?"

Athiel took a length of chain dangling from Ter Greiel's arms in his hand and surveyed it scrupulously. The angelic writing that covered each link seemed almost foreign to him. *How much knowledge have I lost?* He wondered.

Juriel moved to speak, but Ter Greiel beat him to the punch.

"They bare my name and my crimes." He hung his head in...was it shame? "And the names of those I slaughtered."

Athiel dropped the chain and drew back, fists clenched defensively. The creature before him felt more familiar if not yet recognizable. It was not the decay of his flesh or the stitching over his eyes and mouth.

"You allied with Lucifer!" Athiel accused.

"I did." There was no pride in his admittance, only a strong flavoring of remorse.

Juriel stepped forward and clasp Athiel on the shoulder. He kept an eye on Ter Greiel as he spoke as if expecting an assault. "Do you not remember the rebellion? Or your role in it?"

A growl rolled out from Ter Greiel, deeper than any yet heard by Athiel. Tremulous like the warnings of a disquieted volcano. Juriel moved as if to cower behind Athiel, but must have decided to hold his ground. If Ter Greiel had meant to threaten, Juriel felt his words were worth the risk.

"Do you remember those you cast down at Michael's side, or the end you nearly met?"

Ter Greiel approached Athiel and held a length of chain stretched between both hands.

"I will tell." Ter Greiel insisted, which calmed Juriel slightly.

Clouded, frantic images accompanied by the clashing of blades and cries of the dying flashed in his mind's eye. Wings shredded as blurry faces twisted in agony. The engravings on the chain verged on legible. They were names, of that much Athiel was sure.

Without prompt Ter Greiel fell to his knees, bowed his head and held the chain high in the fashion of one who had been defeated and was surrendering his sword.

"Forgive me, brother. Your name was close to adorning my bounds."

CHAPTER 55

Despite the blaring of the television the small apartment felt eerily quiet. Traci was in the kitchen pouring a bowl of melted chocolate chips over a larger bowl of freshly popped corn. It had been Solomon's favorite since he was three and, butchering the language in such adorable fashion as young children do, called it "poplate choc-corn". The name stuck.

Solomon sat at the edge of the couch, stiff as a board, his eyes pointed at the television but it was like he was looking straight through it and miles beyond. He had been nearly catatonic since they left the church, and it chilled her to the core.

A part of Traci remained guilty over the way she had spoken to the younger pastor as she had stormed away. He seemed to genuinely care about their well-being (*sweet* was the actual word she had wanted to use, but she had pushed back the notion of attraction…he was a *priest* of all things). *The other one, Father Donovan, she thought, that was a man possessed. He* hated *us. Why?*

Lost in her thoughts, her hands were on autopilot, and consequentially the last narrow dribble of chocolate fell off the mark and splattered onto her fuzzy pink house shoes. The wet smacking sound brought her back to reality.

"Oh no! No no no!" she pleaded as if that would turn back time.

Instinctively she pulled her leg back to avoid further

chocolaty bombardment, letting it splash on the linoleum before logic took over, and she tilted the bowl back upright and placed it on the counter. She grabbed the towel draped over the oven door handle and tried to pinch out as much chocolate from her shoes as she could before it cooled and hardened. She bit back more than one obscenity as she labored.

Movement in her peripheral startled her and sent her tumbling back. She yelped as her arms swung wildly for purchase, but the momentum sent her teetering back until the stove stopped her falling.

"Mom are you ok?" It was only Solomon, and that was the most normal thing he had said in hours. Actually, it was the only thing he had said in hours.

As her cheeks flushed red, Traci managed a light chuckle.

"Yeah, sweetheart, you just spooked me a little." *Actually you've been spooking me a* lot *today.*

"I heard you saying 'no'. I thought you were hurt."

"No, hun, I'm fine. Just," she raised her right shoe and presented it with both hands. "spilled the chocolate all over myself like a dodo."

"I'm sorry."

His words and tone nicked at the edge of her false smile.

"Why are you sorry?"

He shrugged. "I don't know, just thought you were hurt."

Traci rocked forward, an act which required surprising effort, stood and crossed the small kitchen to him. She touched his cheek gently with her right hand and tried her best to brighten her face.

"I am completely fine. How could I not be? I've got you watching over me. Right?"

He cast his eyes down and shrugged again as his lip curled with uncertainty. She took his jaw in both hands and came to his level.

"You take very good care of me, and I try to take very good care of you. It's who we be, and it's what we do. Simple as that."

He nodded.

"Now go pick out a movie while I finish cleaning up, and then I'll be right there with poplate choc-corn and drinks."

The kid she knew resurfaced, "Can I have Coke?"

Her motherly instinct was quick to select the stock response, *no, it's way too late and you don't need to be drinking Coke anyway,* but she muscled it back, surmising that after all her son had seen of late, a little carbonated beverage was such a mild vice. If anything he'd earned it.

"Sure, bud."

Solomon left to browse through their small collection of DVDs, and Traci went about the task of cleaning. When she walked into the living room juggling the large popcorn bowl and two glasses she was not in the least surprised to see Solomon in the far corner still trying to make up his mind.

"What's stumping you, bud?"

Knees planted firm he spun and held up three colorful DVD cases.

"I can't see what those are. Bring them over." Traci said as she set their feast on the coffee table.

Solomon met her on the couch and laid the movies in her lap. She considered them all but while she had her own favorite amongst the three, she really wanted him to choose.

"Well, you watched Kung Fu Panda two nights ago, so let's veto it. You've been telling me you want to watch The Incredibles again, so how about that?" Although she adored The Incredibles the third selection, The Iron Giant, was her true choice. She was consistently impressed with the technological dazzle that Hollywood studios had been cranking out in recent years with computer animated films, but she had a soft spot for hand drawn cartoons, and The Iron Giant was far and away her favorite.

Solomon must have been reading her mind.

"Nah, let's watch this," he said and snatched The Iron Giant from her lap.

"Sounds good." Traci leaned in and kissed his forehead, which won a comical shudder. That was good. *That* was her son.

They turned off all the apartment lights except the half bath in the hallway (just in case) and started their movie. It was a deceptively normal night, but for now that was close enough. It was a start.

Occasionally she would glance over at Solomon who, once their poplate choc-corn was gone, had sunk back into the couch cushions and now lay like a boneless heap. This was not the same child from two days ago. Not entirely. His face was as much a mask as flesh. She could still hear what he had said to Father Donovan as clearly as if he were repeating it now. She had tried to ask him about it three times throughout the day, but he remained silent and distant. It must have been posttraumatic stress; that was the logical explanation. They both were.

He finally noticed her peeking over and asked, "What's wrong?"

She winked and answered, "Nothing at all," but was lying to Solomon as much as herself.

Out in the possibilities of the night, beyond the protection of walls and windows, where mistakes and fears take body, the demon Uzahl stood in the shadows…watching and abiding.

CHAPTER 56

F ather Gregory Donovan sat up, wide-awake. No alarm woke him, only a deep-seeded command. He was told he would wake then and so he did. There was no drowsiness, no complaints from weary muscles desiring just a little more rest. He felt invigorated. Ready. It was time at last to see the deed done.

He opened his closet and put on the black cassock minus his collar, as instructed as well as black running shoes. It would help him remain undetected by whatever human sentries his demonic nemeses had in place. The angel Rewinel would detain spiritual elements set against him, so long as he did as instructed. He *must* do as instructed.

He took the five-dollar bill from his wallet before placing it back on the nightstand. It was all he was told he would need. Just enough for the train. He was told he might not return for some time, but that the angel would provide everything he would need. It was in every way a test of his faith, and he would pass with unwavering prowess.

As he entered the living room he saw that he had a new message on his answering machine. He almost walked away leaving it unplayed, but curiosity got the better of him. To his surprise it was Joseph. His voice was heavy with equal parts confusion and determination.

"Greg, it's Joseph. I don't know what happened this

morning, but I'd feel a lot better if you and I could talk about it. Ms. Nicholas seemed pretty upset. It's been, well, it's been an insane couple of days, and I'll be honest with you, Greg, I'm at my wit's end. I really want us to figure some things out, and I'd like, if possible, to do that face to face. Preferably tonight instead of in the morning before service. Ok? Call me back on my cell when you can. God bless you, Greg."

Donovan gnashed his teeth. The enemy was full of tricks. It would try to play to his sympathy. Try to get under his armor and wrap its infernal claws around his heart. He erased the message, feeling, as he did so, some small amount of the tenseness in his neck diminish. The only thing the message did make him regret was that most likely he would not be there tomorrow to speak to his flock. And if he was not there then the deceiver would give a sermon in his absence. The thought brought bile to the back of his throat. It nearly caused him to abandon this night's duties.

No, he told himself, *I must walk in faith. The angel was very specific. I must trust that I would be brought back before God's people can be corrupted. There is a plan.* This he repeated time and again. *There is a plan.*

The last thing Gregory Donovan, leader of men, soldier of the Lord, did before leaving was kneel and pray. He prayed to Saint Jude that his task be blessed and prayed to Rewinel for the resolve to see it through.

His prayer done, he stepped out into the night, hands ready for the blood they must shed.

CHAPTER 57

"Does something about this seem off to you?" Paulie Rodriguez, the Rookie, asked while buttoning up his uniform shirt.

"What? They didn't tell you?" Paul Kennedy, the Old Pro, had one leg hiked on the bench, lacing his boots.

"Tell me what?"

"I'm the reason we got this gig. Mayor's..." he snickered, "*request.*"

Paulie stopped and gave him a look like he had bitten into rotten meat.

"As in he asked for us personally?"

The Old Pro nodded.

"Oooo-kay..." the Rookie's suspicions were heightened, but still without direction. "Explain."

"The Mayor and I both attend the same church."

The circuit connected, and the Rookie felt the spark.

"Oh, ok. So this is about all that freaky stuff at Saint Michael's."

Again the Old Pro nodded.

The Rookie went about the business of his belt, but the inquisition continued.

"You know this for a fact?"

Paul conceded, "No, but that would make the most sense."

"So if the guy died, why are we watching the lady and her

kid? What or who exactly are we watching out for?"

It was a valid question. They had not been given much more than an address and strict orders to be vigil for anything "out of the ordinary". When Paul asked the chief for clarification all he got was, "Because that's what the Mayor wants."

Paul could only guess, "I think it's a PR failsafe for the church on behalf of the Mayor. It's been kept out of the media so far, so I think city hall doesn't want to take any chances that there's someone out there who still has it in for that girl." He straightened but felt his thought incomplete. "Or her son."

The Rookie adjusted his hip holster and threw a stick of gum in his mouth.

"If you say so, old timer." He gave the Old Pro a wink.

Paul Kennedy bowed his head and grinned. He liked this kid.

The Two Pauls finished getting ready in relative silence, but as they made their way to the motor pool the conversation picked back up.

"So does anyone really know how that guy supposedly flung himself, what was it, twenty, *thirty f*eet across the church?" the Rookie asked.

"No idea. I don't think anyone in forensics is buying that story." The Old Pro answered.

The Rookie walked around to the passenger door of their cruiser and stopped just shy of getting in to ask, "But you do?"

The Old Pro climbed in, turned over the engine, and waited for the Rookie to follow suit before replying. "Yeah, I honestly do."

"Why? No offense, Paul, but that just isn't physically possible. You know that, right? I don't care what he might've been hopped up on."

"Drug tests were clean. The guy had a history of crack, but he'd been clean for a bit."

Both men were in the car and buckled, but the car had not moved.

"So?"

"Just clearing a point."

"Ok, but you still haven't made yours."

Paul Kennedy turned to look the Rookie straight in the eye.

"I had a hard time believing it. But I do because I know Joseph Behanan. At first I wasn't even sure I believed *him*, but I thought it over and over and, to me, it's a matter of faith."

"Faith? This has nothing to do with faith. It's a matter of physics."

Paul's cheeks clinched, but out of conviction as opposed to anger.

"Faith is the evidence of things unseen. I heard that for the first time in a Sunday school classroom, but I didn't really learn the truth of it until I became a cop."

The Rookie's face had gone blank, but he was listening intently. He always took strict note of any wisdom the Old Pro sent his way. He wanted to learn. He wanted to protect and serve and be the very best public servant he could be. He knew he was young and overly eager, so he looked to the Old Pro for tempering. Yet another quality Paul loved about the kid.

"People can rely too much on logic, and I'm telling you now, if you don't learn to listen to that voice in the back of your head, other people's logic will get you in some bad situations. You're going to see things that defy logic or explanation, and when you do, I hope you already have figured out what you believe."

Paul studied Paulie for a moment, to see if his words took. "That make sense?"

Paulie was stiff, but finally answered, "Clear as mud, Buddha."

The two men laughed. The Old Pro shifted into drive, and the cruiser pulled out to meet its destiny.

"One day you'll learn," Paul said as they turned onto Hobbler Boulevard. "I just hope it's not the hard way."

CHAPTER 58

The northern California night air was thick with salt. Alit by a breeze it swept rampant through the wide downtown streets, sending tendrils past the bright lights of the traffic and storefronts, through the well-groomed hair of the masses and down into the back alleys and underpasses where those thought of as lesser men staked their meager claims. The salt was thick enough to overpower the stench that Blowfish had grown accustomed to (and strangely fond of in its familiarity) and the breeze just violent enough to exacerbate the small tears in his newspaper bed. He heard the first tiny rip and sat up, wanting to be quick enough to keep the damage from worsening. He adjusted a brick so that it lay overtop the edge of the tear. That would hold for tonight and tomorrow he would venture downtown for new "bedclothes". Maybe a USA Today. Its pages usually weathered better than the cheap paper of the Herald-Sentinel. Confident in his makeshift engineering he lay back down and pulled his shirt over his face to ward off the world.

The quiet was relative. There were always bits of conversation going about in their filth-ridden commune, the sounds of traffic speeding by overhead, the vermin skittering about like miniature thieves. Blowfish had adapted to these things as people do who live adjacent to train tracks. After a while it blends into the background, and you just carry on with your life.

Tonight's breeze, however, carried with it more than the salt and the drone, it held a sound that somehow was more distinct to Blowfish's tired ears than any other, even though it seemed a world away. Laying on his left side his left ear keened into the sporadic intonations, and after a minute he was so unconsciously focused on it that it was near-deafening. He groaned and rolled onto his other side hoping his other ear would be more cooperative towards the goal of sleep, but soon it turned traitor as well. Finally he relented and rolled back to his left and pushed himself up to a seated position. He squinted, somehow it made the sound easier to isolate, and its source easier to locate. It was Herschel. He sounded like he was on the far side of their homestead, singing a very off-key rendition of Bill Whither's "Ain't No Sunshine" only after each phrase he would mutter what sounded like lyric-by-lyric commentary.

Blowfish got to his feet and made the short trek to Herschel whom he found sitting on the hood of the old abandoned 1986 Ford Escort that had served as a boundary marker of sorts even before Blowfish had joined this forlorn community.

Herschel rocked back and forth, his pursed lips now stuck in the near-eternal lyrical loop of "I know, I know, I know, I know, I know, I know…".

Blowfish watched for a minute but his balance betrayed him, and when his right foot shifted to compensate it kicked gravel half a foot in front of him to bang against an empty can whose sun-faded label almost still read, "creamed corn".

Herschel flinched and in a surprisingly fluid motion slid off the hood and spun to face with the aggression of a rottweiler rounding on an interloper.

"Just me, Herschel." Blowfish held his hands up in the universal show of *I mean you no harm.*

Herschel, like a broken record, repeated his bridge "I know, I know, I know…" and shook his head disapprovingly. After far more *I know's* than the songwriter scribed Herschel jumped to a higher octave instead of a higher note and "*I* know" became "*they* know". He showed his back to Blowfish and began walking past the decrepit Ford.

"You okay, Hersch?" Blowfish called after him, but Herschel gave no sign that he had heard.

Blowfish started after him and inadvertently full-on kicked the creamed corn can up into the air so that it crashed against the back of the car. This got more reaction from

Herschel than Blowfish was prepared for. Once again the man spun, but this time the song ceased, and his face was full of white-hot rage.

"Man is gonna be condemned for the evil his sins have wrought! Man is gonna scream and cry and *beg*, oh man how man is gonna beg that God will forget each little big-bad we do. And you," he pointed directly at Blowfish now as he prophesized, "you, demon, are gonna burn in hell! I tell you this, you gonna burn burn burn like the devil you are!"

Herschel had taken no steps forward but Blowfish took several back as if he had;as if Herschel's voice were a great repulsing force. He was at a loss for words, but willed some out regardless of whether they made sense. He needed the cushion words—a*ny* spoken in pursuit of truce—may provide.

"I didn't do anything to you, Herschel, it's ok, brother. It's just me, it's just Blowfish." More than once Blowfish had seen Herschel mentally disappear into what he called The Deep Blue. It was that state of inner chaos that consumed a man and sent his soul spiraling out into the farthest reaches of the ocean while his body stayed behind and went about walking and talking and interacting and reacting without true evaluation of surrounding stimuli. Blowfish had been considered a genius once, but now did not realize that he himself often dove into the Deep Blue, mostly with the Godfather of Soul and Sandwiches as his personal tour guide.

Herschel quieted but never put down his accusing finger. He licked his wide lips and blinked rapidly which was good. This was usually a sign that Herschel was coming back from the Deep Blue. You could actually watch as his soul re-organized his thought processes and reclaimed the body. The long finger curled slightly then gave up the ghost of its anger. He slid a palm over his thinning hair and shook his head again as he turned a shoulder to Blowfish.

"She's doin' it. She likes it when I dance for her. And she's doin' so very fine." He said absently.

"Who? Who do you dance for?"

Herschel began tapping the toes on his left foot rhythmically and making little popping sounds with his mouth in double-time. Over the tapping and the popping he hummed a tune from the back of his throat. To Blowfish it sounded oddly like "Sympathy For the Devil" by the Rolling Stones.

"Herschel?" Blowfish reached a hand out, despite the many feet in between them, but Herschel ignored it entirely. His eyes stayed downturn watching his foot tapping.

Tch! Tch! Tch! Echoed from the overpass columns, unnaturally loud, cutting through the city's dissonance.

"Please allow me to introduce myself," a scratchy woman's voice cackled from behind Blowfish, startling him. He could have guessed its owner had he been given a clear moment to think it over.

Sylvie Crindle sat with her knees to her chest, and her back leaning against the nearest support column of the overpass. She was almost invisible in the shadow it cast and had she not spoken the lyrics, Blowfish may not have seen her at all. Now that he did, however, he could not help but wonder if he was imagining the cat-like way that her eyes seemed to gleam in the dark.

She rose to her feet with a nimbleness that should have been impossible for a woman her age and started towards him with a snake-like grace to her sway. Rotting teeth peeked out from behind lips pulled far back in a sneer.

"He's dancing because I asked nicely." She said matter-of-factly. Her tongue clicked against the backs of her teeth. *Tch! Tch! Tch!*

Blowfish had to force back the lump forming in his throat so that his airways were clear enough to breath and speak.

"W-w-why do you…" he stuttered out, "why do you…?" He could not complete his thought. *Why do you watch him dance?* Maybe? *Why do you make him dance?* Was most likely what he was going for but Sylvie Crindle, despite all her manipulative bitterness, could not *make* Herschel do anything he did not want to do.

"Because I enjoy it." She provided the answer to both questions as if she heard each churning in his mind. "Because it's jolly in the shadows, and his mind is full of them. It's like a starry sky but with most of the lights winking out." Her head bobbled to the rhythm Herschel continued to provide.

She stepped up to Blowfish so close that he could smell something akin to rancid meat on her breath. So close that she seemed to see into his Deep Blue.

"What's the sky like in that noggin these days, friend?" She let a long yellow fingernail rap gently against the side of his forehead then brought it back to her lips and actually licked it. She closed her eyes and made a tight "yummy" face.

Blowfish was paralyzed. Not by fear, not entirely, but by some morbid fascination.

"You're crazy," he squeaked out at last.

She winked at him. "No, I'm the only straight arrow in this crooked quiver," she replied while finally backing a few welcome steps away. "You, friend, are about as nutty as they come. Maybe even more than our fella Herschel over there."

Blowfish peered over his shoulder long enough to see Herschel pointing at his tapping foot and making a scolding face towards it as if it were on the verge of being in big, big trouble.

Sylvie's head twisted cockeyed on her serpentine neck, and one ear began to twitch with an agenda of its own. *Tch! Tch! Tch!* It was a wet sound, like water dripping continuously over time, boring into his temple.

"Did Herschel ever tell you how he got here? Hmm?"

"No," Blowfish was honest.

"He was a decently successful man, upper middle class at least, but he had himself a bit of a...*quirk.*" The smile on her cracked lips spoke as to how very much she enjoyed telling this tale. "He has a liking for little boys and hands he can't trust."

Blowfish was dumbfounded.

Sylvie nodded and continued, "It's absolutely true. He was bad. He almost was *real* bad. He could've been *real REAL* bad. All he needed was the right encouragement. He would've made John Wayne Gacey proud, but he had a nephew who was too quick and brave enough to tell. So, like any good coward, friendly ol' Martin Herschel Jenkins left home and hid here. We became friends pretty quick, he and I." She smiled proudly. "I've been easing him along for some years now, but lately, well, something has upset the applecart, and here lately Herschel and I get along better than we ever have. Don't we, friend?"

Herschel ignored her for the continuing sake of his foot. Sylvie returned her attention to Blowfish.

"You're gonna dance for me too, friend. Dance in the shadows and welcome me in."

Now Blowfish was truly frightened, enough so to break his paralysis and start to walk away. Later he would be ashamed to realize that he had abandoned Herschel to his own cowardice, but at the time there was no instinct but survival.

As he left Sylvie Crindle taunted, "Pleased to meet you, hope you guessed my name." *Tch! Tch! Tch!*

Blowfish hurried back through their ramshackle community and past his own piece of Earth. His pace quickened as if he thought Sylvie might leap from the shadows at any given moment and cut open his head to dip her yellow fingernail in the starry sky within and twirl a vortex into his Deep Blue. He walked at a near run in the direction of the pier, having forgotten that he had meant to go there earlier, but now it was a need, not a want. He had to sit where he had seen the man-that-was-not-a-man rise, where the Godfather of Soul and Sandwiches was waiting with a tuna fish on rye hold the mayo…

Where he felt safe.

CHAPTER 59

The doorbell rang. Pushed again. It rang again. Knocked. Reverted back to the doorbell. Pulled out cell phone and called. Home phone rang unattended inside. The only occupants were stillness and its roommates, darkness and quiet. If it had not been a home it could have easily been a mausoleum. Determination gave ground to disappointment and finally to frustrated acceptance.

Joseph Behanan returned his phone to his pocket and started back towards the street which offered only a fraction more semblance of life than Gregory Donovan's home. At least the street had lights and the sound of bugs and lit windows where movement could be spied flittering by. But by comparison Father Donovan's home was a black hole that seemed to suck in the light and the noise and the movement and compress it into nothingness. Having his back facing the house gave Joseph an unexpected chill, forcing him to fight the urge to face the house again to cure it.

He had tried earlier to call and stretch out the olive branch, but Donovan's answering machine had been like a sentry at the gate with orders its master not be disturbed. But Joseph was fervent in his self-appointed task. He could not, no matter how hard he tried, figure out why suddenly Donovan had seemed to shun him, and a time or two he even colored himself paranoid, but the gut truth was undeniable: something was happening, and Donovan was keeping Joseph out of the loop. Like an incompetent...or worse, like an enemy. It was absurd. They were men of God joined together in one parish with one purpose. They were meant to be a united front on the spiritual battlelines but Donovan was acting like a lone crusader with unexpressed goals and reasons, and if the wound between was left unattended it could grow gangrenous. All Joseph knew to do was show up and confront him tactfully (unless tact was not effective).

He debated whether to take a seat on the concrete steps that rode the gentle hill of

Donovan's front lawn, but without knowing where Donovan went there was no true guessing when he might return. Tomorrow was the Sabbath and Joseph had an unrelenting feeling that Donovan would be a no-show. So he walked back to his car and tore a page from the planner he kept in the passenger seat.

GREG,

CAME TO SEE YOU. WE NEED TO TALK. PLEASE CALL ME ASAP.

JOSEPH

...and then got back in his car and drove home to shuffle through sermons he kept pre-cooked for such sudden situations.

Remembering his conversation with Mayor Consuela he flipped on the radio, needing at least a brief distraction, and tuned it to 103.1 The Dove, Lanza del los Santos's contemporary Christian radio station. Jars of Clay was claiming, "I am the only one to blame for this. Somehow it all ends up the same." Joseph had heard the tune, and actually liked it a lot (really liked the band a lot) but could not remember the exact title of the song. Something *Apart* was all that came to mind.

As he drove he tried to lock onto the lyrics and tried to block out the nagging fears, the tormenting hopelessness that seemed without end, and the tiredness (physical and spiritual) that resulted. He tried to think ahead to what sermon might be most appropriate for the morning service. He tried to pretend there was still a God.

Gliding effortlessly alongside the car, the angel Dycliasses tweaked the subtle tonalities of the music so that they might be more soothing to his charge. He made the driver seat marginally softer and the air inside a fraction cooler. He thought back to the sermon's he had, under instruction, helped Joseph write and decided that the message of living without worry entitled "Heavy is My Burden" was best. He knew even reading over it would help comfort Joseph.

Miles away he could smell the building presence of nefarious plot-works that would soon come to a head. It tempted him to leave and investigate. He knew the child and his mother were in danger, but Joseph was also in danger and remained his priority. He could hope that others would be there to act.

Both angel and man knew it would be a long, arduous night.

CHAPTER 60

Riding the train skirting downtown should have brought a fresh serving of childhood nostalgia, but instead the fascination of the view, the joy of rocking with the turns, and sense of speed was replaced with a heightened awareness of how filthy the train car was. It offended all five senses. Sight: It was covered—seats, walls, on advertisements and scratched into windows—with graffiti of various purpose. Touch: The seats were only slightly less grimy than the handrails and walls. Hearing: The clatter of the wheels was a rhythmic hammer to his ears and when the breaks were applied they were a sharp blade. Smell: There was an undeniable aroma of urine and spoiling milk although he could locate the source of neither. Taste: The air itself left a hint of rust and urine on his tongue that was revolting to the point of nausea. And the passengers…the few that ducked in and out of the car he occupied, were varying degrees of riffraff that only fed into the offensive nature of the setting.

The weak fluorescent bulbs blinked out at random intervals, giving him the ominous sense that a malicious, unseen entity announcing its control of the train. It was like being in the rancid belly of a beast. Briefly he wondered how Jonah must have felt.

To Father Gregory Donovan, priest, crusader, it was a more than fitting vessel; a tarnished silver bullet rocketing him into the heart of darkness.

His hands fumbled negligently in his empty pockets trying

their best not to be the devil's idle playthings. He watched the buildings, the city's bones, flash by in the forefront and roll slowly by like tired giants in the distance. It was a thing of beauty, or had been. So many lit windows auditioning for the right to be stars in the sky. The bustle of humanity shouldering its way past itself in the congestion like clotted arteries. It had been an entity. It had had a soul. Now it was a war zone.

In his mind's eye he imagined that hidden behind every door and window was a network of vile minions, toiling like morlocks until the time came when they must surface to feed on the naked souls of mankind. Most victims would never even feel the snapping jaws that would shred them over the course of years until their weary souls were lead to the gates of Hell. The helpless needed a hero.

He laughed aloud as he fought the near-overwhelming urge to whisper, *I'm Batman.*

He cocked his head and loosed a long sigh that collected as condensation on the window. He took a finger and began drawing the iconic bat-symbol. The train jolted in protest throughout the process of his artistry, and when he was finished, leaning back to take in the sight of it, his drawing appeared more like an open maul with fangs like a bear trap. Fat droplets fell from its edges giving it the illusion of having devoured a fresh kill, with blood running down the chin and to the ground. He stared. The mere sight of it—this symbol of justice distorted into something vile—threatened his conviction and again he felt the malevolence pressing in around him. He clinched his jaw and looked around. The window peering into the next car was pitch black. He could feel eyes staring back at him, daring him to continue. Disregarding the few other passengers in the car he stood up and made his way to the center of the aisle. He spread his feet shoulder length apart and kept his knees loose to counter the shifting of the train that attempted to unbalance him.

The other passengers shot weary glances at frequent intervals, failing to remain nonchalant and unnoticed by the obviously crazy man in the priest costume. It was not such an unusual sight, this was downtown after all; however, it was still rather unnerving.

Donovan gazed ferociously into the blackness and

thought, *Read my mind you mongrel of Hell. I am a warrior of Righteousness, and God's word is my sword. You will not, you cannot detain me.* He was a spark in a pit that had just begun to rise and was gaining heat. A flame that could ignite the dead wooden figures that passed by him daily and spread until the city itself combusted and, from there, the world. The path of the righteous was beset on all sides by iniquity, true, but also with possibility. When beholden to his faith a man could walk straight into the lion's den and, scathed or unscathed, come out alive and tell the tale to the masses. He would be a shining example and, in his heart, prayed that others would be drawn to him like moths. It was a rush and conviction unlike any he had experienced before while waging his war from behind the shielding of the pulpit.

The train slowed as it neared his destination. His hands still searched for the nothing in his pockets, and for a moment he questioned whether he should have brought a gun but dismissed the idea quickly. The angel Rewinel would have instructed him to if it was necessary. No, he would trust in what he had been told and let faith fill in the blanks.

When the train came to a complete stop Gregory Donovan nodded in mock-courtesy to the darkness beyond the window, turned, and took the next first step towards his fate.

CHAPTER 61

He pressed <SEND>.

It took a second longer than usual before the silence was interrupted by the ringing of her phone. It rang once. Then twice. *What is she up to?* Thrice. *Maybe she got called in? Naw, she would've at least texted to tell me.* Four–

"Baby!" Even at this late hour Sam's voice was excited and energetic. She seemed genuinely surprised to hear from him, too. Brownie points scored. "What are you doing calling me?" He could hear her wide smile through the phone.

As much as Paul Kennedy loved—no *adored* was the more ardent and precise word, any man could love and be loved in return (thank you Nat King Cole), but to *adore* is to love and cherish and remain captivated by something so precious to you as to be essential to your very lifeforce—his wife, he had his fallibilities that put their own considerable strain on their marriage. Paul was a man who, when driven to do so by necessity, could rend control of any situation from anyone who could not. In the heat of the flames he was all "point A to point B", here's the problem and here's the solution.

Dig in, get it done. But outside of the world-at-large, behind the protective barriers of his day-to-day cop mask, Paul was a very self-conscious and awkward person. He never felt like he had found his place among man, always felt strained to hold long conversations and forced small ones with a general unease that probably made others believe he was fake and snobbish. Few knew this, none of those select trustees being his high school football buddies or brothers in his fraternal order of law enforcement. *You gotta be a man's man out there,* he would think, it was a weakness he had only rarely put into words, but Sam…Sam was the x-factor. The one safe and holy place that made all things acceptable. She was the only person in the world he felt he could totally be himself around. Not his own siblings or parents (whom he loved more than life itself), sometimes not even Kat, but always Sam.

This generalized social phobia had more specified symptoms, foremost of those being his innate hatred of the telephone. Paul was not a total communication-phobe, he just preferred talking in person. Talking on a phone, especially his cellphone was akin to claustrophobia. He felt tethered by some intangible line that wrapped about him like a straightjacket. He was a very visual and busy-bodied creature. His eyes always darted from item to item in any environment, picking up and cataloging the most seemingly trivial detail. It was part of what made him a good cop and, God willing, someday a great detective. But in the curious case of the cellphone, it was a curse. His Sherlockian pupils and puppy dog attention span meant that as he tried to utilize his sense of hearing to engage in meaningful phone conversation, his sense of sight would intervene by feeding his brain waves of visual information and overloading the system. It was frustrating. It was like being at war with one's self. But dare you not call it ADD or ADHD. He was a grown, intelligent man and was totally in control of every chemical coursing through his biology.

The point: Paul Kennedy was a man who hated talking on the phone, and the *"whys"* were beyond comprehension and moot in the eyes of the greatest object of his affection: a woman who craved communication and yearned with happy, loving delirium for the sound of his voice no matter what words it floated to her ear. To Sam, who not so secretly, felt insecurity on much the same level as her husband: his not wanting to talk on the phone amounted to his not wanting to talk to *her*—in her mind. Her insecurity insisted that it meant he did not care *enough*. It was an argument that had reared its ugly head throughout their otherwise happy marriage like a dark, reoccurring season.

But she was always on his mind, and tonight he wanted nothing more than to hear her voice. Even through a cellphone.

"I just wanted to say hey, and tell you I love you," he whispered sweetly.

The night was cool and lifeless. Only a few apartment lights remained on across the street. From the Nicholas's window came the erratic, electric glow of a television. In the passenger seat beside him Paulie "The Rookie" Rodriguez made a show of rolling his eyes but laughed playfully afterwards. The Rookie was young and full of machismo, but when it came to romance, he *got* it. So as the Old Pro continued to sweet-talk the love of his life, The Rookie pulled out his own phone and entered into a text conversation with a woman he may one day discover was his.

Sam breathed in deeply as if his words were a perfumed scent that had been carried to her on a warm wind.

"I love that." She said.

"I know," he smiled shyly and felt the blush raise in his cheeks. "It's part of why I called."

"You *do* love me, huh?"

"More than I can say."

"So how's it going? Your text earlier said something about night watch?"

"Yeah. Think the Mayor set it up."

"Really? Why? Not just why is it needed but also why *you*? Did he ask for you specifically?"

"I'm thinking he did. Remember what I told you happened at the church?"

"Yes…"

"We're outside her apartment. Apparently the Mayor thinks someone may still be after her. Honestly, it's a bit weird."

"Yeah it is. So, ok, why you and Paulie?"

"I guess because A, I was at the church and know a bit of what's going on, at least as much as anyone can who wasn't there when it happened, and B, probably because the Mayor and I are both members there. Kinda like keeping it in the family, you know?"

"Okay, I guess I can understand that." Even though she did, it was obvious Sam did not like it.

"Why do you sound worried, hun?" He asked.

"I don't know. I'm not, and I am. It's just a weird situation is all. I just don't like you being connected to it."

"Hey baby," he steadied and softened his voice, "it's ok. It's my job, and honestly, it's going to be a piece of cake. What happened at church was bizarre, sure, but it happened then and there, and now it's over and done."

"You don't know that."

"My gut tells me so." A white lie.

"Ok." She let herself believe it to satiate her own need for comfort. Then the need to change subjects overwhelmed her. "The Rook's quiet. What's nancy-boy up to?" They both laughed, the tension easing slightly.

One corner of the Rookie's mouth turned up in a grin.

"I heard that," he said, then loud enough for the phone to pick up, "Hi Samantha."

They both laughed a little more naturally.

"Hey Rookie," she called back.

"Kat in bed?" Paul asked.

"Yeah, don't think she's asleep, though. Getting her that laptop may not have been the brightest idea we've ever had."

Paul chuckled. *Yeah, probably not.*

"I'd unplug the wireless router, but I'm sure she'd just leech onto one of our neighbor's networks."

"Well at least she's home, and it's not a school night." Paul conceded. He always did when it came to Kat. Sometimes he was more Girl's Little Daddy than even she was Daddy's Little Girl.

"True, but getting her up for service in the morning isn't gonna be pretty. May just skip Sunday school altogether."

"Naw, don't do that. You're the mama, you're in charge. Throw a bucket of ice on her. She'll get moving."

Sam laughed. "We'll see."

There was a truly comfortable silence. Such times passed easily between them, relished as few couples can.

"I've been thinking a lot about what you said to me." Sam was often a woman without transition and who left a lot open for the guessing.

"Um…" he laughed sarcastically, "I say a lot of things. I said 'I love you', I asked you if you had washed those new red boxer briefs you got me, and I think at one point I even said, 'honey remind me to grab some toilet paper at the end of my shift'."

She was in minor hysterics.

He was on a roll, and when the streak is hot, baby, you play it.

"That was it, wasn't it? You've been wrapped up in the eternal debate of double-ply or not to double-ply."

Sam could not stop laughing. Ease-dropping, the Rookie fixed him with a faux-contemptual sidelong glare.

Sam finally composed herself.

"No, dingbat," she managed and almost instantly her voice took on a glaze of tenderness. "When you talked about how blessed you feel. Even after all this time it still amazes me how you always seem so appreciative of what we share. Can't tell you what that means to me."

"Well it's true."

"I know. I just…well, I haven't told you this because I've been kind of wrestling with it and even wrestling with how much I believe it myself, but I've been having a bit of a crisis of faith lately."

"Wow, yeah, had no idea, baby. What brought this on?"

"I can't explain it. And when I say 'lately' it's really felt like the last few days. It's like something just feels vacant. It's hard to explain. Like, ok, tonight when I prayed, I felt more like I was pretending or rehearsing. I don't know. It doesn't make much sense in my head, so trying to put it into words is a train wreck."

The thought struck an odd chord with Paul, but for her sake he verbally waved it off. "I'm sure it's nothing, hun. Wasn't it just a few weeks ago Father Donovan gave that sermon about how sometimes God distances himself from us to test our faith? You know, to see how resolute we are in our daily walk. If it's anything at all, it's that." Paul was not entirely sure what belief system the Rookie subscribed to if any, so he felt more than a little self-conscious in talking so openly about his faith in front of him. The Old Pro held little love for debating such things with non-Christians, a fact which shamed him. It made him feel like less of a believer. But this was a matter of Sam's faith and as such, he was a virtual apostle.

"Yeah," Sam hesitated, "You're probably right. Just had a lot on my mind lately. Then again, who doesn't these days."

"Very true, baby."

"Paul..." the Rookie's voice was quiet, but stiff as he tapped the Old Pro's shoulder. "Isn't that your pastor?"

His eyes followed the Rookie's sightline.

"Yeah." He replied queerly. "Hey hun, hold on a sec, ok?"

"Everything ok?" she asked while the Rookie continued, "You think he's just checking up on her?"

Paul shook his head in overload, unable for a second to figure out who to answer first.

"Yeah, hun, just one sec." Then he turned to the Rookie, "Probably, but..." *But...what?* he thought.

"We were told to keep an eye out for anyone," Paulie pointed out, "and pastor or not, he qualifies as 'anyone'."

"Baby?" Sam asked into the silence she was hearing from her end.

"Yeah, you're right," Paul answered the Rookie. "Hey sweetheart, I'm gonna have to call you back in a few minutes, ok?"

"Baby, what's going on?" Sam was on the verge of panic triggered by the uncertainty in his voice.

"Nothing baby, Father Donovan just showed up..."

"This late?"

"Yeah, we gotta go talk to him, hun. No worries." The Rookie was already getting out of the cruiser. He finished with Sam hurriedly. "I'll call you back in just a few. Ok?"

"Ok." Sam was not eased.

"I love you, Samantha. More than air, you know that?"

"I do. I love you too."

"Good-bye, baby."

"Bye."

CHAPTER 62

And this is how death comes…

The only light in the apartment came from the television. *The Iron Giant* was nearing its climax but only Solomon was watching; Traci had fallen asleep some twenty minutes before. The over-alert, over-stressed state her body had maintained throughout the day had finally taken its toll, and now rest demanded its due. Her light snore was almost on tempo with the film's score, even though with one particularly grindinginhale she had nearly woken herself. Her head lay snuggly with just the top resting on Solomon's left leg, leaving him unimpeded in his continuous and rather subconscious quest to finish off the last remaining half-popped, chocolate-crusted kernels.

As the animated military forces sat nervously at the foot of the gigantic, metallic alien automaton on screen, his fingers pinched a particularly delicious looking piece (the best kernels were those that had just a lip of white fluff peeking out from its only partially cracked shell) and the thought ambushed him like the bite of a mosquito: it was the first time in weeks, perhaps even months, that Solomon had genuinely felt like just a kid. He savored that realization for a long moment. By some unrecognized grace he had forgotten, temporarily at least, all about the live "television" he watched in the windows of the apartments across the street, about the chase through the city streets, and its climax at the church and most of all, in his

337

cartoon-addled, chocolate crusted euphoria he had forgotten there were such things as angels and demons. He knew this was the kind of innocence adults often moaned about with earnest longing but had not felt since childhood. That safe realm of grey were there was no good or evil, only raw emotion. When a child reached that age of accountability, when right and wrong were a ceaseless distress, that's when it became too late to turn back and sit on the sidelines. He had hit that some time ago, and, with wisdom beyond his years, had pined for it ever since.

And tonight, to slip back into that fond remembrance so easily…

…Solomon felt it. A sharp stab in the base of the spine, a tightening in his chest, a sudden chill in his lungs. It was considerably stronger, Solomon was not sure how he new that, but he did just the same. It brought a tangible weight and stagnation to the air. His mom began to cough in small fits. Perhaps she felt it, too. Putridity overpowered all other aromas as if rotting corpses had been buried beneath the floorboards. And it was smiling a ferocious victor's smile.

He should have felt dread, down to the core, down past the sugar coating of his child's mind and into the pit of his very soul in that place where every mortal man instinctively feels the hunger pangs of hell's feasting worms, knowing they waited for him. But he did not. What he felt was akin to shock; totally devoid of emotion. It was not a feeling that could be cast into a mold of opinion but something of pure, unshakable fact. This *thing* that was coming for him, it held title to him. It held claim.

That was the part of Solomon that had long since abandoned that archaic innocence. The part of Solomon that was as curious about the demons he watched toying with men as he was the angels that stroked their hearts.

The other part was still very much the child. Very much the slave to emotion in all its chaotic forms. And that part of him knew there was much to fear, not for himself but…

"Mom?" he slapped her shoulder rapidly. She stirred but would not wake outright. "Mom!" This time he grabbed her and shook her as violently as he dared.

She awoke with a start.

"Solomon!" She shook her head to throw off the chains of

weariness and blinked widely as her eyes tried to focus. "What is it?"

He wanted to respond, but his brain could not conjure a term to adequately describe the danger that approached. Even if it could his tongue would have floundered in the attempt. All he could manage was to look from her to the door in a quick panic, his eyes wide as saucers, giving his baby-smooth features an ugly, baroque makeover. Even still Traci was quick to pick up the message. She jumped up and ran towards the door, intent on locking it.

Knock, knock, knock.

Hearts, thought, and time all stopped. When bravery finally found some small hold, Traci slid backwards slowly, not wanting footfalls to betray their presence. But it was naïve to believe that just staying still in the near-dark—suddenly the television seemed as bright as a nova star—and keeping quiet would fool the visitor into just leaving. It was all so very déjà vu in the most horrific sense.

Knock, knock, knock.

The rapping at the door was unhurried and non-aggressive. Just a casual night-caller here to see how they have been or borrow a cup of sugar. Nothing important. Certainly nothing malicious.

Knock...

A slight pause.

Knock...

Slight pause.

KNOCK!

The last knock was a bomb exploding against the stillness. It was a hard, deep smack that punched them in the hearts and shook the very walls of the apartment like the footstep of a giant.

"Ms. Nicholas? It's Father Donovan. I really would like for us to talk." The voice was collected and even.

A sickening cocktail of fear, relief, and confusion seized her stomach, and she thought she might retch. Her motherly instinct reached an arm out to both confirm Solomon's presence behind her and to hold him back as if he might be safer those few inches behind.

"Traci, I really believe that things didn't go very well

between us, and I'd like to correct that. Won't you let me in?" The thin string that dangled that naïve hope of avoidance finally snapped under the weight of affirmation. He knew they were home, and he would not go away until his purpose was satisfied.

She turned to Solomon and was shocked by the sternness in his brow. When he looked up at her she mouthed, "Is it *him?*"

She did not specify whether she meant "is it really Father Donovan" or whether it was someone or *something* else. She did not even know why she was convinced that Solomon would know the answer. It was as if he were on some higher plane of consciousness. She could not understand how she knew, but she knew.

Solomon nodded gravely, and in that moment true panic set in.

She pushed Solomon firmly towards the back of the apartment. "Go to the bedroom and lock the door. Grab my cell off the dresser and call 9-1-1." When he did not move she snapped, "Now!"

As the boy set in motion towards the bedroom, the mother hurried into the kitchen.

She called back over her shoulder, "Do not open the door, no matter what!"

Reaching the kitchen she went straight for the knife drawer and pulled out the closest, largest blade she saw. It almost seemed to glow righteously and holding it made her feel powerful like a mother wolf, baring her teeth to protect her cub. Her eyes darted around for any other possible bright ideas and, in the space of only a second, could puzzle out none. She began to run to the back hall, intent on making her stand outside the bedroom door; the last barricade before her helpless son.

As she was halfway across the living room she heard another voice in the hall and its words stopped her dead, but simultaneously filled her with relief.

"Father Gregory Donovan? This is Sgt. Paul Kennedy, LSPD."

CHAPTER 63

"**G**regory Donovan, my name is Paul Kennedy, I am a member of your church," the Old Pro repeated.

Father Donovan had in no manner acknowledged their approach, he only stood facing the door to apartment 403—the very apartment they had been assigned to safeguard—as stiff as a scarecrow and considerably less lively.

The short hallway had dingy walls and was ill lit giving it a look Hollywood horror filmmakers would admire. Although it contained numerous fluorescent bulbs only two were to be working, one flickering sporadically. Paul could not help but question what kind of lowlife must maintain this slum.

"Are you here just to check up on them? Father?" Paul hoped this change in approach might break through, but it was only met with the same nothing so he tried to rise to his station. "Father Donovan, sir, I'm going to have to ask you to step away from the door."

Maybe it was the atmosphere, maybe the action (or rather *inaction*) of the man, or likely both, but without him choosing to do so Paul found his hand rested instinctively on the butt of his .45 Smith & Wesson as opposed to the tazer on the opposite side of his duty belt. He had listened numerous times as this man preached the word of God with such inspiring conviction. He had witnessed as he washed sins away in the baptismal pool. Now, in the claustrophobic confines of this dismal hallway, the man he had looked to as a spiritual leader filled his gut with an unreasonable terror.

And there was the unmistakable sense that there were more than the three of them occupying the hall.

"Sir, please step away from the door and over to us so we can talk." The Rookie also tried to sound stern but the tremor in his voice betrayed his own uncertainties. By strange standards that should have gifted the Old Pro with an ounce of reassurance, he saw the Rookie unsnap his holster and the slow curling of fingers around his .40, and that only made the terror more real.

"I take orders from no man, or even," venom rose in the priest's voice, and his mouth sounded thick with saliva, "vile serpents that walk upright on two legs. My orders come from the highest source. The hand of man will not," his mouth twisted in a beastly grimace, "*cannot* stay me."

And then, slowly, eerily, Donovan turned to them. As the dim light adorned his features the Old Pro could identify a few of the unnerving characteristics that he could not single out before. The priest's cheeks looked unnaturally hollow, especially in comparison to when he saw him only the night before, and— and maybe this was only a trick of the lighting—his skin had a grayish hue that, when combined with his stiff movement, made him appear a corpse. It was not like seeing a man; it was more like seeing a thing wearing the flesh of a man. The Old Pro could not help but remember old photos he had seen from the classic vampire film, *Nosferatu.* It seemed the most apt comparison even without the fangs or elongated fingers.

The priest spoke, "Has he sent you to try to stop me?"

Consuela? Paul thought. What was happening here?

The Rookie seemed more in control of his mental faculties and took the lead.

"Sir, step away from the door and lie down on the floor with your hands behind your back."

How did this escalate so fast? Paul wondered. He felt more passenger in this twisted episode than participant.

Donovan's head tilted down, but his gaze remained fixed on the Rookie.

"My duty is God's will and woe be to any who would oppose me."

The two hall lights flickered as he spoke. The very walls seemed to narrow as shadows appeared to stretch across them like snakes.

The Rookie drew his pistol. "Final warning! On the floor! Hands behind your back now, or I will be forced to shoot. *Do you understand?"*

Donovan's head reared back, his eyes widened grotesquely, and he shouted, *"Get thee behind me, Satan! For my purpose is divine and my conviction stone!"*

Paul drew his own weapon. Sweat beaded in his hairline and ran down his forehead.

"WILL YOU OPPOSE ME? WILL YOU STAND AGAINST THE RIGHTEOUS?" The priest's mouth became thick with foam like a rabid animal, flinging spittle as he cried out. A high pitch rode the top of his voice, violating their ears.

Both officers shouted back their own warnings. Their fingers danced nervously against their triggers. The lights flickered in a maddening strobe. Paul Kennedy pleaded for the man he admired to comply.

The priest took a single step forward before the Rookie opened fire.

CHAPTER 64

T he gunshots rang out, ushering in the end like exclamation points.

A friend with some slight knowledge of self-defense had shown Traci once upon a drug-addled time how to assume a fight-ready stance, and to her credit she tried, but with her fear induced muscle spasms it was all she could do to keep herself standing. There was a presence that enveloped the apartment like a poison cloud as if the real battle was not being waged in the hall, but in her soul. She felt the icy talons of an alien intelligence probing her mental walls, looking for any weakness, and that filled her with a dread that nearly stopped her heart. Her arms shook so violently that she nearly dropped the knife. To compensate she wrapped her left hand around the right and applied as much pressure as she could muster. *It* wanted her to feel helpless, and if not for her higher calling, had she not been a mother, it likely would have succeeded. But there was Solomon to think of, and her love for him was an unconquerable bastion. She would not yield to fear. She would not yield to the man in the hall. She would not yield to the creature in her mind.

Outside the officers were shouting. Although she could not discern their words it was clear that the priest had not been subdued by their shots. They sounded surprised. After all she had seen so recently, she was not. What they faced was not a man, at least not anymore, but an unholy abomination. An old hate in a brand new shiny man-suit. She had not liked Father Donovan after their confrontation in his office, but she did not believe it had been saddling him then, that it was directly to blame for how he treated them. She was somehow certain Solomon would have seen through it if so. Even still, no man deserved such evil be visited upon them.

A low, rolling thunder reverberated through the walls and the floor. The few pictures of she and Solomon that hung sloppily on the walls on thumb tacks swayed and soon fell, their glass shattering on impact. A growl, like a rabid wolf but impossibly deep, rose through the shaking. It sounded wet and sharp.

More shouting from outside and then gunfire. Judging from the duration both officers had likely emptied their clips, but their tones made it obvious that the bullets had proven utterly ineffective.

Words came to her mind and were born through her lips.

"Our father who art in Heaven, hallowed be thy name," she began, feeling much like a child trapped in impenetrable dark.

Running in the hall. The officers were charging the abomination.

"Thy kingdom come, thy will be done, on Earth as it is in Heaven." She continued, her voice shaking to match the rest of her. It sounded feeble, so very feeble, and the words both a bitter omen and claw at acceptance.

A heavy thump against her living room wall, like the smack of a body against it.

"Give us this day, our daily bread. Forgive us our trespasses as we forgive those who trespass against us."

A shout of defiance quickly turned into frantic pleading.

"Lead us not into temptation but deliver us from evil."

A blood-curdling scream of pain.

"For thine is the kingdom..."

A heavy smack against her door, accentuated by another cry of pain.

"And the power..."

Another slam, causing the doorframe to push loose and a crack to tear through the paint up to the ceiling. More pleading, from the sound of it, gargled by blood and tears.

"and the glory forever."

A third slam, the nails of the doorframe were exposed almost entirely. Her locking chain was all that held the door closed.

A hot tear rolled down her cheek. Something inside begged her not to finish her prayer, to leave it unfinished as if it was drawing the creature to her. But her mouth betrayed her.

"Amen."

The door exploded inward, amid the shower of splinters and chunks flew a dark blue shape. It crashed onto the floor and partially uncurled. It was a police officer. Even despite the blood streaking his face, Traci recognized him from the church crime scene though she could not remember his name.

Then *it* stepped through, calm and slow. The foul beast looked to be outgrowing its man suit. Thick veins bulged across its forehead and hands, and the blood seemed to have risen just underneath the entire surface of its skin. Its eyes were a hellish dark red, and its lips were pulled back and cracked. It did not look in her direction and for a fraction of a second she felt invisible. It crossed the threshold towards the fallen officer, and Traci noticed with fleeting relief the rise and fall of his chest. He coughed, throwing blood out and across his cheek. Two steps away from the officer the beast's head suddenly snapped up, and let slip an inhuman hiss at the window across from it. The thing's arms drew up to shield its face.

Another officer appeared in the doorway, leaning against it and favoring his right leg. He was younger, tanned and filled with rage. His bloodied left hand went to his duty belt and pulled out a dark cylinder. With a flick of the wrist that sent a shock of pain over his face, the cylinder extended into a full metal baton. He limped forward as fast as he could, seeming to favor speed over silence.

It mattered little. The priest began convulsing in such a wide and violent manner that she soon heard the snap of ribs. A stream of obscenities spewed from his lips, peppered with warnings and sacrilege.

The younger officer was almost to him and drew the baton back, planning to take out the priest's knees. The priest's torso spun completely around with the snap of more ribs breaking. He roared at the officer through a mouth that had opened impossibly long. Blood and bile splattered out at him. The officer shielded his face and swung blindly with the baton, but before his blow landed the priest dropped limp, and the baton hit solid on the side of his falling head, popping his jaw out of place.

This was no horror film; there was no false sense of safety. The air itself was becoming frigid rapidly. A relentless sound like the spastic beating of wings underlaid the continuing thunderous resonance. Mad screams echoed from all sides but so faint as to sound miles away. But she seemed to sense these things alone. The younger officer was still cautiously making his passage to his partner, but his eyes darted about hysterically as if expecting danger from any direction at any time. Just before he bent down to examine his partner a solid thud shook the floor as if something heavy had fallen to his left. There was nothing there but the physical shock of it upended a table lamp that had miraculously survived the previous tremors. The younger officer started and then hastened to aid his partner all while attempting to make the Catholic's sign of the cross and muttering "Santa Maria".

To her surprise the wounded officer rose with minimal help from his partner. His nose and mouth were bloodied, and he held his neck and right shoulder, likely from where he had impacted the door on the way in.

"We gotta get them out," the older officer winced and doubled over as he spoke, hinting at some internal pain or maybe bruising concealed by his clothing. At first Traci did not realize that she and Solomon were the contextual *them*.

"Ma'am," the younger officer had both he and his partner pointed to the destroyed entryway. He was helping his partner stand, but was soon leaning on him just as much for stability. "Where is your son?"

Traci could not will words from her throat, but managed to point down the hall behind her to the bedroom door.

"Can you get him and follow us outside? Backup is coming but we need to get out of here now."

As if to emphasize his point a large impact crater appeared in the living room wall just around the corner from her. The audible crash of it was highlighted by an otherworldly howl. Her knees buckled, and she nearly toppled.

This was infinitely worse than the church had been. They were caught in the maelstrom of a battlefield entrenched with unseen forces. They were defenseless. Utterly outmatched and with no concept of what was truly happening around them. Her inner bounds were broken, and her mind distanced itself from her body. Without its control she bore witness from a far off, lofty place, watching as her body acted on its own. It screamed, loosing the tide of terror and anxiety she had fought so hard to hide from Solomon.

The older officer ducked away from his partner reflexively at the sound of her shriek. His reasoning finally caught up, and he spun on his heals to ensure that his partner did not fall. When he was satisfied with the younger officer's condition (temporarily at least) he doubled back and nearly ran to her. After three steps he was stopped dead.

"We have not finished our dance." The voice rose over the thundering which began to trail away into silence. The body of the priest rose from the floor like a corpse being lifted on a hook. His torso faced the younger officer's back, his head the older, but his pelvis and everything below the opposite direction. Streaks of dark, almost black blood fell from his eyes like tears.

Traci's heart leapt to her throat which was dry and burning.

"Get them out!" the younger officer made this his battlecry as he pivoted halfway around and launched himself sideways at the abomination. It was a brave move, but brooked no gain. The priest caught him in its arms without looking and did not fall back as force and momentum under the laws of physics should have dictated. Instead it pulled the officer in close and slammed its mouth down on the officer's neck. The officer screamed in agony and the older officer cried "Paulie!" after him. The priest spun its body back around so that it all faced the same direction, as it did so it launched the younger officer through the living room window towards Ludlow Street four stories below.

"*NO!*" Traci and the older officer cried out in unison. The officer charged in recklessly, pulling his own baton as he did. All reason had abandoned him leaving only raw passion burning white-hot. It was a hero's assault: the doomed act of a man brave in dire circumstance. Brave *because of* it. Brave in his insanity. Brave because the soul knew what the mind refused: that escape was as impossible as victory.

The beast licked its lips at the officer's frenzied approach, smearing the blood it had drawn from his partner's veins. The priest's neck was now stained entirely red.

"Come to me!" It called in a voice made of two voices. One human though savage, the other something else entirely.

The officer's attack was heartbreakingly brief. He fought as if fighting a man—as if his reflexes and strength could be enough to dominate—but even his initiative failed him. His first swing was meant for the beast's knees hoping to topple it, and it landed solidly enough, but the knee did not give. He followed through with the force of his swing, dragging the baton across the left leg until its tip cracked against the right with the same ineffectiveness. He brought it high over his left shoulder then back across the priest's right cheek, again with no effect.

The beast took no time to mock or gloat. With blinding speed it reached up and took the officer's right arm by the wrist. One swift tug and the arm snapped backwards with a sharp crack. The officer cried out, but the world went silent in Traci's disembodied ears. All except for the sound of two heartbeats: her own and, through the void, Solomon's.

Solomon!

And just like that her mind rocketed back into her body.

She ran down the hall, turning her back to the fate of the noble officer who was surely about to give his life, and grabbed at the bedroom doorknob. It was locked. She had forgotten to expect this, but was proud of Solomon for remembering. She could hear him sobbing inside. She took two quick steps back from the door then rammed into it as hard as she could. She felt the doorframe buckle but it did not give. She reared back for a second attempt–

"Traci," The beast's dual voice called to her from behind. It sounded frighteningly close.

She turned slowly, leading with the knife. It did not shake. She did not shake. Her moment had come. She was Solomon's mother. She would not cower, no matter the foe. Her life at stake for her son. Her protection would be absolute. Unyielding.

It stood at the end of the hallway, seeming to take up its entire width. An unnatural shadow covered its face, but the white of its teeth shone from beneath the crimson they dripped. Even at a distance she could feel its icy breath. Gooseflesh rose all over her back and shoulders up the length of her neck. It held the officer by the throat, raised against the wall to its right. He was alive, but choking and kicking weakly. His eyes rolled back in their sockets.

"Do you know what is happening?" it asked quietly, in a single voice belonging to the priest.

"You can't have him." She replied, ignoring his query.

"Everything has changed. Everything. There is no more balance. No more salvation. Soon only dominance and damnation. This world we tread will burn will hellfire." It gave the officer a joyous smile. "Even death will not provide release. Heaven's gates have been sealed."

"You *cannot* have him." Traci repeated forcefully.

"He is mine. We created him, you and I. My seed, your lapse. We shared something wondrous did we not?" It chuckled. "You even believed I loved you."

"Why do you want him?"

Its answer bore true pride, "He is meant for great things."

"I am through with this," Traci took a bold step forward, "I am through running from you," and another, "whatever you may be," and another, "whatever face you might wear." The tip of the knife lead her down the short hall to it. It gleamed righteously. "Even if you're the devil himself you can...*not... have...my SON!*"

She stabbed forward at the heart of the beast, but in a blink it brought the back of the officer around into the path of the knife. Its blade penetrated deep with a wet kiss. He might have tried to cry out in his pain, but the beast's grip on his throat kept him silent.

The beast pulled the officer back with such swift force that it ripped the knife from her grasp. It rotated the officer around so that he was facing her, and for the first time she could read the name on his uniform.

KENNEDY.

The two locked eyes, the pain she had inflicted read clear, but she did not see accusation in them or animosity, only surprise and sorrow.

"His name is Paul Kennedy. He is a husband and father. Even a man of faith…" it cocked Paul's head to the side in its grip, "…as it were."

Paul was purple with lack of oxygen, and his mouth agape.

"No…" she managed to whimper. "Spare him."

"In trade for our son?"

Her head dropped. She could not look at Paul Kennedy, father and husband, as she answered. "No."

"I thought not." And with a minute flick of its wrist, it broke Paul's neck and let his body fall to the floor like a discarded ragdoll. In an instant all of Paul's hopes and dreams, his joys and might-have-beens were ended.

"What is your name?" she asked. The cold reality of her fate crept over her in a wave. She was not devoid of fear for her son, but saw and accepted that she was powerless to save him. And for that, she hated herself infinitely.

It answered in the other voice through the lips of the priest. "I am Uzahl."

"You're his father. Will you care for him?" the concept seemed unfathomably alien, but in these last moments of motherhood, it was the only thing she truly cared to know, one parent to another.

"I will teach him to burn down the righteous, as is his part."

"I hope God himself strikes you down."

Uzahl stepped over Paul's body to claim her. Its shadow stretched out and covered her, and inside that blackness all warmth was vanquished.

"Solomon," she said, loud enough for him to hear through the door, "I'm sorry. I'm so sorry."

She only wished she could have shed a tear.

"I love you."

CHAPTER 65

The silence was vicious.

Throughout the turmoil outside, Solomon sat at the edge of the bed and listened, the deceptively serene eye at the center of the tempest. If the apartment window had been his television, this room, cut off from the violence by the frailty of wood, was now his radio, and it played only one relentless song, a wartime ballad of the most gruesome nature. The oldest, in fact. The eternal war brought to you play by play one gut-wrenching battle at a time. And as the technology allowed, he observed all as an unscathed bystander, isolated in what remained of his innocence.

His ears strained to follow each melodic rise and fall as the conflict just outside his sight unfolded. The low muffled notes of the initial confrontation in the hallway between the demon and the police officers were quickly overpowered by the swirling violins and rolling timpani of their entanglement. Soon the violins crescendoed into a wicked frenzy that climaxed with a cymbal crash as the fight broke forcefully into the apartment. The next movement was ushered in by sour, enharmonic brass chords that lay hidden underneath until the violins quieted down to muted staccato strikes. It was the hand of suspense in the composer's foray. And then, just as the sustained enharmonics threatened to shatter the ear a high, bright octave of horns crashed over them like a golden wave. The police and his mom doubtlessly could not understand what was happening at that moment, and during that enflamed verse Solomon wished fully that he had had his television view.

They had charged in without warning—he was not sure what had drawn them into the fray, but he learned long ago that angels were ever-vigilant—and their front had caught the demon entirely off guard. There were twelve of them, radiant like morning stars and rabid in their intent. They fought bravely as one coalesced force, some assaulting directly, others feinting about to confuse, and the others attacked from within in an attempt to sever the demon from its human host. It was a maddeningly beautiful aria in which all the instruments were entwined. The sad, hopeful plight of the officers and the woman—here she was just a chorus member and not the one who had given him his life, physically at least, even if a baneful agent was part of the equation—danced aside the searing rage of the beast in its struggle with the small but determined angelic host. And juxtaposed within the chaos, the high, unheard tenor of the priest lamenting the malevolence of his corruption, only now realizing it was far too late to undo what his jealousy and ignorance had birthed.

As he listened, as far removed as the mind of his mother had become—both floated at such close proximity, but their lives would never again connect—he watched the magnificently savage onslaught of the angels. More than once they had pulled the demon nearly completely away from the priest—an act which none could have known would have ended the priest's life as his body lay twisted about the spine and sternum—and in the attempt had flung the demon into the realm of flesh where he would be significantly weaker. This part of the struggle resulted in physical impacts on the apartment walls, which had no doubt further frightened and confused the mortals around them.

It was a valiant fight, and had this been other, spiritually *normal* times, even the weakest of the angels' ranks could have bested the fiend. But the fundamental laws of the universe, those spiritual absolutes by which all things truly ran, were diluted or perhaps even dissolved, and the demon proved too much. It gained a sudden upper hand from which there was no turnabout, and in short order all twelve of the angels were vanquished.

Next the police officers had met their fate. The first was

flung from the apartment accompanied by a blasting choral hit, the second over the melancholy tremor of an oboe.

That left only one obstacle standing between the demon and the boy.

Solomon had fallen victim to no emotion as the passionate concerto played out. He remained an appreciative, though unaffected seat-filler. But as the oboe faded and finally gave up the soft ghost of its requiem, the music was silenced wholly and no longer did he hear. The child *felt*.

His mother. She was there. Alone and unprotected. She had taken one failed shot at breaking down the door to join him; whether she sought to protect him or die at his side even she likely did not know. She was outside reason.

…And scared.

…And so very ashamed.

Ashamed that it was her hand and her knife that had cut into the policeman and taken him from the lives of his loving family.

Ashamed that she was only mortal and incapable against this devil.

Most of all…*ashamed* that she accepted that she could do no more and had surrendered her most precious belonging, her only son, into the waiting hands of damnation.

He heard her voice for the last, bittersweet time.

She called to him.

"I'm sorry," she said earnestly. "I'm so sorry."

But it was "I love you" that finally broke him.

His lungs fought to breathe, and his throat burned for the air it was denied. His doe-like eyes stung despite the cool tears that escaped them. His hands reached in her direction, but the rest of his body refused to move from the bed. His mouth worked to form her name, the name she had given herself for his sake.

Mommy!

He had not called her that for a few years as he slowly matured, shortening it to the more sophisticated moniker of just *Mom* but now all pre-adolescent tenure fell aside, and the child underneath was crushed in its depravation.

The door lock turned over. The knob made a drawn-out quarter turn, and then the door opened inward in like fashion. The room was the last dying heat of the sun, the doorframe the dusk, and beyond it the carnivorous gullet of night within which he would be devoured whole.

A farewell to forlorn blessings; his father had come at last.

CHAPTER 66

The couch had been an unreasonably expensive purchase. Ok, sure it was fine Italian leather and, sure, at the time Jack's business had been experiencing a very profitable upswing. Sure, it was much more comfortable than it appeared and gave the formal living room an almost regal visual appeal. But to her, in truth, it had always served as a totem commemorating the Olympian rise of her husband's greed and ego. It was the first of many such totems that were bought for no other reason than Jack desired an air of wealth and success that oversold where he was at the time. He was getting there, his patient roster had received a monumental shot in the arm when the only real regional competitor he had—the young and flamboyant Dr. Herald Sears, DMD, who had just purchased the practice of Jack's former competitor, Dr. Gerald Tipton, DDS, as he passed into retirement—fell victim to the avalanche of outstanding debts and uncollected accounts left by his predecessor and soon elected to close up shop entirely and try his luck further north under the protective wing of his older brother, Dr. Jacob Sears, DMD. The series of unfortunate events had decimated the hopeful ambitions of Herald and, in the end, made Jack Edwards, DMD, king of the dental hill in the small rural community of Sherrington, West Virginia.

To celebrate he had bought this first totem, the unreasonably expensive, unrealistically comfortable couch on which Roxanne Edwards now lay under a thinning blanket, trying to sleep.

Roxie was a woman of simple tastes. Over the years many had commented on her humble country style, both in terms of décor and southern sensibilities. This couch was the antithesis of everything she was and liked about herself. Maybe *that* was the real reason she could not fall asleep.

Or maybe it was the guilt.

To be fair and precise the guilt was not her own. It did not spring from the nooks and crannies of her subconscious and therefore definitely did not feel due her. Jack had thrust it upon her. The decisions that had put them both in their current precarious situation had been his own and were made and acted out without her knowledge. Frankly she was dumbfounded that he had been able to pull off what he had without her realizing for so long. She had left her teaching career to serve as his office manager apparently just after the fraudulence had begun and now, lying here in the night, kicked out of her own bed, she questioned whether that was why he had fired Tina and brought her on board in the first place. He must have believed her gullible enough that he could falsify a small percentage of the claims without her being the wiser. It was a bold-faced slap; an insult to both her intelligent and their marriage. All things considered, she was glad he had slammed the bedroom door in her face, she would rather be on this miserable couch without his company than in the same bed with it.

But there was so much more right now to occupy her thoughts. The voice. Could it really have been him? After all these years…

If so then it was a sheer blessing that she had successfully persuaded Jack to not allow their home number to be changed when they had moved into this larger, cavernous home in Willowbrook Manor.

Wake up, Roxie, this gaudy castle is the real original totem. The others are just its babies.

But that voice, you could never forget a voice of someone you had known since the day they entered this world.

The initial shock of it had caused her to faint. When she woke Jack was kneeling over her, wearing genuine concern and then, when she sat up and assured him that she was ok, it was scorched away as the detestation returned, and he stormed away in his self-righteousness.

He did not even help her to her feet. And that told her everything she needed to know about where she stood. Or it should have.

She had avoided him the remainder of the evening, keeping herself occupied in one of the spare bedrooms that she had unofficially claimed as her office space. She sat at the plain, wood finish computer desk that was her single favorite piece of furniture in the whole house (she cherished it for its unspectacular simplicity) and tooled around the internet on her new laptop, wiling away the hours until bedtime, skipping supper altogether.

Around eleven thirty—Jack's routine bedtime—she poked her head out, thinking how much she must resemble a prairie dog at that moment, and when she saw the light on and door open at the far end of the hall she made her move. She crept across the maple floor of the hallway like a thief, sure that the slightest creak would rekindle his rage and cause him to slam the door before she could get inside. Truth be told she really did not have a game plan for once she *was* inside. At that point she figured she would just have to "wing it".

Only the room was empty. The master bath light was off, so Jack had already brushed and flossed, and his corner of the sheets had been folded over as was his ritual, but no Jack, which relieved her immensely. She began to unbutton her blouse and step inside, intent on retrieving a slip to wear to bed when she heard his heavy footsteps climbing the stairs. Her first thought was to run into the bedroom and undress quickly and try to climb into bed, naked if she must, before he could. That felt safer somehow, as if the bed were a haven wherein his anger held no prominence.

What she had not come to realize while picking herself up off the kitchen floor was that his anger was no hot flash that would be quenched by time and reason, it was lasting and inflammable. The heat of his stare said it best, he truly believed that everything that had so swiftly and unexpectedly gone wrong—after months of *his* misdeeds, mind you—could all be placed squarely and *solely* on her shoulders.

He stomped down the hallway like a kid on the verge of a tantrum and shouldered his way past her into the bedroom. She caught the complaint in her throat before it hatched and stood in the doorway silently.

Jack went directly to his nightstand and placed the glass of wine he'd been carrying—another nightly convention—on a coaster he had been using to bookmark the Chuck Hogan crime novel he had been reading of late. That done he came straight to her, never looking up, seeming to proclaim that the shame was just too great to bear, pushed her roughly into the hall, and then slammed the door inches from her face.

The tears had come immediately, despite her shock. She wandered around the house for the next fifteen minutes like a ghost in a tunnel with no light at its end. Once back in her office she opened the antique chest at the end of the guest bed and withdrew the weathered pastel blanket that her mother had made for her when she was three. On some subconscious level she was still functioning, but only enough to satisfy the most rudimentary needs: coverage and rest.

She ambled down the wide, winding stairs and turned towards the back of the house and the kitchen. The kitchen was a scene of modern beauty set against country comfort. The countertops and backsplash were a charcoal marble finish that balanced unexpectedly well with the Brazilian tile flooring. The back wall was entirely glass as to overlook the rolling hillside and forest acreage beyond the massive deck behind the house.

But none of that was of interest to her right now, only the memory of the red blinking light on the answering machine that now sat dark, as if denying it ever had anything to say.

The waning moonlight highlighted the prettiness of her round face. She had been quite the looker in her younger days, so it was said, but time and semi-luxury had added weight to her features making her look more like a mom, despite never having given birth.

The old grey mare she ain't what she used to be, she would hear a voice—a voice that was her own, but joyously far removed from the shackles of this marriage—in her head sing on those many occasions when he felt the need to slip in a seemingly harmless reminder of how her looks were fading. It added value to the summation that he must have felt that, with all his growing wealth, he deserved something—or some*one*—

more extravagant; a silent, subservient trophy wife who knew and appreciated just how good she had it.

After what could have been a few minutes or half the night, she shambled in her zombified state over to the totem upon which she now lay, slowly regaining her faculties.

Focusing on the voice had been a lifeline pulling her back to reality while the reality Jack had suddenly entrenched her in seemed more like a nightmare.

Please God in Heaven let me wake up from this!

But reality is reality, and it is often undeservedly harsh, especially to the gentle of spirit. She would not wake and find that the Insurance Commission was not investigating her husband while the State Board of Dentistry waited on their findings, ready to bring legal action against him. The blessing she received was that of distraction and soon after, a peaceful night's rest.

Her mind clung onto the sound of the voice. Ignoring the deranged animosity it had spewed and honing in on the pleasant familiarity in its opening tones.

As she slipped blessedly into a gentle rapture her thoughts were brief and simple: *My brother is still alive. Tomorrow I will start to look for him. Thank you, Lord, Jasper is still alive.*

CHAPTER 67

The cool night air whipped at Blowfish like a personal attack. As he sat on the edge of the pier it punished him for giving his coat and beanie to the floating stranger he had met here. The one that spoke to him in a voice that had plunged into the Deep Blue and for a time, at least, stilled its turbulent waters. But Blowfish did not regret having given his possessions away. He was made of sturdier fabric than the polyester coat, which had been given to him in the first place by a concerned volunteer woman at a shelter. It never felt like it belonged to him anyway, just borrowed and waiting to move on to the next needy soul. Life was a circle. If you provide to others, often others will provide to you. He liked the thought of that. It did not act like a mandate of karma, but something with a greater awareness. Something with breath and conscience. Something immutably divine.

He smiled proudly as the wind beat against the back of his head, sending the clumped, frayed strands of his hair whipping about his cheeks. He stared out towards the horizon, though it was invisible at this time of night, and wondered if he could see indefinitely in a straight line, to the lives of those on the closest shore, what would they be up to right now? Would he see a man and woman walking hand in hand on a beach? A child skipping stones into the obsidian sea? Or an unfortunate like himself kicking his dangling legs from a pier, feeling like the son of Poseidon?

With his back to the grinding gears of the world of man he was irrefutably free. Not enslaved by the calendars and demands of the clock, nor victim to inflation and taxation. He was a rolling stone, and wherever he chose to lay his hat, well, that was his home.

Too bad I gave up my hat, he laughed to himself.

A tinny crash ripped his attention away from the Pacific and back towards the dock yards. Maybe it was…no. Nothing.

His lip curled down in disappointment. He must have been here for a solid hour now, and still the Godfather had not shown. His stomach gurgled in confirmation. He was hoping to sit a spell and convene with his dearest friend. To stare across the ocean and stake their claims on lands unseen. To puzzle the stars in the sky and draw their portraits amongst the diamond twinkles. To eat heartily and laugh even more so. But his friend was a no-show, and his gut was sore about it.

The wind died down a bit, giving way to the soft symphony of the waves. He found his throat vibrating as it hummed a tune that had been haunting it tonight. The hum was fierce in its resolve and soon forced lyrics from his lips.

"Pleased to meet you," he whispered melodically, "hope you guess my name."

He stopped, having startled himself. He quickly surveyed all the moonlight would reveal of the docks, knowing she was there in the shadows, watching him, orchestrating him with her skeletal fingers across silvery puppet-strings. But no, she was not there, at least as well as he could tell.

To his shame he realized how completely he had come to fear Sylvie Crindle. She looked brittle enough to be blown apart by a stiff wind, but was certain that if she was, it would only be her skin that disintegrated revealing a nightmarish crone with flesh made of writhing snakes and a tongue of flame underneath. There was a word for her. *Evil*. It was as plain and simple as that.

She wanted him. For what he had no idea, but that she did was certain. Aside from Herschel he had seen her weave herself about the lives of the others of their community. After each encounter with her a person seemed to shift slightly into a more volatile personae. In one particular instance Blowfish had seen

Sylvie whisper to Motor-Mouth Gillespie, and soon he stomped over to Shirley May's shopping cart, screamed something at her about being a thief, flipped her cart and started ransacking her belongings. When Shirley protested Motor-Mouth had actually struck her! Shirley ran off with a bloody lip. Motor-Mouth never found what he had supposedly been searching for, but somehow Blowfish knew that was never the point. Sylvie had vanished before the altercation took place, but deep down he was certain that things had played out exactly as she wanted. She was a virus to the body of their community; oil floating on the surface of his Deep Blue. There was a growing certainty within him that soon something would have to be done about her, and he feared that the duty may fall squarely on his shoulders alone.

As hard as he tried he could not even remember exactly how she had first come into their collective lives. He remembered that she was just suddenly there, moving about outskirts of their hobble like a carrion bird circling over a dying animal. As time progressed she drew in closer and made herself more a part of them, but she had never told her history and none had ever asked.

She was the dark end of life's spectrum, and at the other he envisioned the floating man. Only, he had already forgotten the man's face. His brow crimped as he attempted to paint the man's features in his mind. He saw familiar, kind eyes and a sheepish smile. Dark hair that stretched down his jaw to frame his face. Wait…that wasn't…

The face snapped to sharp focus, only it was not the floating man at all, but the young man at the convenient store. What had his name been? Tony maybe? Andrew? He could not remember. Besides, to a man called "Blowfish" what was in a name really?

He put his back to the ocean and drew his legs in Indian-style. The golden skyline shown majestically over the dock warehouses, but his view of the streets was entirely obscured. He scanned the skyscraper and apartment windows slowly even though they were too far away to reveal what lay behind them, but he took them in one at a time and postulated that that generous young man had made his life in one. Maybe a lush high-rise apartment brimming with expensive décor and livened with the merry voices of friends or perhaps a spacious office from which he had wrestled a healthy income from an increasingly tightfisted economy. The young man had not looked overly wealthy, but maybe that just meant he was humble enough not to flaunt his good fortune.

He laid back onto the pier, stretching his complaining legs out and cup his hands underneath his head. Another image came to him. The young man was there, but the "where" itself was difficult to make out. Ghostly images of people fluttered by, but the young man stood out with a pleasant degree of clarity. He could remember being upset but not why. He could remember a woman's voice. Something so warm about her, but that too was lost to him. She seemed important somehow, and that alone was worth consideration. That is, if it was not just some dream he was recalling. Even if it was, so what? It gave him comfort in a world that had given him little. He liked the thought of the young man standing by him like an angel on his shoulder. Yes, he liked that very much. It made life seem like more than a chain of tragedies. Maybe there really was something higher up there.

Grinning, he let that thought carry him into sleep.

CHAPTER 68

Kenneth was up again, racing to the bathroom against the bile rising from his stomach. It was halfway up his throat, and he had only just leapt from bed. His right foot slid on a small puddle just inside the bathroom that was likely water from the last time he had had to clean up after himself, and he nearly went down but managed to catch himself on the doorframe. That delay, however, cost him everything and before he could properly regain balance and continue the bile filled his mouth, gagging him. He coughed which forced his mouth open, and vomit exploded across the bathroom. He doubled over quickly to keep the rivers of it that ran down his chin from dripping onto his silky maroon pajamas.

Sharon was up immediately, woken from the violent upheaval of his flight.

"Oh baby," her concern was the very definition of "heartfelt", "my poor baby." She was at his side in seconds, one hand around his waist to help him balance and the other rubbing sympathetically on his back.

He raised a hand to assure her he was okay and then took a testing step towards the commode. With the step his confidence increased, and he took another, even daring to straighten a few degrees. He hacked wetly as he staggered, Sharon staying with him the whole way before helping him be seated.

She knelt to his eye level then examined his face thoroughly.

"Ken, you look absolutely deathly," she said, wiping at the beads of sweat on his forehead.

The burning in his throat prevented speech so he tried to turn his head and wave her assessment away with a weak flapping of his right hand.

"Don't you dare," she snapped gently like a mother who would not be told no by a child yet refused to scold, "I'm calling Dr. Castle, and that's the long and short of it." She stood and made to leave, calling back to him, "I should have hours ago."

This was the third time Kenneth Phelps had frantically left the bed to vomit since they laid down and the tenth time he had vomited that day. He had suffered acid reflux throughout his adult life, but this was something deeper in his body, a sickly churning that would heed no rest. Sharon had fought ardently with him about calling Dr. Castle after he had fainted hours ago and had allowed Ken to talk her down, but now nothing on this Earth could stop her from making that call for the sake of the man she loved.

She understood what was gnawing at him and shared his sorrow. She had tried to stay awake with him in bed, knowing he was not likely to slumber. But as is the way, the harder you try to stay awake, the quicker you fall asleep, and Sharon was out in less than forty minutes.

Kenneth had laid with his back to her, which he was not custom to do, staring blankly at the wall between the closet and master bath. Disillusionment swam in his stomach like a living thing, batting at its walls, bringing its contents to a boil. And through the minutes that slowed into unforgiving hours one thought reverberated within the hollowness of his heart, *What's the point?*

The day's events floated by with all the impact and reality of a sitcom, though there was little that had occurred. Mostly he had sat in his office chair like the waking dead, nearly unblinking. Sharon had brought him a plate of food—hangar steak dripping with merlot butter and sautéed green beans, his favorite—but he did not seem to notice and never touched it or the water she set with it.

Around 7:30pm when the station's owner, Ansel Kramer, had called, Sharon had answered, held the phone out to Kenneth, and was surprised when he took it. She stood silently, hoping to overhear the one-sided conversation, but could glean little. Kenneth sat there silently, his head swaying slightly as if his neck was at a loss for strength, and on the occasion gave a simple "yes" or "no". When the conversation ended he handed the phone back out to her without pressing to end the call. She bit back the urge to ask what was happening.

She did not need to, however, and after a few quiet breaths he told her anyway.

"There's a rumor coming down the wire that I'm being investigated. Chief Leftwich called Kramer personally to warn him. Advised him to distance himself and the station from me until things get sorted."

A hand went to her heart.

"Investigated? For *WHAT?!*" the words jumped from her throat louder than she had intended, and she blushed both in anger and embarrassment.

"He wouldn't say." Kenneth's eyes were dead. His jaw tense and pulled back, its muscle flexing unconsciously. "He said he had faith in me that this would blow over, that I couldn't possibly be involved in what they are saying, but I don't think he meant that. I think he believes I am."

Her compulsion was to berate him for not asking what the accusations were and she felt ashamed for it. But that's how she was when anything or anyone threatened him. She was fierce in her defense and would always remain so.

Instead she managed to ask, "Are you supposed to call the police? Are they supposed to contact you?"

He shook his head slightly to say he did not know.

She folded her arms and searched for what to say. Again, he beat her.

"It doesn't matter. It's insignificant now."

Her heart shattered. She stepped forward and reached for him, but he stood and walked out of the room.

The remainder of the day they barely spoke. He treated her like a phantom, like a wisp of air and noise. He was not angry with her, but her comfort conflicted with the spiral he had welcomed into his mindscape. So, she became an obstacle that he skirted right up until she made for bed.

He had retreated to his office knowing she would not follow. Around 11:00pm she knocked softly then opened the door enough to put her head in.

"I love you, Ken. I will be in bed if you need me." She laced her words with reserved sweetness. *Please need me.*

She closed the door just as softly then walked the lonesome stretch down the hall to their bedroom. She opened the drawer to her nightstand and pulled out her back-up stash of Prilosec—she and Kenneth both would sometimes forget to take them throughout the course of their busy days, so she always kept a box by the bed—popped a pill through the silver casing and bit down on it, once again hating that she had never learned to properly swallow pills and therefore had to chew and suffer through every disgusting bite. She went to the bathroom sink and filled the small cup she kept there with enough water to wash the taste down with a little extra to rinse her mouth and throat thoroughly. The after-taste dying from her mouth she made her way to the bed and began clearing it of decorative pillows.

The door came ajar. Kenneth stood just outside its frame, head turned down, hands in his pocket. Sharon's heart warmed considerably, and she let it show with a tender smile. It brought him across the threshold to her. He placed his strong arms around her and drew her as close as their bodies would allow. His heartbeat was slow but reassuring against her ear, and she let herself sink deep into his embrace.

"I love you so much, Sharon Phelps," and he kissed the top of her head.

She looked up at him, water playing at the corners of her eyes. "And I love you. So, so much."

He kissed her full and long. Tears escaped down her cheeks and ran the lines of her jaw until they adorned his chin. Feeling them he broke their kiss and wiped them from her face before bringing her back to his chest. His heart seemed stronger.

When they split he went to the closet and changed into the maroon silk pajamas that she had given him last Valentine's Day. It was a small token but it gifted a measure of hope. They climbed in bed, kissed once more then he pulled away, kissed her forehead tenderly and rolled his back to her. She realized then that the strength he had found had only been for her benefit, and the worry that wrought settled into her chest until she lost the battle to sleep.

Now he sat on the commode, the last vestiges of his hope and possibly his sanity rolling off him like a mist as his tongue absently licked the bile from the backs of his teeth.

Sharon came back into the room, cellphone to her ear.

"Thank you very much, Dr. Castle, I can't tell you how much I appreciate this." Then she hung the phone up and set it on the corner of the sink. "He'll be here as quick as he can."

Kenneth nodded, at least he tried to, how much his body obeyed he was not sure.

"I don't..." Kenneth tried to speak but the dryness of his throat sent him into a coughing fit. Once over he swallowed in an attempt to wet his throat with saliva. Confident in his success he continued quietly, "I don't know what's going on at the station, but..."

"Shhh..." Sharon knelt in front of him again, taking his face in her hands and stared into his soul. "Whatever it is, you'll beat it. You know and I know there's not a thing in this world that you've done to deserve this treatment."

He kept quiet, staring intensely back.

"You are a man of integrity. A man of *God.* And I don't care what anyone has told you, that means something. You're here and I'm here and that *means* something."

She bent down and kissed his knee before laying her head on it. Her right hand rubbed his leg.

"If we have breath we have hope. Both for this world and the next. I don't intend to sit idly by and believe there's no reason to carry on. I won't resign myself to such helplessness." She kissed his knee again. "And neither should you."

She let out a sigh and stared at the tile floor.

"It's going to be ok," she assured them both, "somehow."

She wished she believed it.

CHAPTER 69

Father Joseph Behanan sat at his desk staring at his laptop with the bewildered surety of an innocent man trudging to the gallows. His thickly padded headphones sat on the desktop beside the laptop spilling The Who's "Behind Blue Eyes" out into the air. The air in turn seemed to devour it before its waves could echo from the walls. His office never seemed so empty. Like a home full of children whose father had slipped away in the dead of night. Only the father did not willfully leave, he was taken. By aggressive means. But in the end, what was left behind remained the same broken home, its hopes and happiness stolen from it.

So many disbeliefs jockeyed for room in his crowded head, the winner being that how was he, was any of this, any of it at *all*, still here? In the morning the congregation would come for mass. They would be expecting words of encouragement, but how could he bless them with such false hope? If you plucked the heart from a thing, should not that thing die? Even if that thing was everything?

It brought him to the brink of madness. He remembered hearing once that if you think you are going mad, then you are still sane enough to do something about it. Wise words, at least in a different time.

He took his aching eyes from the screen and rested them behind their lids. In this self-inflicted darkness there seemed to

373

be nothing around him. He could feel his weight pushing down on his chair, and even though they rested side by side on the floor, his feet felt at entirely different heights. It gave him vertigo.

He blinked his eyes open and looked at his feet, the funhouse effect lingered, but his sight gave him tether. He noticed the carpet fibers, like caterpillars standing at attention, but his mind saw past them, seeking to peer beneath the carpeting and the floor, and all it could picture was nothingness so black and abysmal it gave him a sense of floating. He was just hanging in the air, waiting for the grand plummet.

His breath caught, and he stood quickly to abate the dread washing over him. He walked around his desk and began pacing a tight circle. Books on his shelves. Church events. Faces of his congregation. He concentrated on them all in turn, needing them to beat back the panic.

A light-grey paperweight sat at eye-level on one bookcase, a gift from his father when he ran track back in high school. It was in the form of a basketball sitting on what appeared to be a rock with one face smoothed out with the words, "You'll always miss 100% of the shots you don't take" etched into it. His father had given it to him before the state meet of his junior year, laughing about the inappropriate basketball, and saying it was the only thing he could find that said what he wanted to say. Joseph had taken it gladly and often read it as a reminder to push forward through odds that appeared to be insurmountable.

A thought flashed over him, and he checked the clock sitting on his desk.

It was so late, but he had been promised long ago that late was *never* too late, and so he made the call.

It rang with all the subtly of gunfire. With each ring he winced, regretting having dialed. After the fourth ring, before the answering machine would pick up, he pulled the phone away to hang it up-

"Hello?" the tired voice greeted, concerned but not unkind despite the hour.

Slowly Joseph brought the receiver back to his ear.

"Dad?" he asked needlessly.

"Joseph," a smidge of relief graced his father's tone, but only a smidge. "You alright, son?"

Joseph released the breath he did not realize he had been holding.

"Yes, I...I..." he stumbled, knowing his father would pick up on it and bit his lip in aggravation, "I'm fine dad."

Fine. The universal word for "not fine at all."

"No you're not, Joseph, I can hear that. And not at this hour."

He conceded, "Yeah, not really."

"Hey, son?"

"Yeah, Dad?"

"I love you, son."

Peace came over him. It was the gentle way in which his father wielded compassion, disarming all the negatives that had burrowed into his chest. It always made the son feel like a child and grateful for it.

"I love you too, Dad."

"Ok, Joseph," Jameson Behanan brought their conversation to an early, quieted ebb, "tell me what's getting at you. You don't sound urgent, but gotta tell ya, that almost makes me worry more."

Where to begin? Or even how to?

"It's almost...wow..." was he really going to say this out loud? To his father, the Reverend?

As his consciousness rolled upon itself like an enraged sea categorizing and sifting through the network of information and possibilities within, his subconscious busied itself with his hands upon the laptop, clicking the internet icon. His email opened before him, the newest a message from Kenneth Phelps. Its subject line read, "Goodies You Wanted". He clicked it without looking. The laptop suddenly blinked to a telltale sky blue with the words SHUTTING DOWN in dead center next to a spinning cursor. This was probably bad, but it held little importance for now.

Half–aware he continued, "It's almost a crisis of faith, in a way." The most garbled, misrepresented understatement in the history of man had just passed his lips.

"Crisis of faith or of mastery of the English language, son?"

The unexpected joke caught him flatfooted and bringing Joseph to silence. Finally the tension broke like a levy, and he erupted with laughter. So did the phone.

He needed this. Score one more for the Rev.

Joseph sat back down in his chair, his feet feeling equal and thus, satisfied.

"I'm in my office, working on tomorrow's sermon–"

"At this hour?" The Reverend broke through.

Joseph nodded before he replied, "Yeah, it's a long story. Some things have..." what was the word? "*happened* lately, and I don't think Greg's going to be here in the morning for mass."

"Greg? Is that–"

"Yes, Father Donovan, he's not been...Dad, I'm going to be straight with you, something's *bad* wrong with him. I don't really know how else to put it."

The Reverend's voice hailed from a different plane where laptops were of equal consequence as dust mites. "How so? This got anything to do with the Vatican bombing? Such a terrible, terrible thing." Jameson Behanan held little esteem for the Catholic doctrine, but the sympathy in his voice was sincere and unmistakable.

Joseph hadn't considered that. Was it related? The destruction of the Vatican could have possibly overloaded Donovan's already overstressed psyche in some way. He decided to shelf the concept for now in lieu of recanting recent events.

As he opened his mouth to speak the laptop came back to life as if defibrillated, the word UPDATES managed to catch his attention. But his father's voice called his name from that other place and brought him back to their conversation.

Joseph began by telling him of the incident in the sanctuary, of Traci and Solomon and the man who pursued them and his subsequent death. He told him about being shut out by Donovan the following morning and Traci's rage before storming off. As he discussed the evidence, it all seemed so insignificant in contrast to his worries, but Jameson listened patiently, giving an *mmm hmm* when appropriate to signify he was keeping up.

When Joseph finished, Jameson asked, "And you think he's suspecting something of you, right?"

Joseph was relieved that his father had deciphered the moral of what, to him, was a convoluted tale.

"Yes. But not that he thinks I had something to do with that man's death. It felt like...jealousy."

"Hmmm."

Joseph kept quiet, letting the wheels in his father's head turn.

"I know I told you this a long time ago, but it bears repeating. A man of God is just that, a man. As mortal, imperfect, and emotional as a wild animal sometimes. But being a man of *God* puts a target square on a man's back. Sometimes it's just the added pressure from being the one people look up to and expect to see living a perfect, Christ-like existence, and sometimes it's like the devil himself wants to ride you into the ground. And some men get so caught up in their title they forget who gave it to them. It's a tightrope walk, every single blessed day, son, but for those of us called to do so, it is an honor without compare. Isn't it?"

Joseph could just see the crooked half-grin on the other end of the line.

"Yeah it is."

"And we push on through trying times. Out of our faith in the Lord. Out of our duty to our church and its members. Out of righteous stubbornness. We push on, Amen." Even in the wee hours with his son the good Reverend was preaching. Glory, Hallelujah!

"Do you trust the man, Joseph?"

"Yes, Dad, I do." That bordered on being a lie. The difference between believing something and wanting to believe it with all your heart.

"Do you have faith in him?"

"I think so." That was more precise, closer to honest.

"Let's pray for him, son, right now."

Joseph closed his eyes, bowed his head and listened, taking in his father's words, filtering them through his heart and redirecting them to the Heavens as if they were his own. Jameson Behanan prayed for Gregory Donovan. Prayed he would show wisdom. For guidance and understanding. For open lines of communication and clarity for his son.

Joseph remembered these words fell not on deaf ears, but on no ears at all.

As his father continued to pray for Donovan, the defenses

that Joseph had tried so hard to rebuild, abandoned him completely. He fell to his knees, his back only remaining vertical due to the chair cushion's support as it rolled back to hit the bookcase behind it. His hands shook so violently he dropped the phone, but the prayer continued uninterrupted as he bawled silently. Every word that drifted up from the receiver added to deception he now held: not telling his father that the faith was worthless now, without a Lord to receive it. That the prayer he spoke was moot. Never in his life was he so convinced that he was betraying the man he loved more than any other. It stabbed to the heart of him.

"Son?"

Joseph shook his shoulders and arms, trying to regain control.

"Joseph, are you there?"

Joseph wiped the drip from his nostrils and corner of his mouth and steeled himself as best he could before picking the receiver off the floor.

"Yes." He managed with care. Any more might give him away.

"Listen, son, I'm old, and I got service myself tomorrow, so I'd better get back to my bed. You do what's left for you to do, and then you get you some rest, alright?"

"Yes."

"Alright, son. I love you, Joseph. And I'm proud of you. I hope everything works out. I'll keep on praying for you both, ok?"

"Ok."

"Goodnight, son."

"'Nite, Dad. I love you." His words trembled, so he hung up before he could be found out.

He wept until his body had shed its last tear. Until he was exhausted into a state of numbness. And that's where he found clarity. In the words of his father.

We push on.

Joseph climbed back into his chair, a new fire blazing inside him, and instead of continuing where he had left off at the rambling beginnings of the misguided sermon he had begun to write, he opened a new blank document. Despite the weariness that assaulted his muscles and watered his eyes, he pushed on through the night, finishing his sermon, back stiff with determination.

He reflected how glad he was that he actually made the call. Their exchange had made a world of difference. If he had known it would be the last time they ever spoke, he would have said so much more.

CHAPTER 70

It was the end of the beginning.

Heaven's walls were alight with chaos, a nigh infinite storm mass that, instead of lightning, bore twisting and stabbing streaks of flame that roared loud enough to deafen those embattled within. Waves of smoke tipped in red crashed in all directions. The roiling sea: the clashing of two armies undulating inward and outward as if the pulsating heart of a beast spilling its blood over both sides of the walls. Brilliant flashes erupted throughout the turmoil, each signifying an angel's defeat as he was ripped from existence.

At the epicenter of the struggle two figures, locked in combat on the ramparts, shone so bright as to cast all around them in shadow. It was the final strokes of their conflict, and in the next hard-won moments, Lucifer would fall.

Circled around them like a floodwall the lieutenants of Heaven fought against those who would soon and hereafter be crowned princes of Hell. At the edge of the skirmish, the angel Athiel stabbed and swung, parried and feinted and wept as one by one his brothers fell beneath his blade. They came at him from all sides in numbers he never would have guessed nor would ever forget. So many had joined in Lucifer's cause. So many had declared feud against the love of the Father. Their blasphemy enraged him beyond measure. Each strike was double-edged with thundering justice and searing remorse. But his was Heaven's cause, the glory of the Lord, the charge of love all-encompassing, and so his blade thrust and destroyed.

As the archangel Michael pressed his final advantage over the Great Deceiver, another force fought through the thicket of his brethren, seeking to take Michael unawares from his flank. He was a swift, unyielding wave of devastation that washed over his weaker siblings. Athiel spied his approach from the bursts of light that resulted in the many deaths he wrought and moved to cut short his advance. The path was swift but hard-fought and soon Athiel stood directly in his brother's way, sword held out in warning. The angel cut through two others that charged his flank without even a glance; his massive blue-flamed sword severing them both from existence in one mighty arc. There was a moment of recognition on both parts that bled into pangs of love, now overcast with the weight of the purpose that each had chosen to champion. And when that hesitation burned away, their contest engaged.

Athiel was smaller than his foe, but held the advantage of speed which he used to great effect in evading each heinous blow. He feinted left then stepped right while spinning and bringing his sword around in a high arc towards his opponent's exposed neck, but with his left hand the angel caught Athiel's wrist and yanked his sword arm wide leaving Athiel vulnerable. As the angel brought his blade in a perfect horizontal swing, Athiel kicked his legs back, bring his body up with them, and the blade passed a hair's width underneath. Athiel swung back down and through the open leg stance of his foe. As he did so he spun in a furious, tight spiral managing to wrench his hand free from the stronger angel's grasp. He passed underneath the angel and scored a weak slice in the angel's inner thigh. Athiel's feet continued to arch upwards lifting him upside down, and as he continued his wild spin he extended his blade, slicing several fiery slits into the angel's wings and beheading another rebel whose own struggle had brought him too close to Athiel's attack.

The opposing angel's lion head roared, and its wings whirled in a thin cone that caught Athiel's blade, stopping it cold after it scored deep cuts. The angel spun around to face Athiel, and as he did his wings ripped the sword from Athiel's hands. He caught Athiel by the throat and flipped him right side up, bringing them face-to-face. Athiel clawed and kicked furiously and even though the angel stumbled, he would not release him. His wings came up and curled around Athiel's head, blinding him but Athiel could feel the heat of the angel's blade as its tip set against his chest.

Over the roar of the battle around them Athiel heard soft words spoken, "Forgive me brother, for I love you." The blade pulled back from his chest as the angel readied the killing thrust-

-there was a great boom that echoed in sound and force and light. It crashed through the armies, and all fell to their knees. The wings fell away from Athiel's head, and the two found themselves shoulder to shoulder on bended knee. Michael's sword blazed with the light of the Throne itself as he held it high like a beacon in the storm. For a moment there was not but silence and awe.

Then in a voice that thundered throughout the Heavens, and the virgin Earth below, Michael commanded, "Wicked creature, abomination to His name, I cast thee out!"

Lucifer screamed, a shrill plea that was echoed by each traitor that had taken up his banner. The angel before Athiel was no different. Fire etched growing tendrils across the angel's eyes moving towards their center. His skin began to darken as if his holy light was being drawn in. There was a building sound like a colossal, furious wind that soon overtook the screaming. The angel's skin began to crack and flake. His hair was blown back by that terrible gale force that Athiel himself could not feel.

Close by Lucifer erupted into a churning pillar of dark flame whose ends trailed off into nothingness in both directions. Athiel's opponent and all the other rebels were being pulled towards it. The angel reached a hand out to Athiel for help, but his hand crumbled list dust and was sucked away into the pillar. Fiery tears streamed from his eyes and were likewise taken and consumed.

The angel, Ter Greiel, lifted his head and cried out across the width of Heaven to the Throne, "Father forgive me!" and then he broke apart in a puff of ash and fell away into the pillar.

Michael's sword, still held high, waited until all rebels followed suit then came down and cut through the column. There was a flash of stygian black across the breadth of the battlefield and then, the pillar and those within, rocketed down out of the realm of Heaven into the bowels of exile.

Athiel fixated on the length of chain held out before and in its dull gleam, remembered these events as if they were recently lived. Their spell broken, he summoned his sword and yanked the chain. Ter Greiel nearly fell but managed to catch himself with his palms. Athiel brought the hungry edge of his blade to rest across the top of Ter Greiel's head. Its flames bore a shallow trench in the prisoner's flesh, but Ter Greiel did not pull away.

"I recall you, betrayer."

"And once embraced me as brother." Ter Greiel remained submissively bowed.

Juriel stood silently but his own blade danced at the ready.

"You would have destroyed me then had Michael been delayed his victory."

"I hesitated. A decision I only now have come to appreciate."

Athiel's fury was swelling. He rocked the blade, so that it parted the flesh.

"You would have me believe you awarded mercy? Even now you play the role of Lucifer's wretch!"

"No!" the denial was sudden and forceful, but Ter Greiel's head remained low. "Forgive me, I have thought over my actions for millennia yet even still my regret struggles with my pride."

Athiel put the sword under Ter Greiel's chin and lifted his head so that their eyes met.

"You could have killed me already. Tell me, castaway, what is your intent?"

The growl building in Ter Greiel's chest was cut into syllables as if he were fighting for breath.

"Redemption."

Both Athiel and Juriel were taken entirely aback. Their swords lowered to the ground. Very cautiously Ter Greiel stood, but even that slow act was enough to startle Juriel back into a ready position. Athiel, on contrast, remained limber.

"You know He will not welcome you back. You are skinned with your transgressions and will forever remain an exile." Athiel said, matter-of-factly.

"He is gone from us." Juriel cut in before Ter Greiel could reply.

Athiel turned to him.

"In what manner?"

A trembling fit ran throughout Juriel as he prepared himself to speak.

"He has been slain."

"That is impossible."

"It is true. Can you not feel His absence?"

Athiel cast his eyes down. "I have not felt Him in many years. I stepped away from His grace, and He has forgotten me." Athiel knew that with the Lord "forgotten" was a word used only for sins once they had been cleansed and were a part of man no more. It was not the word he wanted to use, but it best represented how he felt. Athiel noted that Ter Greiel had not been caught equally unawares by the claim.

"You believe this as well," Athiel asked, "that He has been killed?"

Ter Greiel raised his arms so that the chains might bear his witness. "I know only that He does not sit on His Throne." He then fixed Juriel with a rueful gaze. "Though I will not believe such incongruous claims."

Juriel stepped towards them both and stated his case, attempting to fell Ter Greiel's accusation of false witness.

"Before you arrived in the park I had been counseling with our brethren. We all felt how faint our knowledge and grace has become. It is dying from us. Many have heard demons speak of our Father's death, and they continue to grow in strength and tenacity. We are NOT what we were. Our wings will not carry us home, although none could remember the way. We are locked onto this plane. I have felt *fear*. Fear like man experiences. And worry." His eyes darted back and forth to each listener, gauging their thoughts. "These are not of our nature! Our power is vastly limited and does not renew. We are failing."

His conviction vanished in an instant as if tossed away by a wind. His head hung loosely on his neck. He looked ready to surrender.

"You may not feel these things, either of you. You abandoned His grace long before."

A look between them acknowledged that both Athiel and Ter Greiel agreed with this conclusion. Athiel held his gaze longer, evaluating the being he once had fought and before that he had called "brother".

"If you knew of this, how then do you expect to be redeemed?" he asked outright.

"I do not know. I can only make the attempt."

"If the Father is dead, as we are hearing," he briefly turned back to Juriel, "though without the full measure of proof," then back to Ter Greiel, "then none can forgive you.

You are beyond redemption and would be better served returning to your master's breast."

Ter Greiel lunged forward so suddenly that Athiel could not evade. He seized Athiel by the shoulders, holding him firmly but without real malice. The words he spit came to Athiel through hot and foul breath.

"I do not serve the Deceiver! I was not cast beside him into Hell! I was condemned to the Pit of Tartarus to suffer and indulge in my pity! To spend eternity in darkness accompanied only by the echo of my screams." His fury spent he released his grip and stepped back.

Juriel's blade stood tall with threat. Ter Greiel gave it only a flick of the eyes then regarded Athiel once more.

"Had I been sentenced to his side I may have indeed followed him willingly. I rejoice that I was not." His fingers drug across the iron threads that sealed his eyes and lips. "That I was not gives me hope."

Juriel, voice thick with disgust, asked, "What hope do you entertain?"

"That in His way, He was showing me His capacity to forgive. That if ever I was freed I could return to beg for it. And should He allow, earn it."

Athiel asked, "He freed you, then?"

"No." Behind the iron threads his eyes turned considerably darker. "It was by the hand of man."

"That is beyond all possibilities! Mankind could never find Tartarus, let alone traverse it. And even if a means was found, the Lord would *never* allow such a thing!" Light peered from Juriel's gaping mouth and corners of his eyes as he shouted, and his arms trembled passionately.

"As you have said, the Lord is gone from us. He can bar no

one." Ter Greiel's reply was calm, almost a whisper.

"Blasphemy!" This was nearly a scream, and the light that had been threatening to escape exploded through his surface, engulfing them all. Before it could clear Juriel charged in, sword high overhead. He managed to catch Ter Greiel off guard, but in his haste swung early and instead of landing a killing blow, he cut long but shallow across the prisoner's chest. Juriel spun vertically with his follow-through, but Ter Greiel was no longer flatfooted. Ter Greiel sidestepped the swing and flung his arms forward, the chains attached to them shot out and seemed to lengthen as they wrapped about Juriel's waist, pinning the angel's arms to his side

"I will see you undone this day, betrayer!" Juriel cried.

Ter Greiel's low growl reverberated like grinding stone, and the chains began to shake in echo and glow red hot. Juriel let out a pained scream.

"Enough!" Athiel called out as he reached forward and took the nearest chain in both hands. Underneath his stone exterior there was a hint of disbelief in the set of Ter Greiel's jaw as the chains became dark and cold. Ter Greiel eased the tension in his arms, and the chains fell from around Juriel and shrank back to their former length. Juriel was on his knees, but the hatred still burned behind his eyes.

"Explain your escape." Athiel's voice lay heavy with authority, its tone—not its words— proclaiming that there would be no further conflict between them. Like a whipped dog Juriel eased off his battle-ready stance, his face a mask of shame and bitterness, but Ter Greiel shifted seamlessly into calm as if the encounter had never occurred.

"I cannot."

Juriel looked ready to pounce back into action, but one look from Athiel straightened his spine.

"Then tell all you know." Athiel demanded.

"I was bound. A light pierced the pit from above me. I thought perhaps Michael had come on some errand; although, I did not feel such a presence. Then, within the light, I saw the face of a man. The light consumed me, and when it faded I found myself with the ruins of the church to which I took you."

"Your tale is suspect," Juriel bit out, though his manner

remained considerably calmer.

"That it is." Ter Greiel agreed, devoid of emotion. He regarded Athiel directly, "As I said before, I have heard that the mortals can be quite ingenious even without being gifted of our inspiration. My escape," now he included Juriel, "and the absence of the divine…such things could be conjoined."

He left the two to ponder such implications for a few moments, then spoke before they could.

"You, Juriel, were seeking something before we came. Were you not?"

"I was." There was a great deal of caution in Juriel's reply. "I desire to find Dycliasses," he turned to Athiel, "our brother."

"Then let us continue in that regard." Ter Greiel said. "If you would lead the way."

Juriel drew to full height and stretched his mighty wings in preparation of flight.

"No," Athiel said softly. "I would prefer we walk."

The tips of Juriel's wings curled inward as Ter Greiel asked, "Should we not hasten?"

"Yes, but there is a woman I would speak with on our way," although he said it, Athiel did not know why. It was as if the words were not his own.

"She must wait, Athiel, our task is the salvation of all, not one." Juriel argued earnestly, but his wings were already folding in submission.

"Each one is the salvation of all, Juriel. I have seen this throughout the ages." Athiel cast a glance towards the empty Heavens. "Even when He would not."

Even though he did not speak the word, the accusation of blasphemy was clear on Juriel's face. Ter Greiel was an unreadable stone.

Invoking no argument, Athiel began to walk. The others followed.

EPILOGUE

Pripyat, Ukraine. Kiev Oblast. Early evening in the Zone of Alienation.

Founded in just 1970 it had been home to nearly 50,000, most of whom were power plant workers populating 160 apartment blocks. It was a town designed specifically to this end. A place of rest for the communist proletariat.

Until April 26th, 1986.

Now it lay in abandonment and ruin, quiet and still as the grave. The cold stone of the stark architecture became overrun by nature in a declaration of reclamation. Trees and vegetation sprouted through the bowels of the halls of man, gifting them with the only life they may ever again see. A ferris wheel still stood sentinel over the landscape, now devoid of laughter or joy; the most poignant statement of the demise of the hope and life Pripyat once represented.

Pripyat, this monument to the folly of man.

Pripyat, whose greatest distinction and whose only crime was its proximity to the ill-fated Chernobyl Nuclear Power Plant.

Now it was governed by the howling winds and silent stones. But Pripyat was not wholly unpopulated. Sourceless shadows stalked the abandoned streets by the hundreds. There had been no souls dwelling in this wasteland since the catastrophe, only the passing of guided tours or looters cautiously avoiding patrolling police, so the sin-born had little reason to congregate here. Demons were not idle phantoms, they had tasks to be done, and it was not often that purpose could be found in such desolate places. Tonight something fell from the sky, from beyond the jade barrier that caged them within the physical realm. Its call to them was intoxicating, and they flocked to it from miles away like moths too long in the dark. None knew why they were seeking it, only that they must.

They made a thick circle around a decrepit apartment building. The light, that yearning presence, was above and descending slowly, but as close as they were, as far as they had come, none dared to approach. None knew why.

Then one, the mightiest among them, the mightiest and darkest, stepped forward, sniffing at the sky like a dog. He commanded the others to follow and entered the building. He would see this beacon then devour or possess it as he saw fit. Such was his right.

They filed in behind him and trekked like pilgrims through the moldy halls and up flights of crumbling stairs. Many howled and snarled as they went, like beasts of the field, anxious yet afraid. Their dark mass consumed all light reflecting from the indifferent moon.

The higher they climbed the more the presence beckoned them come, and the more their howls intensified. They drew closer. Their craving more maddening with each inch gained. Its call was a pulsating hum in their acrid, formless selves.

The leader reached the highest stair, and the door that lead to the roof. He hesitated before passing through it, drinking in the magnificence of the mystery beyond. He would savor this. At last he stepped forward through the mass of the door-

-and was cut down.

"Now," was the calm command that echoed from every level of the staircase through sophisticated headsets. From all sides shards of blue light rained into the black mass that trailed down the entrails of the building like a giant serpent. Pained and desperate screams rang out as demons scrambled to escape, crashing outward like black waves only to be eradicated by the unrelenting onslaught. Those in the rear of the procession turned to flee but once outside fell victim to another blue maelstrom.

The darkness was hammered in upon itself from both ends

until it collapsed and was gone entirely.

Absolute slaughter. All in a span of less than thirty seconds.

"Clear up."

"Clear down."

"All clear. Maintain a perimeter until heli-vac arrives."

SWARM Prophet Odin, aptly named considering the patch covering his left eye, stepped into the stairwell, flanked by two Crusaders. The trio climbed the stairs and opened the access door to the roof. It swung open revealing a tree whose cruel twist of roots had overpowered the structural rot and dug into the rooftop and through to the floors below. Its bark was a sickly grayish brown and infected with moss. It was an ogre-ish conqueror proclaiming its dominance over the well-laid plans of man.

The Crusader, Archangel, produced a small, obsidian marble from his utility belt roughly the size of a silver dollar and placed it on the roof inches from the base of the tree and the very thing that had drawn all the demons to Pripyat. He gave Odin a nod.

Odin pressed under his left wrist.

"Bubble's up and stable, sir." Archangel announced, watching the marble.

Odin was satisfied. "You and Guardian take opposite corners. Assist our perimeter. Mop up any stragglers."

Archangel rose and pulled the scoped rifle from his back and inserted his sync-line into its butt. Behind Odin, Guardian did the same. They split off to the northeast and southwest and set up roost.

Odin pressed his headset and keyed into a different channel.

"Safe Haven this is Wayward, do you copy?"

The reply was near-instant.

"Wayward this is Safe Haven. We copy. What is your status?"

"We have secured Eclipse and are awaiting evac. Repeat. Eclipse is secured."

"Well done. Come on home. Dinner's ready. Safe Haven out."

Odin thumbed off the link. To his left he heard the muted report of Guardian's rifle, echoed by a few quick shots from the fire teams below. He crossed his arms behind his back and stepped closer to the gnarled tree to study call sign Eclipse, The Paradox, more closely. So strange a thing that it should look so…innocent and…normal. But these strange times were swiftly becoming stranger still. Who would ever believe that such a small, light-haired child had killed God?

About the Author

Nathan Day has been called a Renaissance Man, passionately expressing himself as an actor, director, screenwriter, songwriter, producer of film and music and now author. A Kentucky native, he won The Young Author's Award in the fourth grade and harbors an obsession for telling and collecting stories through any medium. He has appeared in over 30 film and television projects including Stash and Bulletsong, the latter of which he also wrote and directed. Orphan: Surfacing and the Orphan Saga are his first published works.